The Gold Letter

OTHER TITLES BY LENA MANTA

The Gold Letter

LENA MANTA

TRANSLATED BY GAIL HOLST-WARHAFT

amazon crossing

Previously published as *Γράμμα από χρυσό* by Ψυχόγιος in Greece in 2017. Translated from Greek by Gail Holst-Warhaft. First published in English by AmazonCrossing in 2019.

Published by AmazonCrossing, Seattle

www.apub.com

Amazon, the Amazon logo, and AmazonCrossing are trademarks of Amazon.com, Inc., or its affiliates.

ISBN-13: 9781542042765
ISBN-10: 1542042763

Cover design by Shasti O'Leary Soudant

Printed in the United States of America

The
Gold
Letter

CHAPTER 1

Kypseli, 2016

Bend so that you don't break . . . Where did I hear that? It's a Taoist saying, I think. And yet there are moments when I think it was written for me. But how can I not break? How many times has my life been like a boat without a tiller? A boat without oars, rotten, with the planks of its hull creaking, threatening to break in two with every voyage? On the verge of finding myself alone in a stormy, pitch-black sea that's ready to swallow me up? There have been times when I was certain that I'd already fallen overboard, my body frozen, my limbs heavy, with something dragging me down to the fathomless depths. Other times, though, I floated on the foam. I took a deep breath and swam to the nearest welcoming shore, where the sun was shining and the wind carried sweet smells like the breath of love.

Only now do I know where I am. Like a pilot who is disoriented and doesn't know if what's on the horizon is land or sea. So how can I steer this vessel of my life? In what direction should I turn? High up to avoid the sea, or low down so I don't come too close to the sun and get burned? I look around me. Abandonment and darkness. A ruined house, strewn with old termite-eaten furniture. And yet these old chairs and sofa breathe. I can hear them, feel them. They want to speak to me, but I don't know their language. The only thing I really know is that they are a piece of my inheritance, a page of my history. And if I want to balance myself somewhere between earth and sky, I must read this history. Before that, though, I must discover it, like an explorer, like an archeologist whose duty is to bring to light whatever the earthquake buried in the bowels of the earth. And there is enough to suggest that what happened here is lost in decades of memories, and that it doesn't only concern my family . . . Like two packs of cards that a croupier shuffles with consummate skill. The queens and kings got mixed up, the aces got swapped with the tens, and the jokers are lurking in wait, chameleons who deluded and deceived for decades. But now the cards are in my hands. Crazily, unexpectedly, without warning . . . but right on time. I remember being struck by the lawyer's strange expression when he called me into his office.

"Mrs. Karapanos, you won't believe what it took to find you!" he said.

"The fact is, I never stay long in one place," I answered. "I have no reason to. Wherever I find work, I stop, but not for long."

The man didn't lose any time explaining the situation. He'd wasted enough on my inquiry. Afterward, I stared at him. I'm sure that my expression was more amusing than his when he informed me that I was the heir to a significant fortune, and also this house. Who? I, who, for as long as I could remember, had not been anchored anywhere, had acquired nothing of my own, and was convinced that there was no person on the planet with the same blood as mine . . . other than my mother, whom I had lost when I was young. And from then on, I'd lost the privilege of being called a person.

A strange noise now interrupted these thoughts and memories. I turned, rather nervously, in the dim room. I'd thought I was alone in this mausoleum of a house. I went to open the other dilapidated shutter, even though there was a possibility it might hit some passerby in the head. However, the shutters were stronger than they appeared. When I finally got it open, the spring sun poured freely into the place and performed its miracle. The light revealed a different reality and restored me to my senses after I'd been sitting for so long in the semidarkness. The situation suddenly wasn't so terrible. The furniture was all covered in huge white sheets. There was a lot of dust, and spiders had moved in, but with a thorough cleaning, I could live here. At least until I decided what to do. And the uninhabited house was certainly preferable to the gloomy hotel room in downtown Athens where I had spent the last few days.

I moved on and opened another window, letting in another flood of light. I found myself in the sitting room. The layout of the house was strange—I'd noticed that from the moment I arrived. It was a small villa, squeezed between the tall apartment buildings of Kypseli. Once, it must have been painted dark red, with white trim around the windows and doors. The front doorstep was made of white marble, as was the stairway that led to the main floor. The living room had a slim, semicircular vestibule with a small balcony. I stood there now. It consisted of little more than a small extension from the building with three long, narrow windows, one beside the other. Sturdy masonry framed both sides of the semicircle, and beyond that were two doors that led to corresponding balconies that were a little wider. A passageway with a closed glass door separated me from the dining room. I was in no hurry to explore the rest of the house. First, I had to find what had made the noise. The thought that it might be a mouse made my hair stand on end—they disgust me more than anything else—but a black cat allayed my fears. With a single bound, it landed on the couch and introduced itself with a meow. The two living creatures in the house sized each other up, the cat's eyes green, mine the color of melted gold, justifying my name. My mother called me Chrysafenia. Only recently did I learn that it wasn't some whim of hers, but my grandmother's name. No one ever called me that after her death. Everyone knows me as Fenia.

The cat decided it liked me. It jumped down off the couch to rub itself on my legs and wound its tail around my shin. I picked it up, and it made itself comfortable in my arms. Its fur shone in the sun like black velvet, and my fingers sunk into its fur. I remembered being a child in Germany—and suddenly recalled a little dog trying to comfort me after my mother died. What kind of brute could get angry with a dog and kill it? The same kind that could hurt a child . . .

"I'll call you Tiger," I announced to the cat, who looked at me as if it approved. "Now let's go and see the other rooms. We have a lot of work to do here."

Tiger settled into my arms, making it clear he had no desire to explore the house on foot. I rewarded him with a long caress. I needed the warmth of his touch as I got to know the house that was now mine. I crossed the large room and opened the glass doors that led into the dining room. A long table covered in a white sheet was surrounded by six chairs. On my left was a large window that I hurried to open. Clouds of dust appeared in the sunbeams. A large buffet stood on the opposite side of the room with a mirror hanging above it. Smaller pieces of furniture and ornaments seemed to beg to be unveiled. I ignored them and continued on into the kitchen. There, spiders and dust had settled on the empty cupboards. It was easy to see that the refrigerator and electric stove were only good for the scrap heap. I returned to the dining room.

"Well, it looks like we'll be eating takeout tonight!" I whispered to my cat, who appeared to approve of this decision too.

I returned to the hall, where I faced two closed doors and a stairway that I expected to lead to the bedrooms.

The first door I opened was the bathroom. It cried out for a plumber to perform miracles, but aside from the dust, it was cleaner than the rest of the house. The smell was really unpleasant. I put on a brave face and flushed the toilet. According to the lawyer, the house had not been lived in for twelve years.

"Mrs. Karapanos, the last occupant of the house was your grandfather," he'd said, "Pericles Sekeris. Your grandmother died in an accident in 1973, together with her son—your uncle, Stelios. Your grandfather was cared for by a housekeeper in his last days."

"And how did I become the heir? Isn't there anyone else?"

"Apart from your mother and Stelios, your grandparents had two other children: Hecuba and Fotini. But in his will, he left everything to you."

It seemed that my grandfather had regretted the way he'd treated my mother. And before he died, he left my mother and her daughter—me—whatever fortune was left. The games life plays. But why had he been so angry with her? What had my grandfather seen in the man my mother chose that made him cut her off? Not that he was wrong. My dear mother, your choice was a mistake—that brute wasn't for you. How could you have had a child with him? To be honest, there are moments when I fear I've inherited something from him too.

The last door on that floor hid a pleasant surprise: a small, attractive office. Again I hurried to open the windows, which looked out on the street. Sun rushed in to illuminate the best-preserved room in the house. Here too everything was covered, but it was cleaner, which made me wonder if my grandfather had spent his final years in that room and simply closed off the rest. Opposite the windows was a bookcase with a small, elegant desk in front of it. Under the window were a sofa and an armchair. I pulled the covers off. The upholstery was the color of a ripe, sweet apple. I dared to sit down. The sofa was soft and inviting. Tiger slipped out of my arms and made himself comfortable on the armchair.

"Yes, Tiger, this is where we'll sleep tonight," I said.

He meowed. He was right: now that we had decided where we'd sleep, it was time to attend to what we'd eat. My stomach was complaining.

My first evening with Tiger in our new house was spent eating pizza by the light of the candles that I'd had the forethought to buy, seeing that we had no electricity. In addition, I bought milk, coffee, sugar, and some cookies for the morning, and of course, food for my housemate. I had never done that before. For the first time in many years, I slept calmly, without any fear, not fretting about every noise—and an old house is noisy.

In the morning I woke with the weight of Tiger on my feet, and I sensed that he would be my protector. For whatever reason, this cat behaved more like a faithful dog—something I noticed over the days that followed. Independent by nature, he was also faithful and obedient. When I had to go out for a while, he waited for me to come home and did everything he could to demonstrate the joy he felt at my return. His gaze was wonderfully eloquent, and very quickly, it felt as if we'd spent a whole lifetime together.

As for everything else, I didn't know where to begin. With the lawyer's help, I had wrapped up all the legal matters. Everything was paid for, and the mythical sum of a hundred and fifty thousand euros had appeared in my bank account. It was childish of me perhaps, but that first morning, drinking my coffee in the small office, I double-checked the little bankbook to make sure that I really didn't have to search for work again. The night before, I'd gone up to the second floor. What I found there was in an even worse state of neglect, but even in the evening light, the elegance of the rooms was obvious. There were five bedrooms on the upper floor, and it was clear that many years had passed since anyone had crossed their thresholds. The largest had a double bed—it must have been Grandfather and Grandmother's. The others were smaller and must have belonged to the children: Stelios and the girls of the family. What had the lawyer said their names were? Ah, yes: Hecuba and Fotini. I felt a bit like a burglar as I walked around the empty rooms—guilty, as if I had no right to be there. Tiger, who was rubbing himself on my legs, brought me to my senses. It was mine, this house! Legally. I had to keep reminding myself of that. Just before it got dark, I went down into the basement. There, to the left and right of the stairs, were two more bedrooms. There was also a bathroom and a rudimentary kitchen.

"Tiger, we're the owners of a behemoth!" I informed him while sitting on the sofa, pizza balanced on my knees.

The cat blinked at me and resumed washing himself. I observed how he passed his small pink tongue over his fur until it shone.

"You sure clean up quick," I told him irritably. "We'll see how long it takes me to get this dump back into shape."

The first step was obvious. I might never have had a decent place before, but I knew a visit to the supermarket was required so that I could stock the house with basic necessities. Seeing how at sea I was, the lawyer had arranged for the electricity to be reconnected, and it was supposed to come on today. I left my cat in peace and, having made sure there was enough money in my wallet, set out on foot for the store.

It was easy to find my way. My house was behind Kypseli Square—according to the lawyer, the suburb had once been one of the most distinguished in Athens. The development of the area had begun in 1930, and together with Kolonaki, it had been settled by the most upper-class Athenians. During the 1950s and '60s, a large number of apartment buildings were erected. My family must have bought the house after the Second World War. I was amazed when he told me that my roots were in Constantinople, where the Ververis family I'm descended from moved before 1950. All my life I'd thought I was like wild grass with short roots, and now I found out my roots were as strong as a big tree's. A strange new feeling, and one I would have trouble assimilating.

I passed one apartment building after another, and I couldn't help wondering why my grandparents didn't give up their house when the value of land soared in Athens, trade it in for apartments, instead of remaining in the little villa dwarfed by the monsters all around it. I was anxious to learn more about my family, about my house, but I told myself to be patient. For once in my life, I had to consider priorities.

I came out of the supermarket certain I'd never make it back home in one piece. I was annoyed with myself for overlooking the obvious problem: how to carry everything I had bought. The detergent bottles were cutting my hands, the broom and mop threatened to poke my eyes out, the bucket kept getting tangled in my legs, and I had to stop every few feet to gasp for air.

Just as I was about to abandon everything on the pavement, I sensed a presence beside me. I turned and found myself looking into two dark, almost black eyes. In front of me stood a young man whose clothes had seen better days, as had he himself. He couldn't have been much more than twenty-five, and I knew right away that he was one of the thousands of refugees who ended up in our country if they weren't drowned in the Aegean by smugglers. Those people were fleeing for their lives, and criminals were making money off them.

"What do you want?" I asked, though he certainly couldn't answer me in a language that was strange to him.

The young man tried to tell me something, but hopelessness has a language of its own. I saw despair, hunger, even resignation in his eyes. He approached me, perhaps the same way he'd swum toward a life raft thrown into the icy sea. With gestures, he and I managed to arrive at something of an understanding. He took the extra bags from my hands and seemed anxious to follow. I don't know if I was foolish or paranoid, but something in his look reminded me of myself.

I found myself walking toward my house with quick steps. I almost laughed. In less than forty-eight hours, I had taken into my protection not only a black cat but also another person. We went into the house together, and the young man looked around him with concern.

"Don't look at it like that!" I said as if he could understand. "We'll fix it up like new."

Tiger approached cautiously and smelled my Syrian friend without enthusiasm. He wasn't wrong. The man was in a terrible state. I made sure that the electricity company had done its magic and wondered if the hot water heater could possibly work after so many years.

After a lot of trouble, I found out his name: Karim. There was no way he could pronounce mine. He ended up calling me "madam," which was easier for him. Where we really got into trouble was when I tried to send him to have a bath and gave him a shirt of mine to wear. At first he was surprised, then he got angry, saying something to me loudly in his language while I tried to explain in mine. Tiger got angry too and meowed loudly—the Tower of Babel was threatening to crush us. Again the gestures came into service, along with some mangled English. Finally, Karim came out of the bathroom so clean and fragrant that Tiger consented to reexamine and finally to accept him.

Three weeks. It took me twenty-one days and many nights to put the house back in order, working methodically with Karim. What I didn't expect was the talent my companion displayed at painting. Beginning with the upstairs, he painted the rooms one by one. With patience and care, we managed to make the house gleam. We even cleaned and painted the two rooms in the basement, one of which Karim stayed in. The furniture down there was mostly rotten, but Karim repaired a lot of things. I called a plumber, who took some days to redo the piping and replace tiles in the bathrooms. Meanwhile, I ordered a new modern stove and all sorts of electrical appliances, not forgetting to equip Karim's basement kitchen with a fridge and a stove. The loyal young man surprised me again and again. In the beginning, he was wary and constantly on guard, but with every day that passed, I gained his respect. He was an observant Muslim and was careful to follow his dietary customs. I honored his hours of prayer and treated him like what he was: a human being with equal rights. He was very intelligent and learned Greek fast, in contrast to me—however much I tried, I couldn't manage five words of his language. Sometimes, we had to resort to English, which neither of us knew well.

For his part, Tiger made our lives difficult, since he insisted on literally tangling himself up in our legs. I was often in danger of breaking a limb as, out of the blue, I found a tail and four legs in the way of my own. I'd scold him, and he'd go rub up against Karim, begging to be hugged. In the evenings, he curled up on the bed beside me, and his green eyes spoke volumes. It was his way of saying I'd become family.

I kept the large bedroom for myself and tried to figure out what to do with the others. I might be busy now cleaning up the dirt and dust of many years, but when it all ended, I was sure I'd spend hours in the little office that had offered me its hospitality on those first evenings. While cleaning it, I had discovered a few albums with old photographs. I didn't dare touch them. I wanted to wait until I felt calmer to get to know my family.

Besides, there was also the tin box Karim and I had discovered . . .

After those first few nights on the office sofa, my back was aching, and I wanted to move into Grandfather and Grandmother's bedroom. I ordered a new mattress, sheets, and a quilt, and we dragged the heavy bed, creaking and protesting, away from the wall so we could clean and paint behind it. We took down the little cupboard that held the marriage wreaths, as well as a cross, and Karim laid down newspapers so as not to dirty the wooden floor. But when he set the ladder up and stood on the first rung, it wobbled dangerously. We pulled the newspapers aside and saw that a floorboard had moved.

"That's all I needed," I exclaimed. "Rotten floors!"

"No, madam," observed the young Syrian. "Look!"

I knelt down. The floor was in good shape, but two planks had come loose, and in the gap between the wood and the cement was a tin box, rusty and covered in dust. I opened it. Inside were a few letters tied with a ribbon that must once have been pink. There was also a pair of old earrings, their elaborate design covered in a green substance. I rubbed them on my pants, and the color changed. I wasn't a specialist, but they looked to me like bronze. Once, for about a month, I had worked as a house cleaner in a home with bronze candlesticks.

I closed the box and turned to Karim, who was looking at me expectantly.

"*Argotera*, Karim. How do you say that in English? Ah, yes, *later* . . ."

I stood up, and he was already looking for a hammer and nails to secure the floorboards. Meanwhile, I went downstairs and placed the box in a drawer of the office. I was burning with curiosity, but didn't waver in my commitment to get the house in order before anything else.

We may not have had a fully functioning kitchen yet, but the rest of the house was now like new. Its two inhabitants, however, were in a terrible state. All our clothes, or to be honest, seeing as Karim didn't have any of his own, all my clothes were covered in splotches of paint and plaster, torn and worn out.

The next evening, I went up to my bedroom in my torn clothes. Opposite the large bed was a full-length mirror, and after a bath I dared to approach it—something I hadn't done for a long time. There, I examined myself from head to toe. OK, I wasn't twenty years old. Soon I'd be turning forty-four, but however critical I was, and despite the fact that I'd never taken care of myself, I had to admit I looked younger than my years. My hair certainly needed attention. The dark-brown color was littered with white, and the short style I'd chosen had grown out and been shoved into a convenient braid. My face was clear with delicate features but also with delicate wrinkles. My best feature was certainly my eyes, with their unusual color. I wasn't fat, but neither was I thin. My curves were smooth, and my body firm because of the hard physical work I'd done for so many years. In short, like my house, I needed a good renovation. Now that we had restored the place so beautifully, I didn't look as if I belonged there. My mind turned to Karim, who needed clothes and shoes. I lay down that night having made up my mind that the two of us would go shopping.

But the next day it was impossible to persuade Karim to leave the house. He looked panic-stricken. His head went back and forth again and again, as in a mixture of Greek and English, he said, "No, no, madam. Karim inside—danger outside! I have no papers. I need nothing, everything fine. You go!"

After that came a monologue in his own language that I naturally didn't understand, but the message was clear. If they caught him, they'd deport him, and dressed in rags as he was, he was an easy target. I reassured him, and when I began taking his measurements, he understood. What my long-suffering friend couldn't imagine was how happy I felt. It had been years since I'd bought myself anything new. I set out with the enthusiasm of the newly enlightened for Patission Street and its shops.

It was dark when I came into the house with the taxi driver, who helped me unload all my shopping bags. Karim must have hidden when he heard the man's voice, so when I was alone, I called him to help me with the bags. In the dim light of the foyer, the change in my appearance wasn't apparent, but when we went into the chandelier-lit living room, the young man jumped back and looked as if he didn't recognize me.

"Beautiful madam!" he called out in English, and his dark eyes shone.

I looked with satisfaction at the mirror opposite me. My hair had been cut again at a length that suited me; it shone like a chestnut, glowing with the highlights they had added in the salon. We sat on the comfortable sofa, and I showed all my purchases to Karim, who greeted them with exclamations of admiration. But when I started to take out men's pants, shirts, and shoes, his chocolate eyes filled with tears.

"Madam," he whispered with difficulty, "all that for me?"

"For you, Karim," I answered. "You helped me so much. I've had you at my side for a month. You're a good man, Karim."

His tears fell on my hand when he brought it to his lips to bestow a kiss of gratitude. In broken English, he said, "Don't know what to say. Good person, madam—like my mother."

"Where is your mother, Karim?"

"Back to Syria—died."

I looked at him sadly. In all this time, I hadn't been able to learn much about his past. The obstacle of language was too great. He had made me understand that he had crossed from Turkey to Lesbos and, from there, made it to Athens. He was alone. In Victoria Square, he'd waited for some time, planning to move on to some other European country. But for reasons I couldn't understand, he'd decided to stay in Greece. He explained, as well as he could, that he had found me the first day he'd ventured away from the square. The fact that he had lost his mother made me feel closer to him. So, both of us were orphans. And while he was in a foreign country, I felt just as lonely. I stroked his hair in a maternal way. In a different life, he could have been my son. He smiled at me through his tears, and then with a bound, Tiger landed between us and meowed loudly. We both stroked him, and then I gave him his gifts: an elegant collar that he was patient enough to allow me to fasten on him and a basket to sleep in. This latter gift turned out to be utterly useless. My black cat had no intention of being separated from me or my bed.

Visitors? No, I wasn't expecting any. That's why the doorbell surprised me that afternoon. I was in my little office, with a strong dose of caffeine for company. I'd finally opened the first album, the oldest. Among the unknown faces, I discovered my mother's, and tears came to my eyes when I saw her as a child, then as a beautiful adolescent. They were mostly family photographs, and I soon found my grandfather, my grandmother—the one whose name I bore—and my mother's siblings. As far as I could tell, I looked like my grandmother.

The doorbell was an unwelcome intrusion but also a source of wonder. Who could it be? I pressed a button, and the downstairs door opened. From the landing, I waited for the visitor. A woman was already climbing the stairs, and the ease with which she did so revealed that she was treading on familiar ground. She stopped in front of me, and her expression wasn't friendly.

"I suppose you are Chrysafenia Karapanos," she said brusquely.

"You have the advantage, madam," I answered. "You know me, but I don't know you."

"My name is Hecuba Papadakis. My family name, though, is Sekeris."

So it was my aunt who stood before me! I didn't dare to even give her my hand. It was obvious that there was no room for a sentimental family reunion. I simply stood aside to let her in. She strolled confidently toward the sitting room, but on the threshold stopped and looked with curiosity at the renovation. From where I was standing, I couldn't see if her icy eyes warmed even for a moment, finding themselves in the house where she grew up. Without an invitation, she went ahead and sat on the sofa.

"I would ask you to sit down, but you've already done so," I said slowly, recovering my composure. "Can I offer you anything?" I thanked my lucky stars that my new kitchen was finally finished and stocked.

"No, thank you," came her abrupt reply.

"Then I take it you will tell me why you have come here. From the little I know of my mother's family, you are one of her sisters."

"And this was my house!"

I sat in an armchair opposite her. So, the woman was looking for a fight. Everything about her announced it: her eyes that flashed lightning, her voice, raised to an unpleasant pitch. I took a deep breath and answered calmly.

"Yes, I suppose you grew up here, just like my mother and her other sister—Fotini, isn't that her name?"

"My father threw your mother out."

"Yes, I found out about that. And then that same man righted the injustice with his will."

"It was no injustice. He shouldn't have done what he did!"

"The fact that my mother married someone without her father's approval—"

"Is that what they told you to say?" she snarled.

"Do you have a different opinion?" I asked, but I was beginning to feel disturbed by her presence.

"It's not an opinion; it's the truth!"

"Which I probably don't know. Do you want to enlighten me?"

"I didn't come here to educate you."

"Then why did you come?"

"I came to tell you that you have no right to my father's fortune. This house is mine!"

I nearly lost my patience. I got up from the armchair and folded my arms across my chest.

"Then, madam, contest the will! You had all that time to do so, and you didn't. I accepted what, by rights, belonged to me. My grandfather had his reasons for what he did, and the fact that he died here alone, without his daughters, probably had something to do with his decision."

Aunt Hecuba leaped up, having lost the last vestiges of self-control.

"How dare you talk to me like that!" she shouted.

Tiger appeared, attracted by the noise. His hair, standing on end, showed that he was about to pounce.

"Hush, Tiger," I ordered, and like the faithful, doglike creature he was, he sat at my feet.

The woman took a step back.

"What happened between me and my father is not your business," she said, more quietly this time.

"Correct. But neither can you come in here and threaten me as if I've stolen something. I had no idea about any of this until the lawyer found me. I didn't even know I had relatives. But now that you've come, you should know that I intend to learn all I can about the family."

"Good luck! But it isn't so easy."

"Are you hiding something?"

She didn't answer me, just rose and fled the room as if she were being chased. The sun hadn't set yet, but I was in the dark.

The front door slammed noisily behind her, and Karim appeared.

"Karim hide, madam," he said. Every day, his Greek improved, and our communication got better.

"And you were right to do so. I wouldn't have wanted that witch to see you!"

"I wait behind the door, in case she do some harm to madam."

"I think she really would have liked to."

"Who is she?"

"My aunt Hecuba. I have a family, Karim, but I don't think it's a good thing."

"Very angry *porson*!"

"Furious *porson*, Karim! And I don't know why. What did I or my mother do to her? And what was that about my mother's marriage?"

"I do not understand."

"Nor do I, Karim. Nor do I! But I'll be damned if I leave the subject like that. Tomorrow I'll go to the lawyer's office and see what he knows. When he first contacted me, I was too confused to ask many questions."

"Madam say a lot. I understand little."

"Me too, Karim. I understand little, and I know even less."

The lawyer seemed to have been expecting me. He welcomed me the next day with a smile full of condescension, but his expression became more sympathetic when I explained the reasons for my visit.

"It's a common phenomenon, Mrs. Karapanos," he observed, continuing to smile. "When they learn about an unexpected inheritance, many heirs concentrate only on that and forget to ask about all the details."

"The difference, Mr. Doulabey," I replied, "is that I didn't even know I had relatives. I didn't have a place to hang my hat, as the saying goes, and suddenly, I found myself inheriting a house and a small fortune. On top of that, I have an aunt who blames me for something I don't understand."

"That too is no surprise. The relatives who get the lion's share of an inheritance are not liked by the others."

"Yes, but why did I get it, considering that my grandfather cut my mother off and drove her out of the house, so that she found herself in Germany with her husband?"

"I would surmise that, at the end, your grandfather felt he had wronged your mother. He obviously didn't approve of her choice of husband."

"I don't disagree with him on that," I interjected.

"Those are things I know nothing about, Mrs. Karapanos, and they don't concern me. I executed the will based on the instructions of the deceased, Pericles Sekeris, and I did everything I could to find you and give you what was yours."

"And my aunts? This Hecuba, who came to find me, and the other one, Fotini?"

"Hecuba Sekeris married a businessman from Crete, Dimitris Papadakis, and settled there with her husband and two children. Your grandfather left her a symbolic amount, as you read in the will. As for Fotini, she lives in Palaio Faliro; she's a widow and has no children. She married rather late. She inherited the same amount as her sister. There's a rumor that she has some mental problems."

"And why did the two of them leave their father to die all alone?"

"That I don't know, unfortunately."

"Do I have any other relatives?"

"Your grandmother had a brother, Nestor Ververis, who, after his sister's death, cut ties with his brother-in-law. Again, I don't know the details."

"But you did know my grandfather."

"Yes, I visited him many times before his will was complete."

"What was he like?"

"A proud man. When he was young, he must have been very handsome, but—"

"Please, Mr. Doulabey. You're the only one who can tell me. It doesn't matter what—I just want to learn about my family."

"Yes, your grandfather was a cold man—even hard, I would say. But he was also very clearheaded."

I left the lawyer's office feeling dizzy from all the information rattling around in my mind. Not only did I have aunts, but cousins too. And probably none of them liked me.

Karim and Tiger were waiting for me to return: the first to hear my news, the second because he wanted affection. Fortunately, both could be satisfied at the same time. I took my cat in my arms and looked at Karim.

"Does madam know now why other madam is angry?" he asked me.

"I found out a few things, Karim, but now the investigation really starts. Now I'm curious!"

"Will madam who shouts come back?"

"I don't know. Just as I don't know where to start looking."

"And the . . . the . . . the . . ." He tried to show me with his hands what he meant. "The box," he finally managed in English.

"The box," I repeated, and my eyes brightened. "Bravo, Karim! I'd forgotten it."

I sprang up and ran to the office. I heard Karim calling to me that he would cook, and Tiger jumped out of my arms. The kitchen interested him a lot more than a dusty box.

I undid the ribbon carefully, but it almost fell apart in my hands. I was twice as careful as I took out the first letter. With surgical precision, I unfolded it on the desk. Fortunately, the writing was easy to read, but my eyes widened when I saw the date. The letter was ninety years old. It had been written in the summer of 1926. The sender was one Simeon Kouyoumdzis, and the recipient was a woman with the name Smaragda Kantardzis. I immersed myself in reading.

> *Angel of my life, being that I worship, this is the first letter I have dared to write you, and it was your eyes that gave me the courage. That look that you gave me on Sunday in church made me understand that the question I feel finds a response in your heart. And as soon as I understood that, everything made sense. The nights stopped hurting me, the days spread abundant light, my life swelled with sense and purpose. My ethereal creature, I want you to know that you hold my heart in your hands. I don't dare to hope, but I long for a single word from you to reassure me that I didn't imagine that look . . . that my lovesick fantasy didn't create that imperceptible smile that was addressed only to me . . .*
>
> *PS: A warm thanks from the bottom of my heart to your special friend, Evanthia, who agreed to be my courier and bring this letter to you.*
> *Your eternal slave,*
> *Simeon Kouyoumdzis*

I leaned back in my chair without knowing what to say. I had never read such a passionate letter, and I was overwhelmed. Karim appeared like a deus ex machina bearing a tray with coffee and my cigarettes.

"You're an angel!" I exclaimed and greedily took the first sip. When I had a cigarette between my lips, my friend hurried to light it.

"What the letter say?" he asked in English.

"It's a love letter," I answered.

He didn't have to express his curiosity. It was written all over his face.

"I don't know, Karim; it's very old. But the girl's name was Smaragda."

"Smaragda," he repeated.

"My mother's name. But her last name? That's not my mother's."

Karim realized that I was mostly talking to myself and left me in peace. Another letter found its way into my hands, the second in the series according to the date inscribed on the envelope. Only a few days had elapsed since the first one.

> *Precious gem of my life . . .*
> *Your letter transported me to heaven. Now that I know for certain that you love me, I feel strong enough to take on the whole world! I understand your fears about the objections of your family and mine. I won't pretend to be humble, telling you lies that are not worthy of you. Our love will arouse antipathy. Already my father has mentioned the names of young ladies from among whom I must choose my wife, and yours was never discussed. You see, my darling, all the families he spoke of were those of rich merchants in Constantinople. Except that, for me, the only dowry I can consider is the heart. And mine belongs to you forever.*
>
> *How I wish we could speak, even briefly. So that I could look into your golden eyes and hold your hand. Miss Evanthia told me that we might be able to meet at her house on Wednesday afternoon. Her mother will be away at a tea party with your mother. I'll wait for you, my beloved.*
>
> *Yours forever,*
> *Simeon*

There was no time for delay. I carefully opened the third letter. I wanted to see if the lovers had indeed met at the house of this Evanthia, who probably had a romantic spirit and ignored the dangers as she served love itself.

> *My dear Smaragda,*
> *I still can't believe what I went through yesterday afternoon. As long as I live, I'll be deeply indebted to Miss Evanthia, who gave us the opportunity to sit beside each other . . . where I could see the liquid gold of your eyes, where I touched your soft hand. My heart has been pounding since that moment, and I'm sure that everyone around me can hear it, the romantic prelude created only for you!*
>
> *The only kiss that I dared to place on your tender lips, which have haunted my nights and dogged my days, became lava and burned me. Now I really know you are my destiny and that, if I can't have you, I will be lost. Very soon I will talk to my father and, if necessary, fall at his feet so that he will permit me to take you as my bride.*
>
> *Just be patient for a little while, light of my eyes, and afterward we'll be together for the rest of our lives. I'm preparing a surprise for you with my own hands. Something that will last forever to remember our love.*
> *With devotion,*
> *Simeon*

So they did meet! I leaned back in my chair. I needed a little time to take in what I had learned, even if it concerned two people I didn't know. For my grandmother or grandfather to have hidden them, these letters had to mean something. They certainly weren't theirs. The dates were too early. Could this Smaragda who shared a name with my mother be my great-grandmother? The thought made me sit up straighter. I felt so helpless. I had no one to tell me what had happened in the past, to tell me my own story. My eyes fell on the box again. There were three more letters. These were different, more recent than the others. I ignored the noises coming from the kitchen as well as the delicious smells that were floating out, as they did whenever Karim cooked food from his country. I reached for the next letter.

A new surprise awaited me. The sender was not Simeon Kouyoumdzis, but someone called Vassilis, with the same last name, and the recipient was my grandmother, Chrysafenia Ververis! With trembling hands, I opened the envelope. The letter was dated 1947.

> *My dearest,*
> *I wanted to tell you so much yesterday, but I didn't manage to . . . maybe I'm a coward. And if that sudden thing hadn't happened with your grandfather, I might still have buried all I feel for you out of fear. What I feel is so strong that I don't know what I would do if you mocked my feelings. Also, my friendship with your brother is still an obstacle. In no way would I want something to happen that would disturb that relationship, which I respect and honor, but the heart has its own ways and doesn't calculate. Besides, I know that some mysterious antipathy divides your family, as it does mine. So you can imagine how much trouble I went to trying to keep my feelings for you hidden. In the end, though, I couldn't manage it.*
> *Yesterday, a dream became reality, a torture came to an end, and now I feel so happy. I won't hide the fact that I feel very guilty because I'm deceiving your brother, and abusing the trust of your family, who have allowed me*

*to come into your house. But there's nothing to be done,
for the present.*

*Eternally yours,
Vassilis Kouyoumdzis*

My head was spinning, and despite the fact that there were two more letters, I wasn't in a state to continue reading. Things seemed to be more and more confused. First my great-grandmother, then my grandmother, had fallen in love with someone from the Kouyoumdzis family, but from what I understood, neither of them had married their great loves. Why? What sort of warped repetition of history was this? And why didn't the two families get along? They must have lived in Constantinople, a closed society, with different ethics and customs. I didn't know much about history, and perhaps I needed to learn more. Perhaps, I could look it up on the Internet. I made a mental note that I needed to buy a computer and find someone to teach me how to use it. But who would teach me about the history of the family? Certainly not Hecuba. And from what the lawyer told me, my other aunt, Fotini, was in no position to. Had I reached a dead end?

"Madam?"

I raised my lowered eyes to my friend, who was looking at me sheepishly, wondering if he should or shouldn't rouse me from my confused state.

"Come in, Karim."

"Everything all right, madam?"

"Bah! I made things worse."

"My mother tell me always with full stomach thing go better here," he said pointing to his head.

"And she wasn't wrong, Karim. Let's go and eat, and then I'll see what I'll do."

I followed him into the fragrant kitchen. He put a plate in front of me that I looked at curiously. It looked like some sort of pie made of ground meat.

Answering my silent curiosity, he answered: "Roast kibbe."

"Which is?" I insisted.

"Lamb with onion, pine nuts, spices," he announced in English.

I translated it back to him, and he nodded his head happily.

To accompany the dish, I'd brought Middle Eastern pitas to the table, which, thanks to Karim, I'd started to substitute for bread in our house and which I liked very much, as well as yogurt, which was essential because the food was tremendously spicy.

"Karim, who taught you to cook?"

"I cook in my country!" he told me proudly in Greek, then continued in English. "My mother has a restaurant. After bombs, madam, she die and my brother. I not there. Whole city ruins, madam. My uncle with his childs. I say leave, I run."

"And your father, Karim?"

"Die in bombing one month before." Again he spoke in English. "Karim has no one—only madam."

His eyes had filled with tears. This young man had lived through horrors that couldn't fit into human heads, and I felt a helpless fury overwhelm me, fury toward all those who made war into a profitable business. They stirred up passions in order to sell weapons, and now the refugees were an excessive burden. What did the warmongers believe? That all these people would wait in line to die and wouldn't try to save themselves? That they wouldn't try to escape to the unknown in the hope there wouldn't be bombs there?

Karim had told me previously that he had walked for whole nights, along with a hundred other people, to cross from Syria into Turkey, and from there to the coastline. He had boarded a boat with many others. He had some money his mother had hidden in their house, and he carried a small bag with all his possessions. But the smugglers threw all the bags overboard to fit more people. Beside him sat a woman with a baby that never stopped crying. The man whose boat it was became irritated and told her that, unless the baby was quiet, he'd throw it in the sea. The woman was afraid. She squeezed so tightly that the baby suffocated.

"And what happened to the woman, Karim?" I had asked, horrified.

"Baby die and man grab and throw into the sea. Woman can't bear. Sea too. Drown."

That evening, both of us had wept for that unknown woman and her child who lost their lives so cruelly.

I looked at Karim, who was now wiping tears from his eyes and looking at me guiltily. "I'm sorry, madam. For tell you another bad story. Your eyes full of tears. Next time I tell something, you laugh," he promised and smiled at me.

"It's OK, Karim. I understand bad stories. You can tell them to me whenever you need to."

"You, madam, never tell Karim bad story."

"I'll tell you, Karim. One day I'll tell you. And we'll both cry again."

After the meal, I found myself in front of the old box again. There were two more letters. Karim followed me, carrying a tray with coffee flavored with rosewater, and pieces of Turkish delight. He left it beside me and disappeared. Tiger wasn't there, and I knew he must be pacing the kitchen, hoping that some snack was waiting for him. I lit a cigarette and let my palate enjoy the medley of tastes and smells as the nicotine mixed delightfully with the coffee and the exotic rosewater. I reached out to unfold another piece of my history.

My dearest,
I think I'm living a dream that I never want to wake up
from. So much pain around us, so much sadness inside
you, and our love, a flower that opens.

*I want you to know that everything I have told you
is completely true, and I meant every word. You'll be my
wife, Chrysafenia, whatever happens, and whoever I
must do battle with! Since you love me too, everything
will be all right.*

*And something else—the secret surprise I'm making
for you. I found the design in the drawer of a piece of
furniture we sent to the cabinetmaker to repair. It must
have been forgotten there years ago. It's a locket, my dear
creature, and it symbolizes our love. It will be the first
piece of gold I give you, before the ring that I'll put on
your finger one day. I work on it at night, and I hope
to have it ready soon so I can give it to you. Until then,
know that you hold my heart in your hands.*

Devotedly,

Vassilis

So the piece of jewelry Vassilis's father designed was never made or
given to my great-grandmother. The couple separated, and it was his
son's fate to make it. Probably neither my grandmother nor the man she
was in love with knew that their parents had exchanged vows of eternal
love before them. It appeared that the Kouyoumdzis and Kantardzis
families called out to each other. But why didn't the union work out in
the end? A last letter remained, and I was sure that it would provoke
even more questions. When I saw the date, I was filled with foreboding.
Months had passed. Either the rest of the letters had been lost or . . .
There was only one way to find out.

My beloved,

*I know that you are suffering as much as I am. I don't
understand how fate could have been so harsh with us.
I feel guilty because I turned out to be weaker than our*

love. But I can't, my precious—I was defeated by the only thing I couldn't fight.

We exchanged vows and letters. Paper and ink, sweetheart. Both perishable. At least I know that one letter will remain forever to remind me that once I loved you as much as my life. And if I seem to be a coward, it is because I can wager and lose my life, but not my father's. You and I are both children who honor our parents; we respect and love them. I know you, at least, understand this. And if the rumors I've heard are true, then it's better for you. I will help you to forget me, and you must do so.

I love you and will always love you,

Vassilis

I was so upset that I left one cigarette burning in the ashtray and lit a new one. What was all this about? They separated, but why? What happened to Vassilis's father, and what one letter was he talking about? There was nothing else in the box except the tarnished earrings, and who knew what they were doing there. And what were the rumors Vassilis was talking about?

Karim barely caught a glimpse of my shadow as I snatched the keys and ran out into the street. The sun had just begun to set. The May heat had retreated, but the buildings and the sidewalk still radiated warmth. I couldn't stay in the house anymore. Its thick walls were pressing in on me. I needed to know my past, and there was no one to help me. My mother had never spoken to me about her family in Greece. She had written them off, probably too full of bitterness. Nor did she ever tell me whether she had loved my father. Even thinking about him made me want to spit on the dirty sidewalk as I walked through the neighborhood. No. I shouldn't call him Father. I couldn't even think of him in that capacity. Better to use his name: Renos. That brute!

I wrenched my mind away from that filth. There was no room for it inside me just then. I had other things to think about—most of all, how to go about finding people who could help me. I needed to find my roots and learn the family secrets that had remained hidden for years.

What was wrong with me? Why were all these irrelevant things pestering my mind? Since I'd recovered from madness in my youth, I wasn't in danger of it now. I looked around at the hunched people hurrying home from a tiring day at work. Thanks to my grandfather, I was no longer anxious about day-to-day survival, yet I had to do something—the dusty old evidence I'd found wasn't going to get me anywhere on its own. I smiled at my reflection in a shop window, and I headed home. The whole way, I gave myself a severe talking-to that helped me calm down. As soon as I arrived at the house and saw the uneasy expression in Karim's eyes, I felt guilty.

"Don't worry, Karim!" I said to him sweetly. "I'm fine. I'll go and have a bath, and you get the table ready for us to play a card game."

It was our latest craze. Every evening, we laid the green baize on the table and sat up till midnight among the jacks and the knights, playing gin rummy.

As the bathwater ran over me, I talked to myself.

"What on earth's the matter with me? How silly I am! Getting miserable because I read some letters. OK, it's good to find out about my family, but there's no deadly secret lurking. How ridiculous I am! I was left a house, and because it's old, I turn into Agatha Christie. Instead, I should be thanking God for taking pity on me before I grew old sitting on some park bench."

That night, Karim lost every hand.

All my life I've had a weakness for sweets. You might manage to take my entrée, but my dessert? No way! Besides being a good cook, Karim was wonderful at making desserts from his home country, and there was never a shortage of delicious things in our house. That evening with the coffee, he presented me with a feast of saffron ice cream with lemon zest. I closed my eyes and enjoyed the heavenly taste with the same delight I had felt in bed with an experienced lover. The interruption of the doorbell grated on my nerves. Karim and I looked at each other in surprise. We never had visitors.

"Angry lady again, madam?" Karim exclaimed.

"I hope not!"

Determined to throw her out if it was, I pressed the buzzer to open the front door and positioned myself at the top of the stairs, ready for battle. But a very different woman entered and proceeded toward me. She stopped in front of me, out of breath.

"I'll either have to stop smoking or stop climbing stairs!" she announced.

Her eyes were the color of green olives. She must have been nearly sixty, and wore striking, modern glasses. Her dress was unusual, her makeup careful and distinctive. She wore a long, full dress the color of sand with flat canvas shoes. Around her neck was an impressive necklace that completed the effect. She looked me over with the same care as I had her, but her expression was friendly.

"So, you're Smaragda's daughter," she said, smiling.

I only just managed to nod because immediately came the shock of her embrace. The strange woman opened her arms, hugged me tightly to her, and kissed me on both cheeks.

"Welcome, my girl!" she added to complete my astonishment.

"I'm sorry," I finally managed to say. "I don't know you."

"You're right! My husband tells me I'm like a typhoon: I overwhelm people. I'm Melpo Leontiadis. Your mother's cousin!"

I stared at her, stunned. For one thing, her name didn't mean anything to me; for another, my aunt's nasty visit was still fresh in my mind. At least I managed to behave like a good host and led her into the sitting room. The woman looked around in awe.

"Good Lord! The house is just the same. You haven't changed anything. Your mother and I used to run and play in here while our mothers were drinking their tea on this very couch. I feel as if I've stepped into a time capsule!"

She turned and found me standing there like a pillar of salt.

"Oh dear! I've turned you upside down!" she exclaimed, and her ringing laughter, as open as her spirit, filled the room. She sat down comfortably on the couch. "Are you going to offer me coffee? We both need it, and later, I'll try to answer as many of your questions as I can."

"You know, I had another visitor recently."

"I do know. Hecuba landed on you. My cousin told me, and that's why I can understand that look on your face. When the first experience of your family is Hecuba, how could you not be scared! But fortunately, we're not all like that. In any case, you owe my visit today to her. I had no idea that Smaragda's daughter was here, and it was Hecuba who informed me about the 'misfortune' you've brought us! Don't worry. She can't do anything anymore. Is it really true that you're named Chrysafenia after your grandmother?"

"People call me Fenia," I clarified, and was annoyed because I felt like a little girl introducing myself.

"And you're the spitting image of your grandmother too. You have the same eyes."

The door of the dining room opened, and Karim appeared. This was another bombshell. Karim, who never even took out the trash for fear of being seen, now decided to make a big entrance. He was carrying a tray with coffee, cold water, and sweets. He set his offerings on the little table in front of the visitor and smiled at her.

"Heavens above!" exclaimed Melpo. "Who are you, young man?"

"Karim, madam."

"Are you Syrian?"

"Yes. Madam found me and keep me."

"Like a stray, eh?" She turned to me. "Don't worry! I do the same, and my husband shouts at me and my children." She tried her coffee and sighed with pleasure. "I feel right at home. That's the way I make coffee. A Syrian taught me." And then, as if something awful had passed through her mind, her beautiful eyes opened wide, and she asked me, "But Hecuba didn't see him, did she?"

"No," I hurried to reassure her. "This is the first time Karim has appeared, and it surprises me that he—"

"Thank God! That woman is a huge racist."

"And you, why did you decide to show yourself?" I asked Karim.

"Madam, kind laugh. Came all the way to the kitchen," he answered, and then, with a slight bow, he left us alone.

Melpo had already lit a cigarette and was enjoying her coffee, looking nostalgically around her. She gave me time to take a sip of the fragrant drink myself and light a cigarette, then she wrapped me in her green gaze.

"And now I'll explain exactly who I am. Your grandmother, Chrysafenia, was the daughter of Fotis Ververis and Smaragda Kantardzis. She married Pericles Sekeris, and they had four children: Hecuba, whom you met; Fotini; Stelios, who was killed in 1973 together with your grandmother; and your mother. Do you follow so far?"

I nodded so as not to interrupt her.

"Your grandmother also had a brother, Nestor Ververis. I am Nestor's daughter."

I was silent while I absorbed this information, linking it with what I had read in the letters. Melpo was the daughter of Nestor, a good friend of Vassilis, who loved my grandmother!

"Apart from being cousins," she continued, "your mother and I were also friends. The two years that separated us didn't make much difference. We played together as little girls, we lived through the first changes together when we became young women, and we whispered to each other about our first crushes."

"Then why did you lose touch? I never saw a letter from you. Did you cut her off like the others?"

"There are a lot of things you don't know, Fenia. And I've come to explain them. But first, you must take something that belongs to you."

She opened her bag and pulled out a small velvet box. I bent forward as I was opening it and froze in that position. On the white velvet lay a fine gold chain from which hung a small gold envelope. Melpo took it out of the box, opened my palm, and left it there. It was the size of my little fingernail, and on it, intricately engraved, was a stamp.

"Open it!" Melpo urged me, and I looked at her without understanding.

How could something so very small be opened? She helped me. From the back, the envelope opened like a real one. A tiny diamond was attached like a seal. When I unfastened it, a thin white metal sheet slid into my palm. On it, in fine calligraphy, the phrase *I love you* was engraved.

So this was the letter that Simeon Kouyoumdzis had designed for his beloved Smaragda, and that his son Vassilis had made for my grandmother. But how had it wound up in the hands of my aunt?

"I found some letters," I told her softly.

"So you know what this is."

"Lots of things are missing. I look at the photographs, and I don't recognize faces. Aunt, I tried to find—"

"Forget the 'aunt' part. Here you were, not knowing I existed. I'd prefer for you to call me by my name."

"Me too. Melpo, will you tell me—"

"That's why I've come. Go get the album so I can start introducing you to your family."

Like an automaton I got up, and when I returned, I was carrying my history. Before Melpo began, though, I asked her to fasten the gold letter around my neck. It had found its place at last.

CHAPTER 2

KANTARDZIS FAMILY

Constantinople, 1910

When Smaragda Kantardzis was born in 1910 in Constantinople—and, to be more precise, in Tarlabasi, the suburb where her parents lived— she didn't bring her family any particular joy. After two older daughters, Anargyros Kantardzis was expecting his wife to give him a son, but God didn't grant him that favor. Nor did He yield to the pleas and prayers of Anargyros's wife, Kleoniki, who knew how much her husband wanted a male child to continue his name. Nearly every day, she went to church to pray, but they had no luck.

The family's two-story house stood among those of dozens of other Greeks who had lived in the neighborhood for many years. This part of Constantinople was a transitional area between the opulent life of Stavrodromi and the simpler and perhaps homelier atmosphere of Tataoulon.

Tarlabasi was divided in two. In the upper part, there were buildings several stories high where the doctors and store owners lived, whereas in its narrow streets, bohemian types strolled nonchalantly. In the lower part, along the Tataoulon Stream, beside the disreputable gypsy neighborhoods, lived the petit bourgeois Greeks.

The Kantardzis house was exactly there. Anargyros's work had been handed down from his father to him, and his surname was rooted deep in the past. Anargyros was a genuine artist. From his hands came scales, but also coffeepots, baking trays, saucepans, even lamps. Apart from having a son, his biggest dream was to be worthy of making a bell. A hard worker, he stoked his fire and started work before dawn, while Jemal, a young Turk who worked for him, carried out his duties as an assistant and also as a salesman. On certain prearranged days, Jemal loaded up as many goods as he could carry and went out into the neighborhoods to hawk the wares of his employer, returning only when his hands were empty and all the goods had found new homes. He handed the money over to Anargyros and later, just before it got dark, helped him close up their shop on the main street of Tarlabasi. In exchange, apart from the pocket change his employer gave him, he was allowed to sleep in the back of the shop, where, among the supplies, Kleoniki would set out food for the poor Turkish boy.

Anargyros considered saving money his highest duty. The family didn't want for anything, but he watched every cent, because saving coins led to gold pounds, and those he kept in a place only he knew about.

He was a silent man, closed and unsociable. Kleoniki didn't often hear his voice, and she preferred it that way, because when her husband did open his mouth, it was never good. He would either scold her or criticize her for something. He had married her not, of course, because he loved her, but because that was what her father had decided. Hers was a very poor family from Kuzgundcuk, a fishing village called Khrysokeramos, on the Asiatic side of Bosporus. The wooden cottage housed a dozen people and the same number of stomachs that had to be filled; fortunately, there were enough fish that at least the family didn't go hungry. The matchmaker who made the offer was from those parts, but she'd moved to Tarlabasi. She met Kleoniki on a visit home, and—who knows how—the woman got the idea to match her with Anargyros.

Nobody thought of asking Kleoniki if she wanted to marry the grim Anargyros, with his rough hands and even rougher personality. Besides, it was thought to be a very good marriage, since the groom was prosperous and an orphan.

"A big thing, that, my dear!" the matchmaker informed the girl. "Neither a mother-in-law in your face nor a father-in-law to boss you around. Lady and mistress of your own house!"

Kleoniki really wanted to say that it was useless to try to persuade her. If it had been in her hands, she would never have agreed to this marriage, but her parents saw in Anargyros a chance to unload one of the mouths that demanded food every day.

The marriage took place in 1906, and immediately after, the couple settled in Tarlabasi. The tall, narrow house with two enclosed balconies to the left and right of the entrance became her home. The young woman needed all of her stamina to fix up the dilapidated house, and in the evenings, she tried not to think about what awaited her in the double bed. Her mother, and even more the matchmaker, had tried tactfully to teach her "that" was a sacred duty for a married woman, but Kleoniki was quite certain that such a painful and exhausting procedure could not be sacred. She escaped for a while, however, when she held her first child in her arms. Her firstborn looked very much like her, and even though Anargyros didn't seem happy with the female addition to his family, Kleoniki was delighted with little Dorothea, who had taken the name of the mother-in-law Kleoniki never knew. After a while, the nightly martyrdom with Anargyros returned, and Kleoniki wasn't sure if it was due to his desire for her or for a son who would continue his name.

When 1908 brought a second daughter, Anargyros didn't confine himself to a grimace of displeasure. As soon as the midwife left, having tidied up mother and baby, he unleashed his anger.

"Don't you know how to make anything but girls?" he shouted.

"I didn't want it, my husband—forgive me!" Kleoniki answered fearfully. "Anyway, it was the will of God, my Lord, so what have I, poor me, done wrong?"

"And what about me? When will I see a male? Is that why I married you? So you can line up one deserter after the other?"

Kleoniki hung her head in shame. She knew that they called girls that because their destiny was to follow their husbands and leave, while a son was another thing.

"Don't distress yourself, husband, and you'll see—the next will be a boy for sure," the woman promised in order to calm him down.

The baby she had just given birth to had begun to cry, but she didn't dare take it in her arms in front of her husband. With relief, she watched him turn around and leave.

It wasn't only the birth of his second daughter that had irritated Anargyros, but also the things that were happening in the city, subjects that were not to be discussed in front of a woman. He hid himself among his furnaces and his bellows and tried to forget it, but his neighbor at the shop, also alarmed by the rumors, came to see him. Jemal was away, so the two men could speak freely.

"Have you heard anything, Moisis?" asked Anargyros as soon as the two of them had sat down behind the shop counter.

"They say Enver Bey has declared a revolution."

"And what does he want?"

"To bring back the Constitution of 1876."

"And do you know what the Constitution of 1876 says?"

"They call it Ottoman equality—so we are all equal, no matter what blood flows in our veins or what god we believe in."

"Hey, that sounds good!"

"Anargyros, the Young Turks don't like the Greeks. Anyway, the sultan, Abdul Hamid, hasn't been standing around with his arms crossed. I heard he brought back that constitution by himself and that he'll hold elections! He's issued a mandate."

"OK. I understand. So we'll be the ones who'll pay for his shenanigans."

"That's what everyone's afraid of."

The two men were silent and emptied the glasses of ouzo they had in front of them in one gulp.

A few months later, ignorant of the events taking place in Constantinople, Kleoniki realized with horror that she was pregnant again. This time, she made up her mind not to leave anything to chance. The very next day, she invited Mrs. Marigo, who lived next door, to come over, and entrusted her with looking after her girls.

"And where are you off to, dear?" the elderly lady asked her, full of curiosity, when she saw Kleoniki with her corset pulled tight and a hat on her head, twisting and untwisting the strap of her bag.

Kleoniki had not expected this question, and now she stood looking guilty, her breath labored.

"Really, Kleoniki, do you have secrets from me?" the woman asked, approaching her with half-closed eyes. "I don't suppose you have a lover somewhere?"

The girl was shocked. "What are you saying, Mrs. Marigo? Aren't you ashamed?"

"Indeed, those things are shameful! But what am I supposed to think when you sneak out as soon as your husband leaves the house?"

The girl's eyes filled with tears, and she collapsed into a chair. The other woman sat down next to her.

"What's happened, my heart, that's upset you so much?" she asked with genuine concern. "Pretend I'm your mother. Open your heart to me, dearie!"

"What can I tell you, Mrs. Marigo?" Kleoniki burst out hopelessly. "I'm pregnant again. And if it's a girl this time, I think Anargyros will hang me upside down!"

"You silly goose! Is that all? You gave me such a fright. And where are you off to in such a hurry?"

"I heard there's a gypsy in Dolapdere, in Tatavla. I'll go and find her."

"Are you looking for a potion, Kleoniki?"

"What else can I do? Anargyros wants a son by hook or by crook, and I don't disagree with him, but how can I help it? So I said—"

"And do you know what you're looking for?"

"No. But I'll ask."

"And why, girl, if you wanted something like that, didn't you come to me? Goodness, don't you have a brain in your head?"

"Can you help me?"

"Don't talk too much now—let's be done with it. You'll go to Dolapdere and ask for the house of Mrs. Zeynep. As soon as you see her, you'll tell her I sent you and then ask for what you want."

Kleoniki followed Mrs. Marigo's instructions to the letter, as she did those of Mrs. Zeynep, but the result was that she lost the child, and her health was affected by the miscarriage. Naturally, she didn't say a word to her husband about what the gypsy woman had given her to drink, and an announcement about the lost pregnancy soon followed. The midwife told Anargyros as politely as she could to leave his wife in peace for a while, until she recovered her full strength, before he tried to make her pregnant again.

That evening, Moisis came into Anargyros's shop in a great hurry.

"Are you alone?" he asked, and Anargyros nodded.

"What's happened?"

"A terrible thing, Anargyros! I just found out now. Do you remember what I told you about Abdul Hamid, may he rot in Hell? He performed his miracle. Counterrevolution, he calls it!"

"What's that?"

"He took up arms, closed the parliament, caught and did away with a few ministers, and now the people, supposedly indignant, are slaughtering innocent Armenians at Adana."

"Slaughtering?"

"It's a massacre, I'm telling you!"

"My God, what about us?"

"The Turks will love it if they find out that the army of the Young Turks is marching this way, and the sultan's dogs are cringing in their corners."

"Do you mean we're not in danger?"

"What can I tell you? Our heads are never secure with them, but for the time being, maybe we're safe."

Jemal returned with empty hands, satisfied with himself, but his smile stopped when he saw his boss's dark expression. He handed over the money, and without a word went about finishing the work he still had to do. Moisis left, giving Anargyros a pained look.

The unrest didn't stop there, and Moisis became Anargyros's living newspaper. On April 12, 1909, the army took over Constantinople, and forty leaders of Abdul Hamid's counterrevolution were hanged in the squares, while he himself was declared to have forfeited his rank and was deposed. The remaining leaders of the counterrevolution were imprisoned, and Hamid's brother, Resat, was declared sultan and given the name Mehmed V.

"Now we're in for it!" said Moisis wryly when he relayed the news.

"Isn't he good?"

"Anargyros, this one's never left the palace. They say he's uneducated. A puppet. They'll do whatever they like with him, and who's to say what's next for us?"

"OK, they can bite each other's heads off one by one, but, my friend, who's going to bother us? We have nothing to do with politics. We just look after our own work and don't get mixed up in theirs."

"Don't you understand? They don't want us Greeks. We're a thorn in their side. And now that the Young Turks have risen up, God save us!" Carefully and in secret, under their shirts, they both made the sign of the cross.

Around that time, Kleoniki found herself pregnant again. This time, she decided to place her hopes only in God and prayed and made entreaties, holding all-night vigils so that her longed-for son would come at last. Dorothea and Makrina were certainly her pride and joy, and she prayed for them first, but she also wanted to bring a lionhearted Kantardzis into the world.

The third girl was baptized Smaragda Kantardzis, and as soon as she arrived, everyone forgot about her. As if the baby understood she was an inconvenience, she decided to remind them of her presence as little as possible. She ate and slept, ate and slept. And if she hadn't felt the milk flowing in her breasts, Kleoniki might have forgotten to feed her. Not that she didn't love her third child, but she felt she was a burden, especially on Kleoniki's soul. Anargyros had given up too, and hardly spoke to his wife. What made the biggest impression on her was that, even once the baby had grown a little, Anargyros didn't touch Kleoniki in the evenings. Instead, he would lie down beside her and, in a few moments, begin to snore. Not that she missed it, but she'd been waiting for the moment when her husband would demand a fourth child in the hopes that it would be a boy.

Perhaps, she reasoned, Anargyros had no desire to touch her for fear the result would be another girl. Three were enough and more than enough. He must have made up his mind that he was unlucky, that the woman he'd married would never produce anything except girls, and so he preferred not to risk such humiliation again.

He had no other complaint, it was true. Kleoniki was a capable housewife and a worthy woman, calm and obedient; he never heard her raise her voice. She made no demands; she had no girlfriends except for Mrs. Marigo and her daughter, both of whom he trusted completely.

As to the other subject, he simply had to accept his fate. In addition, he spent time at the brothels, and the truth was he enjoyed it more. Beautiful women, and their attractions in full view, unlike respectable women who even went to bed fully dressed. A prostitute was one thing; the mother of your children was another. A simple matter, the sorting out of things in Anargyros's mind, and just as much in Kleoniki's. Without ever discussing it, they became simply two housemates who were raising three children.

When, one day, her husband blocked their front door with a heavy chest, Kleoniki was disturbed, but she never interfered in his business.

"Why, my husband?" she asked him later, as they were eating.

"The times are difficult," he answered her gloomily.

"What makes the times more difficult than they were before?" she insisted.

"What can I tell you to make you understand? Look after the household and the children, and don't talk! Just put the chest there as soon as I leave, and ask who it is before you open the door."

"But except for Mrs. Marigo and her daughter, who comes to our house?"

"I'm not talking about our people, woman. You don't understand a thing! Whatever tradesman comes past, you have a bad habit of letting him in. Be more careful!"

"Do you know Mrs. Marigo's niece?"

"Isn't she a teacher at Zappeion? What about the girl?"

"Nothing—just that she told her aunt that the new government, the one with the Young Turks, has turned very wild. The schools are being watched—not just ours but the Bulgarian and the Serbian ones too. They want to make us all Turks or kill us off. They're really wild, Anargyros, and treacherous! In the beginning, they pretended they wanted to treat us all fine and equal, and now that they've risen up in the world, they're showing who they really are!"

Anargyros stared at his wife as if he were seeing her for the first time. It wasn't what he was hearing—he was well aware of current events—but that Kleoniki had said it.

"And how do you know about the Young Turks?"

"Mrs. Marigo tells me."

"And how does Mrs. Marigo find out about them?"

"From her husband, Anargyros."

"And do you women talk about politics when you get together?"

"What politics, my husband? We talk about our lives, and we're afraid! We have children, husbands who are going about the neighborhood all day. And isn't that the reason you put the chest there? You're afraid too. Evlampia, Mrs. Marigo's niece, told us something else she'd found out. They say that the local policemen are forcing their way into houses and searching for weapons. Is that true, my husband?"

"It's true, wife. Moisis told me. That's why I'm telling you—be careful!"

"You too, Anargyros."

If only the Greeks had known how to protect themselves. Their information came mostly in the form of rumors. The Greek newspapers tried to protect themselves and their journalists by maintaining a neutral position, but they felt the Turks breathing down their necks, on the lookout for the slightest misstep. Asia Minor had borne the heaviest burden. Vague reports spoke of the expulsion of Greeks from the region. Erythraia and many parts of Asia Minor, from Adramyttium to Myra, had been emptied of non-Turks. Even in places where the inhabitants hadn't been driven out, nobody dared to leave their houses, not even to work in the fields. Everything stopped. Killings, pillaging, torture, and acts of terrorism became regular, everyday phenomena. There were widespread rumors of women and children being abducted. In Cesme and Karabournou, approximately seventy thousand Greeks were deported. The audacity of the Young Turks was evident in the newspapers they circulated in Smyrna, in which they claimed that the Greeks had emigrated but that their fortunes would naturally be safeguarded until they returned. Armed police but also mobs entered shops and houses and ordered people to hand over everything they had before driving them away with orders never to return.

A few months before the beginning of the First World War, the Ecumenical Patriarchate announced that the Orthodox Church was being expelled and closed all its churches and schools. The only ceremonies held were funerals, and even those were perfunctory. The protests to foreign representatives fell on deaf ears. The foreign powers couldn't interfere in the "internal affairs" of Turkey. The war turned everything on its head. The campaign against the Greeks ended with the general mobilization of the Ottoman Empire.

Kleoniki couldn't understand why or how, quite suddenly, her husband had softened. Anargyros, who didn't like much coming and going, abruptly asked her to invite the neighbors for a gathering at the house. Kleoniki nearly jumped for joy and rolled up her sleeves, ready to officially host Mrs. Marigo's whole family for the first time. Apart from her friend and her friend's husband, Myronas, Kleoniki invited their daughter, Paraskevi, with her own husband, Meletis, and their daughter, who was the same age as Smaragda. Anargyros invited his friend Moisis and his wife, Simela.

That evening, while the women gathered to help the mistress of the house, the men sat together in the large sitting room to discuss what was going on around them. More and more, Anargyros felt the need to be surrounded by people; he felt safer like that. He wanted to talk to others rather than be afraid by himself. Naturally, the main subject of the evening was the war and the conscription of thousands of Constantinople Greeks.

"What we went through," began Myronas, "to save my brother-in-law, you can't imagine! Since he was a Turkish national, he had to go to the war."

"You don't say!" exclaimed Anargyros.

"Yes, indeed! Forty-five Turkish gold pounds is the buyout for every year the war continues. What could we do? We gave it to them."

"And whoever couldn't pay," Moisis interjected, "is hiding. In Stavrodromi, they say, the draft dodgers hide in the roofs of the houses!"

"Roof brigades," Myronas's son-in-law, Meletis, added, making a pun on the Turkish name for them, and nobody could suppress a smile despite the tension.

"The truth is," Anargyros continued, "that here in the city, we have fewer problems with the Turks."

"But for how long?" Moisis asked him. "You know what our late, lamented Patriarch Joachim said about the Young Turks: 'We have nothing to hope for from these people's chauvinism. We must fight to keep this house'. . . We all know what he meant. They won't settle until they've gotten rid of all of us. And now, they've got the war as an excuse."

"It's true!" said Myronas, a cigarette in his mouth. "On the coast, they say, people are leaving. They're heading over to Chios and Lesbos. And not of their own free will. A cousin of mine who comes from there told me the Turkish irregulars burst into the houses and grab whatever they find, then they burn them! Fokea is deserted. My poor cousin got away safely with his heart in his mouth, and what he told me made my blood freeze. I tell you, terrible things are happening down there. The Young Turks have gotten into the local people's heads, stirred them up. They use religion to turn them into fanatics, but plunder and rape is their real reward."

The atmosphere became heavier. Kleoniki came in with a tray loaded with snacks to accompany the men's ouzo. As she left, she saw the men, as if they were obeying a single order, raise their glasses and empty them with dark looks, then hurriedly refill them.

"There are moments," Meletis said softly, "when I think about taking my family and leaving."

"And where would you go, sir?" asked Moisis. "This is our place."

"Is it, Moisis? Your place is where you live, raise children, work, and get ahead. Your place isn't where you're scared stiff about whether you'll wake up, whether you'll see your wife and child tortured before everything is destroyed by fanatical Turks who don't think but just obey."

The women came into the sitting room, and the men changed the subject, despite the fact they'd have liked to talk more. They all had the same need: to talk, to exorcise their fears. The interruption, though, was imperative. These weren't things for women to hear and be terrified about. They sat down at the table to eat the tasty things Kleoniki had prepared, but together with the delicious smell of the food, the air carried young Meletis's last remarks.

It was a great mystery to Kleoniki how the three children she had given birth to and who had been raised by the same parents could be so very different. Every year that passed brought a new surprise for her.

Dorothea had inherited only her mother's outward appearance. Tall, brown haired, and plump, with very pale skin, she gave an impression of sweetness and calm, whereas in fact she was a difficult child. In front of her father, she was always obedient, but she opened her little mouth and talked back to her mother without regard for her mother's heavy hand. Whatever she had to say, she said, and never mind the consequences.

Makrina, the opposite of her sister, was short and very thin. Her features were very similar to Anargyros's, but despite that, you wouldn't call her ugly. Her character remained a mystery to Kleoniki, who asked herself where her daughter had come from. Smiling and cheerful, with a song on her lips from the moment she woke in the morning, she never annoyed anyone, and her father may not have admitted it, but he had a weakness for her.

Smaragda was the greatest mystery to her parents as well as her sisters. Externally, she seemed to possess all the beauty Anargyros and

Kleoniki had between them. She was tall—the tallest of the three, with a body that became firmer and more desirable as she grew, and with eyes that were at times honey colored, and at other moments the color of the copper her father worked. Her hair was light; she liked to drip lemon juice on it and sit in the sun so it would turn blond. Her skin was almost transparent, like the girl herself. Despite her perfect beauty, she went everywhere unnoticed. As she grew, they wondered if she had any substance, if she was some sort of spirit. She never complained; she did as her mother asked quickly, never making a mistake. The person who knew her best was a girl of the same age, Evanthia, granddaughter of Mrs. Marigo. They had grown up together since infancy. With Evanthia, Smaragda wasn't ashamed or speechless or transparent. During the hours they spent together, the little girl revealed all the things she might have said the following day, which she would spend in silence.

The big surprise for Kleoniki was that one day—while the two older girls learned to embroider and knit with great difficulty—little Smaragda, seated beside them, taught herself very quickly with a leftover length of wool that had fallen on the floor. When Kleoniki saw her struggling with the crochet hook in her tiny hands, she stared in amazement. As if remembering the child, she moved closer and began to show her. Smaragda was so disturbed by the unexpected attention that at first she froze, but she soon began to soak up the lesson like a sponge. And while Dorothea sat complaining as she tried to do the basic stitches, and Makrina, simpering and laughing, tried to escape her chore, Kleoniki's youngest, her Smaragda, patiently and persistently learned beside her. Smaragda stubbornly bit her lip and wrestled with thread, cloth, needles, and crochet hooks. In the same way, she learned her letters. Kleoniki had to fight with Anargyros for permission to teach her. She waited to catch him in a good mood before sharing Mrs. Marigo's suggestion.

It rained heavily that evening, and Jemal came back early without having managed to sell all the goods. The muddy streets made walking difficult for the few people who were out, and they hurried home. Despite this, the day's profit was very good because the Turkish boy had managed to sell the most expensive items he was carrying, and Anargyros was satisfied. He tidied up the shop and, although it was still early, left to go home. Something about the cold, the dreariness of the weather, and the rain that got heavier every hour made him hurry to reach its warmth and put on his slippers.

When Kleoniki greeted him, he was soaked to the bone. She scolded him. "Mercy! God-fearing creature! You'll catch a chill, and then what will become of me? Didn't you think to take an umbrella?"

She helped him to change and, for good measure, rubbed him with alcohol. Anargyros didn't tell her, but he enjoyed her attentions as he'd loved his mother's caresses. Warm and dry, he sat down to eat and smiled when he saw in front of him the bowl of delicious, meaty soup and beside it the platter with the meat and vegetables.

"Bravo, wife!" he said. "Just the thing for a day like this!"

Kleoniki blushed. Her husband almost never praised her, and every kind word from him was balm to her. Sitting opposite him to keep him company, Kleoniki felt that surely this was the ideal opportunity to speak to him. She let him swallow the first mouthfuls before she began.

"My husband, I want to tell you something, but first I'll ask— would you like to hear this now, or would you prefer we discuss this later?" she began sheepishly.

"If you're going to make me angry, neither now nor later!" he answered, swallowing a large spoonful of his soup.

"It's nothing bad, my pasha, but I don't know how you'll take it."

"Enough! Tell me, then, and we'll see."

"Mrs. Marigo's niece Olympia, the one from Zappeion, said she could teach Evanthia to read."

"So? What's that got to do with us?"

"Well, the girl suggested that, since she's coming to teach Evanthia, she could teach our girls too."

"Why?"

"What do you mean 'why,' my husband? It's good for them to learn something else. The times are changing. We don't know what may happen to us. Let the girls learn their ABC's at least. Look at me; I never even learned how to write my name properly. I don't know how to read a newspaper or write a letter to my mother. And why would I write? How would she read it? Anyway—"

"Wife, learning lots of letters isn't for women!"

"But I didn't say lots, my husband . . . a few . . . just so they can sign their names. Besides, Olympia can only come for a few hours in the evening. I'm not talking about sending them to school."

"I should hope not!" Anargyros snapped. "I won't have my daughters sauntering around the streets like—"

"Stop, my pasha! Where is your mind going? I just said that, seeing as the girl is coming . . . What's more, Anargyros, do you have anything to reproach Mrs. Marigo's niece for? Isn't she respectful and serious, despite the fact that she's educated?"

"It's true," her husband admitted thoughtfully.

"You see? The girl teaches at Zappeion, and she tells us how much people respect the girls from good families who go there. They call them Zappies! And they say the school is a real palace. Such marble, such classrooms and offices for the teachers and the directors. She told us about it yesterday, and we all listened with our mouths open. Zappeion is a real jewel, she says. She also told us something else I didn't understand."

"What's that?"

"That, for years now, the Zappeion has been declared on the same level as the Arsakeion school! That's good, isn't it, my bey?"

"Very good."

"So, just think, our girls will have a young woman who teaches at such a school for their teacher! What do you say, husband? Will you give your permission?"

"Dammit, wife, you've got my head whirling like a top!" he said, pretending to scold her, but he already knew he'd accept. He saw nothing bad in his wife's desire to educate their girls a little. Besides, Moisis's daughter had a tutor coming to the house too.

Discerning the likelihood of a positive answer, Kleoniki wanted to make things more certain. She took her husband's empty plate, and in a few minutes, a delicious piece of halva appeared, which she knew was his weakness, together with his coffee. She'd toasted pine nuts, which he loved, with the semolina, and the cinnamon sprinkled on top released its aroma to satisfy the sense of smell as well as sight. Anargyros looked at her happily, a hint of a smile on his face.

"It seems that you laid your plans carefully. All right, then! I give you permission. Starting tomorrow, the girls can begin to learn their letters."

Kleoniki was so overjoyed she took his hand and kissed it, full of respect.

The lessons began, in fact, the next evening. It was decided that the Kantardzis house was the most convenient place for the lessons, since it was larger, and Kleoniki tried to transform the empty room behind the kitchen into a suitable classroom. This suited Anargyros, because then it wouldn't be necessary for his girls to leave the house at all, especially in winter when it got dark early.

When the three girls found out about it, it was only Smaragda, the youngest, who showed any enthusiasm. The other two exchanged a look full of distaste, but they knew they couldn't escape. Their mother was determined. They submitted to their fate, but from the beginning it appeared they had "no aptitude for learning," as Miss Olympia said sadly. Dorothea was constantly glum and negative, and Makrina was much more interested in her teacher's clothing than what she had to say. In contrast, Smaragda and Evanthia were attentive and studious. The conquest of reading was, for little Smaragda, the entrance to Paradise. It opened doors she could not have imagined. When her father left the house, she secretly opened his newspaper and tried to read it. She didn't understand anything, but she persisted. Afterward, she took her workbook and copied down whole sentences for practice. That helped her very quickly to develop an even style of writing with round and legible letters. Naturally, the lessons were in Greek, but Olympia conscientiously taught them to read and write in Turkish too. Only in history was the whole lesson devoted to Greece and the achievements of their ancestors. It was the only hour when all of Olympia's pupils were attentive; their interest in learning about their people comforted her, as did the performance of the two younger girls.

For Kleoniki, New Year's of 1918 was the best of her life up to that point. Without explanation, which she wasn't interested in anyway, Anargyros announced to her that their neighbor Myronas had invited them to his house for a New Year's meal his wife had prepared, and he'd accepted. Blushing deeply, Kleoniki couldn't believe her good fortune. Before Christmas, she had her clothes ready, although she didn't know that her dark-blue dress would almost scuttle the holiday. She'd had it made recently, following the fashion of the time, which raised the height of the skirt to the ankle. With great difficulty, it must be said, she had accepted the dressmaker's proposed design.

"But Mrs. Kleoniki," the girl insisted, "look around you. All the women shortened their dresses at least three years ago!"

"Yes, my dear, but as a married woman, is it right for me to do such a thing?" she objected, her face bright red.

"It has nothing to do with your being married. The fashion isn't just for the unmarried girls. Anyway, with so much mud in the streets of Constantinople, why should we want dresses that drag on the ground?"

This last remark was the most compelling. Every time she left her house to go to church or memorials, Kleoniki had to spend an awful lot of time cleaning the hems of her clothes. She decided to shorten the simple dark-blue dress herself, together with the rest of her clothes.

That morning, she dressed the children first, adorning them in their jewelry, and combed their hair nicely so they could go to church with their father. Immediately after that, when she was alone, she began to get ready with a racing heart. She was impatient to put on her new acquisition, like a girl going to her first dance. She combed her hair so her hat would sit well on it, and before she put the hat on her head, she put on the dress and looked at herself in the large mirror of her room. In keeping with the more frugal fashions of wartime, jewels and ornaments weren't necessary, but she wouldn't go to a strange house without the good gold chain Anargyros had given her for their wedding. Nor could she not wear the gold earrings her mother had put on her that day. She gave up her large bracelet but wore her gold watch and, naturally, the ring, also a present from her husband, with a large blue stone that matched her dress. She didn't forget to dab a little cologne on her headscarf after she put some behind her ears. Ready and adorned, she stood and waited so as not to crush her new clothes. Every now and then, she bent down and saw that her shoes showed, and she blushed. She felt a little depraved. Never in her life had she shown even an inch of her body, and now she was sure that, as soon as she sat down, her slim ankles would be on public display. A little smile rose to her lips, but she suppressed it as she heard the door. Anargyros and the girls had returned. She rushed to make his coffee and serve the girls breakfast very carefully so as not to dirty her clothes. Perhaps she shouldn't have gotten dressed so early, but she couldn't wait.

It was Makrina who unintentionally caused a fuss. Chewing a slice of bread with quince preserves, her favorite, she admired her mother, who was standing at the window, waiting for them to finish so she could clear the table.

"Father, did you see how beautiful Mama is today in her new dress?" she asked Anargyros, who was busy rolling his morning cigarette.

He raised his eyes, and then he noticed her. Kleoniki saw his look pass over her, at first indifferently, but then it got stuck at the hemline of the dress.

"What's that?" he asked quietly, but his voice had become rough.

"A new dress, my pasha. I told you I was going to have a new dress made, and you gave me the money."

Kleoniki was almost stammering she was so upset. She felt drops of sweat run down her back.

"I paid for that rag? Is that the way you're going out in the street? In half a dress?"

"That's the way they're wearing them now, my husband, so their clothes won't drag—"

"Who's wearing them? Respectable women? Kleoniki, go and change into an old dress so that we don't ruin New Year's Day!"

"But it's not so short, my bey!" she risked, wondering at her own courage and boldness.

"Have you gone crazy, woman? If you try to sit down, everything shows. Sit and you'll see I'm right!"

Kleoniki dared to sit down carefully. The dress came up imperceptibly and just showed her ankles.

"I told you so! You're proud of that vulgar thing?" Anargyros fumed. "What did I tell you? Your legs show! See here, if you want us to visit the people next door, you'll put on a dress that's suitable for a respectable married woman!"

Kleoniki's eyes filled with tears. She got up, resigned to her fate, but help came from where she least expected it. Makrina, who had done all the damage, ran and hugged her.

"Father, please! Mother looks so beautiful today! I don't want her to put on another dress."

The other two girls came and formed a wall around their mother. Anargyros was astonished by this small rebellion happening in front of his eyes.

"It seems to be that, with the New Year, all the ladies here have forgotten who's the head of this house!" he roared.

Makrina moved away from her mother and approached him. A timid smile lifted the corners of her mouth, but her eyes flashed, full of cunning as she exploited the weakness she knew her father had for her. "Come now, Father," she pleaded. "Do you want to spoil our enjoyment on this day of all days? Anyway, don't we deserve a treat? Mother is so beautiful!"

The ten-year-old girl spoke in a way that was quite inappropriate for her age, and even dared to take her father's hand. Kleoniki could see the battle raging inside him. She broke away from the embrace of the other two girls and gave a dry cough to clear her throat.

"It doesn't matter, girls. Your father is right. I'll go and change. You finish your breakfast."

She went toward the bedroom and couldn't believe her ears when she heard a stern voice calling her back: "Seeing that the girls want it too, leave it, wife. Wear your dress, but pull it down as much as you can when you sit!"

And so, 1918 began very nicely for Kleoniki after all. When they arrived at Mrs. Marigo's house, she noticed that all the women were wearing dresses like hers, which were similar in length and design, and she glanced discreetly at her husband to see whether he understood that he had unjustly provoked the scene at their house. His face revealed nothing.

Apart from them, Mrs. Marigo and her husband had invited their cousins, Olympia's parents, and another family, who had a son. While she was helping set the table, Kleoniki managed to ask her friend, "Mrs. Marigo, who are those people?"

"My mother is matchmaking!" Paraskevi interjected, laughing.

"Hush, you!" her mother scolded. "These things aren't said in a loud voice. Wait and see if they like each other first." She turned to Kleoniki and continued in a low voice: "Olympia is at an age to marry, and

Kleonas is a very good boy. My husband and I are hoping something will come of our work, because her mother is bursting!"

"Why?"

"What do you mean 'why'? My niece is nearly thirty. Is it right for a girl her age to remain single? Teaching is all very well, but a woman must marry to have children."

"That's right," Kleoniki agreed.

But Mrs. Marigo and Olympia's mother had tried in vain. Kleonas was not to Olympia's taste, nor she to his. At least the day passed pleasantly, and the men stayed far from unpleasant subjects, wanting to drive away whatever bad things awaited them in the new year. Information about the war reached them in a confused manner, and news about the Ottoman Empire wasn't good. Their homeland was being tossed about like some giant whose legs had been chopped off. The German allies weren't doing well at the front. There were rumors that the United States had joined in the game, but nobody knew whether this was a bad thing or a good thing.

In 1918, the good and the bad came together. Fortunately, the bad came only to the Marigo family, while the good was the end of the war. In October 1918 at Mudros, the Ottoman minister of the navy, Huseyin Rauf, signed an agreement that basically brought the Ottoman Empire to its knees. The terms were humiliating. Among other things, the armistice relinquished the Turkish fleet as well as their weapons to the Allies, decreed the immediate opening of the Dardanelles, and granted free passage for all shipping vessels in the region. The Greeks, who were on the side of the victors, couldn't believe their good fortune. After so many years of oppression, after the expulsions they had suffered, they suddenly found themselves in a strong position. A short time later, the naval squadron passed through the straits. Among other vessels were the Greek battleships *Kilkis* and *Averof*, which anchored in front of the

Dolmabahce Palace, its Greek flag visible even from Hagia Sophia. It seemed like a dream that had taken five centuries, since the sacking of Constantinople, to become a reality. The victory demonstrations were very moving, and most importantly for the Greeks, they were able to participate without fear.

In the Kantardzis household, the first, naturally, to learn and then to sing a Greek song that was popular at the time was Makrina. Her clear voice reached all the way to the street: "To your health, always your health, we spoke of this. It was a dream that we forgot."

Kleoniki scolded her and told her to lower her voice, but the chatterbox Dorothea joined in.

"What are you afraid of, Mother? It's over! We're not afraid of anyone. We won, didn't we?"

"Hush, girl. Don't try to play the teacher with me," Kleoniki retorted. "Turks are passing by. Do you want them to hear you and get angry? Who knows what we'll wake up to next? You're still young, but our eyes have seen a lot of things!"

As she did whenever one of the girls was disobedient, Kleoniki grabbed her slipper and chased them to give them a beating. In any case, her husband seemed in better spirits recently, and she knew he'd been going to admire the Greek flag fluttering proudly in the harbor. Once he had taken her with him, but Kleoniki was more frightened than pleased. There were crowds, and men in uniform. Her gaze fell on a few Turks who were looking askance at the *Averof*, which was an impressive ship. She took Anargyros's hand, and they left in a hurry. When they arrived home, as soon as she closed the door behind them, she blocked it once more with the chest.

"What's the matter, wife? What were you dragging me home for? Didn't you enjoy our walk? You saw the ships, didn't you? The *Averof*?"

"The only thing I saw, my pasha, was the Turks looking at us furiously. Even if they gobble us up, it doesn't satisfy them!"

"You don't know, and that's why you're frightened. We won!"

"Ah, Holy Virgin, you're talking to me like I'm one of your daughters! Do we know how long this peace will last? And what if they win again?"

"Woman, come to your senses! The war's over."

"Yes. And you think they're not in a hurry to start it again? If you want my opinion, these people have no decency. Politics aren't for us. Just do your work, my husband, and nothing more. And tell me, this ship . . ."

"The *Averof*?"

"Yes. Why did you tell me they call it 'Satan's Ship'?"

"Because the Turks were afraid of it! They say they were beaten by a Greek convoy in the Balkan Wars."

"Just listen to what he's telling me—he doesn't hear his own words! Was that another war?"

"Yes, it was!"

"Then you should realize I'm right. War doesn't end, husband. I know that much. Now one has ended; at some point, another will begin. So, listen to me: I may not know many things, but the less you show yourself, the less danger you're in."

Only a few days had passed after the end of the war before another one broke out in their neighborhood, right next door.

Kleoniki was waiting for Olympia to come for the lesson when Mrs. Marigo burst into the house in tears, then fainted in her arms. Kleoniki didn't know what to do. Fortunately, Mrs. Marigo's daughter, Paraskevi, arrived, but she too was in a terrible state, her eyes red from crying and her hair uncombed.

"Dear, what's happened? Will you tell me?" Kleoniki asked.

The older woman's look spoke volumes. All four of their children had crowded around, not wanting to miss a single word.

Kleoniki spoiled their plans. "Dorothea, take your sisters and Evanthia, and go to the back room to study something. We have to talk!"

All four sulked, but Kleoniki's expression made it clear that negotiating was impossible. Whoever opened her mouth to complain would be the first to pay the fine. The slipper was always Kleoniki's first resource, but after that she would pull their braids. The girls lowered their heads and disappeared. Kleoniki heard their door closing and then closed the door to the living room before sitting down opposite the troubled women.

"So, now tell me, Mrs. Marigo! What happened that you came here in such an awful state? Paraskevi, you tell me! Why are you like this, and why did your mother faint? Did something happen to the men?"

"No!" cried Paraskevi.

Her mother jumped in: "How can I tell you something so shameful, my dear? The disaster that befell us! Olympia—"

"What's happened to your niece?"

"Bad luck to her, with the poison she's fed us, the wretched girl! She's been stolen, Kleoniki."

"Bah!" It was the only thing Kleoniki could say as she remained staring at the two weeping women. After a few minutes, when she'd taken in what she'd heard, she repeated it a little louder: "Bah! Stolen how?"

"That's the worst part, Kleoniki," said Paraskevi. "She was taken away by a Turk, my crazy cousin."

Kleoniki closed her eyes as if trying to persuade herself that she hadn't heard right. She held her ears to make sure they were in the proper place.

"What are you telling me, Paraskevi? Come to your senses!" she scolded her. "Olympia with a Turk? Those things don't happen."

"Well, then why are we like this?" continued Mrs. Marigo. "Our young Greek men asked for her hand many times. The girl was as refreshing as cold water! She had a good name, good fortune, good looks, and faith, and she went and got blinded, the cursed girl, by a Turk, an infidel!"

"Yes, but how did it happen? Where did she meet him?"

"He's a teacher too," Mrs. Marigo said. "How and when, don't ask me. I went over to my cousin's house, and she told me all the details. Olympia left a letter. She loves him, she says, and so as not to make things worse, he took her and they left. Do you hear? Do you hear what I'm saying? How much worse could things get?"

"So, where did they go?"

"To Batum. They'll work there if they can, may they be forgiven! How can my poor cousin, who's shut up in her house, forgive them? They can't look anyone in the eye because of their shame. Olympia, with so much education, such a position, to go off with a Turk! And naturally, in order to marry him, she'll change her faith, the slut!"

New tears were shed, and this time Kleoniki wept with them. She couldn't absorb the disaster that had happened to her friends and their family, and she had no words to comfort them.

Anargyros took it even worse than she did when he found out that evening. Kleoniki waited for the girls to go to bed before she told him, speaking with a trembling voice. She saw him roll his eyes, and then his fist fell heavily on the table, making plates and glasses shake dangerously while out of his mouth came a string of curses in Turkish that made Kleoniki bite her lip. It was the first time she had ever heard her husband curse like that. She quickly served him a brandy to calm him down.

"My bey, my pasha," she begged him. "Don't upset yourself so. It's terrible what's happened, but it's not in our home, my husband. Olympia is no relative of ours."

"Don't let me hear that name ever again! We made her the teacher of our children. Fine things she's taught them!" shouted Anargyros.

"Now, why are you mixing things up? Reading and writing is what our girls learned—she didn't teach them anything else."

"A Greek girl who runs off with a Turk, a girl who feeds her parents such poison. Since she doesn't respect God and gives up her religion, she doesn't deserve to be a teacher or come near our girls. Better for her that she ran, so they didn't lynch her!"

The only ones who were pleased by the disappearance of Olympia were Dorothea and Makrina, who were spared the everyday martyrdom of their lessons. More because they felt they should than because they cared, they asked their mother two days later: "Mother, won't we be having lessons again with Miss Olympia?"

"Your teacher got married and moved away," their mother answered curtly.

"And when did such a thing happen?" insisted Dorothea, who'd heard something and wanted to be sure about it.

"And why didn't she ask us?" complained Makrina, upset to have missed out on the celebration.

"Look at her, wanting a wedding invitation," her mother scolded.

"So, we won't have any more lessons?"

All three of them turned to look at Smaragda, who had spoken in a voice plaintive with genuine sorrow.

Kleoniki approached her youngest with understanding. "No, Smaragda, dear. I know you loved your teacher and the lessons, but sweetheart, those things are over now. Whatever you learned, it was worth it."

After what happened, she would not have dared to ask Anargyros for another teacher for the girls or to send them to school, despite the fact that it was her dearest wish, and she was sad because she knew how much her youngest wanted to continue. She jumped for joy when Mrs. Marigo found some old books of Olympia's, which she gave to Smaragda. The girl's face shone, and she hugged her mother with a daring she didn't usually have.

In the years that followed, Olympia's sin was discussed with horror and scorn in hushed voices at evening gatherings and tea parties. Even if some woman, deep down inside, understood the girl, she didn't dare say so. Many romantic souls sighed secretly, calculating what a great love the girl must have felt to run off with her beloved, overlooking the fact that he was a Turk. For their part, the men didn't try to put themselves in the shoes of the man who was probably ostracized by his family for loving a Christian and a Greek, especially in those times, when the Turks had to accept their defeat. From Mrs. Marigo, Kleoniki and Anargyros learned that the girl's parents had been forced to leave Tarlabasi and had moved to Galata. In the aftermath of the event, their small community failed to notice when the Patriarchate, exploiting the strength it had acquired, banned Turkish in Greek schools.

A few months later, though, something new made hearts take wing. The herald for Anargyros, as always, was the well-informed Moisis. One day, he came into his friend's workshop, and beneath his mustache he was smiling.

"Give me a coffee, and I'll tell you the news!" he announced.

"If it's good news, why are you talking about coffee? We'll drink an ouzo. Kleoniki's made me some salt tuna today that'll have you licking your fingers!"

Anargyros left his bellows and fire, and the two men set themselves up with ouzo and snacks behind the tall counter.

"Tell me, then! What have you come to say?" Anargyros prompted him.

"A resolution was passed, brother," said Moisis grandly.

"I have no idea what you're talking about."

"Hey, just listen. A resolution was passed for the union of Constantinople with Greece."

"You don't say!"

Anargyros hastened to clink glasses with his friend.

"Do you think our torments have ended?"

"We won, Anargyros. That hasn't changed. And it's time for the city of Constantinople to be reborn Greek. Time to topple the minarets of the Hagia Sophia! Asia Minor will soon be ours again."

"Do you think so, Moisis?"

"Just as I see you and you see me! Big things will happen, Anargyros. We'll be rubbing our eyes out of disbelief!"

Moisis's predictions came true, but not the way everyone in the Greek world would have liked. And even if, at the beginning, public opinion was clear, suddenly, as if some hand had intervened, the balance was turned upside down.

In May of that year, Greece landed in Smyrna. The *Averof* was there, and the Greek forces were received with an enthusiasm that bordered on worship. The news reached Constantinople quickly. Everyone breathed more easily; fear had disappeared, and hope took its place in people's hearts, together with national pride.

A Greece of two continents and five seas . . . the "Great Idea" swept their wishes along with it—ignoring the 1453 lesson of the Kerkoporta Gate, when the last Byzantine emperor was overthrown by traitors who entered the palace through a small wooden door. It took three years to obliterate the dream—three years of smoke, ashes, blood, and cries of agony. The expulsion that had begun many years earlier and been interrupted by the Mudros Armistice resumed, and it was more merciless than ever. The Asia Minor Catastrophe and the events that followed put an end to the two-thousand-year presence of Greeks in that land. The reckoning was tragic. The politicians and military commanders' dream of retaking the country was paid for with the blood of innocents, as is so often the case.

Anargyros couldn't look Kleoniki in the eye after what happened. Everything she'd said back when he was so certain that Greece would remain victorious went on echoing in his ears. She didn't understand, and wondered why her husband didn't say a word in the house. At first, she attributed his behavior to the fear that had overcome them all over again. They bolted their doors as soon as the troubles broke out. Kleoniki didn't open up even for the milkman, and gave the children tea even though they complained, not knowing the reason. Nor did she open the door for the egg seller or anyone else. But it was impossible to stay shut in forever. Timidly, like snails after the rain, the men began coming out to go to their shops, fearing that they'd find everything destroyed, but nothing had been disturbed, and they all took heart. Still, Anargyros kept his head down. One evening, long after the children had gone to bed, he ate yet another meal silently, and this was the drop that made Kleoniki's glass overflow.

"My husband, there's something you're not telling me," she began, nervously drawing shapes on the white tablecloth with her fingernail.

"What else should I tell you? Didn't we both learn the news about the war together?"

"Anargyros, I'm not talking about the war now. Enough. Whatever happened, happened; ordinary people were killed and houses were burned, but not in Constantinople. Here, nobody bothered us. Why do you worry so much?"

Anargyros rolled a cigarette and lit it, and after he spoke, Kleoniki would have liked one too, to recover from everything she'd heard.

"I have a burden inside me, wife. You were right, and I was wrong. You told me we shouldn't be in a hurry to celebrate because they could start another war and win. And it happened like you said. I scolded and mocked you. I thought, *She's a woman—what does she know about such things?* But now you say they didn't harm any of us, and well . . . I didn't want to frighten you, but the Greeks are leaving Constantinople. A thousand or two every day. Our embassy has closed here."

Silence spread through the room. On the one hand, Kleoniki was shocked by the news; on the other, in the sixteen years of her marriage, Anargyros had never admitted that she could be right and he could be wrong, and for him to do it at this moment meant that things were very serious. She dared to look at him. He was smoking with his head down.

"Don't you have anything to say?" he asked.

"My husband, I am an illiterate woman who knows nothing besides her housekeeping," she answered calmly. "But I think that, at times like these, the question of who's right and who's wrong is irrelevant. Just let the suffering become a lesson. That's the best thing. I don't know what will happen to us tomorrow, but here, where we live, we just need money. It was money that helped Myronas get his brother-in-law out of serving in the army, and haven't we done everything that we needed to all these years by bribing people? So look to your work, and do whatever you can to be a good provider. And guard our money as you always have."

"It's in our room," her husband confessed.

"I know," Kleoniki said, surprising him. "I found it under the floor, between the floorboards."

"You found it?" said Anargyros in wonder, sitting up in his chair.

"Ever since you brought me here as a bride, I've kept this house clean with my own hands. Do you think I don't know every inch of it? Except that I wanted to tell you, my pasha, don't keep it all in one place. A little here, a little there. It's safer!"

Anargyros was thunderstruck. Was this his wife? Where had she hidden all this cleverness? Deep inside, he buried his shame about the way he had treated her for so many years. In his mind, Kleoniki was a slave who looked after him and nothing more. He'd expected his wife to give him a son, and when she didn't, he blamed her. An endless chain of thoughts and guilt, but he didn't have the strength to acknowledge any more. Over time, Kleoniki would become aware of the changes in his attitude, and feel bitter that they'd come so late.

The next discussion between the couple was also about something unpleasant. Anargyros came home from the shop shivering. January of 1923, which had just ended, had seemed like the coldest month ever to him. His wife, who had watched the snow and ice from the window, greeted him with a robe she had warmed near the stove, and his slippers, which were piping hot. She gave him a brandy to warm himself up and then sat down to keep him company as he ate, as she did every evening. He drank his soup slowly, without any enthusiasm, and Kleoniki was surprised. Egg-lemon chicken soup, and Anargyros struggling to get through it?

"Maybe I didn't make the soup right, my husband? Is it too sour?"

"The soup's fine, wife—tasty as ever."

"Then don't you feel well?" She got up to feel his forehead. It was cool.

"There's nothing wrong with me, Kleoniki. Sit down . . . I want to speak to you."

She looked at him with a frown. "Something bad happened, didn't it?"

"Here, where we live, were you expecting something good? Moisis told me today that they signed a treaty."

"What's that mean, my pasha? Is it good or bad?"

"Probably bad. They will exchange populations, he says."

"How will they exchange them?"

"Greeks from here will go to Greece, and Turks from there will come here."

"Even if they don't want to?"

"Yes, exactly. If they'd wanted to, they'd have done it. But now it's compulsory. Our people will leave their houses and fortunes, and Turks will come to stay here. And our people will go to live in the houses of the Turks from Greece."

"Just like that, everyone must leave what he has and go?"

"That's what Moisis says."

"Mercy, him again! He never has any good news to tell us."

"Is it Moisis's fault? Didn't you say that he finds things out and tells me everything I know about what's going on?"

Kleoniki began playing with the tablecloth again. "Just think, my husband. With this paper that you're describing, the one they signed, have you considered that they seem to be punishing their own people too?"

"Why do you say that?"

"Look, husband. Even the Turks who live in Greece think of it as their country, like we do here in Turkey. They were born there, had children, grandchildren. They have friends, neighbors. How will they leave it so suddenly and be uprooted?"

"Are you in your right mind, woman, to think I'd pity the Turks?" Anargyros objected.

"They're people, my pasha, people! There are big fish in the sea, but there are also little sardines. Even in the ocean, the big fish take what they want, but the little ones pay. And on land it's the same. I'm not saying there aren't a lot of people who wanted it, but there are others who thought they'd end their lives in the place they'd learned to call home. When you are forced to uproot yourself, Turk or Greek, both feel the same pain."

Anargyros began rolling a cigarette, trying to understand his wife's words, and realized that she was right. But Kleoniki's thoughts had run ahead of his.

"Anargyros!" she called out, surprising him. "Why did you tell me all that? Are they driving us out too? Is this your way of telling me we must leave our house? Mother of God! Our house?"

"Hold on a moment, my good woman. Where has your head gone? If it was something like that, would I be behaving this way? Would I be sitting, rolling a cigarette? The Greeks of Constantinople are not part of the treaty."

"Praise the Virgin! You gave me a fright, Anargyros."

Most of the news, the worst of it, Anargyros himself didn't know. He wasn't aware that more than thirty thousand Greeks, some of the richest in Constantinople, in fact, had left in the autumn of 1922, but the government didn't want them to come back. Those who had Turkish passports returned, because the Turks couldn't do anything about it. But they exploited the new law passed in April of the same year and confiscated the savings of the rest. There were rumors that the amount that passed to Turkish hands was between two hundred thousand and four hundred thousand pounds sterling. Suddenly, the Greeks of Constantinople, after the Treaty of Lausanne and because of the Asia Minor Catastrophe, had been transformed into a passive minority. And if they gained some "privileges," such as the right to practice their own faith freely, and to teach Greek as well as Turkish in their schools, the word *minority* would characterize their future. A new period was beginning, with Kemal Ataturk sworn in as the first president of a now-united Turkey in 1923, while in the same year, the capital was moved from Constantinople to Ankara.

Kleoniki never forgave herself for not understanding right away, for not reading the signs that led to the family's own catastrophe. She now believed those who said, "From one bad thing, thousands follow." The beginning of the trouble was thought to be Makrina's new friend, who'd moved to Tarlabasi with her parents. Nobody knew the origins of the Yiouroukos family, a couple with one daughter and two sons. Flora, the daughter, was the same age as Dorothea, but it was Makrina with whom she became inseparable. Kleoniki didn't see anything harmful about this new relationship, although she didn't take to the plump girl with the impudent look who often came to her house.

Even though Flora's mother, Katina Yiouroukos, suggested that they spend time together, Kleoniki made it clear she wasn't eager to advance her relationship with the woman. On this subject, Mrs. Marigo, who also didn't care for the new neighbors, was in agreement.

"I don't know, my dear, but there's something I don't like about them," she said. "There's a lot of Turks coming and going over there."

"Because of work?"

Kostakis Yiouroukos was a businessman, but no one knew anything about his business. Some said he was mixed up in the spice trade, while others said tobacco.

"What work could that be, Kleoniki?" Mrs. Marigo objected. "Anargyros also sells what he makes to the Turks, but he doesn't let them in his house."

"Lord preserve us!" Kleoniki exclaimed.

"Dimitrios's wife, Kalliopitsa, told me the other day that a Turk, a really dignified fellow, came with a car and picked them all up."

Kleoniki shuddered and decided to speak to her daughter and extricate her from her relationship with Flora, but it wasn't as easy as she thought. Makrina defended her friend with great fervor.

"You shouldn't be saying what you're saying, Mother," she insisted. "Flora is my friend, and it doesn't matter to me what company her parents keep. She's not to blame for anything."

"All I'm saying is keep your distance, in case anything reaches your father's ears."

"But what did Flora do to make you not like her?" said her daughter. "The poor thing thinks of you as a second mother!"

"Unfortunate for her, because she already has a mother! And if she has one, why does she need a second? You think you're fooling me? Evanthia's been coming here since she was a baby, and she never says things like that, but this Flora, who just arrived, says she thinks of me as a mother? Makrina, be careful! I won't say any more."

Makrina obeyed, grateful at least that she wouldn't lose her friend. That spring, the girls went out together. The first time, it was to attend church for Good Friday, and the second time, they went to pick flowers and make wreaths for May Day.

Later, Kleoniki racked her brain trying to understand how she had allowed her daughter to go walking with Flora. Because, after these two outings, it became a habit for the two to go for walks in the nearby countryside. They never came home late, which gave Kleoniki a little comfort. How could she have imagined? How could she have foreseen the disaster that was coming toward them? Her mind was constantly on her three girls. Dorothea was eighteen; the time was coming for her to get married—something that seemed difficult given her character, which got worse as she grew older and spoiled her beauty. Makrina was seventeen, while Smaragda, the only one of her children who gave her no trouble, was turning fifteen. She was proud of her girls, but she had begun to understand her husband, who had never wanted any. Kleoniki lost sleep when she thought about their future and the dangers they'd face if she didn't stay alert.

The winter of 1925 brought Kleoniki some calm. Heavy snow put an end to the girls' walks, and Flora was a regular visitor to the house. Smaragda and Evanthia would shut themselves up in one room, and Flora and Makrina would hole up in another, the former classroom. Only Dorothea stayed with her mother in the kitchen, and as always, the girl complained incessantly.

Nobody suspected that the writing Makrina had learned from Olympia would someday help her communicate secretly with her lover. And while her mother had been reassured when she stayed in the house with Flora, it was her friend who carried the correspondence back and forth. As soon as the weather improved and the two girls went for their first walk, trysts were resumed, vows of eternal love exchanged, and desperate measures agreed upon. No open road existed, and both of them knew it. Makrina would never receive approval for such a wedding.

Kerem was the son of a very rich family and had met Makrina on one of their visits to Flora's house. They managed to see each other three times. As soon as she heard of Kerem's visits, Kleoniki vetoed her daughter's trips to the neighboring house, but the harm was already done. Flora helped her friend as much as she could. She took her for walks so the couple could meet, and when the harsh winter began, she took on the duties of a postman. Sometimes, Makrina swam in an ocean of happiness; at other times, she staggered through storms. On the one hand, she cared about her family; on the other, she couldn't imagine her life apart from Kerem and his beautiful eyes. For his part, he had secured his parents' permission, overcoming their initial objections. He'd made it clear to them that either he would have Makrina, or he would run away. Facing the threat of losing their only son, they agreed, but with one condition: the girl would have to change her faith for the marriage to take place.

"What will I do? What will I do?" the girl asked and asked again when Kerem told her about the ultimatum.

"Do you love me?" he asked in agony. "Do you love me as I love you?"

"You know I do! But just think what you're asking me. I must deny my mother, my father, my family, and my faith. It will be like killing my parents! They'll be outcasts if I follow you."

"Then let me go to them and ask for your hand."

"You mustn't. My father will kill you if you dare to cross his threshold. No! There's no life for us in Constantinople, Kerem."

"So come with me! I'll take you to my house in Ankara. You'll live in a palace; you'll be my sultana. And as soon as you change your faith, I'll marry you!"

"When you say that, I start to tremble, Kerem!"

"No, my darling, it's nothing. God is Allah, and God is everywhere and always the same, whatever you call him. Think of how beautifully we'll live, my dearest. You won't want for anything, most of all my love! I'll cover you in gold and precious stones. You'll eat off gold plates, and servants will wait on you. Our children will study and inherit a kingdom. I love you, my pretty, and I'll die if I don't have you. Don't you pity me when you know I'm pining for you?"

Each time they met, his pleas were stronger. He held her hands and left little kisses on her cheek, her lips, her eyes. And with each kiss, her defenses fell; in her mind, her mother, father, and sisters faded. Constantinople and her house dimmed into dull, sad colors, while Ankara shone with promises of light.

Makrina decided to leave home at night. She waited till everyone was asleep, her heart beating like a drum from fear and anticipation. She took only a few things in a cloth bag, Kerem having assured her she would be well taken care of. Silk and embroidered clothes were waiting for her, real gemstones and pure gold bracelets. He didn't say a word about the fact that she would have to wear a headscarf.

When she heard her father snoring in his bedroom, she waited a little longer for her mother to fall asleep too. She tiptoed to their room and, by the light of the candle Kleoniki lit every night, saw the couple sleeping. She blew them a kiss, afraid of getting close, and then it was her sisters' turn. She dared to stroke Smaragda's hair and straighten Dorothea's blanket. She left the letter she had prepared, and with her eyes full of tears, she went downstairs and raised the big bolt of the front door. Kerem was waiting for her in his car. Weeping, she got in beside him, and within moments, the night had swallowed them up.

The following day, deep mourning fell on Anargyros's house. It was Dorothea who found the letter. She got up early as usual to rake out the oven and throw more wood on the fire so it would be hot enough for her to make her father's coffee. Then she went to light the stove in the sitting room because the cold was biting. She heard her mother getting up and then, immediately after, her father. The day threatened rain; she could see heavy clouds ready to burst into a storm. Now it was time to wake her sisters. Today was the start of a big housecleaning, and all the women's hands were needed. As soon as she touched Smaragda's shoulder, the girl opened her eyes and got out of bed. Dorothea prepared to do battle, as she did every day, with Makrina's laziness, but as soon as she approached the bed, she realized that what she had taken for her sister's body was nothing but a pillow. Frightened, she brought her hand to her mouth, then spotted the letter. Smaragda, who'd been getting dressed, heard a thud. She turned to see her sister had fainted on the floor. Tears and cries followed. Soon, Anargyros, red in the face, was reading a letter that thrust a knife in his heart, and beside him, Kleoniki cursed herself for not having learned to read.

"Will someone please tell me what happened?" she wailed. "What does this letter say, and where's Makrina? Tell me! I'll scream!"

She didn't manage to. Anargyros let the letter fall from his hands and lurched forward like a tree felled by an ax. Whiter now than the paper that had slid to the floor, he brought his hand to his heart and grimaced with pain.

Kleoniki called out: "Anargyros! What's happening to you, husband? Anargyros!"

She helped him into a chair, and Smaragda ran to fetch cologne. Dorothea struggled to put a glass of water to his lips. Kleoniki opened his jacket, loosened his belt, and rubbed his hands with the cologne. Her husband was panting, trying to breathe.

"Smaragda," Kleoniki ordered, "run and fetch the doctor! Hurry, dear, your father isn't well."

The girl went to obey, but Anargyros stopped her. "I'm fine!" he thundered. "I've recovered. There's no need to broadcast our shame."

"But what happened? Why won't you tell me?" Kleoniki complained.

"Your daughter ran away!" her husband announced.

"Makrina? What? How could such a thing happen?" Now it was she who was beginning to turn red.

"You're asking me? You're the one who was with her all the time. And it's not just that she was stolen, it's by whom! The slut dishonored us! Your daughter was taken by a Turk, woman, and right under our noses!"

Kleoniki received the news like a thunderbolt. Her eyes widened, and her hands rose to her cheeks, scratching them with her nails and making her pain visible in small red furrows. A black cloud darkened her eyes, and at that very moment, there was a clap of thunder nearby, making the earth tremble. Kleoniki fell to the floor, having fainted, and the girls hurried to bring her around, again using the cologne as their remedy. They both understood the urgency of the situation. With a great effort, they brought their mother to her senses, only to see her dissolve in wails reminiscent of a funeral lament. Smaragda positioned herself beside her mother, while Dorothea sat beside her father. He asked her to pour him a brandy, and she obeyed, then made coffee for them both. The sisters hadn't spoken a word, communicating with just their eyes.

"And now?" murmured Kleoniki after an hour of stunned silence. "What shall we do now, Anargyros?"

"What do you want from me? When I said that reading and writing spoil a woman, nobody listened to me, and look where we ended up! What do you expect from a teacher like the one you brought here?"

"Eh, my pasha, can you hear what you're saying? What does Olympia have to do with our daughter?"

"Everything! Didn't she run away with a Turk too?"

Dorothea and Smaragda exchanged a shocked look. So that was the big secret about their former teacher.

"What are you trying to say?" Kleoniki countered. "That Olympia taught them about such things? Besides, the children never even knew what their teacher did. Now they've found out from you. But you still haven't told me what the letter says."

"You don't need to know!" Anargyros roared, grabbed the letter, and tore it up furiously. "From today, we're in mourning in this house. Close the windows and put on black. We've lost one of our daughters!"

"My husband, have you gone crazy? Are we going to cast out our child like that?"

"What do you want, wife? For me to run behind her and give her my blessings? She says she's leaving with the man she loves because, for her, it doesn't matter if he's Turkish and believes in another god, because God is one, whatever his name is."

"Shame on her!" Kleoniki lamented. "Didn't she think of us?"

"Of course! That's why she left, she says. She knew we wouldn't give our blessing to the marriage. She says they'll live in Ankara."

"Did she say anything else?"

"What else did you want her to say? That she'll abandon her faith and become a Turk? How else would he accept her?"

"Yes, but who is he? Where did she meet him?"

"Do you really need to ask, Mother?" Dorothea spoke up at last. "It must be Flora's fault. She and her family have dealings with the Turks."

"Why haven't I heard about this?" Anargyros roared again, hitting the table with all his strength. "You allowed her to be friends with someone like that? You let her go to their house?"

"Wait, my bey, it's not like that!" Kleoniki cried. "I didn't let her go to their house once I learned about their business. I kept her home; Flora would either come here, or they'd go for walks together."

"Walks? Woman, are you trying to make me crazy? What business did our girl have going for walks?"

"But my husband, all the girls go for walks with their friends. Sometimes to church, sometimes to pick flowers. It's not a crime."

"Enough! So, that's how the thing was done. With visits and walks. While I was sleeping the sleep of the just and had faith in you to protect our girls!"

"But Father, it's not right to put all the blame on Mother!"

They all turned to Smaragda in shock. In the first years of her life, Anargyros, who'd never heard the child's voice, asked his wife if their youngest was mute, and she had crossed herself, laughing. Even when Smaragda grew up, she almost never addressed her father, and whenever he asked her something, she'd always answer in a whisper. Now, her voice rang out loud and clear.

"You know," she continued, "I visit Evanthia's house, and we go for walks and pick flowers, but we never talk to Turkish boys. Let alone fall in love with them. Mother couldn't have expected something like this."

"Well said, little girl!" Anargyros said ironically. "So, tell me, seeing as you know so much, how are we to go out and look people in the eye? And Flora's son-of-a-bitch father, Yiouroukos—what am I supposed to do with him? Shake his hand after he's made this shameful match for my daughter?"

Fresh tears came to Kleoniki's eyes, and Anargyros hurried to roll a cigarette with trembling hands. The days that followed were like a nightmare. Anargyros got even angrier. He forbade them to go out at all, and did indeed force them to wear black, as if there had been a death in the family. Kleoniki cried day and night, and Mrs. Marigo and her daughter tried to comfort her. The news got around that Kostakis Yiouroukos had come to their door, trying to offer the shamed father an explanation. He hadn't expected to come face-to-face with an enraged bull. Anargyros had grabbed the man by the lapels and almost thrown him down the stairs, raining slaps on his face.

"You're finished in Constantinople!" Anargyros had threatened. "Everyone will find out about what you did, you and your wife and your daughter! That you came to me today to boast about your achievements!"

Yiouroukos had tried desperately to explain, but Anargyros kept cursing and hitting him.

"The whole neighborhood heard, Mrs. Marigo!" wept Kleoniki afterward. "Good thing your husband and brother-in-law broke it up. The police would have carted my husband off to the station. Where this trouble will end, I don't know."

Anargyros kept his word. The whole neighborhood stopped acknowledging the Yiouroukos family, who were regarded as accessories to a crime that had plunged a respectable Tarlabasi family into mourning. Turks and Armenians didn't stop at their door even to sell them milk. Very soon, they couldn't stand it and moved away. No one ever saw them or heard from them again, but neither was there any news from Makrina. A long time later, Anargyros and Kleoniki heard that their child was living in Ankara and that her name was now Neilan.

As time passed, Anargyros only grew angrier, and finally he got the idea in his head that in order to regain his honor, he needed to marry off his oldest daughter to the best possible groom. He ignored Kleoniki's protests, and barely two months after Makrina left, he hired a matchmaker to find a groom for Dorothea. The amount he offered the woman made her open her eyes wide. She lost no time, and within a few weeks, she brought him a young man. He was from Galata, a bank clerk, and the nephew of a bishop. Anargyros was beaming. He accepted her choice and came to an agreement about the dowry, then announced the news first to Kleoniki and then to Dorothea, who accepted the blow without blinking an eye. She knew there was nothing she could say.

The groom arrived with his parents a few days later to meet his bride. Tactfully, they were left alone for a short time, and in a week, the deal was done. Fortunately, Iakovos was pleasant, but that made no difference for Dorothea. She sealed the match with her lips and her soul, and almost immediately after New Year's of 1926, she was driven to the church by her proud father. She set up house in Galata and seldom visited her parents. It was her small revenge. She had no complaint against Iakovos, but she could never love him.

For the first time in her life, Smaragda was lonely. Without her two sisters, she saw eyes finally falling on her, something she didn't like at all. The only eyes she welcomed were Simeon Kouyoumdzis's.

The first time they met was at a party to honor the engagement of Dorothea and Iakovos. Due to the occasion, Anargyros had given the women permission to enlist a dressmaker. Kleoniki remembered the last time all too well, so before choosing patterns, she showed them to Anargyros, who got angry again. Fashions had changed completely once more; corsets had disappeared, hemlines had risen even higher, colors were brighter. Now, in the twenties, women had to be beautiful and provocative. They even denied their long braids, cutting their hair short with bangs.

"Next you'll tell me you're taking up smoking, wife!" Anargyros scolded.

"That's why I'm showing you now, so you won't get upset later."

"What can I say, after all that has happened?" said Anargyros. "Whatever we were going to suffer we suffered! Now, with Dorothea's marriage, everything will change."

"Whatever you do, my husband, the thorn won't ever leave our hearts," Kleoniki said sadly. "And if I pretend I'm not in pain, it's for the sake of our other daughters. I pray to the Virgin every night that you've made the right decision for our Dorothea—because you were in a hurry, my husband, a big hurry."

"What was I to do, wife? Should we have moved away too, like the teacher's parents? Iakovos isn't just a good, well-mannered boy; he's also the nephew of a bishop."

"So what, he's the nephew of a bishop? What's that got to do with our Makrina? You only think about shame, Anargyros. But I suffer because I don't have my child, my dear one. I miss her laughter, her songs. Just because you forced me to wear black doesn't mean that my child is dead for me. And now you've added more worry to my mind with this rushed marriage. I'm afraid our Dorothea will be unhappy."

It wasn't the first time she'd said that, but it would be the last. The dress was approved, the engagement took place, and the parents of the groom presented the bride, who managed to smile, with gold jewelry.

After the party, Smaragda couldn't get to sleep. Simeon's family had been at the party too. His smiling eyes never left her mind. He was tall, muscular, and well dressed. All evening she'd stolen glances at him, and her heart fluttered every time their gaze met. Afraid, she looked around to see if anyone had noticed. Her father was chatting with the groom's father and seemed absorbed in the conversation, and her mother was busy with the groom's mother and another woman who was probably his grandmother.

The second time they met was again at the invitation of Iakovos's parents, Mr. and Mrs. Prousalis, and this time her heart beat so hard it sent a rush of blood to her cheeks. Unfortunately, there was some disagreement between her father and Simeon's, some political discussion about the fallout from the Asia Minor Catastrophe. The girl didn't understand much, but she saw Mrs. Prousalis signaling to her husband to intervene before it developed into a quarrel.

The only one Smaragda confided in was, of course, her bosom friend Evanthia, whose eyes widened as soon as she heard.

"What are you saying? Do you mean he likes you? If he asks for you, will you accept him?" she asked.

"What do you mean, 'asks for me'? Who do you think we are? Cinderella and the prince? He's from a very rich family—goldsmiths, like their name says, every generation. I heard my mother say to Mrs. Marigo that Simeon's grandfather was goldsmith to the sultana. Imagine what sort of high-class wife they want for their son! What could they see in me?"

The family certainly didn't consider Smaragda. Neither her name nor her dowry impressed them. But Simeon was impressed. By her lovely eyes, her slim but strong body, her lips that smiled shyly and lit up her whole face. He began to lose sleep and his appetite. He sought desperate means to see her, though he knew the match was impossible. He went all the way to her house, hoping that he might spot her at some window looking at the sky, and his lovesick heart wanted to hope that, as she looked at the white clouds, she might be thinking of him.

Dorothea and Iakovos's wedding made his hopes soar into the happy heavens. At the party, Smaragda dared to look at him, and her feelings were written on her face. There was no mistaking them. Those honey-colored eyes sent the message his heart was yearning for: she felt as he did.

Three days later, Evanthia arrived at the Kantardzis house, panting and red in the face. To cover her emotions in front of Kleoniki, she started an irrelevant conversation about a hundred and one meaningless things. Smaragda eyed her suspiciously. Something had happened, and she needed to find out fast. She took Evanthia by the arm, and they shut themselves in the room that was now exclusively hers. She didn't even let her friend take off her pinafore off before asking, "What's going on? You don't usually chatter like that!"

"Give me a minute to recover! You've got me on tenterhooks, I'll tell you that!"

Evanthia pulled an envelope out of her pocket and gave it to her friend. Smaragda looked at her in wonder.

"What's this, friend? Did you bring me a letter?"

"Bravo, detective! But who do you think this letter is from? Your heartthrob!"

"Simeon?"

"Do you have another? Yes, him! My mother sent me to buy some fennel from Anezo's shop, and Simeon stopped me on the doorstep, the naughty fellow. What nerve! It took my breath away. If anyone had seen us and told my father, he'd have hanged me with a leash!"

"Hush now, so I can read it!" Smaragda ordered as she opened the envelope with trembling hands.

"Read it, but after that, he said you might want to answer him."

After a few tense moments, Smaragda looked up with shining eyes. "Simeon says for me to thank you very much for undertaking this mission and bringing me the letter."

"He wrote that? If your mother reads it and kills me, and my mother too, he can keep his thanks! Lunatics, both of you."

But Smaragda wasn't listening. Her eyes ran over the words, and her spirit sang with delight as she read everything she longed for. Her heart couldn't hold so much happiness. She read the letter twice and then pressed it passionately to her breast, as if it were the boy himself. She kissed it a dozen times and whirled around happily. Her friend shook her head.

"Goodness me! What people suffer for love!" she teased, but affection showed in her eyes. "Are you going to tell me what the gallant fellow writes?"

"He loves me, Evanthia," the girl exclaimed.

"Hush, silly! Do you want us to get caught? Your mother will hear!"

Evanthia went to the closed door, listened carefully, then opened it to see if there was anyone outside. She closed it again more calmly.

"We got lucky," she observed, but Smaragda's mind was elsewhere.

She was seated, already writing her answer with a firm hand and a heart filled with happiness. Evanthia tried to say something, but wasn't permitted.

"Hush, Evanthia, I'm writing. Sit and wait till I finish."

Obediently, the girl sat on the bed and crossed her arms, waiting for her friend to complete her love letter. Smaragda sealed it in an envelope and handed it over.

"How will you give it to him without anyone knowing?" she asked Evanthia.

"He told me to go to the church and leave it under the icon of the Virgin. Did you ever hear anything so shameful?"

"But you'll do it, won't you?" Smaragda asked in agony, squeezing her hand tightly and looking imploringly at her friend.

"I guess I have to. But it's all your fault if something happens and they find out!"

But nobody found out because nobody suspected calm, courteous Smaragda, nor cautious Evanthia. Every day, Simeon kept an eye on the two houses, and he grabbed the letter mere seconds after the girl left it under the icon, trembling and asking forgiveness a thousand times from the Virgin. In the half-light of church candles, he read it, his hands shaking in anticipation.

> *Dear Simeon,*
> *I did not dare to hope for so long.*
> *You were in my dreams and my prayers, and at night I asked for comfort as I longed for what your eyes had shown me to be true. And you were not dreaming. What you read in my eyes was true. I feel as you do.*
> *And your heart, which you offer me, I hold beside my own. They will beat together from now on. But you know, just as I do, that it will be difficult for this love to have a happy ending. I'm not, my dear, the bride your parents would wish for you. Neither my name nor my dowry is a match for your name and position. But the heart has its own currency, my dear, and its own place, and I feel happy at this moment because you love me as much as I love you. As to all the rest, we must place our hopes in God.*
> *With my love,*
> *Smaragda*

Simeon brought the letter to his lips, as Smaragda had done with his, and he had the feeling he was holding her hands in his. The sheet of paper had touched her, she had bent over it, it held her breath still. He buried it deep in his pocket, next to his heart, and left. He was unprepared for Evanthia's return; she hurried into the church, and they nearly bumped into each other.

"I'm very sorry," Simeon blurted out.

"Pardon," Evanthia said at the same time.

"Did you come back to see me?"

"Yes, with my heart in my throat, but I had an idea. Smaragda doesn't know anything about what I'm telling you, but I really want to help you two. My friend loves you, Mr. Kouyoumdzis, and I hope your feelings for her are serious."

"I give you my word, Miss Evanthia!" he reassured her warmly. "I love Smaragda with all the strength of my heart."

"Next Wednesday my mother and hers will be away in the afternoon at a ladies' gathering. I'll be alone, and no one will think anything of it if my friend comes over to keep me company."

Hope shone in his eyes. "Are you inviting me?"

"But you have to be very careful. Nobody must see you coming into the house, or we're done for!"

"I swear to you," Simeon declared. "I have no words to express my thanks."

They separated, and Simeon nearly danced in the street on his way home. Just before she left, Evanthia had assured him that, the next day, she would return to receive his reply.

The second letter from Simeon arrived in the same way as the first, but when Smaragda finished reading it, the girl looked at her friend wide-eyed with surprise.

"It says here that we're going to meet at your house!"

"Speak softer, Smaragda," Evanthia begged her. "Don't you know the walls have ears? And yes, it's true. I told him that our mothers will be away on Wednesday, and he can come to my house so you can speak in person."

"How could you be so daring?"

"Don't remind me, because I'll regret it. I invited him, and that's the end of it!"

"And what if someone sees him coming in? What will we say?"

"Are you stupid? We won't have a chance to say anything, because our parents will have hanged us by the neck! So whatever prayers you know, you'd better say them. But I can't bear to see you so upset, and from what I understand, he loves you. Anyway, what harm are we doing? It's not like your sister or our teacher. He's a Greek, and he wants you—I'm just acting as a matchmaker!"

That Wednesday, Smaragda was surprised that her mother didn't notice a thing. She felt as if she had a fever, her cheeks were burning, and it was hard to breathe. When Kleoniki was ready, she took her daughter over to Evanthia's house, where Mrs. Marigo and Paraskevi were waiting to accompany Kleoniki to Mrs. Alexoudis's party. There were detailed instructions about locking the door, not opening it to anyone, and behaving themselves before the two girls finally found themselves alone. They looked at each other guiltily, but before they could catch their breath, there was a knock at the door, and Evanthia raced to open it in case someone saw their visitor. Simeon entered hurriedly and closed it behind him.

"They only just left, Mr. Kouyoumdzis," she scolded him. "What if my mother or grandmother forgot something and they come back? We're finished!"

"I'm sorry, but I couldn't wait any longer. For two hours I've been hiding across the street," he apologized, blushing.

With an understanding smile, Evanthia led him into the main room, where Smaragda stood waiting, obviously very moved. Evanthia muttered something about going to make them coffee, but the two lovers heard nothing. They had already been transported to their own world. Simeon approached slowly and took Smaragda's frozen hands in his. He dared to kiss them, and when he raised his head, he saw her eyes full of tears. They sat down beside each other without him relinquishing her hands. He felt a knot of happiness closing his throat.

"I think I'm dreaming," he told her softly.

"Me too . . ."

"Bless Miss Evanthia."

Smaragda nodded.

The hour she spent sitting beside him was a dream that had become reality, but she still didn't believe it. Whatever beautiful and tender things she heard from his lips she knew would never leave her heart or her mind. When he bent closer, she allowed him to kiss her, and that was the moment when she thought she would die of delight. She wasn't ashamed that she had pressed him to her; everything seemed completely right. They separated before the two hours were up, unwilling to take any risk, and he got up to leave, promising that he would write very soon. Even though Evanthia had returned, he dared to hug Smaragda tightly again, making her friend blush and lower her eyes to study the pattern on the carpet. Immediately afterward, he regained his composure, said good-bye politely, and left the house, taking every precaution. As soon as she heard the door close behind him, Smaragda's knees buckled. Her friend was shaking with nerves too.

"I'm terrified the whole neighborhood knows what happened here this afternoon," Evanthia confessed, her face white.

"Me too," Smaragda agreed.

"We'd better pull ourselves together before our mothers get back! Let's splash some water on our faces, and then we'll eat some sweets to help us recover."

Smaragda didn't object, but the candy she ate seemed tasteless after the far greater sweetness of Simeon's kiss.

The next day, they watched their families like hawks for signs of suspicion, but nothing seemed to be amiss. Another letter from Simeon reached Smaragda's hands without incident, and her eyes were damp with emotion as she read it. She shared her beloved's words with Evanthia.

"This surprise he's preparing, what do you think it is?" her friend asked. "It'll be made of gold, I bet. He makes jewelry for a living; surely he won't leave you."

"Evanthia, did you get stuck on that? Didn't you hear the rest? He'll speak to his father! He'll ask for his blessing."

"Yes, but look what else he said. His father has other ideas about a bride. What's more, my father, who knows him, has said many times that he's a difficult, ill-bred man. Don't get your hopes up, my dear, because a man like that isn't going to care a whit about any great love."

Anxiety and fear filled Smaragda's heart. And as the days passed without any news of Simeon, she sank into a darkness that deprived her of her very breath. She wandered about the house with no appetite, and her mother soon noticed that the girl was hardly eating, that her clothes swam on her, that her rosy cheeks were dulled and faded, and that she never smiled. However much pressure her mother put on her, the girl wouldn't say a word and closed herself up in her room. Kleoniki grew very anxious. She was afraid of how her husband would react if she told him what she'd observed about Smaragda. A month later, she turned hopelessly to Mrs. Marigo and confessed her fears.

"If he's a good boy, one of ours, why doesn't she tell me, so we can see what we can do about it?" she said in tears to the woman who had been like a mother to her all these years.

"Wait a bit, my sweet; it's not the end of the world," Mrs. Marigo said comfortingly. "Most likely, Smaragda loves a boy, but he doesn't want her, and that's why she's fading away."

"Let's hope you're right, Mrs. Marigo, because neither Anargyros nor I could deal with another tragedy like with Makrina."

"Give me a little bit of time, and I'll get a hold of that good-for-nothing granddaughter of mine and pressure her until she tells me what's going on."

Mrs. Marigo did as she said. She and her daughter grilled Evanthia until she cried, but still they didn't take pity on her. Finally, after hours of alternating threats and pleas, the girl couldn't bear it and confessed the love between Smaragda and Simeon Kouyoumdzis. The two women almost shouted for joy because the boy was at least Greek. Afterward, though, Mrs. Marigo grew somber. She remembered something her husband had told her. At the time, she hadn't paid much attention, but now her position was very difficult. How could she be the bearer of such bad news to the lovesick girl wasting away next door?

CHAPTER 3

KOUYOUMDZIS FAMILY

Constantinople, 1926

Simeon Kouyoumdzis returned home after the enchanting afternoon he had spent with his beloved and shut himself happily in his room. The next day, he threw himself into crafting a piece of jewelry for his Smaragda. He didn't want something ordinary, something any other woman would have. He was so absorbed in his work that he didn't hear his mother calling him to eat lunch. Penelope Kouyoumdzis had to send a servant to fetch him, and he came downstairs, ashamed of his absentmindedness. But the whole time they were eating, his mind kept returning to the complex design for his beloved.

"Young man, you seem a bit distracted today," his father observed.

"I'm sorry, Father."

"Did you catch a cold?" his mother asked anxiously and hurried to feel his forehead.

"I'm fine, Mother," he answered irritably. "I'm just not hungry."

"And what's wrong that's made you lose your appetite, my son?" his father insisted. "Did your ships sink in a storm, or is there something else the matter?"

Simeon never admitted it, but he was as afraid of his father as everyone else was. The man's word was law, and though he was not violent, his icy stare was enough to make anyone feel threatened. Even at twenty-six years of age, Simeon had never dared to talk back. Vassilis Kouyoumdzis had a particular way of imposing his will on others.

Simeon looked down and began drawing designs with his fork, unwilling to continue the conversation. He wasn't ready for an open conflict with this father, a conflict he couldn't see any way of avoiding when he declared his love for Smaragda.

"I'll let it go for now," Vassilis said, the satisfaction in his voice obvious, "considering that I'm bringing you such good news."

"Me?" the young man asked in surprise.

"This evening, we'll have the pleasure of receiving the Karakontaxis family."

"And that has something to do with me?"

"It seems, Simeon, that you don't listen when I speak!" his father upbraided him. "Didn't I tell you some time ago that the daughter of my friend Aristarhos Karakontaxis would be a suitable bride for you? They're coming for a small party so that you two can get to know each other."

Simeon was thunderstruck. He stared at his father for several long moments.

"I'm sorry," he whispered as soon as he could speak, "but didn't another family come last week that also had a daughter? The tall one with the big nose?"

"And you said you didn't like her," his father replied. "Even though, in my opinion, it shouldn't be the big nose you should be examining, but the enormous dowry."

"Yes, but I must like the bride, mustn't I?"

Vassilis turned to his wife. "Penelope, leave us!"

The woman didn't even think of objecting, though she had hardly touched her food. Vassilis lit a cigarette and looked carefully at his son before he spoke.

"I think I failed to teach you some things and left that work to your mother, who isn't qualified for it."

"What sorts of things, Father? If I don't like the bride, if I can't love her—"

"Why are you mixing up love with marriage? A man, Simeon, has a responsibility to examine other questions."

"Of morality, for example?"

"That, but also the dowry. We have a position in the city. A name and a solid fortune. We can't allow those things to become a target for every conniving female!"

"Yes, Father, but if I don't like the woman—"

"Now you're talking like a schoolboy. We're men; do you understand? When the lights are out, all cats are gray! You'll marry, have two or three children with your wife, and afterward, do what you like. Who's going to stop you?"

"Is that what you do, Father?" Simeon dared to ask.

"This is not about me."

Simeon suppressed the ironic smile that rose to his lips. His father was already looking at him quizzically.

"Son, are you, by chance, in love with someone? Is that what this is all about?"

"No, Father!" his son hastened to reassure him.

"That's all we need—lovesickness! Anyway, you'll like Aristarhos's daughter. And when I tell you what sort of dowry her father's offering, you'll like her even more!"

"Do you mean she's ugly too?" asked Simeon without enthusiasm.

"Not all that again! What did I tell you? What does beauty matter? Simeon, get your head on straight . . . unless you love someone else, and that's soured all the rest."

"No, Father," Simeon repeated and was silent.

For a second time, he heard a bell strike in his head. He felt like a betrayer, like the apostle Peter. *Before the rooster crows, you will deny Me three times . . .*

"Good, then. Tonight my friend's family will come, and you'll study the candidate carefully. Afterward, we'll talk again and make a decision. Enough!"

Later, to calm down, Simeon immersed himself again in the design of the locket for his beloved. Far from the influence of his father, protected from his overwhelming presence and icy gaze, Simeon felt his conviction and his dreams of a life with his beloved return. Let his father's friends come. He had given away his heart already.

Miss Roza Karakontaxis didn't have a big nose and wasn't ugly, Simeon had to admit. She was pleasant, delicately built, and quiet, as befitted a girl from a good family. Dressed in the latest fashion, her hair set in chic waves, she sat so still that he knew she wasn't a doll only by watching her thin fingers playing with the pearls that hung from her neck. She glanced secretly at him, Simeon observed, and the enthusiastic looks that were exchanged between their parents did not escape him. The Karakontaxis family were not the only guests, but his mother had been careful not to invite another family with a marriageable daughter so that there would be no anxiety.

Despite the fact that Vassilis Kouyoumdzis wanted to speak immediately to his son and find out his impressions, his wife persuaded him not to rush the boy. She also took care to see that, in the following days, Roza and Simeon would meet again at a party. In fact, there was a gramophone at the house where they were invited, and all the young people danced, avoiding the modern fox-trot and choosing simple waltzes so as not to shock their parents.

Simeon's mother discreetly approached her son and said in a low voice, "Simeon, your father says you must ask Miss Karakontaxis to dance."

Penelope gave an imperceptible nod to underline her words, and Simeon understood that he had just received a strict order that couldn't be denied. To make certain, he looked at his father. His expression was icy but clear. With a heavy heart, he approached Roza, who was standing next to her mother, and asked her for a dance. They found themselves whirling to the music without speaking. He faltered in his step when she spoke to him first.

"Are you always so quiet?"

"What should I say? Do people talk while they dance?" he answered, then realized how silly he sounded.

"In our case, I think that's why we're dancing under our parents' supervision. So we can talk before they announce what's 'destined to be,'" the girl said flatly.

"Destined?"

"I mean our marriage. Didn't your father tell you?"

"He said something, but—"

"Did you think you had a choice?"

"That's what I understood."

"I didn't take you for such an innocent! The marriage has already been arranged, Mr. Kouyoumdzis. For form's sake, he's waiting for an answer from you and me," the girl declared, now smiling broadly.

Simeon looked at her, lost.

"Are you sure?" he asked finally.

Roza gestured with her chin.

"If you look carefully, you'll see the future in-laws boasting already. Listen, Simeon, let's go a little farther away and make sure we understand each other. They won't mind."

Stunned, Simeon followed, and Roza sat on a sofa, indicating with her fan that he should sit beside her.

"Now we can talk in peace. This marriage came as a surprise to me too, to be honest. But I don't love anyone else. Do you?"

Simeon hung his head.

"Ah! I understand. You love someone, but you can't have her," the girl said. "Then I'm the luckier one. They told me about you. I'm just relieved you're not ugly."

"But is that how it is? They'll force us to marry? What sort of world do we live in?"

"What can I tell you? Money is all that matters to them. You're like a child. Don't you know how these things are done?"

"I'm surprised that you're talking to me like this!"

"I'm trying to make you understand how useless it is to object. The Turks call it kismet, and we call it *riziko*—fate. We can't avoid this marriage, but we can work together to make it bearable."

"I appreciate your honesty, Roza, which is why I'm letting you know that I plan to fight this."

"Do as you wish, but remember what I said: We have no way out. So, either we marry and make each other miserable, or we decide to be happy. That's what you get to choose—not your bride. You'll see. All right now. Let's go back to the dance floor; our parents are looking at us strangely."

Simeon followed obediently, but her words echoed in his brain, drowning out the music. He felt betrayed and angry. Unless Roza was wrong. He stole another glance at her. Respect grew in him, and if it hadn't been for Smaragda, perhaps he might not have objected to this marriage. At least the woman they had chosen was clever, logical, and attractive, almost beautiful. But she wasn't Smaragda.

Ten times in the following days, he began writing his beloved a letter to explain, and as many times he tore up the letter and turned back to his desk in tears. Well hidden in a drawer of that desk was the design for the locket he dreamed of making, a gold envelope, small and hollow. On the front would be an engraved stamp and her initial. On the back, the envelope would open and a thin gold sheet would fall out. On it would be written what his smitten heart was calling out: *I love you.*

He couldn't, he had to admit, go against his father's wishes. The memory of the conversation he'd had with Roza at the party made him ill. That evening, his father returned home earlier than usual and invited him into the sitting room. His mother was there too. Simeon knew that the hour of battle had come.

"So, Simeon," his father began pompously, "I think you owe us an answer."

The young man tried to clear his throat, but his voice came out hoarsely: "I have to admit that Miss Karakontaxis is very attractive—"

"Bravo, my son! I knew you'd turn out to be sensible," he exclaimed. "Tomorrow we'll go and ask for her hand."

"Wait, Father—please listen to me!" Simeon pleaded, and the other man froze.

"What more is there to listen to? You like her: it's finished!"

Simeon took a deep breath, and as he exhaled, he said what he'd wanted to say for so many days: "I love another girl, and I promised I would marry her!"

The air in the room froze. The couple opposite him remained motionless for a short time, seemingly without breathing. Then his father jumped up, so Simeon did as well. Only Penelope remained seated, her face white with shock.

"Say it again," his father ordered, his voice low and cold.

"I told you, Father. I love another girl. I promised—"

"And who gave you permission to do such a thing? Who told you you could promise to marry someone without my knowledge?"

"I didn't want to provoke you, Father, but I simply fell in love with this girl—"

"And who is she?"

"Her name is Smaragda Kantardzis. We've met as a family at Mr. Prousalis's house. Iakovos married her sister."

Vassilis Kouyoumdzis remained silent for a while, searching his mind for information about the Kantardzis family, and when he succeeded, his eyes opened wide.

"You impudent puppy! You want to take the daughter of that nobody?" he shouted.

"But Father, Smaragda is a very good girl, and her parents are completely respectable."

"So why did her other sister run away with a Turk and convert to Islam? Or didn't you know?"

Simeon's jaw dropped. "She did what?"

"That's right, you idiot who thinks he knows everything! Just because that father of hers bribed Prousalis to overlook it, you think I'd do the same? I won't marry my son to such people!"

"Father, I love Smaragda, and I don't care what you say about her sister or her father."

Bright red in the face now, Vassilis Kouyoumdzis raised his fist, but Penelope leaped between them. She grabbed her son and pulled him back.

"Don't, my boy! Don't go against your father! Ask forgiveness, my pasha. He'll have a stroke because he's so upset, and you'll be responsible. Anyway, the girl we want for you—you saw her—she's a sweetheart! Say yes, my boy! We want the best for you. Don't break our hearts out of stubbornness."

"Stubbornness! Is that what you call it, Mother? I told you I love her, just as she loves me."

"Do you hear your son?" her husband shouted. "Fool, you can be sure her father and mother put her up to it. They've just got their eyes on our position and our money!"

"That's a lie!"

"You dare speak to your father like that, you hoodlum?" Vassilis roared.

This time, Penelope left her son and went to her husband. Summoning all her strength, she took him by the hand, not knowing where she found the courage, and forced him to sit down. Then she turned to her son, and for the first time, she spoke to him in an angry voice.

"Simeon! What sort of behavior is this? What you just said to your father? Shame on you!"

Simeon felt her words like a blow. His mother's eyes had filled with tears. He hung his head and approached his father. He took his hand and kissed it respectfully.

"Forgive me, Father."

Penelope squeezed her husband's shoulder, and he nodded, accepting his son's apology.

"Blessed be the name of the Lord!" the woman exclaimed. "You've both come to your senses. And now let's sit down and talk nicely like a family."

Simeon sat down as if his legs wouldn't hold him up any longer, and with the last shred of courage he possessed, he tried once more.

"I didn't want to make you angry, Father. But I want you to understand me. I love this girl. And if you wish, I'll fall at your feet so you'll give me your blessing!"

Without thinking, he found himself kneeling in front of his father, but Vassilis recoiled.

"What's this now? A full-grown man who talks like a little woman? Men don't kneel!"

"But if I don't have Smaragda, I'll be lost forever!"

"Simeon, for your mother's sake, we said we'd talk nicely. You aren't cooperating."

Again, Penelope went to her son and guided him back to his seat.

"Simeon, it's for the best."

She took her place beside her husband once again and rested her hand on his shoulder. She had already exceeded her stamina, but she was amazed that her husband, who never paid attention to her, seemed today to respect her.

Simeon took another deep breath before he spoke, keeping his voice low.

"Father, please. Smaragda is a very good girl, beautiful and well behaved. She may not have Roza's money, but she's not entirely without a dowry. And I'm sure that you would find in her not only a daughter-in-law but a girl who would love you and help you."

"Before I answer you," his father said, "I want you to tell me something else. How far has your acquaintance with this girl progressed?"

"What do you mean?"

"Simeon, don't play the fool with me; I'm speaking to you as father to son now. I want a straight answer. Is it possible that your relationship with the girl has obliged you to marry her?"

"No, Father! I told you—she's an honorable girl. I swear I didn't touch her."

"Bravo. I believe you." Vassilis seemed satisfied. "So, Simeon, for better or for worse, I gave my word to Aristarhos Karakontaxis that you would marry his daughter. Now I'll ask you another question, and I want you to answer honestly. Whose word carries more weight? Yours or mine? Whose promise must be kept for us to preserve our honor as a family?"

Simeon bowed his head and lowered his eyes. His gaze was empty, as was his spirit. He'd been defeated, and he knew it. He couldn't shame his father; they hadn't raised him that way. And the blood of revolution didn't run in his veins. He would have to bury his heart.

CHAPTER 4

KANTARDZIS FAMILY

Constantinople, 1926

Mrs. Marigo entered Kleoniki's house with her head down. It wouldn't be easy to say the words, but she had an ethical obligation to the woman who'd been like a daughter to her for so many years. Kleoniki's parents lived far away, in Khrysokeramos, that fishing village she'd arrived from, dressed as a bride. Since then, she had only seen them two or three times. It required a long journey, and her mother had another nine children who had married and settled nearby and who now had children of their own.

The two women sat in the kitchen. Smaragda, as usual, was in her room, with no desire to take part in all the things she used to love, including seeing her friend's family. At the same time, Evanthia was terrified to see Smaragda after her betrayal and so, for some time, had pretended to be sick.

"Tell me now, Mrs. Marigo," Kleoniki asked anxiously. "Did you find anything out?"

"Yes, my dear, I did! My naughty granddaughter put up quite a fight, but in the end, we got it out of her. The man in question is Greek."

"Praise the Virgin!" Kleoniki cried and crossed herself.

"Don't get ahead of yourself, sweetheart. He may be Greek, but it's not going to happen! I was pleased at first when I found out, because he's a handsome, nice young man, with plenty of money."

"What are you telling me?"

"Yes, indeed. Lots of money. To tell you the truth, he's not from our class."

"Who is he, then?"

"The son of Kouyoumdzis."

"The goldsmith?"

"Him."

"Bah! Mrs. Marigo, they're like royalty."

"Exactly. Now do you understand? Would such a family accept Smaragda as a bride for their prince?"

"But if the young man loves her?"

"Hush, dear, let me finish. A few days ago, my husband came home and said there was a huge to-do in town about a match that had just been made. The wedding's been arranged for the end of the year."

"So, what does that have to do with us? You're making me dizzy!"

"Kleoniki, you speak before you think. The match was between the son of Kouyoumdzis and the daughter of Aristarhos Karakontaxis!"

Kleoniki froze. She covered her mouth with her hand.

"What are you telling me now? Only a sultan could marry a girl with the fortune of Karakontaxis. And the Kouyoumdzis boy took her? Ah, people like that would never look at us!"

"Goodness, my dear, what you put me through before you understood!"

"Wait a minute, there's something else I don't understand. Kouyoumdzis is engaged, so why is my daughter pining for a man she can't have?"

"Is it really so strange? She loves him."

"If that's all it is, fine, but what if my child is—in trouble?"

"Oh no, my dear. Evanthia didn't tell us anything like that. Don't get bad ideas in your head."

"If the harm's been done, Anargyros will skin me alive, and he'll be right to do it! What was I thinking? How did so much go on right under our noses?"

"For God's sake, stop, woman, and don't make a catastrophe out of it! An innocent flirtation, my granddaughter told me."

"What am I to do now, Mrs. Marigo? Her father must not find out."

"Shouldn't you talk to your daughter? She might not have heard about the engagement."

It must have been an evil hour. How else could Kleoniki explain what happened next? Her husband, who never came home before the evening, had returned early for once. And heard Mrs. Marigo's words. He threw open the kitchen door, and the two women turned white. Kleoniki jumped up, and her coffee cup smashed to pieces on the floor.

"Anargyros!"

"What's going on in here, woman? What's Mrs. Marigo saying? Whose engagement?"

"Sit down, husband," Kleoniki said, resigned to her fate. "Sit down, my pasha, and I'll tell you everything; I won't hide anything from you."

"I'll be leaving, Kleoniki," said the visitor, standing up, but Anargyros prevented her from departing.

"Sit back down, Mrs. Marigo. You were talking to my wife, weren't you? Now you'll talk to me."

"I'll get you a cup of coffee first."

"I don't want any!"

Kleoniki didn't dare even to pick up the broken cup. She sat down opposite Anargyros with her friend beside her, and they revealed what had happened. With each word, she saw her husband's expression darken more and more, and as soon as she'd finished, Anargyros jumped up and charged into his daughter's room.

Ignorant of everything that was happening, and lost in the wanderings of her lovesick heart, Smaragda was reading and rereading the letters Simeon had sent her, letting the tears run down her face. She couldn't understand what could have made her love forget her. On her last trip to the church, Evanthia had found nothing waiting under the icon.

Anargyros nearly tore the door off its hinges. Smaragda froze in terror, the letters in her hands. As soon as her father saw his daughter, her eyes red from the tears that still ran down her cheeks, he stopped himself from striking her. But then his eyes fell on the letters, and he snatched them from her hands. His anger returned, sharper than ever. Anargyros had never hit his daughters, but at that moment, his mind went dark. His hand came down with all its force on Smaragda's cheek. She thought her head would be severed from her body and she would see it rolling on the carpet. Kleoniki let out a cry and threw herself between them.

"Anargyros!" she shouted. "What are you doing? You'll kill her!"

"If she's going to shame me like her sister did, I'd rather see her in the ground! I'll say I buried another daughter."

"I didn't shame you, Father," Smaragda managed to whisper, while her mother tried to wipe the blood that was running from the girl's nose with her handkerchief.

Mrs. Marigo tried to calm him.

"Anargyros, my boy, that isn't the way," she said to him softly. "I'm not family, but I have a duty to tell you that it's not right to hit your daughter."

"Mrs. Marigo, you know how much I respect you," answered Anargyros, "but this sort of treachery I cannot accept. Do you see these? He sent her letters, and in one he says he kissed her! And your granddaughter was the go-between! They met at your house!"

"I know, my pasha, and she'll be punished by my son-in-law, but that's not a reason to cripple your daughter. It was a kiss, my bey, nothing more. And since it will remain between us, and no one will find out about it, it's as if it didn't happen."

"You tramp, how could you do that?" He turned to his daughter again. "Aren't you ashamed?"

"Father," Smaragda, who was on the point of fainting, dared to say, "he told me he would marry me. He loves me, and he'll come to ask for me."

"Dream on!" her father hollered. He was about to resume the beating, but Kleoniki stopped him with a furious look.

She took her daughter in her arms, stroked her hair, and began speaking to her in a tender voice. "He won't come, my darling . . . he won't come, my treasure . . . don't wait for him . . ."

"Why? Has something happened to Simeon?" The panicked girl broke away from her mother's embrace.

"Your lover is getting married!" shouted Anargyros. "He's filled your head with hot air, and now he's marrying someone else!"

The news hit Smaragda like a bullet. The color drained from her face, then she staggered and collapsed at her parents' feet.

"Holy Virgin! My child!" howled Kleoniki and fell to her knees.

Mrs. Marigo pulled Anargyros out of the way, snatched the cologne from the girl's dresser, and knelt beside Kleoniki.

"What have you done, Anargyros? You'll kill my daughter!" shouted Kleoniki, rubbing her daughter's wrists while Mrs. Marigo got water and sprinkled it on the girl's face.

The man stood numb now, watching the efforts of the two women to bring his deathly pale daughter around. With a great effort, she opened her eyes.

"Praise the Lord!" exclaimed Mrs. Marigo.

"Come, sweetheart," her mother said, and nearly lay down beside her to hold her in her arms. "Don't upset yourself. In time, everything will get better."

Smaragda hid herself in her mother's embrace, curled like an embryo, and began to cry softly, but so miserably that even Anargyros softened. Mrs. Marigo stood up with difficulty and took him by the hand.

"Come, Anargyros, my son. Let's go, and I'll make you a coffee so you can recover from the shock. Leave those two—at times like this, a mother's embrace is the best medicine."

A few minutes later, sitting in the kitchen with his coffee, Anargyros lit a cigarette while Mrs. Marigo swept up Kleoniki's broken cup.

"The blood rushed to my head!" he admitted.

"I understand, my bey, but that's the way these things happen. Your daughter didn't do something bad. She fell in love. Is there anything more beautiful than love? And the young man said he'd marry her."

"Then why is he marrying someone else?"

"Because he's a respectful son and didn't go against his parents, that's why. Should we blame him? He loved your daughter, he wanted her for his wife, but Kouyoumdzis wouldn't allow it. And to tell you the truth, I don't say he was wrong. Wouldn't you, in your place, have done the same if you had a son and a fortune like that? He's marrying the daughter of Karakontaxis, not just anyone. Drink your coffee now, my pasha, and I'll go home. And when your daughter recovers, sit down and talk to her, and I'm sure she'll tell you that nothing bad happened— nothing to make you ashamed of your lovely Smaragda."

She stroked his shoulder like a mother and left. Anargyros smoked cigarette after cigarette until he disappeared in the smoke that filled the room.

During the week that followed, he was unable to speak to his daughter. Smaragda ran such a high fever that they called the doctor, and Kleoniki never left her side, dampening her face with a towel dipped in water and vinegar. On the day the fever broke, her mother ran to light a candle, to thank the Virgin for saving her child.

Smaragda began very slowly to get up, to sit in an armchair in her room, and she seemed calmer. In the wanderings of her mind, hazy with fever, she had found a way to accept what had happened. As soon as she felt strong enough, she wrapped Simeon's letters in a silk handkerchief, put them in a box, and hid the box in her wardrobe. As her fever came down, she had heard her mother speaking to her, trying to explain what had happened. Simeon had been brought up with principles like her own. He would never go against the wishes of his father, however much he loved her. With understanding and patience, Kleoniki helped her to understand and even forgive her father for his attack.

Dorothea's visit almost made things worse. She arrived full of happiness, ignorant of everything that had happened, to tell her mother that she and her husband had been invited to the marriage of Simeon Kouyoumdzis. As soon as she heard, Kleoniki cast a frightened glance toward Smaragda's room, grabbed her oldest daughter, and pushed her into the kitchen, closing the door behind them.

"What are you pushing me around like that, Mother?" the girl complained, straightening her hat.

"Hush, girl—you'll make a mess of things! Coming here like that and boasting about the invitation."

"Why? What harm did I do? Don't you know this is the wedding of the century? And they've invited my father-in-law and us. I'll go to the dressmaker tomorrow so she can start sewing my dress."

"Can she sew your mouth shut instead?" Kleoniki scolded. "We don't say those names here."

Dorothea's mother grabbed her by the hand and sat her down. In a barely audible voice, she explained to her firstborn daughter what had happened. When she finished, Dorothea's mouth was hanging open.

"Are you serious? Kouyoumdzis with our Smaragda? And you didn't tell me?" she complained.

"Pull yourself together, girl. We've been scared stiff, trying to bring your sister around. And we still are, but at least the fever's gone down."

"I'll go and see her, Mother."

"You stay where you are. She doesn't speak to anyone, doesn't want to see anyone. She won't even see Evanthia!"

"Eh, I understand that. Evanthia might feel bad now; after all, she betrayed her. And I don't blame my sister."

"That's not fair. Mrs. Marigo put her through a real inquisition. Do you have any idea what Mrs. Marigo is like?"

Mother and daughter smiled at the idea, but soon became serious again.

"And Father?" Dorothea asked.

"What can I tell you? He was very upset by all this."

"I can't believe he raised his hand to the little one! He never hit us."

"Eh, that's why things are as they are. And let me tell you, I was very angry with him when I saw the girl falling like a log at my feet. And afterward, so many days with a fever. My baby was destroyed."

"Why didn't you tell me to come, dear Mama?"

"What should I have said? You have your own home now. Anyway, don't think I don't know that you're still angry with us about the wedding. You didn't want Iakovos, but your father—"

"Let's not get into that now. Just as well he found me a good husband. I don't have any complaints."

"Is that the truth?" Kleoniki asked, encouraged, and squeezed her daughter's hand.

"It is, Mother."

"Blessed be the Virgin's name!" the woman said, crossing herself.

"Yes, but now I must see my sister," Dorothea insisted. "She may not speak to you, but I know she'll speak to me."

Kleoniki never found out what was said between the two sisters. Dorothea spent a long time in the room that used to belong to all three girls. She may have been the more distant of the elder two, but Smaragda respected and loved her oldest sister. After Dorothea left, Smaragda even came out of her room and sat at the table with her mother, who hurried to make coffee and give her a sweet treat. Silently, Kleoniki sent blessings to her oldest child for having achieved such a miracle.

When Anargyros returned in the evening and found his youngest daughter reading a book beside the stove, he was embarrassed. It was the first time they had seen each other since the episode, and he didn't know what to do or say. Kleoniki appeared with his slippers in hand, smiling, but her eyes told him to be careful.

They sat down to eat, but each bite went down with difficulty until Smaragda broke the silence. She had thought it over for so many days. She'd accepted what had happened, and she wanted to make things right.

"Can I speak to you, Father?" she asked as soon as Anargyros lit a cigarette and Kleoniki brought him his coffee.

"It depends what you want to say," he answered curtly, more because he was nervous about what his daughter might reveal than because he was angry.

"Smaragda, sweetheart, why don't we leave such conversations for the daytime?" Kleoniki said.

"Don't worry, Mother. It's just, we can't go on like this." She turned to her father and continued: "I want you to know that I didn't do anything bad, nothing vulgar, nothing to dirty our name. We only met once, and Evanthia was with us. He sent me three letters, and I sent him two."

"Does he have your letters?" Anargyros asked in alarm.

"Now that he's getting married? I very much doubt it. I imagine he tore them up. I won't deceive you: I love him still, and I know he loves me, but he can't do anything about it. It's over, Father. As if it never happened."

"And you aren't angry with him?" Kleoniki asked.

"No." She looked at her mother, and something like a faint smile rose to her lips. "What are you afraid of? That I'll go to the church and throw acid in his face?"

"The thought had crossed my mind," Kleoniki admitted. "Why would I do him such harm? I told you, I love him. I think I'll love him forever."

Smaragda finished what she had to say and then disappeared into her room to cry in peace. The wound had reopened, and it was bleeding . . .

When 1927 arrived, Anargyros seemed to be deep in thought. Kleoniki watched him come and go, but she couldn't get a word out of him. They had spent a lovely New Year's Day visiting Dorothea's house in Galata. Even Smaragda seemed to be finding her old self again, slowly but surely. She embroidered, she read, she helped her mother with the housework, and she even began to spend time with Evanthia once more, having first made it clear that they wouldn't talk about the past.

At that New Year's dinner table, Kleoniki received her first happy news in a long while: Dorothea was expecting a child.

After the holidays, Smaragda went to stay with her sister for a few weeks. Dorothea was suffering from dizziness and nausea and had to spend most of her time lying down. Smaragda read to her in a soothing voice, and the pregnant girl settled down and slept. During that period, Smaragda had the opportunity to get to know her brother-in-law, to admire his calm personality, and to see how much he loved her sister. Dorothea may have been more or less forced to marry, and certainly she wasn't in love with her husband, but she respected him and admired his obvious affection. Their relationship was sweet, calm, even tender, and when Smaragda realized this, it made an enormous impression on her. She had always believed that, without passion, no marriage could be successful. Now she saw another side of it.

Back home, Kleoniki looked at her husband, who sighed as he played with his worry beads. She put aside the little quilt she was knitting for her first grandchild.

"Won't you tell me," she asked abruptly, "what's making you sigh like a foghorn? I've tried to hold my tongue, but where's this all leading? Has something happened at the shop?"

"No, woman—everything's fine at the shop."

"So, what's going on? Thank God we're all healthy, and we're expecting a grandchild, so what's worrying you?"

"There's something I want to tell you, but I don't know if I should."

"Now you've really got me worried!"

"Hush, woman, for God's sake. It's not something bad."

"Tell me then, and I'll be the judge."

"You know Ververis's son, Fotis?"

"Our doctor's son? Pah! Of course. What's the matter with the lad?"

"Nothing's the matter with him, but his father told me he wants our daughter as his bride."

Kleoniki blinked at him blankly.

"Do you understand what I said?" he asked.

"Ha! So that's why you've been looking at me like that for days."

"I was flabbergasted too!"

"But just like that, out of the blue? Anargyros, I don't suppose you said anything to the man? Look me in the eye—did you, by any chance, send a matchmaker?"

"No, I didn't, woman. On my oath! Given what's happened, I'd have to be a blithering idiot to do such a thing. The doctor himself came to my office and said his son saw our daughter and wanted her."

"Our daughter is young, Anargyros. I imagine he knows that."

"He knows that, but he says he loves her. And what am I to say, wife? Smaragda's still only seventeen, but how can you turn away such good fortune? Fotis is the son of a doctor and a doctor himself. Money, name, and the young man is good, handsome, honorable, strong! Like a lion!"

"So, what did you tell him?"

"I asked for a little time to think it over. I blamed my hesitance on her youth, and told him we'd have to speak with her first. If she accepted him, I said, I would as well, with all my heart, but only if she herself consented."

"Bravo, husband! You told him the truth."

"But how are we going to tell Smaragda such a thing when she's still crying over the other one? The doctor came today and asked me again. I made an excuse and told him she was at her sister's."

"Wait till she comes back, and with God's grace, my pasha, I'll work out how to tell her. These are things a mother knows better how to say. Don't do it like with our oldest, when you shouted and told her who to marry."

"Hey, don't tell me Iakovos was a poor match. What a boy! He treats her like a sultana!"

"Yes, dear, I don't disagree, but it's one thing for the eldest, another for the youngest. Dorothea wasn't in love with someone else. How strange that this Fotis suddenly turns up. Couldn't he have waited a little bit longer for her to forget Simeon?"

The couple were silent, buried in their own thoughts. Deep down, Kleoniki felt a great satisfaction. She'd never spoken to anyone about it, not even to Mrs. Marigo, but her motherly pride had been wounded when Simeon took the rich girl instead of her daughter. Such a marriage, now, to a doctor, would come to the attention of that snob Kouyoumdzis. Her Smaragda would live like a real lady, she'd attend the salons, she'd have a name. Kleoniki waited till her husband was asleep and then knelt at the icon to beg the Virgin for courage, so she could speak to her daughter and convince her to accept.

When Smaragda returned from her sister's house, Kleoniki told her as sweetly and carefully as she could, without making her own desire obvious, about the proposal. Smaragda had met Fotis a number of times at the gatherings of family friends and at church. She listened carefully to what her mother had to say and calmly asked her for a few days to think it over. Then she shut herself in her room. On the evening of the second day, she sat down with her parents at the table and announced to her father that he could accept the proposal. The wedding of Fotis Ververis and Smaragda Kantardzis took place a little before the Easter of 1927.

CHAPTER 5

Kypseli, 2016

Melpo closed the first of the albums we had been leafing through for so many hours. The last black-and-white photograph was of Smaragda and Fotis's wedding. In it, my great-grandmother was standing beside a very tall and handsome man. She wore a bridal gown and carried a bouquet. Both looked into the lens, their lips smiling gently, but in the end, I couldn't determine if she looked happy.

I turned to Melpo, who was greedily drinking a glass of water.

"So, she married the doctor after all," I remarked calmly.

"Yes, and had two children by him. My father and your grandmother."

"But what about the gold letter? How did Simeon's son make it, and how did I end up with it?"

"Patience, sweetie. You can't learn the history of an era in a single day!" complained the woman. "Take a look around you. We've even tired out the cat!"

She was right. Tiger had fallen asleep at our feet, bored and seeing no prospect of more treats. Melpo stood up stiffly.

"Wait? Are you leaving?"

"Do you expect me to sleep on this couch? Haven't you realized how many hours we've been sitting here? My tongue's gone furry from talking, and my husband will think I've been abducted."

"No, he won't! You called him." I pouted.

"Yes, but that was two hours ago."

She was right. She had arrived in the afternoon, and now the street was quite dark. Karim must have switched on the light without my noticing it, as I was too absorbed in Melpo's story. Now, surely, my faithful friend must have withdrawn to his room to sleep. Melpo stood beside the window and lit another cigarette.

"One for the road," she apologized.

"Can I ask you one more thing? How do you know all this with such detail?"

She smiled. "My girl, since I was a child, I've loved the old stories. The society of Constantinople was closed, and tales were handed down by word of mouth; it wasn't hard to find out about my family."

"But why did my great-grandmother agree to be married?"

"Pride, I guess. Simeon wounded her, but in the end, she managed to shame him for not resisting, not fighting harder—for not running away with her if necessary. Don't forget that after denial, lament, and self-pity comes anger. It's one of the stages of grief."

I nodded. I knew something about that.

"And Simeon? What happened to him?"

"He and Roza lived well together, but Smaragda was always between them, especially for Roza, who finally found out who her husband's beloved was and never forgave her."

"How do you know?"

"It's in the next part of our story."

"And when will I find that out?"

"Tomorrow. I'll come back."

"Their children?"

"Simeon and Roza had three children: Vassilis, Penelope, and Aristos."

"And Vassilis is . . ."

"I'm leaving, Fenia! If I stay any longer, we'll talk until morning and my husband will have a nervous breakdown. He hates to be alone in the house, and I've left him for so many hours."

"Why don't you bring him with you tomorrow?"

"You and I should talk more first. You'll have plenty of time to get to know your uncles and cousins."

I hugged her on the doorstep, and it felt wonderful. I was holding something of my own in my arms. A person whose veins flowed with the same blood as mine.

As soon as I got into bed, I realized how tired I really was. So much information had piled up in my brain. My hand touched the locket. It may not have brought luck to its owners, but it was just right for my neck. I too had been unlucky in life. I thought of my mother. I was ten years old when she died. At first, I took comfort in the thought that she had become an angel and was watching over me, but later I rejected the idea. If she'd become an angel, she wouldn't have left me like that: prey in his hands.

I closed my eyes, trying to drive away the bad thoughts. Tonight, I needed to sleep with only sweetness in my mind. I remembered her arms embracing me, her lips smiling, her voice singing. But uninvited and unwanted images came into my mind. My mother trying to smile at me, even with her lip split, her face covered in bruises. I remembered her hugging me even when her body ached after the beatings and the abuse. I raised my hands and covered my ears so as not to hear her cries when my father grabbed her, making some meaningless excuse. Every time, her only concern was to shut the two of them in their room so that I wouldn't see, but however much she tried to shield me, I knew that it was not a bedroom, but a place of martyrdom. However she tried to disguise her cries as laughter so I wouldn't understand, however much she tried to silently endure, he would grow wilder, and the blows would come harder and fiercer; there was no end to the torture.

I turned over in the bed. I had managed for so many years to bury the memories deep inside me. Melpo's visit and our journey into the past had brought forth echoes from my own history—I was in fact the great-granddaughter of that other Smaragda, who had loved and been betrayed, and who had found herself beside a man who, I was sure, had never loved her.

A particular memory crashed over my mind: That afternoon . . . I must have been about five. My mother had left me at an upstairs neighbor's apartment. Anna was her friend, the daughter of refugees. She had spent her whole life in Wuppertal, from the time her parents had arrived to find work. The two women were close, which they hid from my father, Renos, who didn't like my mother spending time with anyone. I remembered Anna helping my mother treat her wounds and bruises; Anna would always disappear from the house just before the torturer came home.

I didn't know where my mother had gone that day, but I stayed with Anna, who had no children, and we had a lovely time laughing and playing with her little dog. When my mother came to pick me up from Anna's apartment, she sat down with me on the staircase, and there she told me about the baby that would come to our house in a few months.

"And what will it be, Mama?" I asked her, full of happiness. "A girl or a boy?"

"We don't know that yet, sweetheart. But whatever it is, we'll love it and look after it, won't we?"

"I'll be a big sister!" My chest swelled with pride.

As soon as we went into the house, I saw her smile disappear. My father was there, waiting. She let go of my hand and pushed me gently toward my room.

"Go play, darling, and close the door. You father and I have to talk."

Numbly, I obeyed. It wasn't long before I heard her pleading voice: "Don't hit me, I'm expecting a baby! Renos, please! Stop!"

I hid under the bed and covered my ears with my hands. There was an awful noise and then a piercing cry. I rushed out of my hiding place and saw my mother on the floor in a pool of blood, my father looming above her. Then I heard banging on the door; it was Anna, but she was too late. I ran to open the door and fell into her arms, shouting, "My mother's dead!"

The woman took me in her arms, and despite her shock, she spoke to me calmly.

"It's nothing, sweetheart. Your mother tripped. She fell and hurt herself. Run upstairs and play with my dog while I help her."

She released me gently, and I slowly climbed the stairs. Normally, she wouldn't have sent me alone, but I understood that, at that moment, Anna's worry was for her friend. I heard her shouting at Renos.

"A nice job you've done! You've just killed your child. Call an ambulance! Quickly, Renos! She'll die of a hemorrhage!"

My mother didn't die. She spent a few days in the hospital, while I stayed with Anna, and then she came home, but she was very pale. It wasn't the last time I witnessed these sorts of events. My mother had three more miscarriages, all caused by beatings from the brute she had married. And each time, he appeared to be repentant and calm afterward, but soon enough something would happen, and it would start again.

I turned over once more. I had begun to sweat, so I got up and took a bath in the hopes it would help me sleep. The cool water was a great comfort. I went down to the kitchen and drank some milk. There was no way I could escape Tiger when it came to food, especially milk. I filled his saucer and watched as he lapped it up.

I opened the kitchen window to let in the cool night air and drive away the nasty smell that had returned. For many years, that smell was my nightmare—a dirty breath of stale beer. It seemed to cling to the walls, the furniture, my clothes. I looked around, afraid he was there, but I knew it was impossible. A headstone, back in Germany, was all that remained to remind me that another wretched abuser had once walked through this world.

Renos worked in a factory in Wuppertal, and all day, he didn't touch a drop. The Germans didn't fool around when it came to work, and he was proud of what he did, cutting components for tools. Monotonous work, but dangerous. A moment of distraction and the monstrous press could cut off his hand.

His parents had left Greece shortly after the end of the war. There was nothing left for them in their homeland, but they hoped that their son would manage to return one day, rich, and live in the land they came from. Naturally, they were deceived. As soon as they set foot in Germany, they started working in the factories. Renos's father worked in the factory where Renos himself later found a job, and his mother worked in a textile mill. Germany needed workers to rebuild it after it was leveled by the Allies. At first, the family lived in an apartment with three other couples and their children. Cramped living conditions combined with hard work broke not only their bodies but also their souls. Young Renos, together with the other immigrant children, was looked after by an elderly German woman for a small sum. Unfortunately, what none of the parents knew was that this *dada* hated children. Beatings and abuse on a daily basis, hunger and threats that kept the children from telling. Until the bad thing happened. Because of her great passion for drinking, the woman didn't notice that the two oldest boys had found a box of matches. Her little house went up in flames. The woman herself was burned alive with the two boys, and another youngster died of smoke inhalation. Everything was revealed, and a new woman was found to care for Renos, but it was too late by then. His hard, brutish character had already been formed.

I stood in the kitchen, irritated with myself. What did I want with all that now? Why bother looking so far back? There was no excuse for the harm that man did. He was always a lost cause, breaking his parents' hearts. They sent him back to Greece to some relatives, hoping it might help. Their naiveté came from nostalgia and love for the homeland they had been forced to leave, which took on mythical dimensions as the years passed. For them, Greece was the best medicine, capable of curing any sick soul. And there, tragically, Renos met my mother. How and why they married, I never found out. I only knew that their marriage raised a storm of objection, mostly from my mother's father, the man who'd owned the house in which I now stood. Was my mother so in love with Renos that she refused to listen? That question had always tormented me. What did she see in this brute that made her follow him to a strange country where she didn't know the language and was far from relatives and friends? In any case, I was sure that he never loved her. Of course, he didn't marry her for a dowry, since her father disowned her. Then why?

I left Tiger satisfied and washing himself in the kitchen, closed the window, turned off the lights, and went back to bed. Melpo had promised she'd come in the morning, and I still had a lot to learn about the family I was descended from. I punched my pillow to make it smoother and settled down to count small white sheep.

Despite my late night, I came down to the kitchen a little after eight the next morning. Inspired by Melpo's elegance, I'd taken some care putting myself together. Karim smiled, but his eyes X-rayed me.

"You had a bad night, madam?" he asked, putting a cup of coffee in front of me.

"I've had worse."

"The other madam? Did she leave late?"

"Late enough. She'll be back today, Karim, and she'll stay with us for lunch."

"OK, madam, I make food from my country."

I looked at him and smiled. After finishing my coffee, I was about to get up from the table, but his expression stopped me.

"What?" I asked, looking for my cigarettes.

"Madam won't get up from place if first she doesn't eat! No cigarette before she eats."

This was our daily argument. Karim wouldn't let me put a cigarette in my mouth if I didn't first drink the fresh-squeezed juice he'd made me and eat every bite of the food he'd prepared. I obeyed, and when I began to eat, I realized I was very hungry after all.

The doorbell rang exactly at eleven o'clock. I had begun to get irritable with waiting. To pass the time, I had helped Karim wash the vegetables he was going to cook, I'd dusted the small office, and I'd even made my bed. I greeted my aunt, who came in with a smile on her lips. We sat on the couch side by side, and she examined me with a kind look.

"Your eyes are red," she observed. "Did you sleep badly or cry?"

"It's been years since I cried, Melpo," I confessed without meaning to. This woman had a curious effect on me.

"That's terrible! Tears are medicine, my girl. They defuse a crisis that our mind can't handle. That's why men suffer more from heart attacks. Because they think they're not allowed to cry. The poor things try to keep everything inside, and the pain sits in their heart until it bursts like a balloon. Why haven't you cried, sweetheart? Has your life been so good that you felt no need for tears?"

My smile was so bitter that Melpo remained thoughtful for a while. Then she took my hand.

"I told you so much about your great-grandmother and brushed right past the first question I should have asked. What happened to your mother? How did you lose her? I've heard about an accident."

"The accident was marrying my father."

"She wasn't happy with him?"

"No."

A monosyllabic answer, the bitterness filling my mouth with poison. Melpo got up and went to the window. A soft breeze stirred the curtain.

Without turning toward me, she asked, "Then why did she marry him? Why did she sacrifice everything for his sake?"

"Didn't she tell you?"

"No. When I turned fifteen, I was diagnosed with a serious illness. Something in my blood—a rare type of leukemia. The doctors in Greece had given up, but my father heard about a doctor in Switzerland who was performing miracles with a similar illness. He sent me there with my mother and visited whenever he could. I spent two years there, two difficult and painful years, and when I returned, the world had been turned upside down. Your mother had already married and been kicked out of the house. Aunt Chrysafenia had been killed, together with her son, my cousin. Grandma Smaragda had died from a broken heart, and Grandfather Fotis had suffered a stroke. They put him in a rehabilitation center, but he didn't last long. The whole family had scattered to the four winds. I was lost, as if I'd entered a parallel universe. My father didn't want to see anyone, except for Uncle Pericles—your grandfather—not even the rest of his children."

"How strange . . . You, who managed to even learn about my great-grandmother, couldn't find out about what happened so recently?" she asked with justifiable curiosity.

"My girl, you learn as much as others want you to learn. Besides, don't forget how young I was and what I'd recovered from. For years, they treated me like a porcelain doll. It's amazing they didn't manage to turn me into a cantankerous brat. I had to fight hard for permission to study; they didn't even want to send me to the university, and it was there, in my final year, that I met my husband. When Paschalis came to ask for my hand, they treated him like a child molester! I was twenty-six when we married, but I think my parents still hadn't accepted the idea that someone was taking their little girl away. It was as if time had stopped in 1971, when I became ill."

Melpo's eyes had become sad.

"Won't you tell me something about you? About your mother?"

"It's not easy, Melpo," I replied. "I've tried for so many years to bury the memories inside me. My father was a violent and bad man. My mother was a martyr."

"And the accident we heard about?"

"There was no accident. They said she killed herself, but she would never have done that. She would never leave me in his hands, abandon me without help, like prey to his devilish soul!"

I began to tremble. I tried to control myself, to remember that I was no longer a child but a fully grown woman. Decades had passed; I had sunk and yet I still swam. Nothing worked. Pain overcame reason; wounds gaped, wide open again; I felt blood in my mouth and dug my nails into my palms.

Melpo took me in her arms and hugged me tightly. Her warmth was a lifesaver. Her hands stroked my hair, her lips gave me kisses of comfort. The trembling died down, and my body grew still. Holding one of my hands, she opened the album waiting on the little table in front of us. She picked up right where we had left off: the wedding of Smaragda and Fotis Ververis. Melpo spoke softly, as if she were telling a fairy tale.

"Your great-grandmother married, as I told you, in 1927. They set up house in Pera."

CHAPTER 6

VERVERIS FAMILY

Constantinople, 1927

Smaragda had spent her life in the shadow of her older sisters, and also with the heavy burden of knowing her father wished for a boy that never arrived. And so, she was quite unprepared for the reception she received from her new family. Her husband worshipped her, and as he told her when they married, his love had begun many years before. Whenever his father was invited to the Kantardzis house, Fotis would beg so dramatically to go too that his alarmed father forbade it. Every Sunday, he would sit at the back of the church so he could watch Smaragda without anyone noticing, and when he had the good fortune to see her at some rare social gathering, he couldn't sleep all night, his head full of new images of her.

Smaragda was shocked, but when she thought hard, she could remember a few occasions over the years when the boy stared at her in awe. Her second great surprise was the way her in-laws treated her. Her mother-in-law's weakness for Smaragda mirrored Anargyros's disappointment: she'd been unable to have more children, and secretly mourned the lack of a daughter. This beautiful, well-behaved daughter-in-law was the answer to Mrs. Ververis's prayers.

The large private house in Pera became Smaragda's paradise. Living with her husband's parents didn't bother her at all. At first, the place seemed enormous to her. The living and dining rooms were twice the size of those in her parents' home, and she found the modern kitchen full of devices surreal. The beds on the upper floor were all four-posters, and intricately carved, like all the furniture. Part of the ground floor was reserved for her father-in-law and her husband's medical clinic, which had a separate entrance so that the coming and going of patients didn't interfere with the life of the household. The house was built on a sloping piece of land, which meant there was a mezzanine with rooms for the two servant women, as well as laundry and storerooms. It took Smaragda a week to discover and remember all the rooms in the house. And yet, just a month after her marriage, despite her young age, she had taken the reins as if she were a seasoned housewife, a fact that made her mother-in-law sing Kleoniki's praises.

But Smaragda couldn't fully accept her new life, couldn't absorb all the new things she was learning. Nor could she get used to her husband's adoration, which embarrassed her. Nights were especially difficult, when her loving husband lay down beside her, full of desire for his beautiful wife. What upset her was her confusion. Her heart still ached for Simeon, yet in her husband's arms, she forgot him, and she didn't want the things they did in bed to end. She couldn't understand why, shortly before the wedding, her mother, Mrs. Marigo, and Paraskevi had tried to explain a woman's duty and obligation in that arena. That she must be ready and obey her husband when he had "appetites." Smaragda didn't see it as a duty or an obligation. And if it hadn't been for that Simeon-shaped ache in her heart, she would have been completely happy. She had accepted her marriage knowing that she would never love again like that first time. And at least she knew Fotis and liked him. The time she spent at her sister's further persuaded her that, even without passion, a household could be stable and happy. Deep down, she still harbored anger toward the man who had given her up without a fight, despite all the things he had said. And yet, there were moments when she suffered from the great love she still had for him. One thought of the kiss they had exchanged in their single meeting made her heart beat loudly and her eyes fill with tears. She wondered if there was something wrong with her, if she had gone mad, but she concluded that the heart was one thing, the body another. She simply needed to separate them in her mind. Not long after their wedding, as she blushed bright red, she told her husband she was expecting a child.

Nestor Ververis was born a little after New Year's of 1928, giving his mother quite a difficult time. Her parents had come, and Smaragda's room was transformed into a hospital. Her father-in-law and husband sent for not one but two gynecologists, as well as several midwives. At one point, despite her pain, Smaragda nearly burst into nervous laughter, looking at the crowd gathered around her head, listening to them give commands and exchange advice. It was almost dawn when she bought her son into the world.

The arrival of the new member of the family turned everything upside down all over again. Smaragda's in-laws had lost their minds, and her husband wasn't far behind. She was transformed from the princess she had been for them to a queen, and her every word was an order. They only had to suspect that she wished for something, and it was in her hands. They loaded her with gold jewelry, and Smaragda pretended not to see the name of the goldsmith's shop on the box.

Two years later, a new sun lit their lives, and this time it was a rosy-cheeked girl with eyes like liquid gold and blond down on her head. They called her Chrysafenia, the name of Smaragda's mother-in-law, but also because of her golden eyes.

Absorbed in her children, Smaragda seemed to live in her own world. Social life didn't interest her, and she attended gatherings with Fotis only when it was absolutely necessary. She would never have confessed that her soul trembled in fear of meeting Simeon and his wife. She thanked God every time she arrived at some friendly house and the Kouyoumdzis couple was not there.

She had no girlfriends. Evanthia had also married but lived far away at Agios Stefanos, which had been renamed Yeşilköy in 1926, when a law required that all non-Turkish place names to be changed. Smaragda had regular contact with Dorothea, who had given birth to another child, and with her parents. Her only other social contacts were with some older wives of her husband's colleagues. Nevertheless, she didn't miss the company of a girl her own age. Secure in her household, she raised her children, completely satisfied with her life. But she never threw away Simeon's letters. Tied with a pink ribbon, wrapped in a silk handkerchief, they rested in their box, buried at the bottom of a chest underneath some lacework and her wedding dress.

One day, Fotis insisted they attend a party, but Smaragda didn't want to leave the house. Her little Chrysafenia was still recovering from a bad cold. But her husband was intransigent, and that was rare.

"Smaragda, dear, I tell you it's impossible for us not to go!" he stressed for the fourth time when she repeated her objections. "There's nothing wrong with the child. I'm a doctor, and you must trust that I know what's going on."

"I just can't understand why you're insisting so much about this party."

"All right then, sweetheart, I'll tell you again," he said patiently. "Mr. and Mrs. Bezikis are patients of ours. My father treated Mr. Bezikis's parents, and I took on the young ones. Their daughter recently got engaged, and they are very keen to introduce her fiancé to all their friends. I can't not be there—Mrs. Bezikis begged me to come. She knows we don't go out regularly, and it's so important to them."

"Enough. I understand. Who else will be there?"

"How do I know? The woman didn't tell me who she was inviting. But with a name like theirs and a fortune to go with it, you can be sure it'll be the crème de la crème!"

Of course, that was precisely what she was worried about.

And indeed, Smaragda's good luck had finally run out. They arrived at the Bezikis house a little late because, at the last minute, their daughter asked her mother for a story. Her tiny hands were wrapped around her mother's neck, and she wouldn't let her go. If Fotis hadn't intervened, Smaragda would have gone on telling the fairy tale all night.

The couple entered the large drawing room full of people, turning heads as usual. Fotis and Smaragda Ververis were considered one of the handsomest couples in the city. The hostess introduced them to some people they didn't know, and a few moments later, Smaragda found herself face-to-face with Simeon and his wife.

She cursed the moment she had stopped telling the story to her daughter, and was angry with her husband for insisting she come—all in the few seconds it took Mrs. Bezikis to make her introductions.

"Doctor, permit me to introduce you both to an outstanding member of our society," the woman was saying. "Mr. Simeon Kouyoumdzis, son of an old family who continues the tradition of his grandfathers in the goldsmith business. And this is Mr. Fotis Ververis, one of the best doctors in Constantinople."

"But I know you!" her husband was saying now. "I've bought the most beautiful jewelry from your shop for my wife."

It was the women's turn to be introduced. Smaragda would have been less pale in the face of a firing squad. Her frozen hand found itself in Simeon's, and he politely brought it to his lips as her husband made the same gesture to Roza. Smaragda remembered that kiss in Mrs. Marigo's living room, his words, the oaths he had sworn, and everything changed. Beside her stood a man who not only loved but also respected her, while opposite was a small, cowardly person, a man who had abandoned her without a word of explanation and run away like a child. There was no reason for her to be heartsick, just angry with her own stupidity. She was no longer the young girl in love with something that existed only in her imagination. Now she knew what a man who loved his wife was capable of; her husband had taught her this. She raised her head, the blood returning to her cheeks, and full of determination, she held out her hand to greet Roza Kouyoumdzis. The young woman's face startled her. It spoke volumes, making it quite clear that she knew her husband had once promised marriage to the woman with whom she now exchanged a cold handshake.

Fortunately, Mrs. Bezikis wanted to introduce them to more guests, and so she led them off to the other end of the salon, putting an end to the charade. Now Smaragda could breathe easier, although she felt Simeon's gaze still fixed on her. A nervous laugh threatened to erupt, and to avoid it, she pinched her hand and bit her lip. The next couple were quite pleasant, and they spent a little time talking to them.

A few yards away, Simeon's wife nudged him. He turned and came face-to-face with her anger.

"Stop drooling, you fool," she growled.

"What are you talking about?"

"Do you want me to bring you a mirror? Your jaw is practically on the floor!"

"Can't you lower your voice?" he scolded. "People are looking at us."

"And will these people see me? Or will they be too distracted by how you stare at her?" she retorted in a low voice, hoarse with tension.

"You don't know what you're talking about," Simeon answered. "That story was over a long time ago, practically before it began!"

"Really? Then why did she nearly faint when she saw you? And you—so much emotion about an old story? I'm not an idiot, Simeon, and I know what's going on—not just now, but for years!"

"Roza, do you really want to talk about all this here? Can't it wait till we get home?"

"You may have obeyed your father's wishes because of my dowry, but your mind is still on her. What do they call it? Repressed desire?"

"Roza, will you be quiet now before I say something stronger?" her husband said, growing angry.

"The guilty don't speak, my love!" she shot back. "You'd better pull yourself together, or I'll have to take serious measures."

Smaragda was relieved to see the Kouyoumdzis couple leave early that evening. From that moment on, she was able to have a pleasant time. She danced with her husband and chatted with the other women. When they got home and went to bed, though, her mind was free to examine itself. She marveled at the absence of those feelings she'd had for Simeon. Her logic had overcome them. Yes, she had loved Simeon with all the strength of her childish soul. Yes, she had hoped that the two of them would live happily together, but life doesn't happen the way one hopes. She was lucky she had married a man who adored her and demonstrated that every day; she had two wonderful children, a lovely home. She must stand by what fate had offered her with open hands, and not fret over something that was never real in the first place. She turned over and saw her husband's eyes looking at her in the darkness; it scared her.

"Fotis," she said, upset. "What's the matter?"

"Why aren't you asleep?" he asked calmly.

"I'll fall asleep soon. I'm very tired—maybe that's why."

Her husband sat up. The moon shone so brightly through their window that she could see him clearly. Smaragda got up and put on her robe.

"Shall I bring you some milk?" she asked him in embarrassment. "Or would you prefer something hot?"

"Sit down, dear. I don't want anything. But will you tell me what's the matter? We've been married for long enough that you must know by now that whatever upsets you upsets me too. Something happened tonight, and I want to know the cause of it."

"My pasha, I don't understand what you're saying," she said.

"Smaragda, if you won't tell me, that means it's something serious. You never hide anything from me. And tonight you got very upset. Do you want to know when? The exact moment?"

"No," she admitted.

"Tell me, what's going on with Mr. Kouyoumdzis?"

"Nothing!" Smaragda reassured him, blushing. "I swear to you."

"I'm not accusing you of anything! But when we were introduced, I felt you stiffen. Your hands got icy, and you turned very pale. Don't tell me it wasn't so, or I'll be angry."

"I won't lie to you, Fotis, but it's nothing. The craziness of youth, my pasha, that's all."

"Go on, tell me, so I can be at peace."

"Before you proposed to me, Mr. Kouyoumdzis told me he loved me and wanted to marry me."

"And you? Did you love him?"

"Yes. Fotis, I'm telling you the whole truth. His father didn't want me as a daughter-in-law; he intended him to marry the woman you saw. So, as a young girl, I had hopes, and the loss upset me a lot."

"Is that why you said yes to me? Out of spite?"

"That was part of it," she admitted. "I believed then that I wouldn't love anyone else, and so it wouldn't matter who I married. I knew you and liked you." The tears she was holding back spilled uncontrollably from her eyes, but she wanted to clear up something else. With her gaze lowered, she went on: "You should know, though, that nothing bad happened. He only gave me one kiss. I just want you to know that I didn't—"

He didn't allow her to torture herself any longer. He reached out and lifted her chin, forcing her to look at him. "I know that better than anyone," he told her pointedly, and smiled.

The blood rose to her cheeks again as she remembered the first night he had taken her in his arms. He took her in them again now and kissed the top of her head. Afterward, he left her alone and got up. Smaragda followed him with her eyes as he went to the window and stood there looking thoughtfully at the sky.

"What are you thinking, my Fotis?"

"Tonight was difficult for me. I won't lie; at first, I was anxious about the way you reacted to that man—you were almost trembling. Later, when they left, you went back to being the Smaragda I know so well. I didn't know what to think."

"Fotis, I swear to you that was the first time I've seen him since all those years ago."

Her husband came and knelt before her, making her embarrassed.

"Listen carefully, Smaragda. I said I know you well, and I meant it. I'm not scared that you still have something in your heart for him."

"Truly?" The word escaped her, and she bit her lip, provoking a little smile from him.

"Yes, my love. And if you aren't sure of yourself, I am. My dearest, how can a girlish dream, two glances, and a kiss compare to what we're living now. I am your husband and I love you; that much you know. And I know you love me too. More than you realize. But know this too: I wouldn't put my hand in the fire for him."

"What do you mean?"

"That, as a man, I understood from the first moment. That man still has his eye on you."

"Fotis, what you're saying is not right."

"But it's the truth, Smaragda. I saw how he was looking at you! And he didn't take his eyes off you the whole time he was at the party, the wretch. That's why his wife dragged him out."

For a long moment, Smaragda was stunned, rooted in place, but then she jumped up and ran to embrace her husband.

"I don't care about him, Fotis! I swear! And I would never do anything to dirty the name you gave me."

He put his arms around her. "I know, Smaragda. I'd put my hand in the fire only for you. But please understand—we can't have any contact with that family."

"Of course, why would we? Can we forget about it now, my husband? Can we put it behind us? I feel better for having told you."

Fotis looked at her gazing at him in the moonlight. He raised his hands and placed them on her face. His gaze met hers, and however much he searched the depths of her eyes, he found nothing but her love for him. He bent and kissed his wife. Her body pressed itself against his, telling him what he wanted to hear. He lifted her in his arms and laid her on the bed. Words of love, kisses, and heavy breathing filled the room. The moon hid tactfully behind the passing clouds.

That evening was not discussed again by the couple. Knowing what he knew now, Fotis took care to accept invitations only when he was sure there would not be another unfortunate meeting. He had faith in his wife, but not in the man. However certain he was of Smaragda's love, he couldn't bear to be in the same room with another man who still wanted her. From the first minute of their encounter with Simeon, he could smell that masculine desire, and there was no reason to put temptation in Smaragda's way.

Despite all his precautions, a month later, they couldn't avoid it. Mr. Stathopoulos and his wife had organized a large party with official invitations, and it was impossible for the Ververis couple not to attend. Smaragda had a special dress made for the occasion, and as always, their entrance caused a stir. Both were radiant. The large salon was full of lights and people, and some couples were already dancing to the rhythms of a small orchestra. Despite the large number of guests, after five minutes, the Ververises became aware of the presence of Simeon and his wife at almost the same moment the other couple spotted them. With relief, Simeon saw his wife's annoyed gaze pass over them and continue examining the other people in the room. On the other side, however, it wasn't the same. Fotis clenched his fists when he noticed Simeon gazing at Smaragda hopefully. He took his wife by the arm, and they headed for the other end of the room.

Later on, Smaragda couldn't remember how it all started. How did she find herself alone? Where was Fotis? But none of that mattered. The result was the same. It was as if Simeon had been watching for an opportunity to pounce. As soon as Fotis stepped away, and as she was about to approach some women she knew, the other man intercepted her. Smaragda's palms felt damp. She looked around guiltily, but no one was looking at them.

"Let me pass!" she ordered, but he didn't move an inch.

"I want to speak to you."

"I have to want it too!"

"Smaragda, I want to tell you—I want to let you know that, for me, nothing has changed!"

"Mr. Kouyoumdzis, you insult me. I am married and so are you," she told him, trying to remain calm so as not to give any excuse for comment if someone had noticed them.

"But I loved you, and you loved me too before we married."

"Yes, before. You changed your mind and took someone else, and so did I. What do you want now?"

"That's what I wanted to tell you! I didn't change my mind. But my father—"

Her patience was exhausted. She looked at him with eyes that shot sparks.

"Very well. Let's forget about politeness if that's the way you want it! You were a coward, Simeon, and your behavior now demonstrates that again. Enough! You filled me with vows and promises, you made me believe you, and then you bent your head and obeyed your father's wishes. Bravo! That's what a good son does. But not a man! And since I have a man now, I'm telling you not to bother me again!"

"But I still love you!"

"And what do you want to do about it? Eh? Do you want for us to carry on where we left off? Aren't you ashamed to stand in front of me and say such things? And if you feel bad about the way you treated me, that you didn't have the courage to write me two words of explanation, to save me finding out from someone else that you were getting married, that's none of my concern. I love my husband. And you know what else? I'm sorry for that wife of yours, that you respect her so little that you'd come speak to me like this. Now, step aside and let me pass!"

She was ready to push him out of the way, not caring who saw, but suddenly, Roza appeared.

"What are you doing, talking to her?" she asked him, struggling not to shout and attract everyone's attention. "And as for you, aren't you ashamed, a married woman? Does your husband know that you're trying to ensnare my husband? Of course, what can you expect from a—"

Fotis appeared, smiling. Smaragda saw the darkness in his eyes.

"Mrs. Kouyoumdzis, I'd advise you not to complete that sentence," he said through clenched teeth. He turned to Simeon. "As for you, if you approach my wife again, I'll break your nose, no matter where we are. Now, take your wife and leave, before everyone here realizes what's going on. And from now on, stay out of our way!"

Roza, furious, went to say something, but Simeon grabbed her roughly by the arm and dragged her off to say good-bye to their hosts, who didn't understand what had gone on and wondered at the speedy departure. A few guests who'd been closer to the quarrel informed them that some tension had developed between the couples, but they didn't know any details. Mr. and Mrs. Stathopoulos would continue to be puzzled.

As soon as Smaragda was alone with her husband, she looked at him boldly, and it was her look that brought a smile to his lips. His beautiful wife had nothing to hide.

"I'm exhausted," she said. "I can't believe that just happened!"

"Are you going to tell me about it?"

"What can I say? He appeared in front of me, the wretch, to tell me he still loves me! The nerve! If we'd been somewhere else, I would have slapped his face. Imagine, right here! And then his wife came to insult me—me! Instead of taking her husband away." Smaragda's anger grew now that the initial surprise had left her. Her eyes were flashing; she almost forgot where she was. "And she, the—I won't say it—she nearly flew at me. Such shameless people! And to think that I once—"

"Smaragda, enough, my sweet! Someone could hear you," he gently interrupted her.

As if woken from a trance, Smaragda raised her head, but now her eyes were sad. "It's awful," she said softly. "In my mind, I pictured him differently. I wanted to keep the image of the boy I knew. Proud. Now he hasn't left me anything."

Fotis hugged her, smiling. If he lived for a hundred years, Fotis thought, he would never understand women, the crazy paths their minds could take. He didn't tell her that if he had lost her then, he might have felt like Simeon. Deep down, he understood the man.

CHAPTER 7

Ververis Family

Constantinople, 1940

Smaragda realized something was wrong as soon as she sat down at the table that night. Neither her father-in-law nor her husband said a word. They ate so hurriedly she was sure they couldn't have said what the dish was. Fortunately, the children's chatter filled the gaps. Nestor, who was about to start middle school, had a lot to tell them every evening, and when he stopped talking, little Chrysafenia, still in elementary school, made them dizzy with stories about the teacher she worshipped. That evening, though, they didn't manage to break the men's silence, or even attract their attention. Smaragda glanced at her mother-in-law, who answered her with a similarly puzzled look. She waited patiently for the ceremony of supper to be over and for the four adults to be alone. Then Smaragda took the initiative.

"Can you tell me what happened to make the two of you drink the water of silence tonight?"

"Yes, we'll tell you," her father-in-law answered. "But you must keep calm."

The two women, nervous now, sat beside each other holding hands.

"There's war in Greece now—" Fotis began.

"We know that already!" interjected her mother-in-law, but a light squeeze from Smaragda's hand stopped her from saying more.

Ververis frowned more deeply and continued.

"Not long ago, since the Italians didn't manage to advance through Greece as they'd hoped, Germany joined the fight to help its ally. As I speak, Greece is already under occupation."

"But Father," his daughter-in-law dared to interrupt, "didn't you tell us that Turkey was neutral?"

"Correct, my child, if it doesn't have to do with . . . Some rumors have reached our ears, and we don't like them at all. As you know, Fotis and I have some Turkish patients, educated people who don't discriminate against other peoples and religions. One of them, whose wife I saved from certain death last year, told me something about the Turks thinking of mobilization, something about the money Greeks would need to protect themselves. Half conversations. And he didn't know for sure. But we have to take precautions. Fotis and I have taken all our money out of the bank and converted it into gold. We've hidden the gold in the laundry. I put a little cement down to cover it. I want you to be very careful these days."

"And the children?" asked Smaragda. "Should I keep them at home?"

"No, for the moment there's no need, but we'll see," answered her father-in-law. "I'm asking you to avoid speaking to anyone—the person may be reporting their conversations. Don't forget that the Turks still see us as unwelcome guests; they're just looking for an excuse to abuse us."

The old man was right. In the fires of a second world war that set the whole planet ablaze, Turkey saw a new opportunity to attack their "guests." The mobilization exploded like a bomb in Constantinople in 1941. All young, non-Muslim men were sent to the depths of Anatolia to perform forced labor. It was a form of execution—slower and more agonizing. And if it hadn't been for a disagreement between President Inonu and General Cakmak, who feared the consequences of another genocide, the men would have been cut down in cold blood.

The shockwaves from the mobilization hit Smaragda's house. However much they ran, however much they pleaded, Fotis had to go. She couldn't process it. She felt her heart split in two; her hands didn't want him to leave. She was sure she would never see her husband again, and there were so many things she wanted to tell him. And yet, for his sake, she wanted to look strong. She didn't want him to leave with the image of her in pieces, to go to his fate worrying about his young children, shattered wife, and elderly parents. It was imperative that he leave calmly and concentrate on staying alive.

She said good-bye to him without crying. Her eyes looked deeply into his, and her lips didn't tremble as she told him: "I'll wait for you to return, and I know you won't disappoint me. You never have."

He hugged her tightly and breathed in her scent. He wanted to have it with him where he was going.

Their house was plunged into silence. Her mother-in-law shuffled in and out of rooms, incapable of helping. All she could do was cry and pray on her knees for hours every day that God would protect her child. Smaragda didn't have that luxury. She and her father-in-law now shared many responsibilities, and the children had to follow their routine without fear. She told them fibs about their father—that he was a doctor, so he wasn't in danger—although she knew he was working as a slave. Dorothea's husband had also been sent away, and her sister was inconsolable. News was slow to arrive, and letters were very rare. The only one that managed to find itself into Smaragda's hands was a dirty piece of paper with a few words on it that made her cry bitterly. Her husband, with his even handwriting, only explained a little, but it was enough.

My dear wife,

I don't know if this letter will ever find its way to you. You should know that I'm well, as well as I can be in this hell. We work from five in the morning until seven in the evening, often without food or water, and I still don't know how I bear up, while around me, men I knew who were tough and strong are dying every day. In my ears I hear your last words to me. I won't disappoint you, my Smaragda. I'll come back. I swear it!

Tell your sister that her husband is all right too, and we're together. I look after him as much as I can. You see, my love, here you don't have the right to be a man, only a wild beast that fights for its life. There are no cannons, or bombs, or bullets—just hunger and thirst. If we find a puddle of filthy water, we fall on it like wolves and suck in a little to get through the day. I won't write you any more details. Know that I love you more than my life, and if I survive and come back, it will be because you ordered me to.

I kiss you sweetly,

Fotis

She read the letter ten times to her mother-in-law, who never stopped crying, and the same number of times to her father-in-law, whose eyes also filled with tears. Afterward, he raised her hand to his lips and kissed it, filling her with embarrassment.

"What's this, Father?" she scolded him, flustered.

"How else can I thank you, my daughter?" he asked, wiping his eyes. "My Fotis is depending on you, and if he returns, we'll owe it to you."

"Fotis will come back, Father!" she assured him. "Don't have any doubt about that. He's strong, and he knows we're waiting for him."

She left to go to her sister's and share the news, hoping to give her some courage too. When she returned, a different and unhappy surprise awaited her, this time from her son. Nestor was a young man already, his voice fluctuating between the man's that was coming and the boy's that was leaving. He had heard about his father's letter and asked her to tell him everything. Smaragda embellished the situation without downplaying the struggle Fotis was making to return to them.

The boy looked at her critically before he spoke. "I don't think you're telling me the whole truth, Mother."

"Why do you say that, my boy?" Smaragda said in surprise.

"It's not just my father who left. My friends' fathers are there too. The news that comes from them is much worse than you're telling me. My friend Vassilis's father is nearly dead."

"Who is this Vassilis, my son? Do I know him?"

"We share a desk. His last name's Kouyoumdzis. His father is a goldsmith, and the Turks sent him to the work camps too. The day before yesterday, they got a letter from him, and he was practically saying good-bye to them. What they're going through is too much to imagine. They don't give them decent food, and they treat them like slaves, and even worse!"

Smaragda could scarcely breathe. What game of fate was this? She looked at Nestor with a steady gaze that didn't betray the tumult of her heart.

"And you're friends with this Kouyoumdzis boy?"

"Brothers is more like it!" the child declared without knowing what pain his answer provoked in his mother.

"And what if I told you I didn't want you to spend time with this boy?"

"You'd have to tell me the reason, Mother, wouldn't you? Maybe he's not from a good family? Are his parents bad people?"

Smaragda was silent. Her reasons were ones a mother could never admit to her son. She glanced at the sky, as if trying to understand what sort of trick this was, who had a hand in such a friendship. But no answer came, and Nestor was pressing her for more details about his father. Smaragda looked at him tenderly. Her son was growing up. The down on his upper lip had begun to darken, and each day, he was getting broader, growing tall and strong like his father. She threw her arms around him, and although Nestor usually resisted being treated like a baby, he hugged her back. Her eyes filled with tears, and when the boy saw it, he gasped. He had never seen his mother cry.

"It's all lies, isn't it?" he asked. "Everything you tell me about Papa. You're lying to me so I won't be afraid."

"That's not the only reason," Smaragda admitted, wiping her eyes. "It's what I tell myself so I can stand it. I try not to think about everything he's going through. Otherwise, I'll fall apart—and Grandma and Grandpa depend on me. He's their only child, and they tremble at the idea that something could happen to him."

"Mother, you can depend on me!" her son declared with pride. "I'm thirteen years old now; I'm not a baby!"

"Yes, son," she told him proudly. "Now go and keep your sister company for a while, because she's still young, and she mustn't understand anything. Promise me you won't tell her?"

"Yes, Mother."

"And remember, your father is strong and he'll come back!"

Nestor went to find Chrysafenia, leaving Smaragda deep in her thoughts. On the one hand, she agonized about her husband, and on the other, she was surprised by the news about her son's friendship with the Kouyoumdzis child. Did Roza Kouyoumdzis know? Her thoughts traveled to the depths of Anatolia, where the youth of Constantinople was rotting. So Simeon was there. She went and lit a candle, asking God for mercy.

The months went by slowly for all of them. Whoever received a letter from their man hurried to inform friends and acquaintances. The men always made mention of who else was with them so that the other families would know they were still alive. The atmosphere in Constantinople was numb. Over time, the newspaper headlines became worrying. The Turkish press launched an open campaign of fanaticism. According to the government, the cause of all the country's troubles was ethnic minorities, especially those living in Constantinople. The president, Ismet Inonu, and his prime minister, Sarafoglou, weren't content to exterminate Greek men in the concentration camps of Anatolia. They wanted something more. It was time to bring back a law passed by the Young Turks in 1914 for the development of the Turkish economy.

On that cold evening at the end of November 1942, rain poured from the sky. Smaragda watched the lightning flash from her place at the window. Her father-in-law was visiting a dying patient, and she knew he would be home late. Over the past few days, they had discussed the developments continuously, and Smaragda had a permanent worry line between her brows as she tried to work out what all this meant. She had asked her father-in-law to use his contacts to find out whatever small details he could. She didn't just have her own household to think of, but her sister and her parents as well. Fortunately, she'd prevailed upon them to sell whatever they could and turn the money into gold coins. Even her father, who had objected at first, had sold a piece of land they had in Chalcis. Dorothea, without telling anyone, had sold all her jewelry to some Turkish women and buried the gold coins in her mattress. Smaragda did the same. In complete secrecy, she went herself to some patients of her husband's and sold all her jewelry, all stamped with the name of the goldsmith, Kouyoumdzis. She no longer wore it anyway, and she remembered what her father always said: "In this place where we live, only gold can save us."

A little before Christmas, the local Greek community suffered another wound: the Varlik Vergisi, or Fortune Tax. Two words that spread panic—a devious stab in the back. With no logical excuse but bigotry, people would now be divided into official categories to be taxed based on their race. No exceptions or objections were accepted. The lists of taxes were published, and the time allowed for paying them was just fifteen days. Once the deadline had passed, fines would be added.

Smaragda looked wide-eyed at the paper that her father-in-law gave her. She couldn't believe the amount they owed could be so large.

"And if we don't pay, what's going to happen, Father?" she asked, her face deathly pale.

"They'll send me down the road my son took. And to pay off the debt, I'll have to work for two or three hundred years!" the old man answered. He seemed to have aged ten years in ten minutes.

"Christ and the Virgin!" she exclaimed. "But we do have enough, don't we?"

"We do, my child, and even a little left over—don't worry. But imagine what's happening with so many people who can't pay. They've already begun to sell everything."

"I'll go mad! I must find out what's happening to my father, to my sister! What an evil thing this is! What have we done to these Turks that they persecute us so?"

"There's no reason, my daughter. We're Greeks. That's enough."

With her heart in her mouth, Smaragda ran to her parents' home. She found her father pale and her mother crying.

"Tell me, Father, do you have enough to pay the tax?"

"I have some," Anargyros answered, "but not enough."

"Don't upset yourself, husband! We'll sell our carpets and our silver," said Kleoniki through her tears.

"How much are they asking you for, Father?"

"They want five thousand for the shop!"

"That much?"

"Yes, and next door at Orhan the cobbler's, they only asked for five. Five! Just because he's not Greek! The scoundrels can't get enough of our suffering!"

A few minutes later, Dorothea arrived, out of breath.

"What will you do?" Smaragda asked her sister. "Do you have enough to pay?"

"I'm a little short, but I'll sell my rugs. As if I care about such things now! We nearly lost my father-in-law. He had a stroke when he saw what we owe. It's not enough to take my husband, now my father-in-law might have to go to the camps too? We'll lose him. What if I hadn't sold things when you said? I'd be tearing my hair out!"

"We would too," admitted her father, "if we hadn't listened and sold the land in Chalcis. We're still short, but as we said, we can get enough if we sell a few more things."

"You won't sell anything else," Smaragda replied. "I'm here."

She shared the money she'd gotten from her jewelry despite their objections, and mentally thanked the wife of the French consul, who had bought most of it at nearly its original value.

Though relieved that her own family was safe for now, Smaragda couldn't help but be sad at what she saw happening around her. A huge bazaar was taking place in every neighborhood of the city. Everyone was selling rugs, silverware, jewelry, after they had already sold houses, land, even factories—anything they could. She saw families find themselves in the street and, sometimes, not even that was enough. As was to be expected, the price of all that treasure fell precipitously, and people were forced to sell their entire fortunes, the labors of a lifetime, for ridiculously little. Many couldn't come up with the amount demanded, and even elderly men were sent to Erzurum, that remote province of Anatolia, to a town that became synonymous with their martyrdom: Askale. Many never returned.

Smaragda had begun to lose her courage; her nerves had frayed with the waiting. Two and a half years had passed since she had said good-bye to her husband. Apart from that single letter, no message from him had reached her hands. Iakovos had written again to Dorothea and mentioned that Fotis was all right, but that was eight months ago.

Christmas of 1943 was approaching, and Smaragda wondered how they would get through the holidays. Her son, true to his promise, was a big support, but she could see that he too was struggling. His friendship with Vassilis Kouyoumdzis grew even stronger, and one day, young Vassilis appeared at their door. The tray nearly fell from Smaragda's hands. The son was the spitting image of his father. The two boys shut themselves in Nestor's room, and didn't come out until Vassilis had to go home.

Immediately afterward, Nestor turned to his mother and asked her a question she couldn't answer.

"Mother, I want to ask you something, but it's difficult . . . ," he began in embarrassment. "I didn't want to say anything—you have enough on your mind—but I can't keep it to myself any longer. Do you know why my friend's mother won't let me in their house?"

Smaragda stood like a pillar of salt before him.

"What are you saying, my boy?" she asked, stalling.

"Vassilis," her son explained patiently, "asked his mother if I could come over. Mrs. Kouyoumdzis said that no son of Ververis could set foot in their house."

"She said that to him?"

"That's what I'm telling you. What went on between you, Mother? And don't tell me nothing. I saw your face when you heard I was friends with Vassilis."

"Nestor, my dear, the facts are not for young children. The truth is that we don't have a good relationship with Mr. and Mrs. Kouyoumdzis. Something happened a long time ago, but it's not your business."

"You won't tell me?"

"I can't, my dear. I'm not telling you not to be friends, nor am I forbidding your friend to come here, but that's all."

Her expression was so grave that her son understood it would be useless to insist. Besides, since his mother had accepted his friendship with Vassilis even though she didn't like it, he would have to accept her silence, however great his curiosity was.

That night, Smaragda tore another page from her calendar—December 23—and then, as she did every night before she went to bed, she checked that all windows and doors were secure and closed the door to her room. She stood by the window and turned her face to the dark sky from which rain fell, filling the streets of the city with mud again. Her thoughts flew to her husband. There were rumors, although people didn't dare to hope, that the exile of their loved ones was about to end. World opinion had turned against the Turks, particularly in America, about that treacherous blow inflicted on minorities, using an outrageous law.

She had just put on her nightgown when she heard a knock at the front door. It was so loud her hair stood on end from fear. The household was immediately awakened, and her father-in-law appeared in the corridor in his pajamas. The children jumped out of bed too.

"Nestor, take your sister and lock yourself in my room," ordered Smaragda, her voice fierce, and the two children rushed to obey.

Already their grandfather was holding an old sword in his hands.

"You hide too, daughter!" he ordered her.

But Smaragda shook her head. She needed to protect her children; she would not hide like a frightened little woman. She picked up a heavy vase and charged down the stairs.

"Who is it?" she demanded from behind the door on which someone was now pounding even louder.

"Smaragda!"

The vase fell from her hands and smashed to smithereens as she recognized the voice of her husband.

She flung open the door, and without looking, blinded by tears, she fell into his arms, moaning. She kissed him like a crazy woman and tasted the tears that fell from his eyes too. A few minutes passed before he pushed her away.

"My Smaragda," he said hoarsely, "don't! I'm dirty, covered in fleas."

Her hands seized him again, she felt him all over to see that he was all right, and she would not have stopped if a sob behind her had not brought her back to herself. Her father-in-law, until now a silent witness of the scene, could not hold back any longer. Father and son embraced.

"My boy!" the man whispered as he kissed him. "I didn't believe I'd see you again."

His mother's frightened voice could be heard at the top of the stairs: "Smaragda? Are you all right? Who is it?"

Fotis stepped into the house. When his mother saw him, her jaw dropped, her eyes fluttered, and her arms opened wide as she ran to her child.

"My sweet! My treasure!" she kept saying, as she kissed him and hugged him frantically.

"Enough hugs!" said Fotis after a time. "The whole household will catch my fleas!"

"Now wait a minute—there are two more members of the family who need to see you!" Smaragda declared and ran to fetch the children.

She found her son standing with the fire tongs in his hands, ready to protect his sister, whom he'd hidden in a wardrobe. She looked at him with admiration and pride.

"Come, son!" she said. "There's no reason for us to be afraid anymore. The head of the household has come back!"

Nobody slept that night. They lit the boilers and heated water for Fotis to take a bath, while his mother emptied the kitchen of whatever food there was; she would have fed him with a spoon if he'd let her. With special joy, Smaragda heard that her sister would be welcoming Iakovos home too. They had come back together, one giving the other courage so that their already tortured bodies could endure the long and demanding journey home.

It was dawn when the couple withdrew to their room to rest, where Smaragda could explore his face and body. He was very thin, his bones nearly poking through his skin. His hair was grayer than his father's, and his hands were covered in wounds, as were his feet.

"I'm fine," he told her calmly. "Everything's over now."

Without saying a word, Smaragda pulled him into bed and took him in her arms as she would a baby. She stroked his hair and hummed softly until he fell asleep.

The war finally ended a few months later. Everyone, victors and vanquished, had to lick their wounds and get back on their feet. The world had been turned upside down yet again. The dead were countless; the earth had filled with lakes of blood. It would take time to recover.

At seventeen, Chrysafenia Ververis was a beauty, having inherited her mother's fine features, her lovely figure, and her thick hair that shone gold in the sun. Her large eyes, with their black lashes that shaded two marbles of liquid gold, enchanted everyone she looked at. Her father called her his "golden girl."

Beside her, her brother was the image of his father: tall, dark, well built, with a calm face and a polite smile. His friendship with Vassilis Kouyoumdzis had become an unshakable bond, something that had embarrassed Fotis on his return from Anatolia. But Smaragda had warned him, and Fotis agreed they shouldn't hold the sins of the parents against the child, so the boy had become almost a member of the family. He came over at any opportunity, and the two boys spent hours together. When they were a little older, they went for their first walks together. Sometimes, if she begged, they even took Chrysafenia with them. Smaragda wondered what was happening at the other house. Simeon had returned a little after Fotis and would certainly have found out about their sons' friendship. Even more, though, she wanted to know what Roza said about them. Kleoniki Kantardzis, Smaragda's mother, used to often repeat a phrase when her daughter was young, one that she couldn't understand: "From one bad thing, thousands follow." As she grew up, she'd forgotten about it, but now it rang in her ears.

Completely unexpectedly, her father-in-law died in his sleep. He came home one day for lunch, they ate, and he lay down to rest. When he hadn't awoken by his usual time, his wife went to check on him, and found her beloved with a smile on his lips, already far away. Everyone was at home. Smaragda and Fotis were drinking their coffee in the sitting room, and her cry made them jump up. They found her kneeling beside the bed, holding her husband's hand and weeping. The children came running in, Nestor and Vassilis, who was visiting, as well as Chrysafenia, who began to cry pitifully.

She had been close with her grandfather since she was a baby. She stopped crying when he held her, she learned to take her first steps with him, and she ran to his arms for comfort. Later, when she went to school, her grandfather was the one who patiently helped her, and thanks to him, homework was transformed into happy games. It had never crossed her mind that one day he would leave her, and now she saw him motionless, without a spirit, unable to hug her.

The young girl threw herself on his body and begged him to wake up. Frozen in shock, none of them knew how to deal with the sudden loss. Smaragda knelt beside her mother-in-law and lamented the death of a man who had treated her perhaps better than her own father. Fotis tried to revive him, but quickly realized medical attention was no longer needed. He sat on the bed, crossing his hands, those hands that had helped so many people but which were now incapable of helping his own father. Nestor sat beside him. Now Chrysafenia was wailing as she begged her grandfather not to leave her, and she reminded him of all the things they had done together. Suddenly, everyone realized that the young girl was in crisis.

Vassilis, who'd been standing frozen in the doorway, decided to act. He approached Nestor and touched his shoulder. They exchanged a glance and understood each other. The two managed to lead Chrysafenia from the room and splash a little cold water on her face. Nestor gave her a sip of brandy. They took her to her room; she seemed a little calmer now. Her brother, though, was still concerned about his father and the two women.

Vassilis read his friend's mind. "Go! Go and be with your family. I'll stay with her."

Nestor didn't wait to be told twice. Vassilis sat there holding the trembling girl in his arms. He thought he must be dreaming. He had never told anyone about his feelings for this precious burden in his arms. It was as if he had loved her forever, from the first moment he'd set foot in that house. He buried his face in her hair, which had come loose from its ribbon and fallen over her shoulders and around her face. He raised one hand and pushed her hair aside. With the other, he held her very tightly and felt a great happiness. He was ashamed of the desire burning inside him. A man had died, and his mind was on . . . He dared to plant a kiss on the top of her head. The girl stirred in his arms and looked at him with clouded eyes—the brandy she had drunk, not having had any experience of alcohol, had made her dizzy. The liquid gold of those eyes enveloped him, covered him, turned him into a golden statue. His heart ached with love, and now she was in his arms.

"Vassilis?" she whispered hoarsely, looking for an explanation.

He couldn't speak. He was incapable of articulating a single word. He lowered his head and came closer to the golden eyes that remained fixed on his. He continued his progress until his lips finally touched hers. He covered them with his and began, delightedly, to drink in those rosy folds that had haunted his dreams. He felt her heart beating wildly. Her hand rose, and her fingers hid themselves in his hair.

Chrysafenia had known for some time how much she loved Vassilis. She didn't dare to hope, or even allow herself to dream. He was her brother's friend, and besides that, she knew there was something between her parents and his. If they found out she loved the son of these people they disliked so much, the trouble she would be in was unimaginable. So there was no way. The young girl had pushed this love further and further away, and buried in the darkness, it became stronger, and returned to claim her. In her dreams, free of every restraint, she traveled with him, she heard him confess his love, she felt him kissing her as he was now. The effects of the brandy became stronger; she was dizzy—she felt as if she were flying across the water on a gentle sailboat. With the security that this must be another dream, she decided to enjoy it. How could it be anything but a dream? Vassilis had never revealed that he felt anything special for her. And now he was holding her in his arms, his lips more demanding with every second that passed, threatening to devour her completely. She felt his breath burning as he kissed her neck, then returned to their target once more.

Suddenly, what she had put aside in the past few moments returned to her mind, and she pulled away, scarlet. In the next room, they were mourning her grandfather, and she . . . She burst into sobs.

"Don't! Don't!" he begged. "Don't cry—I'm sorry. But I've wanted to tell you I love you for so long."

The sobs stopped abruptly. She raised her eyes and looked at him. "What did you say?"

"I love you, Chrysafenia, my dear. For years, from when we were all little and you ran behind us begging to play too. And as you grew up, I nearly lost my mind. I had to bite my lip every time I came to your house and had to behave politely, while really I was dying to do what I just did. Forgive me if I've offended you. I swear to you, if you don't love me, I'll never bother you again."

She raised her hand and covered his mouth. He looked in her eyes and saw all his dreams becoming reality before he took her again in his arms.

From the moment the tragic news of Dr. Ververis's death spread, the house was filled with people who had come to commiserate, and the family accepted the condolences of many who had been cured by his hands. His wife was a complete wreck; she had stood beside him for more than fifty years, and now she felt that her whole world had died with him. The constant presence of the Kouyoumdzis boy made no impression on anyone because they knew about his friendship with Nestor. Only Chrysafenia felt split in two; her heart danced in a happy cloud, while her soul ached from the absence of the man she worshipped.

After the funeral service and the burial, when they returned to the house for the customary coffee, Vassilis saw an opportunity to give Chrysafenia a letter. She hid it under her pillow to read when she was alone. She felt a little disturbed by this game, but understood that there was no other way.

The only person with enough distance and insight to notice was Smaragda's mother. Kleoniki didn't say a word, knowing it was not a suitable moment, but not one of the couple's illicit glances escaped her. She was very upset. Scenes from the past came into her mind, and she crossed herself as she thought of the way history seemed to want to repeat itself. Her daughter had told her what had happened when they ran into Simeon and Roza all those years ago. And now she saw his son with her granddaughter, walking the same path, now even more dangerous.

She waited a few days before visiting her daughter to warn her. Smaragda wasn't leaving the house because her mother-in-law wasn't at all well. She was fading by the day, buried in her grief, and she hardly ate. With a thousand pleas, her daughter-in-law managed to make her drink a few spoonfuls of soup or milk, while Fotis gave her mild sedatives to help her rest and recover her spirits, but her condition continued to deteriorate. The elder Chrysafenia didn't want to live, and day by day, she slipped away, hurrying to join her husband.

Mother and daughter sat down in the living room to talk. Smaragda was overwhelmed, as much by her grief as by the struggle of trying to keep someone she loved alive.

"Daughter, I didn't come here today just for a visit," her mother began awkwardly. "I need to speak to you, and I don't think the subject can wait."

"What's happened, Mother?" she asked anxiously, "Is Father . . . ?"

"Your father is fine, sweetheart, but it seems that something is happening here right under your nose."

"In my house?"

"In your house. The other day at the funeral, I saw things that will light sparks if you don't manage to stop them, my dear."

"Will you tell me?" Smaragda said impatiently.

"Kouyoumdzis's son, daughter, has his eye on our girl!"

Smaragda stayed still for a moment as she took this in. Then she blushed and sat up straighter. "What are you saying? Vassilis is Nestor's friend!"

"Did I say he wasn't? But the looks he was giving your little girl weren't just friendly. Anyway, dear, I wanted to warn you about this even before I saw them. It's not right, sweetheart, to let him in your house. For years, while the children were small, I didn't speak up, but now—he's a man, and our girl's a woman. And what a woman! As they say, the fruit ripens. And he's not blind!"

"Mama, you're making me dizzy! I have so much on my mind—"

"I know, daughter, but shouldn't I tell you? They don't keep gunpowder near a fire, right? Anyway, they're young, just the right age. Would it take much for something bad to happen?"

"If it's true, what you say," Smaragda began, a bitter smile rising to her lips, "what a cruel trick of fate this is! Like mother, like daughter? Like father, like son?"

"Eh, it seems the blood of one attracts the other. What can I say?"

Smaragda didn't sleep a wink that night, and she didn't say a word to her husband. First, because she had to confirm everything herself, and second, because she was afraid of Fotis's reaction. She didn't know what she'd do if it turned out to be reality and not just a grandmother's fears. She decided to keep her eyes and ears open before she intervened, but again, events overtook her.

Twenty days had passed since her father-in-law died, and Smaragda had reached her limit. Her mother-in-law was in such a state now that she could hardly raise herself from her pillow. Sometimes she ran a high fever, and in her delirium, she'd howl for her husband. Smaragda couldn't even look after herself, let alone work out whether there was a love affair going on.

Chrysafenia opened her door and listened carefully. Complete quiet reigned in the house. She made her way cautiously along the corridor. The way her heart was beating, she felt like it should have woken everyone. She tiptoed downstairs and opened the door for him. Her father was the first to go to sleep, and her exhausted mother was sleeping beside her grandmother, ready to comfort her when she woke in the night. Her brother was also sleeping heavily.

Vassilis slipped hurriedly through the open door and embraced her. He had been waiting for two hours until everyone in his beloved's household was sleeping. He'd escaped too, without considering the consequences should his absence at midnight be discovered. He had to see her alone, had to kiss her again before he lost his mind completely. Soon, his family would surely figure out what was the matter with him. More and more absentminded, he'd started to make mistakes in his work. He had finished school, and as was expected, he worked beside his father so that he could continue the family business. Despite the fact that he loved his trade and the hours he spent working the gold, recently, it had been impossible for him to focus. The melted metal reminded him of her eyes, the shine of it like the shine of her hair, and every precious stone recalled the clarity of her skin. His father was getting frustrated with him, and Vassilis was afraid that, soon, he would demand an explanation.

They sat side by side on the steps of the entrance hall so that, if they heard a sound, he would be able to flee. His arms were wrapped around her while his lips sought hers, and time stopped for them both. Chrysafenia felt as though her body had become ethereal, as if her spirit was flying in a sky lit with love. She couldn't get enough of kissing him; she didn't want to lose a moment of that tremor that moved her whole being.

"I love you," he told her yet again in a small pause between their kisses.

"I love you too, Vassilis, but I'm very afraid. If they find out, we're finished. And what we're doing tonight—I'm ashamed. It's not right for me to meet you secretly. Here we are kissing, and my parents are sleeping upstairs, unaware."

"I know, my precious! I don't like it either, especially deceiving my friend, but tell me what to do and I'll do it. You know I'm going to marry you, my love. I'll speak to my father, and I'll come to ask for your hand, but how can I right now, when your house is in mourning?"

"The trouble is, I fear another period of mourning is about to begin."

The girl's fears were confirmed a few days later. Her grandmother breathed her last in Smaragda's arms. But before dying, for the first time after her husband's death, she was completely lucid. She smiled at Smaragda, she stroked her hair, she thanked her for all her care and love, and she gave her her blessing. Then the body ceased while her soul flew to meet the man she loved so much. Before the official days of mourning for the doctor were up, people gathered again at the house to bid farewell to his wife.

Still more grief descended on the household, and this time, Smaragda had to turn all her attention to her husband, who couldn't bear losing both his parents within a month. And as time passed, the love between the two young people grew stronger. They invented all sorts of ways to spend even a little time together, and between kisses and burning caresses, they exchanged vows of love and dreams of a beautiful life. They deliberately avoided discussing their fears about their families' objections in an effort to exorcise the trouble that, inside themselves, they knew they couldn't avoid. Those fears were confirmed two months after the death of Chrysafenia's grandmother. Smaragda had begun to return to her usual routines, and the first thing she wanted to do was to speak to her daughter. She hadn't forgotten her mother's words for a moment, and she decided it was time to straighten things out.

What she didn't expect was the discovery she made when her daughter was at school. While cleaning the floor one day, she found a small pearl button. She recognized it from one of Chrysafenia's dresses, so she went to her daughter's room to find the dress and sew it back on. As she was looking, it fell out of her fingers onto the bottom of the wardrobe. Looking for it irritably, her hands found a velvet box. She pulled it out, and the blood drained from her face when she saw, on the dark cloth, the familiar name: Kouyoumdzis. Trembling, she opened it. On a bed of white silk, she found a thin gold chain from which hung a small gold envelope. On the back there was a tiny diamond. In surprise, she saw that the envelope opened, like a real one, and out of it fell a gold sheet with one phrase on it: *I love you.*

The woman began to tremble. Her legs wouldn't support her anymore, and she sat on her daughter's bed with the necklace in her hands, staring at it as if hypnotized. Suddenly, she had the desire to bang her head against the wall, to cry out, to smash the letter to pieces, to curse fate for playing this dirty trick on her. Instead, she took a deep breath and put the necklace back in its box, but did not put the box back in its place. She staggered out of her daughter's room.

So, it was true. Her blood froze at the idea that things might have progressed a long way. Might even have gotten out of hand. She sat in her armchair, and that was where her daughter found her when she came home from school. She was shocked—her mother never sat down at such a time—but any expression of surprise died in her throat. The velvet box in Smaragda's lap looked like a bloodstain. Numbly, Chrysafenia approached.

"And now tell me, am I mistaken?" Smaragda asked in a low voice. A threat floated in the air.

"No. I won't lie to you," the girl answered.

"Vassilis gave you this."

Chrysafenia nodded, then knelt in front of her mother.

"Mama, please, I want you to understand me. I love him, and he loves me too!" she said, and her eyes filled with tears. "He says he'll marry me, but with so much mourning, how could he come to ask for my hand?"

Smaragda felt the room spin at the words she heard from her daughter's mouth. Something dragged her violently into her youth, when she'd thought Simeon would be hers forever. The nervous laugh that rose to her lips was interrupted by Chrysafenia, who continued her passionate speech.

"Vassilis is a good boy, Mother—you know he is. He's been coming here for so many years—you know his character!"

"And this character," Smaragda interrupted her angrily, "didn't hesitate to betray us, did he? Under our noses, betraying our trust and his friendship with your brother. And tell me, since we're speaking plainly, how far did this good boy's hand go?"

"What do you mean?"

"Daughter, I think you understand very well. I'm waiting for an answer."

"If you mean what I think you do—" The girl swallowed drily. "Nothing bad has happened."

"Enough! And your meetings? Where did they take place?"

"What do you want me to tell you, Mother?"

"Tell me the truth! You never leave the house by yourself, and when he's here, your brother is too."

"Um—he used to come secretly at night. We sat in the entranceway, Mama. We didn't do anything bad, I swear to you! We just talked and—oh dear! Do we have to talk about this?"

"So, have we reached that point?" Smaragda said, horrified. "Upstairs, your parents were going through agony with Grandpa's death, and I was lying beside your dying grandmother, and you—how could you do this to us? Weren't you ashamed?"

"Have you ever been in love, Mama?"

The simple question stabbed Smaragda in the chest. She looked at her daughter. It wasn't the time for revelations. She preferred to attack.

"How dare you! I expected you to learn what love is," she shot back, "instead of telling me such shameless things. And if he was someone else, perhaps I'd say you're young, both of you, but since you love each other . . . But child, you know very well that we can never consent for you to marry a Kouyoumdzis!"

"But what have they done to you? Was it so terrible?" the girl objected, standing up from her position at her mother's feet.

"That's none of your business."

"But it is, Mother! I love Vassilis, and he loves me. That's all there is to it. And he'll marry me!"

"He won't marry you, my child. And even if we gave our consent, he wouldn't marry you!"

"Why not?"

"Because he's a Kouyoumdzis. He says one thing and does another. Listen to me! His mother won't let him. I promise you that!"

"And I promise you she won't stop us. Neither she nor his father. And that gold letter you're holding, it's to remind me forever of how much he loves me. Vassilis has made up his mind to fight his family for our love, and he'll do it!"

Smaragda wasn't angry now. Her eyes filled with sadness. She understood her daughter, who was in love and so like her. But she was certain of the result. Then, the problem had been Simeon's father, who wouldn't allow his son to marry a girl from a lower class; now it was Roza, who would never permit her son to marry the daughter of the woman her husband had once loved. She stood up and approached her weeping daughter.

"I'm sorry that I've made you cry, but with that man you've gotten mixed up with, it's unavoidable."

"How can you be so sure?"

"Let's say an inner voice tells me. In any case, I'll give you a chance."

"What chance?"

"I won't say a word to your father, because if I do, you should know there'll be real trouble. And I won't tell Nestor that his friend betrayed him. But Vassilis may not come here ever again except on the day he comes to ask for your hand—together with his parents. Don't you dare be foolish enough to meet again in secret, or I'll break the promise I'm making you now. Send him a message that the lies are over and he must talk to his parents."

CHAPTER 8

KOUYOUMDZIS FAMILY

Constantinople, 1947

Before he closed his store to finally go home, Simeon Kouyoumdzis carefully examined the work his son had done and was satisfied. Despite the fact that the boy had been absentminded lately, his experienced eye discerned that Vassilis had even more talent than he as a goldsmith. It was obvious that he loved the precious metal very much. When he was quite young, still a schoolboy, he had watched his father and grandfather work, and tried to learn as much as he could. They could have sent him abroad to study, but were delighted that Vassilis wanted to stay and continue the family tradition. He had devoted himself with great enthusiasm to learning all the secrets of the trade.

They had a very important order to deliver in a few days. The Tsalikoglu family were celebrating their son's engagement, and they wanted all the pieces to be unique and worthy of a princess, seeing as the bride was from one of the most important families in Constantinople.

Simeon examined all the precious stones his son had set in the bride's ring and sighed with satisfaction.

"Bravo, my son!" he said to him.

He looked around at the place where he spent most of his day. Although he had put the key in the door a little before eight that morning, and now the clock showed eight again, he didn't feel ready to return home. His aging father still came every day, and his hands were still steady, but he tired easily and his back ached, so he left much earlier. They all lived together in the large, two-story house that had filled with children's voices over the twenty years of his marriage. In addition to Vassilis, they had two other children: Penelope and Aristos, who was finishing school and wanted to study to be a teacher.

He sat at the desk in the back of the store. It used to be in his room, but after his wedding, they had moved it to the store. It was rare for Simeon to sit there. Usually, Vassilis used it to write invoices and make designs. Simeon lit a cigarette and leaned back in his chair. From where he sat, he could see the whole place. Up front were the shop windows and display cases filled with gleaming jewels, and further back beat the heart of the workshop. When he took over the business, he had added a door so as to close off the workshop when he wished. The store was at the very center of Pera, and after his renovation, it was the most up-to-date in the neighborhood. Next to his children, it was his proudest achievement.

His thoughts turned to his marriage, and a bitter taste rose to his mouth. He got up to pour himself a brandy and sat back down. He let his mind wander. Sometimes, when he saw his son, who was so like him, he remembered his own youth, and his mouth filled with poison. Simeon knew that if he ruminated on Smaragda, he would lose his courage to go home.

As it was, every day was more difficult. Roza looked for excuses to quarrel; their arguments had grown nastier with the years—especially since she found out that their son was friends with Nestor. There were times when it was hard to stop himself from grabbing her by the throat to make her shut up. She could go on for hours, asking questions and answering them herself, shouting, cursing, threatening.

In the beginning, Vassilis had tried to explain it to them, but when he got older, he had simply declared that Nestor was his friend, whether they liked it or not. He had to respect his mother's wish not to invite his friend to the house, but they could not kill a friendship that had deep roots. Every time he went to the Ververis house, Simeon would pay dearly for it. Roza never stopped talking and shouting. Simeon's own parents held their tongues. They had both grown weary of this unpleasant daughter-in-law, but they didn't say a word. They simply lowered their eyes when she looked at them. The fault was all theirs; they had no right to complain. Besides, the only thing that father and daughter-in-law agreed on was their disapproval of this friendship.

Simeon poured himself another brandy. Absentmindedly, he rummaged through the papers lying on the dark surface of the desk. Sketch after sketch. His eye fell on a different type of paper, older, and he felt his hair stand on end. Where had this come from? The memories flooded in, threatening to drown him. This sketch had been made with his own hand, many years ago, for a girl he loved so much that his heart itself had held the pencil when he drew. Except that the necklace had never been made; the gold had melted in the furnace of his father's will. What was it doing among his son's sketches? He folded it and put it in his pocket. It was past nine o'clock; he needed to go home. Dinner would be ready, and his family would be gathered around the table. If he was any later, he would have to swallow, together with the food, his wife's provocations and insults.

"Did you finally find the door?" Roza asked him as soon as he entered, repeating the beloved phrase with which she greeted him nearly every evening.

"Good evening to you too!" he answered. The paper in his pocket burned him.

"That's all we needed," she sneered, "your wisecracks! Don't you see how many people are waiting for dinner? How many times should we heat it up? Who are we that you don't think of us? And if you don't think about me, don't you at least feel sorry for your parents? They want to eat, to take their medicine, to—"

"Roza, don't start, please! Can't you let one evening go by without complaining? Here I am; you can see me. Call the children so we can sit down at the table to eat our food without you poisoning it!"

She glared at him with half-closed eyes. She wasn't used to him answering back. Something was different. She pursed her lips unhappily and left to call the family. Simeon loosened his tie a little and went into the dining room. His wife's pursed lips didn't mean the fight was over; it was only delayed. She always pursed them, and now they were ringed by small wrinkles. When he married her, she was almost beautiful, but now the poverty of her spirit had made her ugly.

They all sat down and the meal began, the silence broken only by the children's conversations, mainly Aristos's and Penelope's, because Vassilis was silent and thoughtful, hardly touching his food. Simeon tactfully watched him, and as he began to put things together in his head, he realized that his eldest son was in love. The thought brought a faint smile to his lips. He wondered who it was.

"Do you see something funny?" his wife said, bringing him back to reality.

"I was thinking," he said and bent over his plate.

"Why don't you tell us so we can all laugh?" she provoked him.

"Do you, of all people, remember how to laugh?" he asked, and all of them turned to look at him in surprise.

That piece of paper in his pocket had filled him with a strength he hadn't felt for years. It reminded him of the impulsiveness of his youth.

"Did you say such a thing to me?" Roza shrieked. "And in front of the children? How will they respect me, how will they listen to me, when their own father speaks to me like some servant. No wonder your son does whatever he wants. Why don't you ask him what time he came home today? A quarter of an hour before you! And where was he? At the other people's house. Whether I speak or shout, you do nothing about it! And you sit there smiling instead of paying attention to your precious son!"

"Aren't you tired of always saying the same thing, Mother, for all these years?" said Vassilis, drawing the fire to himself. "Nestor and I aren't going to give up our friendship over something that happened between you. It's not our business, as you told me. So, now the hour has come to tell you that it's not your business what I do with my friend!"

Roza reacted as if someone had slapped her. She leaned back in her chair, white in the face. The two other siblings lowered their heads, waiting for the storm, which wasn't long in coming. Roza jumped up with her eyes flashing fire.

"You dare to speak to your mother like that? Is that what we've taught you? But what can I expect given where you choose to spend your time. Who knows what that shrew, your friend's mother, says to make you behave like that!"

"Roza!"

It was Simeon, who was standing now and fixing her with his eyes.

"Mrs. Ververis is not to blame for anything, and it's not right for you to slander her like that!"

Roza pursed her lips again, but help came from an unexpected quarter.

"Even so, that's no way for a child to speak to his mother!" the elder Vassilis Kouyoumdzis said in his deep voice, turning angrily to his grandson. "And as long as I live, I won't permit it!" He thumped his hand on the table. "Ask your mother to forgive you, young man, right this minute!"

To everyone's surprise, the boy bent his head and murmured a few words of apology to his mother. Peace reigned until they had finished their meal, at which point they all hastened to get away from one another.

Vassilis locked himself in his room. Tonight was the big night. In his pocket was the necklace he had made, safe in its velvet box, resting on the white silk lining. He had agreed to go secretly again to her house. He wanted to see her eyes when she opened his gift. He wanted to taste her gratitude—his body was galvanized at the thought. But it would be hours before everyone in both their houses was asleep.

The front door of her home seemed like the gates of paradise to him. And how couldn't it when there was an angel waiting on the doorstep inside. He rushed into the semidarkness and sat, as usual, on the marble staircase, while the small candle that she always carried stood guard, casting its glow on faces that burned with love. He took her in his arms, and her kiss was the breath he lacked. He caressed her hair, buried his face in its silk, and smelled her perfume. He felt her trembling in his arms as his kisses and caresses became more daring. She pulled back, blushing, her thick eyelashes shading her eyes. He pulled himself together with difficulty. It was time . . .

"For me?" she asked, and her voice was a whisper full of ecstasy as she saw the beautiful locket.

"For you, my darling," he answered, a lump in his throat.

He showed her how to open the tiny envelope so that the letter fell into her hand.

"Gold of my life," he said to her as he helped her put it on. "This way you'll know every moment that my soul is in this gold letter. For me, this is our engagement. From now on, I'll think of you as my wife."

The girl leaned toward him, carried away, delighting in his stolen kisses. She couldn't let him stay long. She was afraid. And he knew it. But he also knew that dawn would find him still full of thoughts of her, and once again he would ache from her absence.

He had no time to feel anything that night. With a thousand precautions, he returned to the house and plunged into his room, his mouth still holding the memory of her kisses. He wanted to lie down and let his mind advance to when she would be all his, when her body would belong to him forever. He closed his door, switched on the light, and turned to find his father looking at him grimly. He staggered back from the shock. His father stood up and approached him.

"Where were you?" he asked simply.

"I went for a walk to, um, get some air," he answered, knowing how silly his excuse sounded.

"In the middle of the night? Did it occur to you that, apart from the fact that it's improper, it's also dangerous? How long has this been going on?"

"Not long," Vassilis admitted, searching his mind for the best way to face this new situation. This wasn't his mother in front of him but his father.

"Are you going to brothels?"

"What are you saying, Father? Of course not!" he answered hurriedly, red in the face.

"That would be more logical than walks for a man your age! And if you weren't at such disreputable places, where were you? And be careful; we're talking man-to-man now! I want a straight answer."

He took a deep breath. The time had come to do battle. He hadn't expected it so soon, but perhaps it was better. The secrecy would be over. He looked boldly at his father.

"I'm in love with a girl," he said in one breath.

Simeon smiled at him now. "I'd suspected something with all your absentmindedness. Why didn't you say something sooner?"

"Because I didn't know how you would take it."

"But what girl would meet you at such an hour?"

"I go to her house."

"And doesn't she have parents?" Simeon squinted suspiciously at his son.

"Don't get ideas in your head, Father. She sneaks out of her room like I do. She opens the front door, and we sit for a while on the steps of her house." He hesitated for a moment. "Father, I want you to know that I love the girl and I will marry her. I wanted to tell you earlier, but her household is in mourning, and it's not the right time to ask them."

"Wait, slow down," Simeon said, soberly now. "First of all, who is she? You're still very young for marriage."

"Age has nothing to do with it, Father! Tonight I gave her a gold necklace, and I told her it was a token of our engagement."

"What gold necklace?"

"I found a design in the drawer of the desk. The one in the workshop."

Simeon was beginning to have difficulty breathing.

His son continued blithely: "A small gold envelope. I don't know who designed it, but when I saw it, it was as if the piece was made for her . . . I worked hard and kept it a secret from you and grandfather, and today it was ready. Chrysafenia is my life, Father."

The room began to spin with this coup de grâce. That name. It couldn't be a coincidence; it was rare, as her mother was rare. Simeon had to support himself on the back of the armchair that was in front of him.

"Are you saying that the girl you love is the daughter of Fotis Ververis?"

He had neither received an answer nor objected before the door opened wide, and a furious Roza fell on Vassilis howling. She managed to give him two slaps and would have continued to hit him if the young man hadn't grabbed her hands to protect himself. Roza had woken up, and not seeing Simeon beside her, she had gotten up to look for him and heard voices from her son's room. She had listened at the door and heard everything. But when she'd heard the name that was a red flag to her, she rushed in. Now she howled and cursed while her husband pulled her away from Vassilis. Her shouts had woken the whole household, and they gathered in Vassilis's room.

"Now we have a quorum!" Vassilis observed with a nervous laugh.

"Will someone tell us what's going on here?" his grandfather demanded.

His wife intervened. "It's not possible with so many people in the boy's room. Let's go down to the living room so that we can talk like human beings."

"More talking is all we need!" Roza screeched.

"Daughter-in-law," the woman said, "we need to understand what's happened. Such goings-on in the middle of the night!"

It was the grandfather who waved everyone downstairs. They switched on the lights and took their places. Vassilis remained standing, motionless as a condemned man in front of a firing squad. Simeon hurried to fill a glass with brandy and swallowed it in one gulp. That suspicious pain near his heart had returned. From far away, it seemed like he heard fate laughing.

"And now, tell us what happened," the older man commanded.

It was Roza who opened her mouth, full of bile.

"I'll tell you what happened. Your grandson went and got mixed up with that slut, the daughter of Ververis. Tonight he told his father, and even said he was going to marry her! He made her a necklace, the fool!"

A sinkhole opened in the middle of the living room. Only the two youngest members of the family didn't understand why the fact that their brother loved a girl had provoked such tumult. After all, the doctor's family was a good and wealthy one. The children remained silent, while around them the objections had just begun.

"And?" asked the grandfather now.

"What more can I tell you? It's not—"

"Not you! Him." The grandfather now turned his fire on his grandson.

"My mother told you everything," Vassilis said, seriously. "I love Chrysafenia Ververis, and I want to marry her. You may not like her parents, but that has nothing to do with us."

Vassilis was horrified to watch both his grandfather and his mother turn on his father.

"You see what you've done?" his wife asked spitefully. "When I said he shouldn't go over there, you ignored me, and look where that got us! And don't say you're sorry. You're enjoying this, but you won't win— neither you nor her. That wedding will happen over my dead body!"

"Simeon!" his father shouted. "Do you hear what your wife is saying to you? I'm saying the same thing. That family didn't come in the door then, and they won't come in the window now!"

Vassilis gaped at them all as if he were dealing with crazy people.

"Just a moment," he said. "What's going on here? What are you all talking about? What happened with Chrysafenia's family? What has her mother done to you?"

"Your father can tell you if he dares!"

"Truly, though, Roza, what has she done to you?" Simeon asked, and his voice was a calm, discordant note in the charged atmosphere.

"You're asking me, on top of everything? In front of the children? Ask me when we are alone, and I'll tell you! I've had to hold it inside me all these years!"

Simeon turned to the two younger children. "Aristos, Penelope, this conversation isn't for you. Go to your room."

The siblings looked at each other unhappily, but they certainly didn't want to draw fire on themselves by objecting. They just hoped everyone would keep talking loudly so that they could listen from the top of the staircase.

"Out with it, Roza," Simeon said to her as soon as the children had left.

"Here? We're not alone."

"Yes, but what we have to say is everyone's business now. And if you don't want to talk, I will. Vassilis deserves to know."

He turned to his son, who was looking at him with wide eyes. This wasn't at all like his quiet father.

"So, my son, once upon a time . . . ," Simeon began under the shocked gaze of his family, "when I was very young, I met and fell in love with a girl. She was my life, my breath; I woke up and went to sleep thinking of her. Like you, I promised to marry her, but when I told my father, he wouldn't let me. You see, he wanted your mother as my bride. However much I insisted, he didn't yield. He had given his word to your other grandfather, and I had to respect that so as not to shame my family."

"But how could you forget the woman you loved?" his son asked, and when he saw his father's face flush, he answered his own question: "You didn't forget her."

"It was for her that I designed the gold letter, only I never managed to make it."

Now Vassilis's eyes nearly jumped from his head. "That was your design I found in the office?"

"Yes, and you found it and gave it to the girl you love. The Turks have a word: *kismet*, destiny. The girl I loved is Smaragda Ververis, the mother of your Chrysafenia!"

The bomb his father had thrown hit Vassilis right in the chest. He opened and closed his eyes rapidly in an effort to believe what he was hearing.

Now Simeon turned to his wife. "And since all the cards are on the table, why so much rage? Why such hatred for a woman who never harmed you? After all, you won. You married me, and after all those promises I made her, I abandoned poor Smaragda without saying a word!"

"I'll tell you, since you understand yourself so well!" Roza shouted. "Why did you marry me but never love me? I gave you three children, but you never looked at me the way you looked at her that night we saw them. Do you remember? You melted, and I froze. You lay down every night in our bed, but if you remembered there was another living person there, it was only a body to satisfy your appetites. And every

166

day, I froze more and more until I became like a body without a soul! I
have been miserable with you, Simeon, like every woman who knows
that her husband loves somebody else. Don't ask me what that woman
did to me! She sucked you dry! She didn't leave anything for me. I hate
her more than I've hated anyone in my life, and if I could, I'd have torn
her to pieces! But even then, you'd have loved her. That's why, as long
as I live"—she turned to her son now—"this marriage will not happen!
And you can cry and plead all you like. Neither she nor her daughter
will set foot in this house!"

Roza was about to storm out, having said her piece, but a sound
stopped her. She turned to find her husband had fainted on the floor.
Frightened, she ran to him. She knelt and tried to bring him around.
Simeon moaned faintly.

"He's alive!" she shouted. "Run, Vassilis! A doctor. Quickly!"

Vassilis ran as if demons were chasing him. Fortunately, their
doctor lived nearby. Behind him, pandemonium reigned as Roza and
his grandparents tried to revive Simeon with no success. His heart had
broken.

The days that followed were dark ones for the family of Simeon
Kouyoumdzis, as his illness turned out to be very serious. According
to the doctor's opinion, his heart was very weak, and they would have
to be careful if they wanted him with them for many more years. The
doctor prescribed rest and, above all, calm.

Vassilis could never forget his mother's words that evening while
they were waiting for the doctor to examine his father.

"Make no mistake!" she hissed. "Your father will die tonight, and
you'll be the cause. So many girls in the city, and you had to find her!"

"But it wasn't Father who had a problem with it; it was you!"
Vassilis responded.

His grandfather grabbed him forcefully by the arm.

"That's enough!" he said to the boy angrily. "You're not going to kill us all so you can live with your great love! This story is finished, and her name won't be mentioned again in this house! If it weren't for her, your parents wouldn't have quarreled and your father would be fine. Since you're becoming a man, you had better learn that a man respects the name of his parents. Nobody consents to this relationship. So, will you go against us?"

Vassilis lowered his head. Now his own heart hurt. He felt it bleed as all the obstacles appeared in front of him. *If I were just a little bit older,* he kept thinking. Then, the doctor came out to speak to them, and with his every word, Vassilis felt himself sinking deeper. The following days, he said, would be critical for the patient, who was perhaps the only ally Vassilis had in his love. But Simeon was too weak to support him now. Besides, he himself needed to support this tranquil, quiet figure who was his father, now lying deathly pale, with his heart weak and broken. Not only now, but all these years.

CHAPTER 9

VERVERIS FAMILY

Constantinople, 1947

It worried everyone when Vassilis stopped coming to the Ververis home. Even Smaragda. Nobody had said anything to him; he hadn't met with her daughter—she was convinced of that, and yet he didn't come. Three days passed before their curiosity was satisfied. Except that Smaragda would have preferred that nothing of what happened, happened.

It was almost Christmas. The New Year of 1947 would arrive in a heartbeat, and she still hadn't finished cleaning the house. Although she had a servant girl to help with other chores, ironing was her work—she didn't trust anyone else, and now the lace of the bedclothes needed starching, as did the curtains, but she kept putting it off. Fotis wasn't at all well. Some sort of cold had been bothering him, despite all the hot drinks and orange juice that she'd used to keep the doctor on his feet while everyone else in Constantinople was sick and needed his services. That morning, she had sent him off as always, but he felt hot to her.

"Fotis, dear, perhaps you shouldn't go out?" she asked him anxiously. "The way you are feeling, you'll do more harm than good."

"All my patients are in the same situation," he replied good-humoredly. "Whether they caught it from me or I from them. But there are two visits I can't avoid. I'll probably come home after that to lie down."

Behind his back, she crossed herself, as she did with her children. Nestor was now a medical student, and her Chrysafenia was finishing school without having decided what she wanted to do afterward. Smaragda closed the door and drew the jacket she was wearing more tightly around her.

"This isn't cold; it's poison!" she said to herself.

She hadn't finished her coffee when there was a knock at her door. She thought it might be Fotis, regretting his decision not to stay in bed, and she sent the servant to open it. She came out smiling to greet her husband, but her smile froze on her lips. In front of her, dressed in the latest fashion, was Mrs. Roza Kouyoumdzis.

"Good morning," she said. "Come in."

She waved her servant off, which surprised the young Armenian girl—she'd expected to be sent for drinks and food. This wasn't at all like her mistress.

Roza gave a disparaging look around her and made a small move toward the interior of the room.

"Sit down!" Smaragda said with icy politeness.

"I didn't come for a visit," answered the other woman drily, "so don't put on the ladylike airs with me. I know you aren't one!"

"I don't accept insults, especially in my own home. Say what you have to and leave!"

"If you think you can get out of this so easily, you're wrong!"

"What do you want, Mrs. Kouyoumdzis, and why have you come to my house so early?"

"Playing the innocent, eh? I know everything now. And I've come to tell you to put your schemes out of your mind! My son's not for the likes of you and that daughter of yours!"

Smaragda looked at her blankly, as a storm broke out in her head. So, the young man had spoken to his parents, and the result was exactly as she had expected.

"First of all, I only found out about this a few days ago," she responded. "I don't like it either."

"Oh, give it a rest," Roza said. "Who do you think you're fooling? Me? No, you're the fool. My husband left you because he realized you had your eye on his money, so you set your daughter up to become Mrs. Kouyoumdzis and steal our fortune instead!"

"What are you saying?" Smaragda asked, shocked by the spite and craziness of the woman standing opposite her. "We both know it's not like that. Simeon and I were young and in love. And if it weren't for his father, we would have married. But all that happened a long time ago. You married him. You had three children, and now, because of some quirk of fate, our children have fallen in love. My daughter doesn't need your money!"

"Do you really think I'd believe you? Listen to me: Call her off. Tell her to leave my son in peace, or else something terrible will happen and it'll be your fault. As soon as my husband found out, he collapsed. The doctor said we mustn't have any trouble; he has to be calm. That's why I came here to tell you to back off. As long as I'm alive, this marriage won't happen, so call your daughter off!"

Roza spun on her heel and almost bumped into Fotis, who had returned unheard. She screwed up her face and nearly spat her words at him: "May you enjoy them both, mother and daughter!"

Roza stormed out, and Fotis and Smaragda remained alone, staring at each other. Smaragda said the first thing that came into her mind, which was numb with shock: "You're back."

"Is that all you have to say to me?" her husband asked, taking a step toward her. "What was that? What's happening in my house?"

Smaragda was suddenly exhausted. She collapsed on the couch. Fotis put down his bag, took off his coat and hat, and sat opposite her.

"Are you going to tell me?" he insisted.

"Wait, my bey, until I recover a little. Can't you see what a state I'm in? She upset me; may she fall on hard times, the crow!"

"Yes, but by the time you recover, I'll probably collapse. What was she saying about our daughter?"

"Fotis, dear," Smaragda explained sheepishly. "I want to tell you something, but I want you to keep calm, my pasha."

"Wife, I don't even like the way you're beginning."

"Be patient, my husband, because it gets worse!"

Smaragda kept getting stuck as she tried to explain to her husband what she herself had learned a few days earlier. The more she said, the more she saw her husband grow red in the face. Finally, she ran to bring him a cognac to calm him down. With trembling hands, Fotis lit a cigarette and smoked it without speaking. Smaragda was silent and crossed her hands in her apron, waiting for his verdict. But he still didn't speak.

"Fotis," she begged him, "won't you say anything?"

"Like what, woman?" he finally said, his tone full of bitterness. "I don't want to ask you, but I must. Do you swear to me that you didn't know anything?"

"May I not go to heaven if I didn't tell you the truth!" she hurried to reassure him. "If I hadn't found the box with the necklace, it would never have entered my head. Have you forgotten that I was suffering beside your mother? My mind was on nothing else. But the girl told me she loves him."

"And you? Did you remember your youth?"

"To tell you the truth, my pasha, I did. I said that fate is something you can't cheat, but I forbade her to see him or speak to him again. I said that if he came to ask us for her, you would be the one to decide."

"But you would want this match?"

Smaragda shrugged helplessly. "She is in love. And I would want this for her if I weren't certain that it would never end in church. And now that woman came to assure me I'm right," she finished hopelessly. "I'm afraid for our daughter. She is sensitive, and she'll be wounded."

"As you were wounded?"

"Why must you bring that up now? It's an old story. Anyway, I married you, and you've given me so much happiness. That love was forgotten. Nothing even happened between us."

"What are you saying to me now?" her husband asked, sitting up uneasily. "That things went too far with our daughter? Did he lay a hand on her?"

"Oh no, Fotis! I didn't say they had reached—the inevitable. But such a long time under our noses, hugging and kissing—does it take much for a girl? Her heart is in his hands."

"Good Lord, what an awful thing has happened to us," murmured her husband, lighting another cigarette.

"And I'm afraid of that monster who just left. She'll make fools of us! From now on, she'll be gossiping all over town, saying we've had our eye on their fortune, that we encouraged our daughter to catch their son."

"That's all we need! It was an evil hour when we let that boy set foot in our house."

"It's not the boy's fault; don't blame him. It's more my fault. My mother even told me: '*Don't put the gunpowder beside the fire.*' I didn't catch it in time. We had all that upset with sickness and death, and the two of them found an opportunity."

"Then we shouldn't have allowed our son to bring his friend here."

"What happened, happened."

"Anyway," Fotis added grimly, "given what we've seen of Roza, even if Vassilis were to beg me for Chrysafenia on his knees, I wouldn't give her to him. Life with a mother-in-law like that would be hell."

"Do you think he'll rebel and come to us like a bridegroom?"

"What are you saying, woman? He's not even twenty. Do you think he'd dare show his face here, against his father and mother's wishes?"

Smaragda shook her head sadly. So, it was her story all over again.

Chrysafenia read the letter three times. She'd been astonished when she saw Vassilis outside her school. Her heart beat wildly. Days had passed, and now he was right in front of her. She blushed, and when he dropped a piece of paper at her feet as he walked past, giving her a conventional greeting, she pretended her handkerchief had fallen and grabbed it delightedly. She noticed that he seemed a little upset. She didn't have the patience to reach the safety of her room but walked with one of her fellow students to the entrance of her house before waving good-bye. There, on the marble steps where she had visited with him, she sat down and, with trembling hands, unfolded the sheet of paper. She read it, and as soon as she finished, she read it again. With every word, an invisible knife sliced into her body, cutting her open inch by inch until there wasn't a drop of blood left in her. It all drained onto the white marble.

A little later, the servant girl stepped out to run an errand. She roused the household with her cries, thinking Chrysafenia was dead. Fotis came down the stairs two at a time, while Smaragda rushed after him. Shocked, the two parents carried their daughter to her bed, and the doctor took the place of a father. He brought his bag and examined her. Immediately afterward, Smaragda was horrified to see him give the girl an injection.

"Don't worry, it's just to settle her heart. She'll recover."

"But what happened?" his wife asked. "For a girl to faint away just like that!" Then she brought her hand to her mouth. "Fotis"—she turned to her husband—"I don't suppose—"

"No. There's no possibility of a pregnancy," he reassured her. "Something else happened."

At that moment, the servant appeared weeping.

"What happened to the young lady?" she asked.

"Nothing, just a little dizzy spell," Smaragda explained. "What are you holding?"

"Her bag. And this too."

She gave the sheet of paper to the parents and left with her head down. Smaragda looked at it and turned to her husband, disturbed.

"Look! A letter from Vassilis. Listen to what he writes:

'My dearest, know that I'll love you as long as I live, but we can't go on. The dreams will remain dreams, because there's no path for our love to walk in this life. I told them everything, and the result is that my father is in bed with a troubled heart. My mother is furious, and what is killing me even more is that we're paying for old sins. I will love you forever. Vassilis.'"

Smaragda raised her head and looked sadly at her husband.

"Didn't you expect it?" he asked her.

"I did. And I can't help thinking: The boy is better than his father, even if he's younger. At least he's written her a few lines, like a man, so she doesn't keep waiting for nothing."

Chrysafenia began to stir, and they turned their attention to the girl. Smaragda hid the letter in her pocket. Fotis sat beside his daughter, who looked at him with a dull gaze.

"Just look at the young lady coming back to us!" he said tenderly.

Smaragda sat on the other side of the bed and held her daughter's hand.

"Sweetheart, are you all right now?" she asked in agony.

The girl looked first at her father and then at her mother. Despite the dulling of her mind, she remembered his words clearly; they had wounded her, taken her breath away, together with her soul. In her parents' eyes, she saw that they knew, and she lowered hers. Tears began to flow and quickly lost themselves in her golden curls. She wiped them angrily and sat up with difficulty.

Fotis stood up. The scene felt like a trial to him, and he didn't like it.

"I'm going into the living room. Smaragda, stay with the child. I'll ask Anous to fix me a hot drink."

Mother and daughter were left by themselves. Chrysafenia didn't raise her eyes from her crossed hands until Smaragda very tenderly lifted her face, obliging her daughter to look at her.

"Are you and Father very angry?" the girl wanted to know.

"Do we look as though we're angry? But I'd be lying if I didn't confess that we're very upset."

"You knew it would end like this?"

"I prayed to the Virgin that it wouldn't."

"And Father? Was it you who told him?"

"Sweetheart, why don't we leave this conversation for later? You haven't recovered yet."

"I want to know!"

"No. I didn't tell him—I didn't have time. He came home early and found Vassilis's mother here."

"Mrs. Roza? Why did she come?"

"Because Vassilis told them everything, and the household was turned upside down. Didn't he tell you? We read his message."

"What did his mother want?"

"To tell me to make you leave her son alone because, as long as she lives, there will never be a wedding. That's why! That's why that shrew came first thing in the morning to insult me!" Smaragda burst out, but then she bit her lip seeing the tears in her daughter's eyes. "Ah, my

176

treasure!" she cried and hugged her. "I don't want you to cry. You're still young. Life is waiting for you. Don't think it will stop with Vassilis."

Despite her words, she let her daughter sob with grief, stroking her hair and kissing her softly as her own eyes continued to fill with tears. She mourned for her daughter, but it was her own memories that came to life, memories of feeling ready to die because of Simeon. She felt powerless to take away her daughter's pain; she knew that whatever she said, the girl wouldn't be persuaded. Experience was something no parent could bequeath to their child. She was a powerless observer, suffering and watching her beloved child learn through pain.

Chrysafenia drew back from her mother's embrace and wiped her eyes.

"I'm ashamed in front of Papa," she said sadly.

"Your father and I both understand. Not that we like it, but because you kept your self-control and listened to me, no harm was done. It's just that it makes us feel very sad to see you like this."

"Mama, I'm hurting"—her voice was filled with more pain— "here." She pointed to her heart.

"I feel for you, sweetheart," whispered Smaragda and squeezed her hand. "I've known pain and grief too."

The girl looked at her attentively.

"Mama, when I asked you, back when you found the gold locket, if you ever loved—"

"Yes, my girl. I was in love, and perhaps it's time for you to learn the whole truth. If I had told you sooner, perhaps we would have been saved your tears now."

"What happened with Papa?"

Smaragda smiled at the girl. For no child does a parent have a previous existence. To Chrysafenia, her mother was her mother, never a girl like her.

"Nothing happened with your father. But before him, I was like you. Full of dreams. And I loved—"

"Someone other than Papa?" the girl asked in surprise.

"Yes. And I loved that someone with my whole heart, but in those days, my sweet, even love was from afar. He sent me three letters, and I answered him, and we saw each other at some party, and at church. I had a friend, Evanthia. She helped us. And once, we met at her house."

The girl sat up, listening with great interest. Her own pain subsided as she felt strange, learning details about her mother's past. She couldn't imagine her at that age, let alone in love. Her eyes were filled with a strange light as she thought back to her youth.

"Was he handsome, Mama?" she asked.

"Very. For me, he was the handsomest man in the world! That day at Evanthia's house, he gave me my first kiss." She looked at her daughter. "Does that seem strange? I was young once too. I thought I would faint. I was in heaven. He told me he'd marry me. He loved me so much, and if I didn't marry him, he said, he would die! And I accepted it. I believed him with all the strength of my heart."

"And what happened?"

"His father wouldn't allow it. I didn't have as big a dowry as he wanted for his son. And the man had already promised him to a friend. My beloved couldn't go against his father. He married the woman his father had chosen for him."

"And you?"

"I thought I would die. I became ill. He didn't say anything to me, not even two words on a piece of paper that would explain it. I was burning up with fever, and he was engaged."

"And Father?"

"Your father was the son of our doctor. He had loved me since he was young, and he asked for me."

"But how could you accept him when you loved someone else?"

"What did it matter to me who I married, since my heart had died? I said to myself, *I know Fotis, and I like him.* It took me time to realize how much I really did love my husband and how happy he made me. Whatever I tell you, my darling, you won't understand, but dreams are one thing, and life is another. And the dreams that stay in our heads and don't come true will only haunt us if we let them. If we keep thinking of what we've lost, we can't enjoy what we have."

"And the other man? You never saw him again?"

"What gave you that idea? Of course I saw him. At a party with his wife. And then I understood that I no longer felt anything for him, for this man who'd betrayed me, who didn't fight for our love. He seemed so small compared to my husband, who had given me his whole soul! I was angry with him and with myself. He told me he still loved me."

"Really?" the girl responded. "He said that?"

"Yes, he did! The nerve of it! A married man with children, the same as me. His wife and my husband were in the room, and there he was telling me he loved me! I nearly gave the wretched fellow a slap on the face to teach him a lesson."

Chrysafenia's face was lit by a tiny smile. She couldn't imagine her mother young, but the feeling she described was very familiar. Smaragda stroked her cheek.

"That's the way. Smile a little, you who were going to die."

"And what happened after that, Mama?"

Smaragda hesitated. "This is where the story gets more difficult. You see, my girl, the man I loved when I was young is Simeon Kouyoumdzis, Vassilis's father!" Smaragda spoke slowly, as if underlining every word, and she saw her daughter's eyes widen.

"Mama?" she whispered, overcome with questions and shock.

"Now do you know why I was so sure that your love wouldn't end in marriage? Then, the problem was Simeon's father. Now it's Vassilis's mother. She blames me, as if it was my fault that her husband loved me before he loved her!"

"What are you telling me?"

"What I should have told you at the beginning. But it wasn't easy to tell a daughter such things. Still, considering where we are now—"

"But how did it happen? You and me both?"

"Your grandmother Kleoniki understood it first. It seems as if our blood attracts his family. But there's no happiness there. That's why you have to get him out of your heart, my girl."

The pain returned, and fresh tears began to fall from Chrysafenia's eyes. Now she had fate to curse as well.

In the living room, Fotis saw his son run in panting. The servant had managed to get word to him about his sister.

"What happened, Papa?" Nestor asked. "Anous told me Chrysafenia isn't well. What's wrong with her?"

"Sit, son, and calm down. Nothing's wrong medically with your sister. But she will need some time . . ."

He explained everything, and as much as he tried to downplay the situation, he wasn't surprised to see his son growing furious. It wasn't only Nestor's sister's pain, but his friend's betrayal. The young man jumped up and left as if he were being chased, indifferent to his father's shouts. Smaragda appeared in the living room, very upset.

"What's going on, dear? Why are you shouting?"

"Nestor has heard the news."

"Lord! And what did you tell him?"

"Anous had already told him about Chrysafenia, so I had to explain everything."

"Bravo, husband! It's good that you told him about it. And where did the crazy boy go now? Mercy! Don't tell me."

"I fear you're right. He's gone to find the other boy to demand an explanation."

"But Fotis, you should have held him back! He'll be in their hands now, don't you understand?"

"Are you going to blame me now? What should I have done? He jumped up like a tiger and raced into the street!"

"Then why are you sitting there, for God's sake? Go after him! Stop him before he gets there!" she ordered, and then smacked her cheek in despair. "Oh, the shame of it! Virgin Mary, intercede for us so that we don't have another crisis!" she pleaded and ran back to her daughter, who was crying inconsolably.

Nestor didn't know how he had reached the Kouyoumdzis house. Without thinking, he began knocking on the door. A servant girl opened it, and before she managed to say a word to him, he had pushed her aside and dashed into the house, shouting his friend's name. Vassilis appeared to greet him, and Nestor grabbed him by the lapels.

"Aren't you ashamed, you scum?" he howled. "I brought you into my house, and you fixed your eyes on my sister!"

"Nestor, I didn't mean to!" shouted Vassilis, trying to free himself. "Let me go, Nestor! I'll explain."

Instead of letting him go, Nestor punched him in the face with all his strength, and Vassilis collapsed on the hall floor. No sooner had he gotten up than Nestor hit him again. Blood began streaming from his friend's nose, but even that didn't stop Nestor. He saw the boy trying to find his balance and grabbed him by the lapels again.

"I brought you into my house; I had to fight to make them accept you. I trusted you and thought of you as a brother, and this is the way you repay me?" he shouted, shaking Vassilis like a rag.

Roza came running to the top of the stairs. Her eyes opened wide when she saw her son, covered in blood, being hit by a stranger, and she started screaming. Behind her was Simeon, who pushed her aside and came down the stairs with difficulty. At the same moment, Fotis arrived and grabbed his son, just as he got ready to attack again. His grip immobilized the boy.

"Nestor!" he shouted, and his voice was so loud that the boy seemed to recover his senses.

He remained in his father's hands without making the slightest movement. Roza took the opportunity to run to her son. She helped him to stand and tried to wipe his face with her handkerchief.

"I'm all right, Mother," he said, grimacing.

She turned like a wild beast on the two uninvited guests. Fotis stepped between his son and the furious woman.

"You'll pay for this!" Roza howled. "How dare your son come to my house and hit my child? I'll call the police to take you away!"

"Mama—" Vassilis tried to stop her.

"Don't you speak to me!" she said, turning to him now. "You went and got mixed up with a slut, and her hooligan brother beats you up. But what can you expect from—"

"Roza!"

She turned and stared at her husband.

"Here," Simeon said, still more sharply, "are four men. There's no place for a woman. Go, and leave us to speak to each other!"

"How dare you say that to me!" she gasped.

"Do you see any other woman here? So leave! And don't worry. I know how to defend my house too."

She hesitated for a while, but she saw she had to obey. She shot him a furious look and stalked off.

Simeon first turned to his son. "Are you all right, Vassilis?"

"Yes, Papa. I'm fine," Vassilis replied. Then he turned and looked at his friend's father. "Mr. Ververis, I want you to know that I loved your daughter and I still love her. And you, Nestor, I want you to understand. I'm not dishonest—I thought we could be happy."

"Do you see now that that could never be?" Fotis asked him calmly.

"Yes, but that doesn't mean I love her any less. Nestor, I didn't want to betray your household. I wanted to marry your sister. Was that bad?"

"It was bad that you didn't tell me like an honorable person," Nestor said.

"And how would that have changed things?" Vassilis turned to his father. "I know that deep down, you wanted to let me marry her. Isn't that right? You understand me better than anyone else."

"Even if it were true, your mother would never have agreed. Nor would your grandparents. And I think you can imagine what sort of war would have broken out if I had consented to this match."

"I know. That's why I'm obeying, just as you did."

He hung his head and quietly left the room. Behind him, Simeon gave Fotis an apologetic look. But Fotis's own face was full of reproach.

"For the second time, this family has hurt my family and my wife with its cowardice," he said to Simeon grimly. "So, son against father. If you really think about it, I must thank you. My daughter would have had a terrible life in your household."

He took his son and they went, leaving the other man alone. Tears streamed from Simeon's eyes. He had damaged two lives with his cowardice. If, even now, he had shown some strength, he would have helped his son to win where he himself had failed. He looked toward Vassilis's room. An unholy satisfaction overwhelmed him, together with all his other feelings. He wasn't the only coward who had sacrificed his love. Now his son had too. At least he wasn't alone.

Smaragda looked at her mother with eyes full of tears. The old lady was holding herself together with difficulty.

"And when, by God's grace, do you leave?" Kleoniki asked.

"The boat leaves in two weeks," Smaragda replied.

"Have you packed all your things?"

"Nearly. Ah, Mama, I think I'm being cut in two!"

"Stop that, silly girl!" Kleoniki scolded her. "What are you saying now? You're going to your home."

"My home is Constantinople, Mama, and you know it! I was born here, I grew up here, and you and my sister are here. In Greece, I'll be alone."

"You'll have your husband and children. What do you mean, 'alone'?"

"I won't have you! But there's no other way. We have no choice."

Their worst fears had come true. Roza Kouyoumdzis made it her life's purpose to destroy their reputation. She vilified the Ververis family, making up ridiculous stories that she told other women. The rumors, like flies on rotten meat, laid their dirty eggs, and the rot spread everywhere. Twice, Nestor heard fellow medical students carelessly slander his sister. At parties and ladies' afternoon gatherings, it was a favorite topic of conversation: the doctor's crazy daughter who'd pursued young Kouyoumdzis, driving the family to distraction—especially the young man, who didn't want her.

Chrysafenia had locked herself in her room and given up school, where conversations stopped as soon as she appeared. Sly laughter and curious looks had become her daily martyrdom. She was engulfed by a wave of hatred for Vassilis's family, as well as for the young man himself, who failed to put a stop to his mother's disgusting gossip. And then there was his subsequent behavior. He sent her another letter, which she read scornfully, not letting the insidious pain beneath her heart rise and soften it. Her anger, however, didn't reach the point of making her tear it up and throw it away as she had done with the previous one when he had announced the end of their relationship. She put it with the others, and in the same box she also kept his gold locket.

Fotis had surprised the whole family when he announced it that cold evening in March. They were moving to Greece.

"What are you saying, husband?" said Smaragda. "They still have a war going on there. Brother slaughtering brother!"

"Do you think I don't know about the civil war, woman? But it's in the mountains. It has nothing to do with Athens, where we'll be living. Besides, we can't stay here. That witch has left us with no choice."

"But how will we just uproot ourselves?"

"Wife, do you know that every day Nestor and I have to hold our tongues so we don't have fights because of Mrs. Kouyoumdzis's monstrous lies! What do you want? Should we get arrested every day?"

"And Nestor's studies?"

"I'll arrange everything."

Smaragda looked at her daughter, who had lowered her head, while tears flowed again from her eyes. She had lost a lot of weight, and every day she tried more and more to stop the tears, but she couldn't.

"I'm sorry, Father," she whispered. "I didn't want this. Now, because of me, we're going to lose our home."

"It's no use looking back, my daughter," her father answered calmly. "It seems as if what happened was our fate. Don't be bitter—I'll take care of everything."

And Fotis did as he said. He left nothing to chance, and he told no one how he managed it. For months, he solved problems. He ran to friends and acquaintances, asking favors or for them to return his. He had a good friend at the Greek embassy, Mr. Raizis, who performed miracles, helping Fotis organize his finances and send all his money to Greece. The rumors had reached Mr. Raizis's ears, but he had known Fotis since their school days, and he didn't believe a word of it. Mr. Raizis had no children, but he understood his friend's desire to protect his, and was determined to help. He even managed to find them a house.

"And where is this house?" Smaragda wanted to find out.

"Why? If I told you the neighborhood, would it mean anything to you?" Fotis asked.

"Husband! Just like that, we're supposed to go live in a house we don't even know anything about?"

"Alekos Raizis told me it's in the center of Athens. Kolonaki is the name of the area. It's an apartment."

"An apartment?" Smaragda asked, startled.

"There isn't any other way, sweetheart. Our daughter is a full-grown woman. The time will soon come for us to find her a husband. With all the filth that cursed woman has smeared on her, how will that happen here? And our son? He'll be a doctor soon. What sort of respect will people here show him? There are only a few of us Greeks left in Constantinople now, Smaragda, and most of them have swallowed this woman's poison, and they look at us with suspicious eyes."

Smaragda had realized he was right—there was no way out. She felt herself choking with anger at the thought that leaving would make them look guilty. Nor did she want to think how much more people would talk when they left; Roza would say she'd been proven right.

Kleoniki got up now and embraced her child. Her heart felt like it might break. A voice inside her said that she would never see her child again. But she understood her son-in-law. He had a duty to his family, and she too was aware that the situation in Constantinople had become intolerable for them.

"And you, Mother?" Smaragda asked through her tears.

"Us? Is this a time to worry about us? We're fine! And Dorothea will still be nearby. You must stand by your husband and children! A woman's place is where she makes her home. And you'll make it from scratch, and I'll be more at peace. Forget this city! What good have the Turks done us? We've lived in fear, and we'll go on living in fear. But in Athens, you won't have anything to be afraid of, and your children will be better off."

Smaragda hugged her tightly, crying mournfully. She would see her again, she was sure of it. Crossing the border wasn't easy, but she had to hope. She looked at her mother, trying to smile.

"Mama, when we have things in order, you'll come with Papa to see us and stay as long as you like. Tell me you'll come!"

"Bah! Of course I'll come!" Kleoniki promised, making her voice cheerful. "A chance to see Greece! I've heard about it for as long as I can remember, and now I'll have a child there. So, you go and I'll follow, my girl. Don't cry anymore. It's not the end, my dear, but a new beginning! You'll see."

Except that, when they boarded the boat, when the whistle blew and Smaragda watched Hagia Sophia grow smaller, she didn't see any new beginning. She saw only a blackness erasing her whole life up till that point. At that moment, they all appeared like disembodied figures—her parents and Dorothea, who wouldn't let her out of her arms when she heard the news. Even Makrina's smile and songs came clearly to her. Then she saw her friend Evanthia, even her teacher Olympia, who had praised her for her excellent handwriting, and finally him: Simeon, as she had known him, holding her in his arms and telling her he loved her. And when they disappeared, she saw herself as a bride, crossing the threshold of the house she was leaving forever and where she had spent most of her life. Where she had thought she would die one day.

She remained on deck thinking about all she loved and could not take with her. Fotis and the children stood beside her, all of them hugging and crying as they said good-bye to their city. Because Constantinople was their city.

CHAPTER 10

Kypseli, 2016

When Melpo's story ended, a lump was stuck in my throat, and I teared up. I gave a dry cough and rubbed my eyes. Melpo looked at me tenderly.

"I can see your grandmother's story has affected you," she observed quietly.

"Yes. The women of this family have had terrible luck."

"Why do you say that? Your great-grandmother Smaragda lived happily with Fotis Ververis."

"Yes, but—"

"And who told you, Fenia, that we are owed happiness in this life? It's not a birthright, my sweet, it's an achievement. And like a mathematical equation, it has many, many variables."

"I've never thought of it like that."

"If Smaragda had chosen, let's say, to cry and suffer for her lost love instead of getting on with her life with Fotis, she would have remained unhappy. She dared to take a step, and she had the ability to recognize and appreciate her husband's love and the life he was offering her. So the equation was solved."

I looked at her and smiled, and she squeezed my hand before she went on.

"Many things will happen to us in our lives. Some of them are terribly painful. But remember that life, rightly or wrongly, is for the strong. For those who manage to overcome hurdles, to survive, and finally to win. And despite the fact that you keep your mouth hermetically sealed about your past, I'm sure that sitting opposite me, right at this moment, is a winner!"

Right on cue, Karim entered the small office. The whole time Melpo and I were talking, he'd only appeared once, slipping in for a moment with chilled juice and a few biscuits. Now, however, he was standing and looking at us with Tiger licking himself at his feet. The cat had certainly tasted our meal already.

"Madam," said Karim. "Food ready."

"Yes, Karim. We're coming," I told him and stood up.

A glance at my watch made my eyes open wide.

"Good Lord, it's past five o'clock! Weren't you hungry, Melpo? I'm a terrible hostess!"

We followed Karim while Tiger, as usual, tangled himself in our legs.

We sat in the large kitchen, which smelled wonderfully of cinnamon and allspice. Fresh green salad awaited us, along with a superbly cooked chicken, and beside it a pilaf with almonds and pine nuts. It was my favorite, and I thanked Karim with a broad smile. As always, the whole time I was eating, he counted the bites. I practically had to unbutton my pants to take the last mouthful. As I told Melpo, my Syrian friend's cooking was responsible for the five or six pounds I had put on.

"They'll do you good," she answered. "If I can judge anything, it's when a person needs coddling, and you, my lady, are shouting for it. So let someone take care of you!"

We finished off our meal with a cup of my beloved fragrant coffee, and I was ready for the rest of the story when I heard the doorbell ring. Melpo and I looked at each other in surprise. I signaled for her to stay where she was and went to open the door.

Charming Aunt Hecuba . . . She launched herself into the living room like a typhoon, leaving pleasantries aside. She looked around her again and then condescended to glance at me, as I waited with my arms crossed over my chest.

"Are you alone?" she asked abruptly.

"Why? Did I have company the last time you came?" I responded.

I saw her tighten her lips. She sat herself down comfortably on the couch, but I didn't follow suit. She wasn't my guest, and I had no obligation to behave in a civilized way with her.

"I'm listening," I said drily. "Coming here in the boiling heat at such an hour, you must want something!"

"I came to make you a proposition."

"Let me hear it."

"Won't you sit down?"

"I hear better standing up. Tell me what's on your mind."

"As I told you, this house is mine!"

"No, as the lawyer told you, this house is mine," I corrected her.

"You know what I mean. I grew up in this house; it was my mother and father's."

"Precisely! It was *my* grandmother and grandfather's," I repeated.

"Are you going to listen to me?" she asked irritably.

"I am listening to you, but tell things as they are, not how you would like them to be!"

"You pretend you don't understand? I grew up in this house. It's meaningless to you. You had no idea who you were."

"And what does that have to do with it?"

"I don't want my father's fortune in your hands."

"He, however, had a different opinion and left it to me. Why do you have such a hard time respecting his decision?"

Her eyes half closed as her gaze passed over me. The smile on her lips was unpleasant.

"I can see you're clever, but you won't get around me with your cleverness!"

"I don't need to. The subject is not up for discussion."

"Yes, it is. I want the house!"

"Do you realize that the present conversation, apart from being ridiculous, is going nowhere? The house belongs to me, and that's not going to change!"

"Wrong! It can change. Name your price, and I'll buy it!"

I stared at her, stunned. "Have you sunk so low?" I asked her in horror. "Why? What does this house have? A treasure?"

"Don't talk nonsense! My reasons are emotional."

"And you, who are overflowing with emotion . . . ," I remarked sarcastically.

She stood up and took a threatening step toward me, but I saw her freeze as she looked to the door behind me. I turned in shock, and there was Melpo in the entrance to the living room, her arms crossed and an ironic smile on her lips.

"You?" Hecuba shrieked. "What are you doing here?"

Melpo approached us.

"Didn't you yourself tell me Smaragda's daughter was here? I came to see her. And I ended up witnessing a silly scene. Are you in your right mind, Hecuba? Have you come to tell your sister's daughter to give up her house and her inheritance?"

"Don't you get mixed up in this! She's a stranger. An intruder!"

"For you! For me, it's a pleasure to meet the daughter of my dear cousin. But what the devil is wrong with you? Not just now, but all along? You were always jealous of your sister, but it turned into a sickness."

"You don't know what you're saying!"

"Neither do you. So many years have passed, Hecuba! Your sister paid dearly for her mistakes, and so did your father. He died all alone here. And after writing him off for whatever reason, you come back now wanting a share of an inheritance that doesn't belong to you. Uncle gave you a good dowry when you married."

"They forced me to marry!"

"And Papadakis was unlucky enough to get stuck with you!"

"Don't bring my husband into this!"

"And don't you interfere with Smaragda's child!" Melpo retorted, raising her own voice now.

I finally recovered from my surprise at Hecuba's proposition, but also the new information about my mother and her sister. I had to take a stand before the women came to blows. I didn't really want to, but I saw them both bracing to do battle.

"Just a moment, ladies!" I said loudly. "I'm here too. And I have the last word. So, my dear aunt Hecuba, I'm sorry—no, I'm not sorry to disappoint you! The house is not for sale. Not now, not ever! However much money you offer me. I'm not trying to bargain either. I will remain in my grandfather's house, so get that through your head. I don't know much about the family I just acquired, but I intend to find out. And the only way you'll cross this threshold again is if you can come to terms with the past and whatever hang-ups you have about it. And you'll only come here as what you are: my aunt! Have I made myself clear?"

To underline my words, I pointed to the door. I saw her undecided for a moment, but when she looked in my eyes, she saw that the battle was lost. She turned like a young soldier, and a few moments later, I heard the front door close with a bang.

Like a balloon gone flat, I let the air out of my lungs with relief and turned to Melpo.

"My Lord, what was all that? She's not a woman, she's a witch!"

"You said it!" she agreed.

"What happened with her and my mother?" I wanted to know.

"Nothing that I know of, but for as long as I can remember she was deathly jealous of Smaragda. I remember Grandmother

Chrysafenia—we always called her Chrysi like Grandfather wanted—would never leave the two of them alone together when they were small. When your mother was born, Hecuba was four years old. And from what my mother told me later, the polite little girl was transformed into a wild beast. I was the youngest in the family, but I remember a lot of instances from our childhood. When your mother went into the first grade and they bought her a bookbag, Hecuba cut it into pieces. Of course she got into terrible trouble with Aunty, but she didn't care. Whatever Smaragda had, Hecuba wanted. She never left her in peace."

"But there was another sister too. Why didn't Hecuba do the same to Fotini?"

"Don't ask me! I never understood."

"And how did my mother respond?"

"Bah, Smaragda was all goodness. In spite of all her sister's abuse, a lot of which her parents weren't even aware of, she always found reasons to excuse her. Your mother—and I said it to her back then—was capable of forgiving the devil himself!"

I nodded. That I knew from personal experience.

"And the house? Why does she want it so badly?"

"So that you can't have it. Her jealousy of your mother has been passed down to you now!"

"Except I'm not my mother. And I'm not about to forgive the whole world."

"Good for you! Bravo!"

Karim came into the room, looking pale. He held a tray with sweets, but his hands trembled.

"Everything all right, madam?"

"It's all right, Karim. Don't be afraid. She left, and she probably won't come back."

"She is not a good person. I was afraid, madam, very afraid."

Melpo approached him, squeezed his shoulder, and smiled at him.

"Come on, Karim!" she tried to tease him. "You survived bombs in your country, and you were afraid of Hecuba?"

"Fear not for me. For madam," he whispered, and his eyes rested on me affectionately.

I approached him too. My caress was aimed at his cheek. The young man blushed and lowered his eyes. I took the tray from his hands.

"Everything is all right, my friend," I assured him. "We're going to keep talking in the office. You go and collect Tiger. I'm sure with all the hubbub he took the opportunity to enjoy the food we left on the table."

With a shudder and a cry, Karim dashed out of the room, knowing I was right about our naughty black cat.

I shut myself up again with Melpo in my grandfather's small, welcoming office. We ate our dessert without speaking, in a companionable silence, enjoying its delicate taste. Karim called it *mahalebi*, and it smelled of rosewater and was topped with grated, toasted pistachio nuts from Aegina. We finished it at almost the same moment and looked at each other like ornery children.

"I never say no to dessert," Melpo exclaimed, smiling broadly.

"It does seem that the same blood flows in our veins!"

As soon as I said it, I felt my face fall. Since losing my mother, I hadn't met a single person I felt anything in common with. Until now.

"Won't you tell me what happened?" the woman urged me.

"I don't know if I can bear it." I sighed. "Renos, my father, was a monster, a mistake of nature. There was nothing human about him."

It came out of me in torrents—all the things that had happened, and my words caused a deep line to form between Melpo's eyes. She listened practically without breathing so as not to interrupt me.

"It was right before my tenth birthday. My mother had promised she would make me a big cake for the occasion, and I was going to invite my friends over for a party. But I came home from school that day and found a crowd of people gathered outside the house, including some policemen. My mother's friend Anna was sitting on the steps crying. As soon as she saw me, she ran and hugged me. I remember that I had never been so afraid in my whole life. I asked for my mother, and instead of answering me, she just cried. She told me my mother had gone away, but I couldn't believe it. I shouted that it wasn't possible for her to have left me. I had a birthday in a few days, and she was making me a cake. They said she had committed suicide. That she had left a note and jumped from the balcony. I never believed it. Neither did Anna. She told the police about the violence she knew of. She swore that the handwriting in the note may have resembled my mother's, but it wasn't hers. Nobody believed her, and the police didn't pay much attention. One fewer refugee. What did it matter to them? Who would miss her? Only me. And I wasn't worth taking into account."

"And your father?"

"Are you sure you want us to go into that chapter, Melpo? It might be too much for you."

"You're here, in front of me. And if you can handle it, I can too."

I lit a cigarette with trembling hands and stood up. If she embraced me, I knew, I wouldn't have the courage to dive into the deep waters of his evil.

"Naturally, nobody could make Renos feel guilty. The German police asked him some questions and let him go. I forgot to mention my grandmother and grandfather—his parents. That's because they were nearly invisible in my life. I don't remember affection, hugs, or really any interaction the whole time my mother was alive. After her death, Renos turned to them. I was still young; I needed someone to look after me. But my grandfather was very ill with cancer. If I remember right, he died almost right after I went to live with them. Grandmother packed her things and made her dream a reality: she returned to Greece."

"And you stayed behind with your father?" Melpo dared to interject.

I looked at her smiling, but without any joy. "Just him and me. I went to school, then came home to do all the housework."

"And Anna? Didn't she help you?"

"Secretly. I learned a lot from her: how to wash, iron, and cook. She always disappeared before Renos got home because if he found her in the house, I would pay."

"He beat you?" asked Melpo in horror.

"Since my mother wasn't there anymore, he needed someone to torture. In the beginning, it was beatings and threats. I tried to anticipate his every wish. I didn't speak, didn't breathe, hoping he'd forget my presence. I prayed he would come home blind drunk, because then at least he'd collapse on the couch snoring quicker.

"The years went by, and when I turned thirteen, Anna and her husband moved away. There was some sort of inheritance, I think. They went to America. It was another huge loss for me. We spent the evening before they left crying. I had another reason to cry, of course. She left; I stayed. I think that, if she'd known what would happen, she would have kidnapped me. You see Renos, my doting father, soon discovered that I had grown up enough that he could have his way with me as he did with my mother."

I fell silent as the weight of those memories overwhelmed me. My body began to tremble again. I wrapped my arms tightly around it to hold it together. Melpo stared at me, frozen, her eyes wide.

"Fenia," she said softly, her voice almost a whisper, "you can't mean—"

"Every word," I said, speaking slowly. "The beatings were only the beginning."

I stopped speaking, biting my lips. Years had passed, nearly three decades, but it was as if not a day had gone by. His dirty smell returned to my nostrils, the hands that felt my whole body, the pain, the sounds, the memories like knife blades that made me hemorrhage again as I had then.

Melpo jumped up. Her arms hugged me, her lips kissed me, and her voice drove away the horrible things. She pulled me into the protection of her embrace.

I became that girl again, the one who trembled in the dark because it meant the time was coming. I heard my voice again begging him to leave me alone. I called him "Father" so that he would remember who he was and how he was supposed to protect me, not throw me on the bed and fall on top of me. A dirty beast with an even dirtier soul. After that first time, it happened almost every day, and all I did was pray for death. But God didn't listen to me, and I stopped believing in him. I was filled with anger, even at my mother, who had left me in his hands. Maybe she had committed suicide, I thought, unable to live like that anymore. I envied her. She'd had the strength to put an end to it. I didn't. It took two years for him to get me pregnant. I was fifteen. I didn't know what to do, where to turn for help. That was the first time I thought seriously about suicide. Some days I'd walk home from school and dream about jumping in front of cars; other days, the thought horrified me, and I returned to where I knew what was waiting for me. Once, I took his razor in my hands. I admired the cold metal; I imagined it cutting my skin. I could even see my warm blood flowing and taking with it the wretchedness that was my life. But I put it down. It was so simple, so easy, and I? I put down the razor and ran far away from it. I wasn't ready to be reunited with my mother. I blamed myself for being a coward, for not having the strength to save myself. And the more I believed in my cowardice, the more I hung my head and believed that I deserved all that torture.

"Nobody deserves that!" Melpo said firmly.

Then I realized I had been speaking aloud. What I thought I was saying in my mind, I had dared to utter. Safe in her arms, I could continue, however strange that might seem. Not a single living being had heard my secret. I made myself more comfortable in her tender embrace and spoke again.

"I told him. I had no choice—it was starting to show. I'd never seen him like that. When he began hitting me and howling that I'd done it to shame him, I thought that if I lost my mind, at least I'd have nothing more to fear. His rage overwhelmed me. He behaved like a father whose daughter had humiliated him. He beat me half to death. It was then I discovered how much the human body can endure under torture. I did nothing to save myself. Since I couldn't end it all on my own, he would do it—and it would be the first good thing he did for me. But I didn't die. I woke up in a hospital, or rather, in a parallel universe."

"Why?" asked Melpo, and then bit her lip because she had interrupted me.

But I finally had opened the chest of memories, and they flooded out, angry that I had kept them locked up for so long.

"In the hospital, he acted crushed, full of concern. In his statement to the police, he was so clear and vivid: an intruder had stolen all his savings and beaten his daughter violently. And imagine, now he'd rushed me to the hospital like a madman only to find out I was pregnant. He had everyone's sympathy. A despairing father whom fate had struck twice. First his wife's suicide and now his daughter . . .

"When I recovered, but before the police came back to take my statement, he informed me that if I didn't corroborate his story, what I'd gone through would be child's play compared to what he would do to me. He stayed beside me the whole night, threatening without mercy. In the morning, when the police came, he put on the most extraordinary act. And I did as I was told. I never forgave myself. When I got out of the hospital, I was more obedient than ever. I had decided on my own punishment: I deserved him."

"That's terrible, maybe even more terrible than the abuse," Melpo said.

"I know. As soon as I recovered, my life ran like clockwork. I went to school, came home, cooked his food, cleaned, studied, and waited for him. If he had drunk a lot, he fell asleep. If not, he attacked me. I didn't resist. It felt like my soul wasn't in my body. Only two senses didn't abandon me: smell and hearing. I still wake up suffocating in the stench of his body and his breath, hearing his animal grunts. All my other senses died. And the more obedient I was, the filthier he got. In any case, he had nothing to fear anymore. In the hospital, I had learned that his attack had cost me not only the baby I was expecting but any future children. I could never become a mother."

Melpo's body stiffened when she heard my last words, and her arm, around my shoulder, drew me closer to her. The silence in the room was almost devout. Even the slight rustling of the curtains could be heard.

I got up and went to the door. There was Karim. He was paler than I'd ever seen him. He was holding a tray. His clenched eyelids tried but couldn't hold back the tears. His body was shaken by heavy sobs, as if an electric current were passing through it.

I took the tray from his hands, and only then did he realize I was standing in front of him. He fell to the ground.

"Sorry, madam. I did not want—but you were speaking, and I waited for you to stop before I knock on the door. And then I heard, and wanted to die, madam. So much pain. Forgive me for hearing. You must forget, madam. Not remember the bad things. I am here, beside you. Nobody will harm you!"

I looked at Melpo, who was following the situation without knowing how to deal with it.

"Take the tray at least!" I told her.

She sprang up and took it. Finally, I could bend down and try to bring my friend back to himself.

"Karim, please! Get up."

With Melpo's help, I detached him from the floor. We sat him down in a chair, but we couldn't stop the tears.

"Can I bring you some brandy?" Melpo asked.

"Are you crazy? He's a Muslim—he doesn't drink alcohol."

"So give him a cigarette, then."

"He doesn't smoke."

"For God's sake! Doesn't drink, doesn't smoke—how does his mind get any relief?" Then she turned to him. "Karim, pull yourself together, young man. You've been through great suffering also, as I understand it, and you know that having someone else crying all over you about it doesn't do a bit of good!"

Her voice held some special power. It was much like a mother's; perhaps that was the secret. Karim stopped crying. He wiped his eyes, and finally looked at us.

"You are right," he murmured. "But you, madam, how did you bear it?"

"However much a person is tortured," I said, as if talking to myself, "a person doesn't stop struggling to survive. When we live peacefully, our stamina seems weak. Nobody knows what reserves of strength we have until we need them." I looked into my friend's eyes. "Wasn't that true for you, Karim?"

He pressed his lips together and nodded.

"How did all this end?" Melpo wanted to know.

"Has it ended?" I asked sadly. "Inside me, it's still there. On the outside, another four years must have passed.

"As I got older, the beatings stopped. He got in bed beside me every evening, even just to sleep. I waited until he was asleep and went to spend the night in the living room. I'd get into the bath and scrub myself for hours, sometimes until I bled. The unholy acts took on a larger dimension. He wanted more than compliance—he wanted participation. He wanted me to say I loved him, that I enjoyed the things he did to me. It reached the point where he gave me presents. He called me his wife. He was terribly jealous, and didn't let me go out, even to school. A strange hostage situation began. I existed only to serve and feed his appetites. And the worst part was, I gave in to it. He was my whole world, and I became like a slave whose only destiny was to serve her master. He reduced me to nothing. I'm nothing."

"That's enough, Fenia."

Melpo's weak voice brought me back to myself, to the room where we sat. My chest of memories was open at last, and even the deepest, the most evil had been set free.

"I'm sorry, but you wanted to know."

"How could I imagine?" she asked. "What finally happened?"

"One night, he was late getting home. There wasn't a drop of booze left in the house, and I was anxious for him to bring me something—I'd been drinking more and more, needing it. As soon as he came in, I snatched the bottle and began to drink. After that, I did everything I'd learned to arouse him. He died on top of me. His heart."

Melpo raised her hand to her mouth. Karim looked at me, his eyes popping.

"On top of you?"

"Yes. A nineteen-year-old girl pinned under a dead man. With all my strength, I pushed him off me and saw his glassy eyes staring at the ceiling. My eyes filled with tears, and I laughed. My mind had been split in two for so many years, so my reactions were split too. My eyes wept, my lips laughed. Some time must have passed before I pulled myself together. I got up and dressed before calling a doctor to confirm his death. Nobody suspected anything. I buried him and then had to think about what I would do. Suddenly, all my senses began to work again. I needed to get away from that house, but I didn't have a cent to my name. I knew a trade, though."

"What do you mean?" Melpo asked, shocked again.

"Exactly what you think I mean. I decided I'd work for two years as a prostitute and save up enough money to make a new life. Then I'd leave Germany forever. At least that's what I said."

"But that's not what happened?"

"No. Two years became five, and five became ten. I moved to Munich, where I could work in a better brothel and have better customers. When I turned thirty, something broke again inside me. I went back to the only source of comfort I knew: drinking. I stopped working. I lost all my customers. My money ran out quickly, and I found myself on the street."

"I don't believe it!" Melpo cried. "My child, what you've been through!"

"For three years, I was homeless. I ate out of garbage cans, slept on the street. I wandered around in darkness."

"And how did that end?"

"However impossible it may seem, God must have remembered me. It was the evening of my thirty-fifth birthday, and my clothes caught the eye of some junkies. They beat me up and left me naked, almost dead, in front of a house."

"And someone found you?"

"Angels found me. The couple who lived there came home and picked me up without a second thought. He was a doctor, and he stitched me up. They washed me and dressed me and put me in a sweet-smelling bed."

"Praised be His name!" Melpo cried, and her eyes lit up again. "Tell me it was the end of your martyrdom!"

"Yes, it was," I murmured, and I saw Karim murmuring thanks to his god too. I smiled before I continued.

"Yannos and Savina Pantazis were Greeks who had been living in Germany for years. They didn't ask any questions, just took me in. And when I recovered, to repay their hospitality, I took care of the house. I looked after them as if they were my children; the only thing I didn't do was feed them with a spoon. Gratitude flowed from every pore of my body. After a few months, Savina announced that, after years of trying, she was expecting their first child. I cried before they did for their good fortune. Somehow, both of them thought I had brought them luck. The child that was born was a thrice-blessed little girl; she was the sun that shone on all three of us. Knowing I would never be a mother myself, I loved her like my own."

"But how did you end up alone in Greece?"

"That's another story, and it's already getting late."

As if waking from a deep sleep, Melpo looked at the darkness that had descended outside.

"True, but I can't leave your side. Not tonight, anyway. I won't leave you alone after all the things you've remembered."

"I stay here. Not leave madam," Karim reminded her, sounding slightly offended.

"Melpo, I didn't wait for today to remember. I carry this around every day."

"It's not the same," she retorted. "It's one thing to bottle something up inside, another to have it pour out and drown you!"

"What about your husband?"

"Let him sleep at his sister's! Tonight, you're going to put me up here."

"But no more talking," I made clear.

"No, I can't bear any more," she agreed sadly.

"And I will cook," Karim announced.

"You always assume I'm hungry," I told him. "I'm not hungry."

"Yes, but the other madam? You will let her go hungry? Shame on you!" he said in English, provoking me.

I smiled at his shrewdness.

"Actually, I'm going to cook!" Melpo declared. "I need to do something. Spaghetti is just what the doctor ordered."

I followed her obediently into the kitchen and sat watching my mother's cousin and my ward sharing my care. My mouth was so bitter and my throat was so dry that I doubted I could eat at all. I felt strangely empty. *Like a burden has been shared,* I thought. For so many years, I had buried everything, and in a few hours, I had revealed it all to these wonderful, unexpected new friends. I had never stopped to wonder why I'd taken Karim in so quickly. Tonight, though, when I remembered Yannos and Savina, I realized I'd been trying to repay their kindness.

The hot plate of spaghetti that landed in front of me made my stomach stir strangely. In the end, I ate with such gusto that even Karim was impressed.

"Tomorrow, though, will you tell me what happened to my grandmother and her family?" I asked Melpo, swallowing the last mouthful.

"Of course," she answered, smiling. "We'll go to bed early, and tomorrow, first thing, we'll open the album of your life. I promise."

Despite fearing insomnia, I slept deeply. Melpo lay down beside me; she didn't want to leave me for a moment, but when I woke up, no one was there. Enticing smells drifted up from the kitchen. I smiled and got up. I looked at myself in the mirror. Suddenly, I felt like a twenty-year-old whose only concern was what to wear on that hot July morning. I took a bath and tied my hair up with a ribbon. I skipped downstairs and stopped short, admiring their achievements. Toast, omelets, hot croissants, and a delicious fruit tart awaited.

"Who's going to eat all that?" I asked.

"Good morning, is what people say," Melpo scolded, then gave me a kiss on the cheek. "We're all going to eat it together, sweetheart!"

It was one of the most wonderful breakfasts of my life. Melpo kept us laughing with endless stories about her family. She had two grown children: Alkis and Petros. They were both married, and one was about to make her a grandmother.

She was the first to rise after we'd drunk our coffee.

"And now come, and we'll finish our story, because today I'm going home, little one," she declared.

I obeyed eagerly. "On one condition. I want to meet my cousins," I told her. "Can we all get together tomorrow?"

Melpo agreed. And in the little office, we opened one last album.

CHAPTER 11

VERVERIS FAMILY

Athens, 1948

On the boat to Greece, once she had overcome the initial shock of leaving her birthplace and separating from her mother and sister, Smaragda recovered her energy. Her life had taught her not to cry for lost paradises, but to create new ones. However, when they arrived at their destination, she discovered that paradise was already waiting for her.

Alekos Raizis had a sister in Pangrati who was away, and she'd offered them her house until their own was ready. Smaragda saw with surprise that there were even servants waiting for them when they arrived at Mrs. Sekeris's small palace.

"Goodness, husband, who is this woman? A princess?" she asked.

"How should I know, Smaragda?" Fotis answered. "When Alekos told me we could stay at his sister's, I wasn't expecting such luxury."

They all woke refreshed the next day, curious to finally see the apartment where they would be living. A lot of things had to be done so they could move as quickly as possible and not overtax the hospitality of Mrs. Sekeris and her husband. Smaragda realized that she didn't have to worry about anything. Breakfast was served in the dining room, and it was the first time, after two decades of marriage, that she hadn't made her husband his first coffee of the morning.

The biggest surprise came a few hours later as they crossed the threshold of their apartment building in Kolonaki. Smaragda's jaw dropped when she saw the foyer with its shining marble and the plaster decorations that adorned the walls.

"Where are we, my pasha?" she asked with a dry mouth. "What sort of palace is this? Is it ours?"

"No, Smaragda. This is the lobby. All the tenants come through here. Our apartment is on the third floor."

They went up first, with the children behind them, looking without a word at all the wonderful things around them. But nobody could suppress a cry of admiration when they opened their door. The polished wood of the floors and the huge, bright living room left them speechless. Smaragda nearly fainted from joy when she entered the kitchen with its marble countertops and cupboards. In Constantinople, her kitchen was dark. This one shone with the light pouring through the ample window. Full of pride, her eyes caressed her future kingdom, and then she took her husband's hand and struggled to speak.

"Thank you," she said, and he put his arm around her shoulders.

The scene was interrupted by Nestor, who rushed in excitedly.

"Papa, Mama, come and look at what else the house has!"

They followed, and when Smaragda saw the bathroom, with its large white marble tub and modern fixtures, she had to lean against the wall so she wouldn't fall down.

"What's this?" she exclaimed. "Blessed Virgin!"

Fotis didn't spare any expense in furnishing their house. The kitchen, his wife's kingdom, had a new stove, shining pots and pans, and a new icebox that made Smaragda cry when she saw it. The dark wooden box even had a big tank in the upper part and a little tap so they could have cold water. In the middle there were shelves for food, and at the bottom was another tap for the melted water to run out.

"Goodness, my pasha! These things cost a fortune!"

"You deserve it, my lady!" Fotis told her. Seeing her eyes light up made him feel happy too.

They all rolled up their sleeves to clean their house and make it comfortable. Smaragda worked tirelessly and sang like a canary, and beside her, Fotis was proud. Nestor and Chrysafenia exchanged glances full of understanding. Their parents seemed transformed, and that night, Chrysafenia said to her brother, "How I envy them! After so many years together, the love in their eyes brings tears to mine."

"Your time will come," he said, and hugged her affectionately.

On the boat, the two of them had talked about what happened. There, traveling between sea and sky, they could open their hearts to each other. Nestor didn't hide how much her actions had hurt him, while Chrysafenia patiently tried to make her brother understand that unfortunate love so he wouldn't go on hating Vassilis. After so long, she had accepted the fact that Vassilis too was a victim of circumstances. She admitted that, whatever happened in the future, a part of her heart would never stop loving him. For the first time, Nestor began to wonder about love and its power. He himself had remained, until then, unharmed by its arrows and influence.

There were only two things in the apartment building Smaragda had an issue with, and she didn't get over them for a long time. One was, naturally, the elevator, which she refused to get into, however much her husband and children tried to persuade her.

"You won't get me into a box until my time comes!" she declared and continued to climb the marble stairs each day.

The second problem was the balcony. From the first time they went out to admire the view, Smaragda clung to her husband.

"That's enough now, let's go inside!" she barked, dragging them in.

"What's wrong, Mama?" asked Nestor. "Don't you see how beautiful it is? With the breeze on your face? Anyway, what are you afraid of? There's a railing—"

"Railing smailing! What if you get dizzy and fall? They'll have to scoop you up with a teaspoon! My house is just fine; I open my window and get plenty of air. And let me tell you: if I want to go outside, I'll go downstairs to the street and take a walk."

Nobody insisted because everyone knew Smaragda didn't change her mind easily. The trouble came when she had to clean the balcony. She went out pale; she came back pale. At last, Chrysafenia took over the job, sparing her mother.

When everything was ready, the family moved into the large apartment. On the first floor, Fotis discovered a smaller apartment available and decided to make it his office. Alekos Raizis from Constantinople worked magic there too, and very soon, his friend again acquired patients, most of them from the upper crust of postwar Athens. Their life assumed its usual rhythm, only Nestor decided not to continue his medical studies, however much his father tried to persuade him. The young man had decided to become a pharmacist. And although Fotis was very unhappy at first, as he got used to his new homeland and talked to people there, he realized that his son was wise to choose such a lucrative profession.

The year 1949 found the family in high spirits. They celebrated New Year's for the first time in Greece, satisfied on all counts. They'd even begun to make their first friends. At first, people had laughed at the strange dialect of Greek spoken by the beautiful woman from Constantinople, but very soon, Smaragda's smile and courtesy won her respect. Every afternoon she came downstairs to collect the half block of ice for her icebox. She was friendly with the iceman, and despite the complaints of some of the other women in the neighborhood, he made a habit of delivering ice to her first. And she always kept a little piece of homemade dessert for him. Her cooking became famous, since when she turned on her oven, the whole apartment building smelled fragrant. One day in the lobby, a neighbor asked what she was cooking that made all the noses in the building twitch. Smiling happily, Smaragda didn't just tell her about her spiced meatballs, but invited her in to try them. Before long, she became the secret cooking advisor for many women in the neighborhood, making numerous ignorant husbands happy, as their wives' cooking was now full of exotic smells and tastes.

Smaragda looked twenty years old again. She and her daughter walked all over Athens, and they never tired of the freedom they enjoyed. The shop windows made Smaragda gawk like a child. She enjoyed everything, and Chrysafenia was drawn along with her. Day by day, the girl left behind her sadness about her lost love. New experiences penetrated her mind and spirit, making the image of Vassilis fade slowly but steadily. And yet, there were moments when she still yearned to feel him close to her. Then she would open her little box, read his words, and wear the gold letter. The feel of the shining metal on her skin evoked the memory of his kisses, and her eyes would fill with nostalgic tears.

For his part, Fotis began to go down to Syntagma Square and to frequent Zavoritis Café, at the intersection of Ermou and Nikis. The owner had recently renovated a luxurious tearoom, and Fotis would take Smaragda and his daughter there for cake. At other times, they liked to sit at Zacharatos's, where the specialty was called a "submarine"—a large spoon of mastic dipped in a glass of cold water. Chrysafenia was crazy about them, whereas Smaragda had discovered Coca-Cola and enjoyed one every Sunday. She had a weakness for sweets, and nearly every day, Fotis brought her an ION almond-chocolate bar in exchange for a gentle kiss.

The first time they went to the movies and heard actors speaking Greek, it was like a dream. The film, *Madam Sousou* with Marika Nezer and Vasilis Logothetidis, was the first of dozens that followed.

The letters Smaragda sent to her family in Constantinople kept getting longer as she described every detail of their new life and begged her parents to think seriously about coming to visit. But it seemed there was always a reason they had to put it off. Fotis also corresponded regularly with the friend who had helped them so much. He learned that Alekos's sister and her husband would be returning to Athens in mid-January, and decided the least they could do was to invite them over for dinner as thanks for lending their house.

Lizeta Sekeris and her husband, Kleanthis, accepted with pleasure, and when the day came all of them sat together in the large dining room. Lizeta seemed very pleased with everything and praised the hostess's cooking. But what everyone noticed the most was how she couldn't keep her eyes off Chrysafenia. She spoke to her at length, asking about her interests and wanting to hear her impression of Athens.

The evening ended with the Ververises promising to accept the Sekeris family's invitation to a party in honor of Kleanthis's youngest brother, who was returning from America. Pericles Sekeris had just turned thirty, and he was a very talented civil engineer. The couple had no children of their own, so they doted on Pericles.

That evening, when the Sekerises returned home, Kleanthis looked inquiringly at his wife.

"Do I dare to ask," he began with a smile, "what you have in your clever mind?"

Lizeta let her hair down and began brushing her thick curls.

"I don't know what you're talking about!" she replied.

"Very well then, I'll explain it to you," he answered her seriously. "The whole evening, you scarcely paid attention to anyone but Miss Ververis. It was obvious that you were finding out all you could about the girl."

"What's so strange about that? Or didn't her beauty make an impression on you? Did you see those eyes? Like melted gold! What's more, she's polite, charming."

"You don't have to enumerate her qualities," her husband interrupted her. "You're not matchmaking for her. Not to me, at least . . ."

"OK, fine! It crossed my mind. Don't try to tell me you didn't think about it too!" She pouted and went on brushing her hair irritably.

Her husband went up to her, took the brush out of her hand, and rested it on his wife's vanity table. They exchanged a look in the mirror, and then he kissed her gently on the crown of the head.

"I admit it. That the young lady is just right for our Pericles."

"Then why do I hear a 'but' coming?"

"Because you and I know that my brother didn't go to America of his own accord. We sent him there to break up that unsuitable relationship."

"That was three years ago!"

"So? How do you know Pericles won't fall right back into the arms of the beautiful cabaret star?"

"No way will she be waiting for him, the slut! She no doubt latched on to some rich man the day after he left."

"Lizeta, how can you talk like that?" her husband reprimanded her.

"Why? What did I say? Our Pericles made a mistake, and he admitted it. Last year, when he came to visit, did you sense that he was angry with us? Or maybe you thought he was still longing for her?"

"The truth is, no."

"You see?" his wife said triumphantly. "I know what I'm doing, Kleanthis. As soon as he sees her, I'm sure your brother will be impressed. What a girl! And just what he needs. To settle down and occupy himself with his work. Since the war, Athens needs his talent more than ever. Don't you see all the building going on around us?"

"My sweet female Machiavelli!" her husband teased. "I won't put any obstacles in your way—you know that. As for my brother, he doesn't stand a chance against you!"

A week later, Pericles Sekeris returned. He'd left as a young man in love, angry that no one accepted his feelings for the beautiful, redheaded Liana, who danced and displayed her charms. Now, he was a different person. Mature and charming, calm and settled. Three years of "exile" had done him good. Alone in a foreign country, he could think clearly. Without the allure of Liana to cloud his judgment, he could understand his family's objections. They realized before he did that what he thought of as a great love was only desire; the distance and new experiences that he was offered broadened his mind. In America, he saw remarkable sights, made friends, and attended a lot of seminars in his field, but he missed his homeland. He corresponded regularly with Kleanthis and Lizeta. For him, they were like another set of parents, and—more than that—they were friends.

He appeared at their house the day after his return and was lost in their hugs and kisses. He felt like a boat entering its harbor. As if he hadn't been away for a single day. His parents' home was suffocating, but his brother's was different. And as soon as the initial flurry had settled, and Lizeta had persuaded him a little, he shared his feelings.

"It's not that Mother and Father have said anything directly, but I see it in their eyes. I went out to see some friends, and they looked at me as if they thought I would end up at Liana's house. How can I persuade them that story is over? Even yesterday, when I arrived, they looked at me strangely. As if they were wondering if their home was the first stop, or if I'd already been to hers. They've gone a little bit crazy. I don't know how I'm going to get used to living there again."

"No problem," Lizeta replied without thinking. "Just come live with us. This house is huge, and we won't try to control you, and I promise we won't imagine the worst. We know how much you've changed. We trust you!"

The two men sat staring at her.

"What's the matter with you?" she continued, ignoring her husband's pointed looks. "It's the only logical solution. Pericles will feel more relaxed, and we'll have his company."

"And our mother will have a fit!" the young man responded, but there was a wide smile on his face.

"I'll speak to my mother-in-law and make her understand," Lizeta said with determination. "But first, do you agree?"

"But how can I stay with you? Won't I be a—"

"Don't say the word *burden*, kid," Kleanthis butted in, "or I'll box your ears! It'll be our pleasure."

"All right then. I accept. I have no words to thank you!"

Lizeta smiled and met her husband's meaningful gaze coquettishly.

The plan went exactly as she wished—and her mother-in-law immediately agreed when Lizeta let her in on the secret of Chrysafenia Ververis.

"But what will people say?" the elder Mrs. Sekeris had complained when she first learned of her son's plans. "Instead of staying with his parents, he's going to his brother and sister-in-law? Have we quarreled? Aren't you afraid that maybe our friends will think that you and he—"

"Mother!" Lizeta raised her eyebrows admonishingly. "Such slander shouldn't even be spoken. It offends your son as well as me, and I've never given you reason to doubt me."

"I'm sorry, Lizeta, but I—I don't understand. Why should my son live somewhere else? I missed him for so many years, and he's finally back."

"I didn't want to mention this yet, but maybe I'd better," her daughter-in-law said. "To be honest, I have plans for Pericles, and having him in our house will make it easier."

"Plan? What plans?"

"To have him marry, Mother. What else? Pericles needs a beautiful, good girl beside him so he can start a family. He's been a rebel for too long."

"Yes, my girl, I don't disagree, but where will we find the bride?"

"I have her all ready, but you won't get another word out of me with your cunning!" she teased. "When I pull it off, you'll be the first to hear. Until then, I don't want to hear any complaints!"

Thanks to her intervention, the move took place shortly before the party Lizeta had organized. She told Pericles it was to welcome him home and also to introduce him to people who would be useful to him in the future. He accepted happily.

On the evening of the party, Kleanthis found his clothes laid out on the bed as usual.

"Tell me, my love, why are my socks and my undershirt inside out?" he asked her.

"Because if I put them like that, it means you'll wear them like that!" Lizeta answered curtly, putting on her silk stockings.

Her husband noticed that they were also inside out.

"If you don't tell me, I'm not wearing them!" he said stubbornly.

"Heavens, Kleanthis, you want to know everything!" she huffed to cover her embarrassment, and then went on without looking at him. "It's for luck. Mrs. Sakalis told me the other day: if you're matchmaking, and the couple are going to meet for the first time, you wear some garment inside out so it will take."

Kleanthis's laugh was clear and cheerful. "What am I going to do with you?" he murmured and hugged her. "You're like a kid, do you know that?"

"But why won't you do me this favor?"

"Did I say I wouldn't do it? I just wanted to know the reason I'll be going around with my clothes inside out."

"Eh, nobody will suspect anything. Unless you plan to show them your socks?"

Smaragda got ready for the party with the excitement of a young girl about to go to her first dance, and her mood quickly spread to the other members of the family. When they came to Greece, Fotis had insisted that both she and her daughter have lots of new clothes made. The war had ended, and skirts again rose a couple of inches, stopping a little below the knee. Color once more played a prominent role. Smaragda smiled at her reflection in the mirror. The women of her generation had lived through so many eras in fashion.

They entered the Sekeris family's bright living room with broad smiles. Fotis and Smaragda were quite sure that no girl could outshine their beautiful daughter, and no young man could match their son's charm. Chrysafenia was wrapped in a pale-yellow silk gown with her blond hair combed back so that it caressed her half-naked shoulders. Nestor, elegant in his dark suit, also smiled with pride at his sister, who held his arm.

Lizeta and Kleanthis greeted them at the entrance to the large room, and there, beside them, stood Pericles. Laughter, handshakes, and hugs among the women, but Lizeta's senses were on alert as she introduced the would-be couple. At their first handshake, she exchanged an optimistic glance with her husband. It didn't require any special insight to recognize that her brother-in-law had taken notice of the lovely girl. She took care as they welcomed the guests to give him information about the family, and in a way she knew would excite his curiosity. Her husband, listening, admired her cleverness. After that, Lizeta devoted herself to other arriving guests and didn't say a word to the Ververis family. She managed to hide a sly smile when Pericles, as soon as all the guests had arrived, lit a cigarette and said to her, as if absentminded, "A lot of people came."

"And all of them, Pericles, are your potential friends and customers," she answered cheerfully.

"Are the Ververis family good friends of yours?"

"More friends of my brother Alekos. They're from Constantinople."

"Ah, so that's why I detected an accent when they spoke."

Lizeta decided to play her secret card. The one even her husband didn't know about and which her brother had entrusted her with. She looked around in case anyone was listening, and then fired her arrow, straight and true: "Yes, from what Alekos tells me, they left in order to rescue their daughter from an unfortunate love affair. The poor girl was terribly upset. She loved someone, but his parents refused the marriage because they had some personal issue with Chrysafenia's parents. The mother of the young man slandered the girl so much that her father decided they should leave and make a new start in Athens. But don't say a word—I'm the only person who knows."

Then Lizeta moved away quickly, pretending that she had to speak to Mrs. Halaris. She was confident that the seed had been planted. Pericles and Chrysafenia were like twin spirits, both of them hurt by love. From that moment, he didn't take his eyes off her, and when his older brother approached the doctor's family, having been directed to do so by Lizeta, he took the opportunity to join the group as well. He heard Smaragda say: "I must tell you, Mr. Kleanthis, we had parties in Constantinople too, but not like this. A thousand congratulations to Mrs. Lizeta!"

"Yes, my wife is very social," Kleanthis agreed, feeling like an actor in some performance. He turned to Nestor. "And you, young man? How are your studies going?"

"I'm very happy, Mr. Sekeris," Nestor answered politely.

"And friends? Have you made friends?"

"I don't have any complaints. At first, my fellow students were a bit standoffish, but now they've accepted me."

"It's difficult," said Pericles, entering the conversation, "to be alone in a strange country. At first, when I went to America, I didn't know anyone, and the language gave me trouble. Books are one thing, but it's different when you have to not only speak but think in a language that's not your mother tongue. I spent quite a few months shut up in the house alone. Of course, it's easier for you because at least Greece isn't really a foreign country."

An appropriate topic for conversation had already emerged. Fotis wanted to hear all about America, and Kleanthis let out a sigh. He glanced at his wife, who was nearby, and took her satisfied smile as an answer.

Lizeta let them talk for a while, then she intervened.

"Tell me," she said, addressing the younger members of the group, "are you really going to hang around us old people all night?" She pointed to the other side of the large room, where younger guests had gathered and were already dancing. "Off you go! Nestor, take your sister and go and dance!"

"What about me?" said her brother-in-law cheerfully. "Where should I go, Lizeta? With the young ones, or should I stay here?"

"You're the guest of honor, choose for yourself!" she answered, laughing. "But you kids go!"

It made a great impression on her when Nestor and Chrysafenia turned to their father. With a nod, Fotis gave them his approval. She didn't move a muscle when she heard Pericles say, "Do you mind if I follow them? I know quite a few of the young people, and I can introduce them around."

Lizeta didn't mind. Not at all.

That night, when she lay down beside her husband, he teased her: "Tired out from all that plotting?"

"Listen, Kleanthis," she replied, "the evening was a complete success in every regard—"

"Oh boy, what's next?"

"Next?"

"Lizeta!"

"Fine, it's no big deal. So I invited them for dinner next Sunday."

"Together with their children, I suppose."

"Now you're just being a pain. Would they come by themselves? Don't you see what sort of family it is? They don't move an inch without their father's blessing."

"Don't be annoyed, my sweet Machiavelli! I don't doubt you or your . . . strategy."

Lizeta waited in agony for that Sunday. She'd played all her cards just right. She said nothing to Pericles about the invitation. She made sure that he'd find out about it in an indirect way when she called the cook in to arrange the menu for Sunday, and only when she left did Pericles ask, "Are we expecting company on Sunday?"

"Nothing formal. My friend Mrs. Ververis will come with her husband and children. Will you be here? Or will you go to your mother's?" she asked casually.

"Oh, if it's no trouble, I think I'll eat with you. They seem like really nice people."

Lizeta lowered her eyes so he wouldn't see how they sparkled. Now to plan the next steps.

Lizeta had fate on her side, though she didn't know it. After the Sunday meal, it was obvious that both the older and the younger members of the group got along well. The visits became more frequent, and it wasn't long before Pericles proposed to Nestor that the three of them go out to the theater together, a suggestion that was accepted with enthusiasm. Lizeta noticed that there weren't many conversations between the prospective couple. It was as if they were observing each other meticulously.

And so, the trio found themselves at the National Theater watching *The Engagement* by Dimitris Bogris. Then the courteous Pericles invited them for dessert at Zacharatos's café, where they chatted, excited about the play they had just seen.

Without lifting a finger now, Lizeta followed the developments. Pericles began visiting the doctor's house by himself, and he took Nestor out with him. Understandably, it wasn't long before memories of Vassilis were awaked in the young man. He found excuses to avoid Pericles. He wouldn't allow his sister to come with them; he became dejected.

One afternoon, Pericles invited Nestor over to talk, and they shut themselves in Pericles's room—with Lizeta outside the door following the conversation shamelessly.

"Now," Pericles began, "I'd like an explanation for your behavior. And I'll thank you not to underestimate my intelligence by telling me it's all in my head! Lately, you've been avoiding me, refusing my invitations, and when I come to your house, you're almost hostile. Have I done anything to you? Have I said something wrong?"

"Not in the slightest!" the young man admitted, obviously embarrassed.

"So, I think you owe me an explanation. In the beginning, you seemed to respect my friendship very much."

"Yes. And if it was just the two of us, I wouldn't have any reservations."

"I don't understand."

"Look, Pericles, I have nothing against you, and the truth is that, despite the difference in our ages, we have a good time together," Nestor admitted.

"I'm waiting to hear what the problem is!"

"It has to do with the past."

He was completely honest with Pericles and told him the whole story of his sister and Vassilis.

"But don't imagine," he concluded, "that anything scandalous went on between them."

"I would never doubt your sister's honor!" Pericles hastened to reassure him.

"But it still cost her a lot. It's why we ended up in Greece. But it also cost me a lot because I felt that a trusted friend had exploited me."

"I understand. And you thought that the story might be repeated with me."

"Something like that. And I'm begging you to keep what I told you between us. My father wouldn't approve of my telling you something that is family business."

Pericles looked at the young man and smiled.

"So, let's clear some things up, Nestor," he began seriously. "I'm not some kid like your friend. I won't lie to you: your sister is a lovely, beautiful girl. But I'm a man and not a boy, and I have no intention to exploit either you or her. For the time being, I enjoy your company—both of you," he stressed. "If something changes, if I realize, for example, that I've fallen in love with Chrysafenia, I give you my word that you'll be the first to know—after her. Are you happy with that?"

"I think so."

"And just so you know, I also had a girl I thought was the love of my life, but I was young and inexperienced. Later, I realized I'd been deceived: I mistook infatuation for love, and I don't want to go through that again. I'm at an age now when I can't afford mistakes, and through our friendship I have the opportunity to get to know a girl and be certain of her character and opinions, as well as being quite sure of my real feelings. So, I'm not hiding the fact that your sister interests me."

"I respect your honesty."

"That's why I asked you to come, so that we could speak openly. And if I did declare my love to her, I wouldn't allow my parents or anyone else to get in the way. Do I make myself clear?"

"Yes."

"So, can we continue to go out together without any obstacles?"

They shook hands, and Lizeta slipped away smiling. Things were going even better than she'd expected.

A bad cold was the excuse. Nestor came down with a fever on the day Pericles appeared to accompany the two siblings to a performance of *Stella Violanti*, at the National.

"What bad luck!" he said when he saw his friend lying down with a wet cloth on his forehead.

Beside Nestor sat Smaragda, looking after him anxiously.

"Yes, my child," she agreed. "I keep telling him to wear a scarf when he goes out. Spring may be here, but the cold is still biting. But he doesn't listen to me, the crazy boy, and now look! Maybe he'll learn his lesson. And you, dear boy, why didn't you warn your friend that you couldn't go out? Why make him come here for nothing?"

"Because I thought," Nestor said, coughing, "there's no reason for our Chrysafenia to miss the performance. Unless Father won't allow it."

"I'll go and ask him, sweetheart."

She glanced apologetically at the guest. Behind her back, Pericles looked inquiringly at his friend.

"Does it seem like a forgone conclusion?" he asked with an ironic smile.

"I'd say the gift of an opportunity. Anyway, we've talked and agreed about things."

"And not the slightest thing will change."

In the living room, Smaragda approached her husband, who was reading his newspaper.

"Fotis, dear," she began in a supplicating tone, but he gave her an annoyed look.

"Smaragda, I told you to be patient. His fever will fall. Just now I gave him—"

"No, my dear. That's not what I wanted to ask you. Look, Pericles came to take the children to the theater, and Nestor said, seeing as he can't go, that Chrysafenia should go with Pericles by herself."

Her husband put his newspaper aside and stood up. He looked deep into his wife's eyes.

"Our son said that?"

"Yes, dear."

"And what do you say?"

"I say she should go," she answered calmly.

"Then she can go."

With this approval in hand, Smaragda went into her daughter's room.

"Chrysafenia dear, Pericles is here."

"I know, but since Nestor—what a day he picked to get sick!" she said irritably.

"It's not like he wanted to! And your brother doesn't want you to miss the theater. If you want to go—"

"By myself, with Pericles?" the girl asked in surprise. "What about Father?"

"Your father said that, if Nestor approves, you can go. Just dress warmly because I can't deal with any more illnesses," she concluded severely, leaving her daughter to get dressed.

As soon as she was alone, Chrysafenia ran to the mirror and made a strict appraisal of her appearance. She felt so strange. For the first time in her life, she was going out with someone who wasn't a relative but a handsome young man. Just thinking about it made her cheeks burn. She had gone out many times now with Pericles, but always with her brother as well. She was a little nervous.

She took her overcoat and gloves, put on her hat, and then became angry with herself. What had come over her? It wasn't a date. She was just going to the theater with a friend. The man had never given her the right to suppose he had eyes for her. His behavior was always courteous and proper. Shaking off her nerves, she went to meet him, and they left together.

The performance of Mary Aroni, who played Stella Violanti, was very moving. Chrysafenia felt her eyes dampen a number of times, and at the end, tears flowed freely down her cheeks, and she applauded enthusiastically. Pericles offered her his handkerchief, and she looked at him, full of gratitude. At that moment, the man felt something strange, something that drew his eyes into her damp ones. They looked like melted gold, those eyes. And when Chrysafenia wiped her tears, he glanced secretly at the handkerchief she'd returned to him to see if specks of gold had stayed behind in its white folds.

They came out of the theater and began to walk. Instead of Stadiou Street, Pericles preferred to go via Omonia Square, where the cafés were buzzing with life.

"Can I treat you to something sweet?" he asked the girl.

"Isn't it late?"

"Come on, this is Athens! Don't you see how many people are enjoying the evening?" he said, and led her to a café-bar.

They sat at a quiet table, facing each other, and ordered. Chrysafenia looked around her at men and women who were talking and laughing, although she raised her eyebrows at some young women who were smoking.

"Don't you approve?" Pericles asked.

"It seems strange to me. In Constantinople, women smoked too—but not respectable women," she said, blushing deeply.

"I saw that the play affected you very deeply," said Pericles, changing the subject, and he watched the girl's face grow sad.

"But it was so miserable. She loved someone who wasn't worth it, and then he died. Fortunately, she never learned what a fake he was."

"Those things happen. We often give our heart without considering if the person we fall in love with is worthy of it. Fortunately for some of us, we make our discovery before we ruin our life. Even before we waste a lot of years," he said to her sweetly.

"You speak as if you know . . ." Her look was inquisitive. "What did they tell you about me?"

"About you? I was speaking about myself, Chrysi."

"That's not my name," she replied.

"But that's what I'd like to call you! Does it bother you?"

"No. I'm just not used to it. What were you saying about yourself?"

"Years ago, I met a girl. I thought she was my great love. I believed that without her I'd die, and I wanted to marry her. But they didn't let me."

"Why? Didn't she have a dowry?"

"My parents didn't get that far. It was enough that she worked in a cabaret."

The girl's eyes opened wide in surprise. "Are you telling me the truth?" she asked, and then a smile spread on her lips.

"I expected all sorts of reactions, but not for you to smile!" he scolded her.

"But Pericles—you? You got mixed up with a girl like that, and you expected them to give their permission for you to marry her? Those things just don't happen!"

"But I loved her. I was crazy about her. I chased after her for a whole year."

"And after that? What happened?" she wanted to know.

"They sent me away."

"That explains America."

"Yes. My father had a cousin there, and they packed me off."

"Yes, but you weren't a child. How did they overcome your desire to stay?"

"Are you joking? My mother collapsed, ready to die, my father nearly beat me, and then there was Lizeta and Kleanthis. They were patient, and over the course of endless discussions, they persuaded me to leave. I love them and respect them very much. I agreed to go, because it was only temporary."

"And then temporary became three years?"

"Away from her . . . influence, I realized that I'd made a mistake. Passion is one thing, love is another. And you?"

"What about me?" asked Chrysafenia, and her expression became cautious.

"Were you ever in love?"

She looked around. Suddenly, all the people and smoke felt suffocating. She asked if they could leave, and he hurried to accommodate her. He paid, and together they walked out into the freezing Athens night. They turned on Stadiou Street and began walking toward Syntagma without speaking.

"Forgive me," he said.

"Why should you need forgiveness?"

"Because I've made you sad with my tactlessness. I shouldn't have asked such a question."

Then, without any preamble, Chrysafenia told him the brief history of her relationship with Vassilis and its unhappy ending—although she left out the part about her mother and Simeon. She claimed not to know the reason for his family's antipathy.

They stopped walking, and Pericles sought her eyes.

"And now? Do you still love him?" he asked. He could see that she was struggling to answer him.

"To tell you the truth, I don't think Vassilis will ever leave my heart, but as my mother keeps saying, there's no use crying over a lost paradise. We can make a new one." She met his gaze with confidence.

His hand rose instinctively and stroked her cheek. A streetlamp bathed her face in pale light, making her look as if she were entirely made of gold. Without thinking, he bent and kissed her. Her soft lips met his shyly, and that gave him the courage to put his arms around her and extend the kiss. She pulled away first, full of shame.

"I'm sorry," he whispered in embarrassment.

"That's the second time you've apologized tonight," she said, with a note of admonition in her voice.

"Yes, it's becoming a habit. First I make you unhappy, then I—"

"You didn't make me unhappy," she interrupted quickly. "I just don't understand why you kissed me."

"Because I felt the need to. Because you're very beautiful, Chrysi."

"And whatever girl you like, you kiss them?"

"No. Only if she's like you and is made of pure gold. And now, let me ask you something. Do you think the two of us could . . . make our own paradise?"

She didn't answer him immediately. First, she examined his whole face and especially his eyes, which were looking at her pleadingly. Then she nodded in agreement. This time, Pericles embraced her with more confidence and covered her lips decisively. He kissed her without hurrying and felt very satisfied when she trembled in his arms. A rowdy group that passed by shouting and laughing brought them to their senses, and they pulled apart with embarrassment. Pericles took her arm, and they walked on, but all the way back, he found opportunities to hug and kiss her. Almost drunk with joy, he left her at her door. He wanted to come up, but Chrysafenia stopped him.

"But why? What will your parents say if I leave you at the front door?" he complained.

"I'll make up some explanation. It's just that I'd feel very strange if we were all together right after what happened between us."

"All right. But when will I see you again?"

"Come tomorrow to see my brother, and we'll arrange something," she promised and ran up the marble stairs.

She arrived panting at their apartment door.

"Isn't that awful box working?" her mother asked.

"I was afraid, Mama, to get into the elevator so late," she lied, "and to have it get stuck in the middle of the night. What would I have done?"

"Why didn't Pericles come with you?" her father asked, frowning.

"I didn't let him. I thought you'd already be in bed, and I told him to leave."

"Bah!" Smaragda exclaimed. "Do you think we'd go to sleep before our girl came home? You are a bit late."

"It's like when we go out with Nestor. We always go for dessert after the theater."

"Was the play good?" her mother asked, and Chrysafenia sat down to tell them about it.

It took a whole hour for her to get away from her parents and shut herself in her room. She ran to the window and pulled open the curtains. The moon, half-hidden in the clouds, seemed to be watching her. She drew away from its inquiring eye and lay down on her bed fully dressed. Her mind returned to the events of her evening, and she touched her lips, which had, for the first time since Vassilis, accepted kisses from a man. Her cheeks caught fire. She felt ashamed, but she had to admit that Pericles had put her in a state. In the dark, she found her box and opened it. She moved the other letters aside and touched the one made of gold. She took it in her hands, and it felt different. Something tender warmed her, but it had the smell of a girl about it. Tonight, in Pericles's arms, she'd felt like a woman.

Nestor looked at his friend, who was standing in front of him looking sheepish. Without beating around the bush, he asked, "What happened with my sister last night?"

"Didn't I tell you that, if something changed, you would be the first to know?"

"So, did it change? You went to the theater and worked your magic?"

"Nestor, don't tease me, please!" he admonished his friend. "I haven't slept all night. Your sister is a wonderful girl."

"And you only just realized that last night?"

"It's not that. It's just that it was different!"

"Explain it to me," Nestor said, suddenly serious.

"That's why I came. To tell you. I'll speak to my parents this very day."

Chrysafenia came shyly into the room, already blushing.

"Come on in!" Nestor called. "You're right on time. Pericles here tells me you had a lovely time last night!"

"What did you tell him?" the girl asked nervously, turning to Pericles.

"You're talking to me now," Nestor said sharply, playing the angry brother. "Aren't you ashamed? I leave the two of you alone once, and what's the result?"

"But we—" Chrysafenia tried to speak, but a knot blocked her throat, and she dissolved in tears.

Pericles hurried to put his arms around Chrysafenia. "Now look what you've done!"

Nestor came up to separate them.

"Can you two quit it before Mama comes in and we find ourselves in a mess?" he asked, and then turned to his sister and gave her a hug. "Oh, come on, I'm not really angry. Anyway, Pericles told me that he's come to ask for you."

Chrysafenia stopped crying and asked, her eyes on Pericles, "Is he telling the truth?"

"Of course! What did you think? That I was some dishonorable fellow?"

A smile appeared on her face, and she broke away from her brother to throw herself back into Pericles's arms, laughing happily.

"Enough, you two!" Nestor objected. "What if someone comes in and sees? We still haven't gotten you engaged . . ."

They separated guiltily, like naughty children.

"Someone had better tell our parents," Chrysafenia said.

"If you're talking about mine, they'll find out today. And tomorrow we'll come back here."

"Good heavens! And Mama and Papa?" the girl asked nervously. "Who'll tell them?"

"You," Nestor answered her.

"I'm embarrassed. You tell them!"

"What nonsense, you two!" Pericles asked. "In any case, I'm leaving. I'll go to Lizeta and my brother's first, and then straight to my parents. Sweetheart, make sure you've told your folks by tonight so they can be prepared. We don't want to surprise them!"

Her gave her a quick kiss and disappeared, leaving the siblings alone together. Nestor gave her a hug.

"Is this what you want, sister?" he asked her affectionately. "Do you think you can be happy with him?"

"I think so. Pericles is a good man. I've been watching him for a long time, and I saw a lot of things I liked, but I didn't dare to hope. After what happened in Constantinople with Vassilis, and the fact that he was a friend of yours too, I was ashamed."

"For you to say his name without crying, does that mean you've forgotten him?"

"You don't forget your first love, Nestor, isn't that what they say? But it's over, and there's no point looking back. Isn't that what Mama says?"

"Yes, you're right. Let's go and tell them now."

The two of them went into the living room, where their parents were drinking their coffee, oblivious to what had happened. As soon as she saw her still-recovering son was out of bed, Smaragda jumped up and hurried to bring him a blanket, but he didn't let her.

"Sit down, Mama. We want to talk to you. I'm fine now."

"But son, only yesterday you were burning up with fever!"

"Sit down, Smaragda!" Fotis interrupted her, seeing the expression on the children's faces and realizing that something serious had happened. "Go ahead, Nestor, we're listening."

"My sister asked me to speak on her behalf."

"What's happened? You're upsetting me! Tell me so I know what more I have to bear!" Smaragda began fanning herself with the newspaper her husband had left on a table.

"Be quiet, my good woman, so we can find out!" Fotis demanded impatiently.

"Don't worry, Mama, it's good news!" Nestor explained. "Won't you let me tell you properly? Tomorrow evening, Pericles's parents will come to ask for our Chrysafenia. He told me himself."

"And how would he know?" Smaragda objected, so upset she didn't understand.

"Has the news unhinged you, woman?" Fotis said indignantly, and his look brought her back to herself.

"Ah! Pericles!" she cried, and then, "My treasure!" And with tears in her eyes, she stood up to embrace her daughter.

Fotis approached, and when his wife stood back, he looked his daughter in the eyes. "Are you certain, my girl?" he asked seriously. "Do you want him?"

"Yes, Papa—if you agree."

She lost herself in her father's embrace, calm now. Finally, she could leave the past and the pain it had caused her behind. After so long, she could look her parents in the eye without being ashamed of what she had unwillingly provoked. With her marriage, she would close the open accounts of the past and look optimistically toward the future. Like her mother, she might have been unlucky in her first love, but she would make her own paradise. The Kouyoumdzis family could no longer harm them.

The wedding of Chrysafenia Ververis and Pericles Sekeris took place on the eve of the May Day holiday of 1949, a week after Easter. All of Athens's high society was invited, and Smaragda's only sorrow was that no one from her family came, however much she begged her mother and sister to make the journey. They didn't want to tell her the truth and poison her joy. Unexpectedly, Anargyros Kantardzis had breathed his last one evening on the doorstep of his house. Smaragda found out after the wedding and cried bitterly for the father she wasn't able to say good-bye to. Fotis suggested she make a trip to Constantinople to see her family, and though Smaragda thought seriously about it, she didn't manage to go. Two months after her wedding, Chrysafenia announced she was pregnant, and nothing could have separated Smaragda from her daughter at such a time. She had to be near her every moment if possible. She measured the days and weeks in her mind while her hands stroked her daughter's ever-rounder belly or knitted the baby's clothes. Constantinople receded further and further in her mind.

CHAPTER 12

KOUYOUMDZIS FAMILY

Constantinople, 1949

Roza looked at her husband and, once again, pursed her lips discontentedly.

"You're still not going to say anything to him? Aren't you going to advise him?"

"And what do you want me to tell him, exactly?"

"Simeon, don't act so calm—I know you've had it with our son's behavior!"

"Oh, so you remembered that he's also my son. But what am I saying—when you want something, you remember just fine."

"Is this the time to be quarreling?"

He looked at his wife, surprised to hear her speak reasonably and sensibly. Perhaps she finally understood how serious the situation was.

"I've spoken to him, Roza," he admitted grimly, "and not once but many times. Sometimes gently, sometimes angrily. It's made no difference."

The two parents fell silent, their eyes lowered. Vassilis had changed suddenly. After the affair with Chrysafenia, they no longer recognized him. In a single night, their quiet, invariably polite son had been transformed. He'd started to frequent shady dives. He would come home drunk at dawn, and he'd lost interest in the work he had loved so much.

"Yes, but we have to do something," Roza said again. "I'm afraid for him, Simeon."

"Me too. Besides, he's spending money like a madman. The other day, he took something from the shop."

"What did he take?" she asked.

"A diamond piece—very expensive."

"And what did he do with it? Did he sell it?"

"He told me it was a present for a girlfriend of his. I was angry with him—I called him a thief."

"Simeon!" Roza sat up, shaken.

"Why? Wasn't it theft?"

"What did he say to you?"

"You won't believe it. He looked me right in the eye and then reached out his hand and took a bracelet. Do you know what the wretch said to me? 'Put that on my tab too, then! I'm taking it in front of you so you can't call me a thief again!' Can you imagine?"

"He spoke to you that way?" Roza said in horror.

"Just like I said. Totally without respect. I cursed him, I called him a son of a bitch, and he laughed in my face and left. I was so furious I saw stars! How I held on to myself and didn't grab him by the neck, only God knows. Good thing my father wasn't there, or he'd have had a stroke!"

"What shall we do, Simeon? What's happened to our Vassilis?"

"Do you still not understand?" her husband asked bitterly. "He's punishing us. We stood in the way of his love."

"And I'd do the same again!" she said.

"So stop asking me the reason for our son's behavior!" he said. "You know; you caused it."

"Now you're blaming me?!"

"Don't you know the sin you're carrying? Roza, a parent isn't God. It's not right to control his life like that. He loved her, and you got in the way. We all let you destroy that family, and look at the result! He hates all of us now. In his way, he's saying, 'You didn't let me have the one I loved? I'll show you what I can do,' and he'll keep at it until you wish that he had her again."

"That will never happen. Even when I'm dead, I won't change my mind!"

"And we're all paying for your obsession. Because of a grudge, you didn't let your child be happy."

"A grudge? Is that what you call it?"

"What else is it? A childish tantrum, and you made it into a rallying cry! Did I ever deny you because I loved Smaragda? When I married you, I honored my marriage vows. I was never unfaithful. Do you still have doubts about that?"

"No, I didn't say anything like that," she admitted and lowered her head.

"Then why did you cause so much harm?"

"Because you didn't love me."

"And who did you punish, Roza? Me, through your child? You placed your ego higher than his life. I told you all this back then, but did you listen to me? No! It was like talking to a wall. You got everyone worked up with your shouting."

"Do we have to go over all of it again? The question is Vassilis."

"Yes. Now Vassilis has become another person."

"Yes, but how far is this going to go? I'm afraid he may get into trouble at those places he goes to."

"You may be afraid, but I'm certain!"

They were silent, each lost in thoughts that grew more distressing every day. There were nights when Vassilis didn't return home. The elder Vassilis Kouyoumdzis shouted, threatened, and quarreled with Simeon, who he said didn't have the guts to rule his household and rein in the useless boy.

What happened next was worse, and it caught them completely unprepared. One Sunday, after Vassilis didn't come home the previous night, they sat at the dinner table in a bad mood. The other two children didn't dare open their mouths in front of their father and especially their grandfather, who was glaring at everyone. They heard the front door open, and a few seconds later, in came Vassilis. But he wasn't alone. Beside him stood a short, very dark girl. The silence that had prevailed until then became even deeper. Vassilis smiled cheerfully while the girl bit her lips nervously.

"The whole family's here!" the young man declared, slurring his words. "We're right on time!"

First Simeon stood up, then Roza.

"What is this behavior, Vassilis? How can you appear in front of us and your grandparents drunk?" she chided him in a measured tone.

"Don't upset yourself, Mother," he answered her with an ironic smile. "When I share my news, then you and Papa and Grandpa and all of you will want to drink as well. They toast to engagements, don't they?"

"What engagement are you talking about?" Simeon asked. "And who is the girl beside you?"

"Ah, yes. A serious omission. Let me introduce you to Miss Lefkothea Yerimoglou, my future wife!"

He would have met with less objection if he had brought a cannon into the house. Roza collapsed in her chair while Simeon stood upright, unable to accept the news. Vassilis's brother and sister only opened their mouths and eyes wide, while his grandmother burst into tears. His grandfather glanced at him and then stood up, threw down his napkin, and left the table. Passing by his son, he spat at Simeon's feet in disdain.

"Son, are you serious?" Simeon finally asked.

"I think I made myself clear. Lefkothea and I are getting married next Sunday. And before you argue, I'm telling you it can't be any other way because our bride is already expecting my child!"

Not even Simeon could bear the second blow. He sat down and emptied his glass in a gulp.

"Vassilis, it's better if I go," the girl said softly. "I'll come again another day."

"You don't have to go anywhere. From now on, you're going to be my wife, and my parents have to respect you. You're going to give them a grandchild," Vassilis retorted and then turned to his father. "Won't you give me your blessing?"

Simeon rubbed his forehead, trying to get a handle on things.

"Excuse me, my girl, but this has come rather suddenly . . ."

"Yes, I understand," she murmured.

"Why don't we all go into the living room?" asked Roza, who had also recovered enough to say what she had to.

The two couples moved into the other room. Nobody else followed. They didn't dare.

"And now, I'd like to learn a few things about your future wife," Simeon said seriously after signaling for his own wife to be silent. He could see she was ready to burst.

Vassilis began to speak about Lefkothea as if she weren't present, and with every word, his parents sank lower. The bride was very poor and had no parents. She worked in a hat shop to survive and lived with a distant aunt. The whole time he spoke, Roza's eyes passed over the girl like an X-ray, and finally drew her lips so tight they disappeared. The girl's clothes were old, and her shoes had seen better days. Her handbag was torn in places, and the lining showed. As the gaze of her future mother-in-law weighed more and more heavily on her, the girl tried to hide her shortcomings, but she knew it was impossible.

An unbearable silence fell again on the room. Lefkothea got up determinedly. She was suffocating and longed to get out into the street, to smell fresh air. Vassilis was certainly her Prince Charming, but his castle was a prison. When they had met by chance on the street and he began to pursue her relentlessly, she couldn't have imagined an ending like this. He waited for hours outside the shop where she worked, he followed her whenever she had to deliver an order, and finally, he managed to buy her dessert. Very soon, she fell in love with him and gave herself up to his arms. Her pregnancy made her feel hopeless because she was certain that the young, handsome man would abandon her. But she was wrong. He told her immediately he would marry her, and now she found herself opposite in-laws who, understandably, would not approve of this wedding. Everyone looked at her as she stood up, and Vassilis seemed surprised.

"Lefkothea, what's the matter? Aren't you well?" he asked uneasily.

"I'm fine, but I'm leaving. I'll walk around a bit, then I'll go home. Come to see me in the afternoon, and we'll talk. Now you should stay and talk to your parents," she told him firmly and then turned to the couple. "It was a pleasure to meet you, Mr. and Mrs. Kouyoumdzis."

Her eyes pleaded with him to let her go. He kissed her tenderly and escorted her out. Before he returned to the living room that would shortly turn into a battlefield, he took a deep breath. He approached his parents, looking first at his mother because he knew it was from her that the attack would begin. He wasn't wrong.

"Tell me, did it take you a long time to find her?" Roza shot out.

"Don't you like your new daughter-in-law?" he asked calmly.

"What's there to like? What street did you pick her up off of? Can you even tell me? She's like a gypsy. Didn't you see the rags she was wearing?"

"I'm not marrying her for her beauty or for her clothes!" her son answered, smiling.

"Then why?" his father wanted to know.

"Because I love her. Why else?" he responded with an innocent smile. "Besides, I'll buy her clothes and shoes. The best!"

"Of course!" Roza burst out. "We've got a fortune for her to spend. You fool, that's the reason she's with you!"

"Thank you very much, Mother. The respect you have for me is unbelievable!"

"I'm going to go crazy! Listen to how my son treats me! Did she give you some magic potion to drink?"

"Is it impossible for her to love me and I, her?"

"Oh, enough of that. Weren't there enough nice, rich girls to choose from? If you wanted to get married so young, why didn't you tell us to find you a nice bride?"

"Because I wanted to find her myself!" Vassilis was beginning to lose his patience. "After all, you didn't like Chrysafenia, and she was beautiful and rich. Now you're insulting Lefkothea."

"Lefkothea!" Roza said ironically. "Couldn't they find some other name to call that gypsy? And what will people say, eh? Didn't you think of that? The son of Simeon Kouyoumdzis marrying a girl with no family."

"If you don't like a doctor's family, what could possibly be good enough? And as for what people will say, you know yourself. You'll take care of all that. You managed to drive the doctor's family out of the country with your slander. Well, now you'll do the opposite. You'll praise your daughter-in-law until everyone accepts her! Next Sunday I'll marry her, and I'll bring her here so we can all live together. Nothing else will happen because, in a few months, Lefkothea will have my child. And that's that."

Roza collapsed in an armchair and burst into sobs. Simeon stood up and approached Vassilis calmly.

"Vassilis, my son, if you loved her, I wouldn't say a word, I swear to you. It has nothing to do with her being poor. But you don't love her. You were in a hurry to punish us, and so you'll punish yourself even more. You're doing this out of spite, and a life without love is not worth living."

Roza sprang up as if a snake had bitten her.

"Your father knows what he's saying," she shouted hysterically. "He married without love too, and suffers nobly for us all to see."

"This again, eh? Leave it, Roza!" Simeon shouted at her, then turned to his son. "You're talking to me now. As you said, there's no way out. The girl is expecting a baby, and the wedding must take place. But look at me. You'll make her your wife, and you'll respect her. Love her for the children she'll give you, and treat her like a precious jewel. Leave your mother and me out of it. This isn't about us. The subject is Lefkothea."

They exchanged a long look. Vassilis felt so close to his father that he lowered his head in shame.

"I only met her briefly," Simeon went on, "but I understand she's a good girl. And she loves you. But you didn't do the right thing, bringing her here. You shamed her and let us shame her. You know what it looked like to me, Vassilis? You didn't bring her here as your wife and the mother of your children, but as a weapon to hurt us. Shame on you. If you want us to treat you as a man and respect your decisions, behave like one! You want to make her your wife? So treat her as a wife! Do you understand?"

"Yes, Father. And I want to tell you—"

"Don't tell me anything! Go to your wife and ask her to forgive you. And to forgive us as well."

"Is it time now to—" Roza began.

"Roza!" Simeon thundered. "I'm speaking! And in this house, I'm the boss. Do you remember?"

He turned to his son again. "Pay attention, because this is what's going to happen. You'll take her to buy a dress and shoes and a bag and a coat. And you'll bring her back here next Sunday. We'll do things right this time. And we'll arrange the wedding. OK?"

"Thank you, Father," Vassilis said, his eyes full of tears. "And I want to tell you something. I do love Lefkothea. She may not be Chrysafenia, but something inside me responds to her. Her love is tender, like a balm. She treats me with kindness and understanding."

"Then bravo, my son! You have my blessing," Simeon said and hugged him. "Off you go now! Run and find her."

"Mama?" Vassilis asked, but she turned her back on him.

"Leave your mother," Simeon said. "Go!"

Vassilis flew off. He hadn't lied. Chrysafenia would live forever in his heart, but this girl who was waiting for him had managed to ease the pain. He lay in her arms and calmed down. Her love was so great that it was enough for them both.

As soon as they were alone, Simeon turned to his wife. Roza was sitting on the couch, and he sat beside her. He didn't speak, just looked at her as she kept crying, and he tried to find in himself what he felt for this woman he had spent his whole life beside. He wanted to say something, but just then, his father charged into the room, Simeon's mother behind him. Simeon armed himself with patience. Another battle began. He let the old man holler, threaten gods and demons, and say terrible things about the bride-to-be and the child she was expecting. Afterward, Vassilis Kouyoumdzis the elder looked at his son, who observed him silently with arms crossed.

"So?" he roared, growing less certain in the face of Simeon's unexpected reaction. "Do you have nothing to say?"

His son rose and, without hurrying, stood in front of him, fixing him with his gaze. His tone was calm but decisive. "I was waiting for you to finish before I tell you exactly what's going to happen. Vassilis will marry the girl he got pregnant, and they'll come to live with us. He'll work as usual at the shop, and I'll gradually withdraw from the business, as will you. It's time for us to hand over our kingdom. And when the girl comes here, we'll treat her with the respect due a firstborn son's wife who will give us our first grandchild. If you don't like that, tell me now, and I'll take my family to live somewhere else."

"You dare speak to me like that?" said his father, shocked.

241

"I don't like it either, but there's no other way. It took me too long to stand up to you, and we all saw what good came of it. But no more! I won't let even worse things happen."

Silence followed his words. Roza stopped crying, and Simeon's father turned around and left, his mother running after him as usual. Simeon straightened his back and left the room too, without saying a word.

The wedding of Vassilis Kouyoumdzis and Lefkothea Yerimoglou took place a little before Lent. The groom's family didn't spare a penny. At Roza's instigation, the bride acquired a completely new wardrobe, and since there was no time to have a bridal gown made, they altered Roza's. Simeon knew his wife's egotism would help ensure all was done correctly. He understood that if she accepted her daughter-in-law and began to present her in society, nobody would dare to say a thing. She threw a party before the wedding to present her, and dragged her along to all the gatherings she herself attended.

During all this, Roza realized that many of the things she told people to praise Lefkothea for were true. The girl was very polite, and she showed great respect for her mother-in-law. She developed a special relationship with her husband's siblings. Even better, she was a good influence on their son. Vassilis stopped going out all night and went back to his work as before. When Lefkothea moved into the house after the wedding, it became apparent that she was also a good housewife and, despite her young age, an accomplished cook. Her sweets in particular amazed everyone. In the end, Roza yielded completely, and accepted that Lefkothea was the best she could hope for for her son. Only the grandfather didn't give up an inch. He did his best to ignore Lefkothea. When he couldn't, he spat out his words with disdain. His disrespect made Vassilis tighten his lips and his fists, but Lefkothea would look at him pleadingly and he'd back down.

Another Simeon Kouyoumdzis came into the world one evening in October of that year, when it was raining cats and dogs. They had sat down to eat, and every so often a thunderclap made them jump in their seats. Lefkothea couldn't swallow a bite, and Roza was the first to notice.

"Daughter-in-law, why aren't you eating?" she asked.

"I can't, Mother, I—"

Her voice was cut off by the pain, and all of them froze. Roza recovered first. She turned sharply to her son.

"Go, Vassilis! Take Lefkothea to her bed, then run and bring the doctor and the midwife. Penelope, run and put a pot of water on to boil! Aristos, help them!"

She left her mother-in-law out of her instructions, despite the fact that the older woman had already stood up. The woman looked at her husband, who was eating his food as if nothing had happened, and for the first time in the fifty years of their marriage, she raised her voice to him. "And you, are you going to just sit there?" she asked sharply.

"What do you want me to do?" he replied moodily.

"I don't know! Your great-grandchild is coming. What's the matter with you, Vassilis? Aren't you ashamed? What's the girl done to you? She brings you whatever you want, she's polite to you, and you—"

"Woman, spare me!"

"No! You spare us! If you don't understand happiness when it hits you on the head, then you're not a human being!"

He jumped up and looked at her angrily, but he didn't manage to speak because his wife couldn't be held back.

"Don't look at me like that. I'm not afraid of you anymore. My soul has been disgusted for so long! You walk around here like some rooster and think you're accomplishing something. Pull yourself together, Vassilis. You should know we put up with your anger like we'd put up with a madman. For now, go to your room so you don't spoil everyone's happiness."

The old woman was out of breath with the effort of saying more than she'd ever said, perhaps, in the whole length of her marriage. Roza had stood frozen in place, and Simeon, who had just come downstairs and heard everything, couldn't believe his ears.

"Penelope went upstairs with Lefkothea, and Aristos has come down to keep an eye on the boiling water," Simeon said numbly.

"I'm going to bring towels and sheets," Roza said as if she were in a dream.

The grandfather looked at all of them and then left. After a few moments, they heard his door close with a bang.

"I'm going to the girl," said the grandmother simply, and shuffled out.

"How about that!" said Roza as soon as they were alone.

"If someone had told me, I'd never have believed it!" Simeon said. "Was that really my mother?"

"What can I say? I guess the pot boiled over at last. Enough now! I'm going to fetch what's needed."

Vassilis arrived with the doctor and the midwife, and they shut themselves in the bedroom. The men waited in the living room. Vassilis busied himself wearing out the carpet with his pacing while Simeon, sitting on the couch, kept on tapping his fingers on the dark velvet upholstery. Aristos, the calmest of all, thoughtfully served them a little brandy, though he failed at his first attempt. A piercing cry from the young bride made him jump, and the glass he was carrying fell out of his hands and smashed to pieces. Silent, the three men counted the minutes with their eyes glued to the big clock. The hands didn't seem to be moving, yet every now and then, the clock contradicted them as its musical sound struck the hours and half hours. Aside from the chimes, the quiet was broken only by Lefkothea's cries, which became more and more piercing.

"I can't bear any more," Vassilis whispered, his eyes damp.

Simeon stood up and took him by the shoulders. "Don't be afraid, son. That's the way these things are. When you were being born, I also thought I'd lose your mother. Women are amazing, Vassilis!"

He wanted to tell him something more, but an especially penetrating cry interrupted him. The three of them froze, looking at each other, faces pale with fear. Just then, the wail of a baby echoed through the house, and the men broke into broad smiles. Simeon embraced his son, laughing.

"Congratulations, my son!"

Roza came running in with tears in her eyes.

"Congratulations, my son! It's a boy!"

"And Lefkothea? Is she all right?" asked Vassilis.

"Fine! There were a few rough patches, but that's what the first birth is always like."

The husband started toward his wife and son, but his mother stopped him.

"Wait, boy. Don't be in such a hurry! We'll wash the baby and get your wife ready, and then you'll see her." She turned to her husband, whose eyes were also damp. She approached him, and he embraced her tightly.

"Congratulations, wife!" he said, and Roza looked at him in surprise. She couldn't remember her husband ever embracing her like that before, and she smiled at him through her tears.

From the first moment, the baby changed a lot of things in the Kouyoumdzis household. It was like a fresh breeze blew through and caressed the rooms. It even affected the grandfather, who gave his blessing with satisfaction to the new generation that had come and presented Lefkothea with a beautifully engraved gold bracelet. Nobody knew what had a greater impact on him, the birth of Simeon the younger or his wife's words; in any case, his behavior improved noticeably.

The second good thing that happened, in addition to the baby, was an excellent prospect for Penelope. Lykourgos Meletoglou, a wealthy raisin merchant, asked for her hand. Penelope, who had met him at the parties of their friends, accepted with pleasure, although her parents had some doubts. The groom had made it clear that, after the wedding, he would take her to Patras, in Greece, where his business had its headquarters.

September 1955 found Vassilis's family complete. Lefkothea had borne him two more sons, Loukas and Damianos, although they had lived through the loss of a newborn daughter from diphtheria. The household was plunged into mourning, and the couple particularly took a long time to recover from their loss.

Penelope had married and was living in Patras. They learned her news from the long letters she wrote, and Simeon and Roza had gone twice to visit her when her daughters were born, staying for two months each time. They returned happy and told the rest of the family about what they had seen and what a good time they'd had.

Roza had changed a great deal. Happy with her grandchildren, she had recovered the glow of her youth. She no longer pursed her lips, and she smiled more frequently. She had become very close to Lefkothea, and nothing about their relationship resembled the ugly moments of their early days. In the afternoons, with the children playing at their feet, they drank coffee and chatted like two good friends, while beside them, Grandmother Penelope giggled like a schoolgirl. During those hours, their grandfather stayed in his room reading the newspaper, not wanting to listen to women's conversations. Only in the mornings now did he go down to the shop, mostly just to take a walk, since his eyes were failing and his hands had lost the suppleness they'd once had. Besides, Simeon and Vassilis were more than capable of managing the business. Young Aristos didn't want to join them, so he'd studied economics and was working in a shipping office.

That morning in 1955, Roza noticed that the men of the family were distracted. They drank their coffee mechanically and smoked, each deep in his own thoughts. She looked at them, one by one, and realized it wasn't the first day she'd seen them like this. She was annoyed with herself for not having realized sooner. But little Simeon, who they called Simos so as not to confuse him with his grandfather, had come down with mumps, and his little brothers had caught it too. The whole household had been in turmoil for weeks. Now, however, Roza was worried. She looked at her daughter-in-law; Lefkothea had made the same unpleasant observation.

"Tell me," Roza began, "has something happened to make you two look as if you were in mourning?"

The men exchanged a furtive look, upsetting her further.

"Simeon, I'm speaking to you!" she said to him shrilly. "What's happening?"

"It's not the time, woman," he said and lowered his head.

"Vassilis, dear," said Lefkothea shyly, looking at him with pleading eyes. "If something bad is happening, I think we should know about it too."

"I have nothing to tell you. Nothing has happened, but there are a lot of things we don't like lately in the city," he answered her. "Mama, don't be angry with Papa; we're not hiding anything on purpose. We just don't know ourselves."

"Why don't you tell us about it so we can understand, son? What's going on that you don't like?" his mother asked, more gently this time.

"I'll tell you myself," Simeon cut in. "For days, the city has been full of riffraff. They hang around in the alleys, and their faces are angry. They look at us strangely and keep passing the shop like they're studying it."

"Holy Virgin!" Roza said softly and saw her mother-in-law covertly crossing herself.

"We asked one or two of them where they were from, and they named some villages in the wilds of Anatolia. We don't see any women, only men," Simeon went on.

"And what do you think it is? What do they want around here?" Roza asked, her mouth dry.

"We don't know! Haven't we been telling you that all this time?" Simeon responded without hiding the tension he felt. "Yesterday, a really good customer of ours, a Turk, came in to shop for his wife, and as he was paying us, he bent forward and told us to be careful because something bad was going to happen. However much I insisted, he wouldn't tell me anything more."

"And there's another thing," Vassilis interjected. "For some time now, the newspapers have been especially furious with us Greeks."

"What have we done to them, the cursed wretches?" Roza objected.

"They say we're responsible for the Turks' poverty: we make fortunes, and they starve! They talk about Cyprus."

"What's that?"

"It's an island, Mama! They say it's theirs."

"Then let them have it and good riddance! Why are we Greeks to blame? Did anyone tell them it was ours?"

"They're looking for an excuse. There's a leader in Cyprus—an archbishop. His name is Makarios, and the Turks hate him."

"Vassilis, I don't understand. What does any of this have to do with us?"

"Roza," Simeon began, "don't make yourself dizzy. Just pay attention to me, and I'll tell you what has to happen. We don't know anything for certain, but there are a lot of signs that we can't overlook. So, I don't want any of you to go out today, and until we see what's happening, Vassilis will stay with you. Father and I will go to the shop," he concluded determinedly, and when he saw his oldest son ready to object, he didn't allow it.

"Vassilis, we already agreed: You'll stay with the women and protect them. We'll keep the shop open so as not to give them a target. If the slightest thing happens, you know what to do. And you, Aristos, be careful. When you get out of work, come straight home, OK?"

Everyone was silent, shaking their heads as Simeon and his elderly father got up to leave. Roza followed them to the door and made the sign of the cross.

"Good luck on your way, my husband," she said to him, struggling to speak. "Be careful! If you see anything bad, you come straight home too! Do you hear?"

Without another word, Simeon hugged her and left a tender kiss on her head before he hurried off. Roza stood there, unable to move. In all the years of her marriage, she didn't remember her husband ever having said good-bye to her with a kiss before he went to work. She made another cross behind him and behind Aristos and repeated the gesture almost at the same time as her mother-in-law. They closed the door and gathered around Vassilis.

"Now, tell us what to do," his mother said as soon as she had recovered her composure.

"I want you all to gather your gold jewelry and whatever coins we have in the house."

They all rushed to obey and brought the boxes with their jewelry and gold. Vassilis took a pillow from the couch, emptied it, and put all their valuables inside. Then, with his wife's help, he carried water, bread, and a few blankets to the basement. Lefkothea watched her husband in surprise as he took some planks from the wall and an empty space appeared. It was just large enough for five people to squeeze into, one beside the other.

"Vassilis, tell me the truth," Lefkothea said nervously. "Are we in danger?"

"I don't know, dear. By God, I don't know. We didn't say it upstairs, but we found some writing on the walls of our shop. It's on all the Greek shops. As if they had marked us."

"Did you wipe it off?"

"Of course we did. But that's not the point. They know which stores are Greek and which are Turkish. My father told me to get this hiding place ready for whatever might happen."

"Vassilis, I'm afraid. The children, my pasha!"

"Aren't I here? Would I let anyone hurt you?"

He knew that protecting them might be out of his hands, but the women mustn't suspect that. They came upstairs and found Roza and his grandmother collecting the silver.

"What are you doing?" he asked as he saw his mother open the large stove. She put the silver inside and piled a few half-burned pieces of wood, left over from last winter, on top.

"I'm hiding it, my sweet. Who knows what might happen. It was my dowry!"

Vassilis smiled and hugged her affectionately. Difficult hours and days might be ahead.

As it happened, they didn't have to wait. Everything broke out in the next few hours. A few yards away from them, in Taksim Square, students began to demonstrate. Soon, the townspeople joined in, along with policemen in civilian clothes. Something had begun much earlier, though.

Three days before, the wife of the Turkish consul in Thessaloniki, Greece, had been photographed outside the house that Kemal Ataturk was thought to have been born in. A bomb had gone off, breaking a few windows of Ataturk's house, and the *Istanbul Express* produced a special edition with a photograph on the front page. Except the photo had been horribly doctored—it showed the house of the Turkish leader catastrophically damaged. The article blamed the Greeks, and was accompanied by nationalist symbols and slogans. Interestingly enough, the edition circulated almost an hour before the bomb, planted by a Turkish usher, even went off. Meaningless details.

Constantinople responded with a demonstration that soon escalated. Trucks full of axes, shovels, clubs, crowbars, and cans of gasoline were waiting to arm the enraged citizens who poured out, uncontrollable and unrestrained, into the streets to spread death and destruction. The first stop was the Seven Hills Café, which they leveled. Next, they split up. Some charged ahead, breaking the doors and shutters of stores belonging to Greeks and other minorities. Behind them, others entered the shops and threw the merchandise into the streets. Finally, the last group destroyed or looted what remained. A river of hate flowed, drowning Constantinople and the Greeks. Howls could be heard, and they trampled anyone who went out into the streets. They broke into the houses and threw furniture out the windows, snatching whatever they found. Some brave people came out to shout that they were Turkish citizens; they wanted to protect their families, but their fate was the same as that of their property. The mob could not be controlled.

Vassilis heard the voices from a long way off. He ran to the open window and leaned out, then pulled back, white in the face. Wild shouts were approaching. There was a coherence and predictability to the sounds. First, he heard the angry voices cursing. He could make out "Greeks, tonight you'll die!" and "Today, your property; tomorrow, your heads!" After that came fearful sounds of doors giving way, then furniture being smashed, then howling. He froze, and his brain froze too. It was his mother who brought him to his senses. She tugged at his sleeve.

"Vassilis, what's happening outside?" she asked. "What are those voices?"

When her son didn't answer, she shook him with all her strength. As if he had suddenly woken up, the young man looked at her and around the room. Lefkothea was standing with her three sons clutched tightly to her in fear, and beside her, their great-grandmother was trembling. They were his responsibility; he had no right to falter at such an urgent moment. His voice came out angrily: "Women, downstairs, quickly!"

He grabbed his oldest son by the arm and took his grandmother with the other. Lefkothea ran down the stairs, clutching little Damianos. Vassilis pulled aside the boards and helped the women get into their suffocating hiding place. With one hand, he replaced the boards; with the other, he held Simos, who was hiding his face in his father's neck.

"Don't make a sound!" he ordered them unnecessarily. Nobody could breathe from fear.

A few minutes later, they heard their front door give way and footsteps overhead. They stiffened beside one another. The voices reached their ears, and their blood froze when they heard what the intruders were saying. Wood broke, glass smashed, and amid the noise, the mob howled like jackals tearing flesh from a carcass. Time stopped. Vassilis didn't know how long they stayed in their hiding place. An hour, a day, an eternity? It stunk—his three small children had soiled themselves in fear. They were suffocating, but he didn't dare push the boards aside until long after the house had quieted down. He turned to his wife.

"Lefkothea, take Simos, and I'll go and see what's happening," he whispered to her, about to hand over their son to her already full arms.

"Don't, Vassilis!" she said, terrified.

"They left, my dear. Don't you hear the silence?"

He gave her the child and slowly pushed the boards aside. Nobody had come down into the basement. He climbed the stairs slowly and felt his strength abandoning him. Nothing remained to remind him of the beautiful house he'd known. All the furniture had been thrown into the street, and what they couldn't lift, they'd smashed to pieces. There wasn't a pane of glass intact, and many of the windows had been torn from their frames. The stairway leading to the bedrooms had been partially destroyed by axes.

Timidly, he put his head out of a window and was stunned by the horrible scene. The street was hidden beneath furniture, rugs, and other household goods. A small fire was burning inside the store opposite. From time to time, a stifled sob came from some victim. In the darkness that had begun to fall, he could make out the body of a man, but it was impossible for him to be alive because of the unnatural angle of his head. Covered in sweat now, he withdrew into the house and went to free the women and children.

"What if they come back, Vassilis?" asked Lefkothea, breathless.

"When fire spreads, it doesn't turn back. It seeks more food for its fury," he told her, his throat dry. He looked at the faces he loved and tried to prepare them.

"I don't want to frighten you, but there's nothing left in the house," he said to the three women. "I don't know what they did upstairs, but downstairs they threw everything out or smashed it."

With slow steps they emerged from the basement, and the first sobs came from his grandmother when she saw her house in ruins. Roza looked at Vassilis, and he could tell her thoughts had turned to the other members of the family.

"I'll go and see what happened at the shop," he said, but she objected vehemently.

"You won't take one step!" she ordered him, and her hand squeezed his arm with such strength that it hurt. "Your father and grandfather know better than you do how to protect themselves!"

"Yes, my treasure," pleaded his grandmother now. "We don't want to be worried about you. Stay here, and we'll see what's to be done. The others will come."

Lefkothea confined herself to looking at him so intently that it was if she said everything. Then she said, "I have to go upstairs to clean up the children and give them a little something sweet to recover."

"I doubt we'll find anything sweet," her mother-in-law said, "but let's go upstairs to see what's happened and I'll help you change them."

Fortunately, the upper floor was untouched. It seemed as if the intruders didn't have time; their fury, unsatisfied, had drawn them onward to the next house. When they came downstairs, having put the children to bed, they found Vassilis trying to put the front door back on its hinges. They helped him put it in position and then returned to the empty living room. Only the heavy stove remained undisturbed, its treasures hidden in its belly. Roza looked at it with a wry smile. Her silver had been saved.

For the next two hours, they did what they could to make the place habitable. They were frightened when they realized someone was trying to enter the house. Vassilis ran to the door, prepared for the worst, but he found his brother carrying their father on his shoulders. Simeon was deathly pale from a wound over his brow that was bleeding heavily despite the fact that Aristos had bound it tightly with his handkerchief.

"What happened?" Vassilis asked in a choked voice.

"Help me lay him down now, and I'll tell you later," answered the young man, panting from the load he had carried for so long.

"Let's take him upstairs," Vassilis ordered, and they carried the unconscious Simeon in their arms.

Roza appeared and covered her mouth to stop the cry she was about to utter.

"Is he alive?"

"Only just," Vassilis answered. "Bring whatever you can find to help him."

Without breathing, she ran to the kitchen, which had almost been destroyed. With shaking hands, she tried to find a pot to boil some water in while her daughter-in-law searched for alcohol without any success.

"Where's Grandmother?" Roza asked. She'd found the gas ring but not the matches.

"I made her sit down in a chair that wasn't broken!" Lefkothea answered, handing her the matches. "How is Father?"

"I don't know. The boys took him upstairs."

"Go to him!" the girl said to her. "I'll boil the water. And I'll bring towels."

Roza didn't wait to be told a second time. With her stomach in her throat, she ran to her husband's side. He had recovered a little, but he was struggling to breathe. He had been wounded very badly, it seemed, and his grimaces told her he was in pain. She sat on the bed and took his hand in both of hers. It was also covered in blood.

"Simeon . . . ," she whispered to him, holding back a sob, and he opened his eyes and looked at her.

"I couldn't save anything."

"It doesn't matter, my husband. It's you who must be saved."

"Roza—." He tried to speak, but another spasm of pain cut him off.

"Hush, my pasha, don't speak. Everything will be all right."

"I don't have time, Roza, and I must tell you," he went on, using his last reserves of strength to speak. "You were wrong. I loved you. And I made a mistake by not telling you, but I didn't realize it myself for a long time, and then I was ashamed. I want you to know, though, even now, at the end. I loved you and I love you now. And I thank you because I lived happily with you. You are a good and decent woman, and I didn't behave as I should have with you. I filled you with a bitterness you didn't deserve . . . forgive me!"

She saw his eyes fade before his hand became lifeless in her own. She bit her lips to keep herself from howling. She pressed her hand to her chest and bent to leave a kiss on his lips.

"Kiss your father," she told the children. "He's gone."

Vassilis felt his eyes burning; his chest was struck by a sudden pain. He bent and kissed his father's forehead, and then it was Aristos's turn. Vassilis saw his brother stumble and hurried to support him. Roza jumped up beside her son.

"What is it? Are you wounded too?" she asked him in agony.

"No, but my eyes have seen such things that I don't know how much more I can bear. We didn't only lose Papa tonight," he whispered, and had to sit down.

Vassilis put him in a chair and knelt in front of him while Roza remained standing.

"Tell us, what other terrible things did you see?" she said, her voice trembling.

"I don't know how to tell you. I left work secretly. There were disturbances in the neighborhood by my office, but not like here. I went to the shop. When I got there, I thought I'd lose my mind. The whole street was full of broken glass, and all the stores had been looted. They had destroyed our shop. I found Father in the workshop under a counter they'd thrown on top of him. He could hardly breathe."

"And Grandfather?" whispered Roza.

"He was lying beside the door. Probably he'd tried to stop them. They'd beaten him and then trampled him in their frenzy."

Roza felt as if the bullet that had been chasing her had finally found its target. She swayed, and the two boys only just managed to catch her in their arms before she fell down in a faint. They had no choice but to lay her down beside her dead husband. Vassilis took a bottle of cologne from her dresser to rub her wrists, and Aristos snatched the jug of water from the basin and wet her face. She seemed to come around. Her eyelids fluttered, memories overtook her, and the tears came. The two brothers watched with horror as she curled up beside Simeon, holding him in her arms and lamenting him silently with her face buried in his neck. With great difficulty, they tried to pull her away, and they managed it just as Lefkothea came hurrying in. One look was enough for her to grasp the extent of the disaster, and she ran to take her mother-in-law, who was now crying loudly, in her arms. With her husband's help, she lifted Roza from the bed and put her in an armchair. Nobody was aware the grandmother had come silently into the room until they heard her cry out. They all turned and saw her fallen on her son, repeating the same phrase: "Why, my treasure? Why? What did you ever do to them?"

She stroked his bloody hair and kissed him without anyone stopping her. They didn't have the courage to tell her that there was another person she would soon be mourning. The moment of truth was not long in coming, and they didn't need to say a word. At some point, Grandmother Penelope froze. Without stirring, she raised her head and looked at her family. Her eyes moved over them, one by one, and stopped on Aristos.

"My husband? He died, didn't he?"

Instead of answering, they all bent their heads, and the woman received the second blow like a dagger to the chest. Her eyes rolled, she grimaced with the pain, and then closed her eyes tight. They ran to her, Lefkothea grabbing the cologne, but the old woman hadn't fainted. She stood up with difficulty and approached her daughter-in-law, who was crying silently.

"That was it, my daughter-in-law," she said and her voice shook. "We've been left alone, and now we must be brave for your children."

They embraced each other, mingling their tears and their laments, unable to believe the disaster that had befallen them. Through the veil of her tears, Roza saw her whole life with her husband passing by. His last words turned her tears into flames. "Why?" she moaned. "Why?"

The double loss in their household attracted a lot of people to their side. Every one of them was mourning their own losses, and they also mourned the total destruction of their lives. The Greek Kristallnacht, as it was later called, was the longest night in Constantinople. At daybreak, martial law was hypocritically declared by the government. What was there even left to destroy? Every hour, someone brought another sad piece of news as the catastrophe of biblical proportions grew. Despite their own pain, the Kouyoumdzis family couldn't help but shudder when they heard of the deaths, the rapes, the desecration of Christian tombs. At the funeral of Simeon and his father, each conversation revealed another aspect of that terrible night.

"In Balukli, they smashed the graves of the Greek patriarchs and threw their bones into the streets," said a choked voice.

"And in the cemetery at Sisli," said another with a sob, "they dug up the most recently buried and stabbed the corpses. They cut them into pieces, the devils."

"Three of them raped Rafailoglou's daughter, and the girl went mad," said a weeping woman.

"And Moisis the money changer's wife. They left her in the middle of the road."

"They destroyed the Church of the Holy Trinity in Stavrodromi."

"They stripped priests and made them go out into the streets shouting that Cyprus was Turkish."

"What are you saying?" said an old man. "The heathen antichrists handed over a little child of nine to a man they call 'the Gorilla' so the beast could abuse him in front of everyone! Should we be crying about churches? People are dead!"

Silence fell for a while as they tried to absorb what they were hearing. Without intending to, they sat close to one another; they needed to know they were not alone.

A tragic figure, aside from Roza, was Grandmother Penelope, who had lost her husband and child in one day. Dry-eyed, she followed the funeral mass; dry-eyed, she watched her two loved ones disappear into the bowels of the wounded earth. Everyone there said she would soon be gone herself, and they were not wrong. The very next day, she was dead. She had done her duty, buried her loved ones, and it was as if she'd ordered her heart to stop beating so that she could go and find them.

It took nearly ten days before the others could stagger to their feet, let alone walk. Vassilis had become head of the family now, against his wishes. His wife and his mother watched him pace the house like an animal in a cage. One evening, at the end of that black September, they put the children to bed and sat in the kitchen.

"We have to think about what we're going to do," he began calmly, and everyone was surprised at the sound of his voice. They had been struggling for so long to get a word out of him.

"But what can we do, brother?" asked Aristos. The young man wasn't in a good state. He couldn't even pass a Turk in the street. He ground his teeth and rushed away to stop himself from attacking strangers. For his part, Vassilis hadn't even gone to visit the family shop.

Images of his father, covered in blood, and his dead grandfather came to life to suffocate him.

"We must," Vassilis went on, as if searching for his words, "stand on our feet again. I thought of something, and I want your opinion, especially yours, Mama."

"Mine?" Roza wondered. "What could I tell you, son?"

"I want us to leave," Vassilis finally said, and taking courage from his brother's expression, he went on. "There's no place for us here. And I can't wait for us to be the next ones to die when the Turks rise up again. I won't watch them slaughter my children in front of my eyes!"

"Bravo, brother!" Aristos declared, and for the first time in a long while, they saw the light return to his eyes. Then he too looked at his mother. "Mama, Vassilis is right. We have to leave!"

"And where would we go, my child? Our house is here, our shop. Your grandfather and your father gave their lives defending it!"

"Yes, but there's nothing left."

Roza was about to answer, but she stopped suddenly. They all looked at her anxiously, thinking she wasn't well, but her expression had filled with something they couldn't interpret. She stood up suddenly.

"Aristos, Vassilis, we're going to the shop!" she ordered.

"Stop, Mother! There's nothing left, I told you," he protested.

"Are you coming with me, or will I go alone? I must see it. Bah! Where did my mind go?"

She dashed to the door. The two men hurried after her. Lefkothea stayed behind with the children, terror gnawing at her heart.

They reached the main street of Pera, where their beautiful store had once stood. They were surprised to see the shops around it functioning, even if in a rudimentary way. But the old owners were no longer there, and in their place were new ones: Turks.

"Do you see why I said we had to leave?" asked Vassilis, his tone sharp.

"Hush, Vassilis, and come with me!" she ordered.

They arrived at the door of what had once been the best jewelry store in Constantinople. After taking their grandfather's body away, they had lowered the metal shutters and locked them. Roza felt her eyes burn thinking of the martyrdom of her loved ones, but she took a deep breath.

"Open the shutters!" she said firmly.

The two men obeyed with heavy hearts. The store looked like a gaping wound. The sound of broken glass from the former windows echoed hauntingly.

"Is there a light?" Roza asked, and her voice trembled slightly.

Aristos turned the switch, and two or three lights that had escaped the mob's frenzy lit up.

"Good. Turn them off again," she told Aristos, and he obeyed.

The three of them remained in the semilit space. Roza didn't waste any time. She didn't give in to her memories, just marched to the back of the store, where the workshop had once been.

"Mama, why are we here?" Vassilis asked irritably.

"Hush, Vassilis, and do what I tell you! Bend down and get under that counter. Aristos, help your brother clear away the broken things. You want me to leave my home, but without money, you can't live anywhere."

She looked around and found a crowbar that had probably fallen from the intruders' hands. She gave it to Vassilis.

"Pry up the floorboards!" she ordered.

Vassilis and his brother lifted a few boards and stood staring at what they had revealed.

"What's that, Mama?" they asked almost with one breath.

"Don't you see? Stand aside now while I open it."

Roza knelt and carefully entered the combination her husband had taught her. Instead of putting his safe in the wall, Simeon had chosen to bury it below his feet. Every evening, before they went to sleep, he made her repeat the combination until he was sure she knew it as well as her own name.

The little door opened, and Simeon's treasure appeared. Packets full of gold coins and a velvet purse full of precious stones.

"Mama!" Vassilis gasped.

"What did you think, eh? So many years of hard work. Didn't you think there'd be some money?"

"That's not just money, Mama, it's a whole fortune!" Aristos observed.

"Hide it on you, and let's go! We have a lot to do before we can set out on a journey."

"Does that mean you agree that we should leave for Greece?" Aristos asked her.

"Why not? What's left for me here? My daughter's in Greece! Even better. Only—" She broke off her sentence and hung her head.

Vassilis understood and put his arms around her while he exchanged a look with his brother. What tied her to this ground was that it was where her parents, her husband, and her in-laws lay.

"We'll take them with us," he said softly, "and we'll have them here forever." He pointed to his heart.

"Yes, son, you're right. Let's go home now."

They hid the treasure carefully on themselves, then opened the shutters of the store. They hadn't managed to close them again before a Turk who had taken over the store next door blocked their way.

"What are you doing here?" he asked roughly.

Vassilis was about to answer curtly when he felt a sharp elbow in his ribs.

"Good morning, sir," Roza said sweetly, surprising her sons. "This store belonged to my husband, and I thought I'd say good-bye before I sell it. I have a daughter in Greece; we'll go and live near her."

"If it's like that, I'll buy your store. Will you sell it to me?"

"Do you have to ask, sir? You'll do me a favor for taking away my worry."

The Turk standing opposite them seemed pleased. He named his price, and the woman had to pinch her son's hand so he wouldn't go on the attack. It was a ridiculous price and not a tenth of the store's real value, but Roza kept smiling.

"Sir, if you'll pay a little more, I'll give you the store and our house! It's not far at all. A big house, two stories. Do you have a family?"

"Of course I do!"

"Then it's just what you need! Why don't you come with us, so you can see if you like it."

Holding Vassilis's and Aristos's hands as tight as if they were five-year-olds, she walked ahead. The Turk followed with a heavy tread and a hostile look.

"I'll throttle you if you say anything!" Roza hissed to her sons. "I'm in charge now!"

Lefkothea nearly fainted when she saw the Turk entering the house. Her mother-in-law's look told her to stay silent.

"Here we are, sir! This is our house," Roza said, looking confidently at him. "There are four bedrooms upstairs, pasha. A real palace—you'll enjoy it. What do you say? Do you like it?"

"Hey, Greek woman, are you trying to trick me by any chance?" he grumbled now.

"Me, pasha? Let me take you to see the title deeds I have! The house and the store are both mine, and I'm selling them to you. Is that a bad thing? Since we're leaving, wouldn't it be a pity for them to fall into ruin? You seem to be an honest worker. Why should I let some Jews rush in here and ruin it? At least you'll do some work on it!"

Her gaze was fixed innocently above his head, and silently she asked forgiveness from the many Jews they had lived among peacefully for years. She saw he was persuaded. They agreed on the final details and made an arrangement to see a lawyer the following day. When he left, Roza collapsed into a chair.

"Daughter-in-law, bring me a glass of water. My mouth has dried up."

Lefkothea rushed to carry out her order, and as soon as her mother-in-law had drunk a little and recovered, she turned angrily to her sons.

"You nearly wrecked everything," she chided them. "Are we going to achieve anything with these cursed people by being macho? Thank God I was able to salvage things, and we'll make something out of it. Off with you now! Hurry and figure out how we're going to leave. Lefkothea and I have a lot of work to do."

"What work?" Aristos wondered.

"Sewing!" Roza answered mysteriously.

They made their journey by train, because there was no way Roza would get on a boat. Two days before they left, she prepared the ritual boiled wheat and took it to the graves of her men. Then she was ready. They took nothing with them except their clothes and their silverware, but their overcoats were very heavy. For days, the women had been struggling with the linings. They'd managed to sew all the gold coins into them. Roza had even slit open their handbags, hiding the precious stones inside. Not until they crossed the border did they take a deep breath. And when they got off the train, exhausted from the long journey with three small children, they realized there was no time to rest. Only by rallying their forces and working hard would they be able to stand on their feet again in this place that they imagined was their homeland but in fact was a foreign country.

CHAPTER 13

VERVERIS AND SEKERIS FAMILIES

Athens, 1955

Smaragda left the letter she was holding on the table in front of her. In great detail, her sister told her what had happened in Constantinople a few months earlier. Smaragda couldn't believe her eyes. The newspapers in Greece had said very little, as if the journalists were in a hurry to change the subject. But the little they did report was enough for the family to be alarmed about their relatives. Fotis immediately sent a telegram, and fortunately, they answered quickly; otherwise the Ververises would have gone crazy with worry. Since her husband's death, Kleoniki had moved in with Dorothea. Galata hadn't been spared the anti-Greek riots, but no harm had come to Smaragda's family.

"Why don't you read the rest?" her husband asked when he saw her staring at the first page.

"I already did," his wife replied flatly.

"So, are you going to tell me? What does Dorothea say?"

"My family is fine, but the families we know . . . the news is not good."

"Don't tell me! Who was harmed?" Fotis asked anxiously.

"A lot of them. Enough to say that there's scarcely a Greek house in the city that isn't in mourning. Among them, she writes about the Kouyoumdzis family. Simeon and his father were in the store—remember? In the middle of Pera?"

"Heavens, woman, of course I know the Kouyoumdzis store—it was the biggest and best! Go on! What happened?"

"The older you get, the more surprised you are by things, husband. Be patient with me. I'm upset too. So, they rushed into the store, the cursed wretches, and trampled the old man. Then they beat Simeon!"

"Are they alive?"

"Neither of them," Smaragda said sadly, and Fotis came to put his arms around her.

"And Vassilis?"

"From what my sister wrote, he and his brother are fine. Vassilis has three children now."

"Three children? That seems awfully fast."

"That's how it is, my husband. Life doesn't stop for a lost love. He found someone and was comforted. But there's more. My brother-in-law found out that the entire Kouyoumdzis family has come to Athens."

Silence followed this announcement. Fotis moved away from his wife and sat down opposite her.

"Where in Athens? Did she tell you?"

"She doesn't know any more. Fotis, what will we do?" Smaragda asked uneasily.

"We? What do you mean? Vassilis is married. He has three children. And our daughter has four. Are we going to worry about old love stories now? Anyway, Athens is huge. Where would they even meet?"

"It's not only him that I'm afraid of. His shrew of a mother came too. Do you think she might start slandering us again?"

"No, my sweetheart. She married her son off, so what reason would she have now? She was a wretched woman, but people change, my dear.

There's nothing to be afraid of. Our children are married and have their own lives."

Smaragda looked at him and nodded, smiling at the thought of their children. Nestor had recently married, and his wife, Yvonne, was expecting their first child. Chrysafenia, whose husband called her Chrysi, had made her a grandmother four times. Baby Smaragda, named for her grandmother, was her favorite. The next eldest, and the only boy in the family, was Stelios. Then came three-year-old Fotini, and Hecuba, who had already turned five. The Sekeris family lived in Kypseli, in a newly built palace that her son-in-law had designed. Pericles had turned out to be a very good husband and a hard worker. He could be a bit rigid, and sometimes rather abrupt, but his wife mostly knew how to soften him.

Chrysafenia scolded her daughter, who was bothering the baby. From the beginning, Hecuba had been annoyed with the newest member of the family. Fotini was quite indifferent to her—she only liked ordering her around. Stelios was a boy, and she didn't quarrel with him, but with the oldest one her mother could never let down her guard. Perhaps because Smaragda monopolized everyone's attention with her sweetness, her beauty, and her habits. She was a calm baby and liked to smile at whoever bent over her cradle. And the more she smiled and enchanted her parents, the more jealous her older sister became. Pericles had made his own position clear: the largest share of his attention was reserved for his son. That, Hecuba could accept. But Smaragda? No.

Chrysafenia got up and took the baby in her arms so as to save her from the hands of her sister. Right on time, Lizeta arrived for a visit. Pericles's beloved sister-in-law, who'd become Chrysafenia's friend as well, took care to pass by regularly and help the young mother, since her brother-in-law wouldn't even hear of a nanny.

"My children are going to be raised by their mother," he declared, dismissing any objections. "I have taken care of everything they need, I've hired a woman to look after the house, but the children are their mother's business."

Chrysafenia didn't object to most of his ideas, although his tone often troubled her. She didn't have to reproach him about other things, but she would tremble when Pericles got his mind set on something. Then, nobody could dissuade him. One of his fixations was the proper raising of the children.

"Welcome!" she called out as she saw Lizeta coming into the living room. "God must have sent you."

"Are the little beasts tormenting you again?" asked Lizeta, laughing, but they both knew she meant the oldest one, and she turned first to her. "How's my girl doing?"

Hecuba looked carefully at her and then consented to approach and submit to her hug.

"What did I bring for my sweetie?" Lizeta asked and pulled a pad of drawing paper and some colored pencils out of her bag, knowing Hecuba couldn't resist them.

She could spend hours drawing, and a brand-new drawing pad was a great incentive. Lizeta's magic bag was full as always. It contained a little rag doll for Fotini and a lollipop for greedy Stelios. Complete calm reigned for the moment. The children were busy with the gifts, and their mother put Smaragda down in her bassinet.

"May you live a thousand years, Lizeta!" she exclaimed. "They'll drive me crazy. Shall we drink some tea? This cold is really settling in, I think."

"Well, it's nearly Christmas, Chrysi."

The two women sat down to their tea while the children played quietly. They chatted about the holiday and the dinners they had to cook. After that, the conversation turned to fashion, and Lizeta had news.

"I didn't tell you! There's a new jewelry shop on Ermou Street. A big one! The builders have been working day and night, and it'll open next week in time for the holidays. They say a fellow countryman of yours is opening it with his brother. They came after the troubles in Constantinople. You must have heard what happened."

"Yes, my mother told me. Fortunately, my family is all right."

"They say these people weren't so lucky. They lost the father and grandfather, and the sons packed up and came to Greece."

With every word Lizeta said, Chrysafenia's head spun a little more.

But the woman didn't notice a thing. She went on: "His name is Vassilis Kouyoumdzis. Do you know him?"

Stolen kisses in a candlelit staircase. Tears, and a letter made of gold still hidden in her wardrobe. Did she know him? As well as she knew her dreams.

Chrysafenia Sekeris's life felt like the pages of a calendar blown by the wind. She didn't understand how the years had passed. She'd watched her family grow, she'd watched the old ones, like her grandmother in Constantinople, die, and she'd watched life itself continue. She told no one that she knew about Vassilis coming to Greece. She didn't even discuss it with her mother, since Smaragda had kept the news from her. When she went down to Ermou Street, she saw his store from a distance and made sure not to pass in front of it. She didn't want to risk meeting; she didn't trust herself. Despite the years she had spent with Pericles, she hadn't truly fallen in love with him. She respected her husband, honored him, but she'd realized very early on that her experience of marriage would not be like her mother's.

Pericles Sekeris's love, if it existed at all, was possessive, absolute, and filled with great egotism. As long as everything was going his way, their life was good. He wasn't violent, but he could be very unpleasant when someone disagreed with him, especially his wife. Everyone thought her lucky for having a husband who made a lot of money and who was charming, polite, and gallant. At home, though, he bossed everyone around, and it never crossed his mind that someone could disagree or have a better idea. Of course, his wife dressed in the latest fashions, and had nice jewelry and an appearance that matched his social position. His children went to the most expensive private schools, and only the best people came to their parties. But Chrysafenia herself sought the company of Lizeta and her sister-in-law, Yvonne. Only with them did she let herself go and forget her anxieties. In the afternoons when they met at her house, they giggled like schoolgirls, sometimes even making fun of their husbands.

Yvonne was Chrysafenia's age, full of zest for life; she was also independent and very clever. She had met Nestor at the university, where she had also studied pharmacology, and with her dowry, the two of them had opened their pharmacy. She only had one child, Melpo, named after her late mother. Her mother-in-law chided her in a well-meaning way after Yvonne made it clear that, after Melpo's difficult birth, she didn't see herself having another child.

"What are you waiting for?" Smaragda would say to her. "Are you such a coward? Have another one. I'll raise it."

"Leave it, Mother!" the girl answered, laughing. "The raising is easy. The birth is what I won't go through again. Not to mention the five months I was forced to lie in bed! May my daughter live a long life, but she nearly sent me unprepared into the other world! Besides, you have Chrysi's children to comfort you."

"My daughter's name is Chrysafenia! Chrysi is like the name of a disease!" the woman said. "Don't listen to that arrogant son-in-law of mine who thought he'd baptize her again!"

However much she tried to hide it, Smaragda could not warm up to her son-in-law. In fact, the more she got to know him, the greater her antipathy was. Fotis tried to soothe her worries, but the truth was, nobody wanted much to do with Pericles. Even Nestor, who had been close with him once, distanced himself after the wedding. Pericles's arrogance annoyed him, and he didn't like the way the man treated his family. He was more like a despot than a husband and father. What pleased him was his wife's friendship with Chrysafenia, and he couldn't imagine what a struggle his sister had gone through to hold on to that friendship. In the early years, Pericles had accepted Yvonne. But over the years, he began to drop hints that he was not in favor of her frequent visits. As the years passed and the friendship became stronger, the hints became complaints. He disapproved of Yvonne, believing she was a bad influence because she'd continued to work after her marriage instead of looking after her household. On top of that, she refused to have more children with her husband.

"I don't know what you see in her!" he'd fume as soon as he found out the two young women had met.

"If you knew her better, Pericles, you'd be friends with her yourself," Chrysafenia would answer calmly. "We're the same age, we have a lot in common, and she's my brother's wife. Besides, her daughter plays well with ours."

She tried to keep her self-control each time, but finally Pericles issued yet another order.

"Chrysi, you pretend you don't understand, so you force me to tell you clearly and categorically: I forbid you to spend time with that woman!"

"What you're saying is impossible!"

"What did you say?" he asked.

"You heard me. Yvonne is my friend, my only friend, and I don't intend to turn my back on her for no good reason."

"No reason? Did you know, my dear, that only the day before yesterday when they went to dinner at my mother's house, your little brother and his wife didn't hesitate to speak out against the regime. They're going to get us all in trouble! I repeat: that friendship is over!"

"And I told you that's not happening!"

Her husband stood up and came toward her with his lips drawn tight, a sign that he had begun to lose his self-control.

"And you dare to go against your husband when he gave you a specific order?" he asked, his eyes narrowing threateningly.

"I'm not a soldier to give orders to, nor am I a slave. I've accepted the lifestyle you want for me, I've given in to a lot of your strange requests, but enough is enough. This goes beyond anything. My sister-in-law has done nothing wrong except for not liking your beloved regime—and if you don't know, neither do thousands of Greeks. She and I don't even discuss politics, yet you continue to find reasons to dislike her. Tonight you've gone too far. I will continue to see Yvonne, where and when I wish, and you can do as you wish."

"Explain yourself, woman!"

"I see no need. We understand each other very well after so many years of marriage. You can hit me if you like!"

"Just a moment," he interrupted her in surprise, "I've never touched you!"

"If you had, you would have had another thing coming!" his wife answered angrily, unafraid. "But there are many ways of making life difficult for another person, and you, my dear husband, have tried them all. I did everything to please you, but I was never good enough, correct enough . . . what you wanted me to be enough. You didn't like the way I spoke, so I changed it. You didn't like my family, so you pushed them away. You scarcely let my mother enjoy her grandchildren because you're afraid they might pick up her accent or 'bad habits.' On top of that, you won't let anyone else look after the children, even while I go shopping. But I won't accept anything else. I'm no longer the twenty-year-old girl who bowed her head. I'm who I am, whether you like it or not. If not, I'll take the children and go back to my parents!" she finished, out of breath, but certain that she had won.

Pericles blinked in surprise. The shocked expression on his face made her want to laugh, but she held her tongue.

"Wait, Chrysi—" he tried to say.

"My name is Chrysafenia! For God's sake, every time I hear 'Chrysi,' I think I'm going to get jaundice."

"Now you're going crazy, my dear. That's what I've always called you, from our first date. Do you remember?" he asked, trying to soften her.

"Do *you* remember?" she retorted. "Where is the sweet, tender man I thought I was marrying? You've turned into a tyrant, someone we're afraid to speak to. And now you're giving me orders? Enough, Pericles! Yvonne is and will remain my friend—do you hear me? I expect you to treat her with the respect that's due to my brother's wife. Just as I respect your relatives and friends and all the people you drag over here without even asking if I'm sick or if I'm in the mood to entertain your riffraff!"

"I don't even recognize you!" he shouted.

"Let me introduce myself then. I'm your wife, not some lapdog for you to give orders to!"

"These aren't your words, though!" Pericles insisted. "That's why I don't approve of your friendship with Yvonne. She's a bad influence on you and makes us quarrel."

"What about your new friends? You spend so much time hanging around with junta supporters, you've become just like them. You're the boss, you give orders. Except that this is our house, not some rocky island where they sent the political prisoners! Enough. *Tamam!*" she concluded, using a word from her Constantinople dialect, which he had forbidden her to speak.

She turned her back on him and left the room with her shoulders straight, leaving Pericles behind to wonder what hit him. It was true that his friends had changed over the last years, and when, a year earlier, the military dictatorship had taken over the country, his friends found themselves in high positions. Chrysafenia had never seemed to share his enthusiasm for the regime. She was a perfect hostess when they came over, but she didn't want to have much to do with them, however much

Pericles insisted. Politics didn't interest her, but every form of violence repelled her, and privately she criticized his choices.

After this, a clear victory on Chrysafenia's part, Pericles took refuge in a strategic retreat. He had no desire to be a target of ridicule in his circle for having a marital crisis. In his wife's face, he saw she was quite ready to carry out her threat and leave him. In a burst of honest self-criticism that night, he accepted the fact that Chrysafenia had been something beyond dutiful toward the family she had created. A capable housekeeper, a fine mother, and as a wife, she had she accepted her responsibilities without making any demands, even in their private moments. It was a successful marriage from every perspective, and there was no need to blow it up without serious cause. Besides, Yvonne, he had to admit, was also a good wife and mother. The two women's meetings seldom took place beyond the four walls of his house, and his sister-in-law was almost always present too. So what was he afraid of?

As a gesture of goodwill, and to persuade his wife to abandon her bad mood, he himself appeared at the women's next gathering with a box of sweets in his hands. Yvonne opened her eyes wide.

"Pericles! What's this? You've brought us *galaktoboureko?*" she asked.

"And not from any old sweet shop—from Kosmikon!"

"You went all the way to Patission Street?" Chrysafenia said suspiciously.

"Why not, my dear? I knew you were getting together today, and I thought I'd sweeten you up. And now I'm off to leave you in peace so you can talk."

He kissed the top of his wife's head affectionately and disappeared.

While they were enjoying their favorite delicately flavored sweets, Lizeta turned to Chrysafenia.

"Whenever my husband brings something sweet home, it's an attempt to pacify the beast he's managed to wake. What did my brother-in-law do to you?"

"Like you said, Lizeta. He woke the beast!"

"It's about time it woke up!" the woman replied. "You've indulged his bad habits, my girl. 'Whatever Pericles says' is no way to spend a life. And make sure you drag him away from the company he keeps, because it won't turn out well for him."

"That's very difficult," Chrysafenia admitted.

"But what does your husband think? That these clowns will be in charge for the next few centuries? The people will rise up, and the despots' friends will pay right along with them."

"Lizeta, are you a leftist?" asked Yvonne, shocked. "I can't bear the junta either, but . . ."

"Do you have to be a leftist to detest some half-crazy types who've overrun us by force?" Lizeta responded indignantly.

"Certainly not, but it's only the leftists who criticize them aloud. Be careful, Lizeta. Don't get into trouble," Chrysafenia warned her, with Yvonne nodding in agreement.

The discussion ended there because a skirmish broke out upstairs between Hecuba and young Smaragda, and it took their mother's intervention to stop it. When Chrysafenia returned to her friends, she was frowning.

"What happened?" asked Lizeta.

"The same thing every day!" Chrysafenia burst out. "This daughter of mine has grown up, but she hasn't developed any brains. I can't understand the hatred she has for the little one. She's my child, but I tremble at the thought that, once she finishes school, she'll be at home all day!"

"Doesn't she want to go to college?" Yvonne asked.

"She doesn't want to hear about studying. Her father told her she must, but she won't budge."

"So, try to marry her off," Lizeta advised.

"Yes, tomorrow if possible!" Chrysafenia said ironically. "But she doesn't want to hear about marriage either. What will I do with her? She's only interested in making life difficult for her sister. And the little one is so quiet and sweet. She doesn't hold any grudge against her sister, but the situation makes me ill. Whatever Smaragda has, Hecuba takes. And whenever any of us lets slip some good words about Smaragda, I see Hecuba turn yellow with hatred."

Nothing had changed as the children had grown up, and it wounded their mother deeply, making her wonder what she herself might have done wrong. Hecuba would turn eighteen soon, and although she wasn't physically ugly, her expression and constant complaints made her unattractive. The next child, Fotini, was pleasant, but she seemed to be lacking in volition, while fifteen-year-old Stelios was a calm child with a weakness for his mother and his youngest sister. But the joy of the household was fourteen-year-old Smaragda. She had inherited all her mother's beauty, especially her eyes, which were like melted gold. She always had a smile or a song on her lips, and she paid no attention to her older sister's scorn. She had accepted the fact that Hecuba was like that and avoided arguing with her, even when the girl stole things that belonged to her, from a piece of chocolate to a scarf or a jacket. The little spear-carrier for the four children was Yvonne and Nestor's daughter, Melpo. She was twelve, and she clung to sweet Smaragda. As she grew up, Melpo never hesitated to take on Hecuba, defending her beloved cousin as much as she could.

On New Year's Day, Pericles broke open the lucky pomegranate at the front door with pride. Everything was going well for him. Despite his wife's objections, his business had doubled thanks to his friendship with the officers. Signs bearing his name were everywhere, on the best new buildings, and his accounts at the bank grew fatter and fatter. In addition, his son had announced that, as soon as he finished school, he would take the entrance exams for the polytechnic school so as to continue his father's business. Fotini, who had finished school with excellent grades, would continue to study piano, which was what she liked best, while Smaragda decided she wanted to be a teacher.

The only black spot in his life was his eldest child. Hecuba seemed not to care about anything. She didn't want to study and refused any suggestion of marriage. Her staying at home caused a lot of friction with her mother, who watched her daughter doing absolutely nothing. Only when Smaragda returned from school did she liven up, eager to create problems for the younger child. Every time Smaragda brought a friend home, the older sister forced her way into the room and listened pointedly to their conversation. In the end, there was always a fight—even Smaragda's patience had its limits. Once, as soon as she had gone into the room with her cousin, Melpo turned the key loudly and locked the door. When the two girls came out later, Hecuba grabbed them both by the hair, and there was a great commotion.

One afternoon, at the beginning of March 1971, a huge fight broke out in Pericles's house. Smaragda and Melpo had been invited to visit a friend for her birthday. Hecuba was furious that she wasn't invited and insisted on accompanying the two younger girls to the party.

"You weren't invited," said Smaragda for the umpteenth time. "Why would you even want to come?"

Instead of answering, Hecuba gave her young sister a hard slap, just at the moment when their mother came into the room.

"Hecuba," Chrysafenia exclaimed, approaching the girl, "what sort of behavior is that? Say sorry to your sister immediately!"

"That'll be the day!" she answered cheekily. "It's her fault."

"Mama, please talk to Hecuba. She's being crazy. She keeps insisting on coming to the party even though no one invited her. What does she have to do with my friends? Nobody there wants her."

In her fury, Hecuba shoved her mother away and flew at her sister. Chrysafenia was thrown to the floor and hit her head on the wardrobe. Pericles ran in to see what was going on, shocked to see his wife on the floor. He helped her up, then turned to his daughters.

"How did your mother fall?" he asked, and his voice shook with anger. "Hecuba!"

"I didn't mean to, Papa! It was—"

She didn't manage to finish her sentence. Pericles's hand came down forcefully on her cheek. It was the first time he had hit anyone, and the mother and sisters froze.

"I'll never forgive you for that!" he said, and with every word it was as if he hit her again. "How dare you raise your hand to your mother? It's the first and the last time. The next time, I'll finish you off!"

"She only meant to hit me, Papa," Smaragda interjected.

"Smaragda, don't make excuses for her!" her father shouted, and turned to the guilty girl again. "And who gave you permission to hit your sister? Who do you think you are, Hecuba? Pull yourself together before we have more serious trouble! And now apologize, because I'm ready to hit you again!"

In a voice that was nearly inaudible, the girl was forced to apologize not only to her mother but also to her sister before she was allowed to leave the room. Pericles and his wife left the room immediately while Smaragda, with a heavy heart, began to get ready for the party. Before she left, she knocked on Hecuba's door. When she opened it, she found her sister crying inconsolably. She wanted to go up to her, to try and make up, but Hecuba curled around on her bed like a snake and, with eyes scarlet from weeping, looked at her sister with so much hatred that Smaragda was rooted to the spot.

"I hate you more than anything in my life," she hissed. "The slap I got from Father was because of you—remember that! Now get out of my sight, and I hope you never return."

Smaragda hung her head. She didn't want to admit that the game with her sister had been lost, not now, but years ago. She couldn't understand the hatred she saw imprinted on the face of a being who shared the same blood.

"Are you crazy?" Melpo said when they met up. "Hecuba's been a mean-spirited old maid from the day she was born! Don't pay attention to her."

"But she's my sister," the girl complained.

"And Abel had Cain for a brother! Did that stop the murder?"

Smaragda smiled and looked lovingly at her cousin, who was dragging her by the hand into the house where the party was being held. She crossed the threshold without suspecting that a few yards away, in the room full of young boys and girls, her intended was waiting.

Time stopped, and the room full of people disappeared when she saw him sipping his drink a little ways from the others; it seemed as if he was waiting for her. From the first moment her eyes passed over him, she was captivated. This young stranger drew her to him like a magnet. Her friend ran to greet the two cousins and introduce them to the guests they didn't know. They reached him, and he stood up. He was very tall, and Smaragda had to crane her neck to meet his eyes. Blushing, she said hello and realized, full of joy, that he'd noticed her too. Help came unexpectedly. Another girl arrived just then, and the young hostess ran to welcome her, while some of Melpo's other friends dragged her away. They remained standing, facing each other. Around them young people shouted and laughed, while far away, Smaragda could hear music from a gramophone.

"Would you like to sit?" she heard him say and obediently took a place nearby, but not next to him.

From that moment, it was as if no one else existed. He asked questions, and Smaragda answered, and when the music grew louder, he moved closer so he could hear her. Smaragda didn't have much to tell him about her life, although the young man seemed to want to find out every detail about her, even the most trivial.

"Won't you tell me anything about yourself?" she dared to ask him at one point. "I only know your first name."

"That's unforgivable!" he said happily. "My name is Simos Kouyoumdzis. My family are all goldsmiths."

Smaragda didn't sleep that night. Lying in her bed, she relived again and again every moment she had spent with him, having already been cross-examined by Melpo. Her cousin spent that night at their house, and as soon as they'd closed the door to Smaragda's room, she began to bombard her with questions.

"Oof!" Smaragda protested at one point. "I've told you everything. What else do you want to know?"

"Will you see him again? Tell me and I swear I won't ask you anything else!"

"He asked me to meet him in the National Garden tomorrow the afternoon."

"Holy Virgin! And how will you go? What will you say to your parents?"

"You told me you wouldn't ask me anything else, and now you've asked me two questions."

"They're very important, though. Tell them you're going to the movies with Kiki," the girl suggested.

"What if they ask us what movie we're seeing?"

"Sheesh! Are you going to let that get in your way? Tell them you're going to see *Lieutenant Natasha* again."

Nobody questioned her choice. The film was a hit, and some people had seen it two or three times. Permission was given without too many questions, and Smaragda, her heart beating so loudly she thought it would burst out of her chest, ran to meet Simos. She found him waiting with a rose in his hand. Her heart stopped at that moment, in that hour they spent together, walking and talking about everything and nothing. It seemed so natural when he bent to kiss her, and she responded eagerly. She knew that she was completely in love.

Stolen meetings, secret kisses—they floated on a cloud. Melpo was the only person who knew everything, every detail, and she sighed, hoping that she too would soon experience a love as romantic as her cousin's. She noticed how Smaragda glowed, the permanent smile giving her an almost angelic look.

But as fate would have it, her smile would fade, as her family's fortune took a turn. Everything began when Melpo suddenly fainted. The doctors were clear: there was no hope for the fifteen-year-old. Everyone froze. The only person who never accepted it was her father. Nestor turned the world upside down until he discovered a Swiss doctor who had performed miracles in similar cases. He took his wife and daughter, and they left Greece. Chrysafenia was immensely grateful to Pericles, who, as soon as he found out about it, used all his contacts to get the papers they needed to travel immediately.

Smaragda was left without her beloved cousin, and the agony she felt about her fate brought her even closer to Simos, who did everything he could to give her courage.

"I can't believe it," she said again and again, crying in his arms.

"Sweetheart, don't cry," he whispered. "You'll see—everything will go well, and Melpo will come back to us strong and healthy. I asked about this doctor. If anyone can cure her, it's him, Smaragda. Don't lose your courage! Melpo *will* come back to us."

He kissed away her tears and held her tightly. And Smaragda nestled into his arms and took strength from him and from the stolen hours they spent together, sometimes in the National Garden, and sometimes on long outings to Kifissia. Simos drove; his car had become the nest that held them safely inside, protecting from prying eyes a love that grew stronger every day. They began to make plans for their future. Following the family tradition, he planned to expand the business and open another store in Patission, with his family's blessing; they were proud to have an heir worthy of the Kouyoumdzis name. Smaragda had decided she would take the exams to become a teacher, and the two pictured their life together in beautiful colors.

CHAPTER 14

Kypseli, 2016

"What do you mean, that's all you know?" I said in horror.

"Didn't I tell you I went to Switzerland? When I left, your mother was happy and in love."

"Yes, but to end up married to my father, she must not have stayed with Simos. Do you think that the families got in the way for a third time?"

"I don't know. I never heard a word from anyone."

"Just imagine, though. Three generations of women fell in love with a Kouyoumdzis man and didn't manage to marry him. What sort of curse is that? And to think that, to separate my grandmother from Vassilis, they were forced to uproot themselves from Constantinople. And yet their children found each other in Athens!"

"My girl, sometimes you meet your fate on the road you took to avoid it."

"And now? How will I find out what happened to my mother? Why did she separate from Simos, and more importantly, why did she marry a monster?"

Neither of us had an answer, and right then, the doorbell rang.

"If it's Aunt Hecuba again, I'll curse her even worse this time!" I declared.

Irritated, I ran and pressed the buzzer for the front door, but when I stood at the top of the stairs, I saw not my aunt but a man who looked like Saint Nicholas! Tall, with a small paunch, snowy-white hair worn long like his mustache, and a neatly kept beard. He reached the top of the stairs where I was waiting for him, wheezing but smiling politely as the saint might be expected to. He looked at me kindly from behind his glasses, his sweet brown eyes crowned by white eyebrows.

"Mrs. Fenia Karapanos?" His voice was in perfect harmony with the man I took him for—deep and cultivated.

"Yes?"

"My name is Paschalis Leontiadis . . . I'm Melpo's husband."

A cry of pleasure escaped me, and only my age prevented me from falling into his arms to welcome him. I confined myself to squeezing his hand and taking him into the living room where Melpo was waiting, not at all surprised.

"Right on time!" she said to him cheerfully.

"You knew he was coming?"

"I asked him to. I sent a text message. Since you wanted to hear the rest of the story, I thought it should happen gradually. So, this is your uncle Paschalis."

We sat in the small office, and in a little while, I called Karim in. I explained to the newcomer about my young Syrian friend, and Paschalis grinned.

"It runs in the family," he declared.

"What my husband means," Melpo intervened, "is that you, like I, have a tendency to collect abandoned souls."

Karim seemed to like my uncle and aunt, and he offered us his famous coffee. The whole time we were enjoying it, speaking of things large and small, I had the opportunity to observe the couple opposite me. So well matched and so close. Still flirting, with love in their eyes—the warmth between them seemed to envelop me too.

"So?" Paschalis asked at one point. "What happened with the story? Did she tell you everything?"

"I shared all I knew," Melpo admitted. "Unfortunately, I don't know the most important part that concerns her mother."

"Right. As soon as your cousin met Simos, you got sick and left."

"I see you're well informed," I teased him.

"Indeed! Melpo has told me the whole story in as much detail as she has you. I won't hide the fact that, to please her, I tried to milk some information from my father-in-law, Nestor, but I was met with a wall of silence."

"But why, for God's sake?" I objected. "Is the secret they were hiding so great? What happened? Why did my mother marry Renos?"

I noticed the glance between the couple, as Melpo appeared to communicate something to her husband.

I lit a cigarette in the silence that followed. The album was in front of me on the table. My eyes ran over the faces I knew now from Melpo's stories. Nestor and Yvonne with Melpo as a baby, and beside them, Grandmother Chrysafenia with my grandfather and their children and—I sat up and looked harder at the photograph.

"Melpo!" I said, a little louder than necessary, and the woman opposite me jumped.

"What's the matter, dear?"

"Look!" My finger pointed to a woman she had told me nothing about. "Do you know her?" I asked. "Who is she?"

Melpo approached and put on her glasses to see better. Her face lit up.

"That's Kali!"

"Who?"

"Kali was her name. She was with them almost from the first day of Pericles's marriage to your grandmother. She came from a village near Ioannina, took a position with them as a young girl, and stayed to the end. When everyone left your grandfather by himself, she stayed to look after him. She never married."

"And where is she now?"

"How should I know?"

"We have to find out, Melpo. She must know everything, especially what happened to my mother."

"You're right," my aunt agreed with enthusiasm. "But where would we find her?"

"How old would she be now?"

"Nearly eighty."

"Do we know her last name?" asked Paschalis.

"No," Melpo admitted sadly. "A dead end."

"In my life, the dead ends are sometimes the way forward," I observed, and stood up to get my phone.

In a little while, I was speaking to my grandfather's lawyer. I had reason to smile at what he told me, which I conveyed to my companions as soon as I ended the call.

"Well, luck is on our side. Mrs. Kali is fine, given her age. When my grandfather died, he left her enough money to ensure her residence at a retirement home in Holargos. The lawyer's sending me the address."

Right then, my cell phone made a noise, informing me that the message had already arrived.

My legs trembled when I crossed the threshold of the retirement home. I didn't know what to expect there. I imagined a scene of abandonment quite contrary to reality. The surroundings were pleasant, music was playing, and voices could be heard singing. Melpo was beside me again—she said she wouldn't leave me alone until I found the explanation I was looking for. A fashionably dressed woman about my age appeared.

"Good morning," she welcomed us. "My name is Despina Karolou. How can I help you?"

"I understand," I began, "that one of your residents looked after my grandfather until he died. To be honest, I only recently found out about my family. I was in Germany; you see, I grew up there. So, I want to speak to Mrs. Kali. I hope she can—that she's in a position to—"

"Kali?" asked Mrs. Karolou warmly. "Kali is our heart and soul! As we speak, she's rehearsing with the chorus! Head into the lounge, and I'll bring her to you, assuming she'll take a break from singing."

We stepped into a large room, very bright and cool. From the balcony door we emerged onto a veranda that looked out on a well-kept garden. Old people sat at tables and on comfortable chairs, some reading, others playing cards, while a group of women had gathered to talk as their hands busied themselves with crochet needles. Melpo and I chose a table a little apart from the others and sat down to wait.

A woman approached a short time later, and we looked at her in surprise, not knowing what to say.

"Why are you looking at me like that?" she asked. Her voice was strong and clear. "You interrupted my rehearsal. Who are you, and what do you want?"

Kali Grigoriadi may have been over eighty, but she radiated the liveliness and energy of a woman half her age. Her white hair was well kept, and her dark eyes sparkled. I noticed that, besides her lips, her nails were painted and not particularly short. She wasn't very tall, nor very thin; she was wearing a colorful floral-print dress and flat shoes. I coughed drily to clear my voice, and I tried to begin, but I choked a little and started really coughing until my eyes watered. Melpo patted me uneasily on back, and Kali got up and, with surprising agility, brought me a glass of water.

"Are you all right?" she asked. "What happened, girl? Did I frighten you?"

"No, it's not your fault," I hastened to reassure her. "Although I imagined you very differently."

"Like what? A wreck? I chose to come here not because I couldn't look after myself, but so I could have the luxury of spending my last days looking after other people. You see, all my life I was a servant."

"Yes, you lived in the house of Pericles Sekeris," I said to her, smiling.

"How do you know him?" she asked suspiciously, and for the first time, she turned to Melpo. Something stirred in the depths of her eyes. "Just a minute!" she cried out. "You remind me of someone."

"I'm Melpo," she said. "Chrysafenia Sekeris's niece."

"But of course! How are you, my girl? I remember you as a little thing running to play with the children. You woke up the neighborhood with your shouting." She turned to me. "And you also remind me of someone."

"I'm Fenia—Chrysafenia. That's what my mother, Smaragda Sekeris, named me."

Now her reaction was different. The old lady opened her mouth wide, and her eyes shone as tears came to them. She stood up, obliging me to do the same, and hugged me tightly.

"My little one!" she kept saying as she kissed me. "It seems like only yesterday your mother was born. I took her in my arms for a while to give your poor grandmother a rest; with four children, she didn't have a moment to breathe. Your mother was such a sweet baby! And such a sweet child later on!"

"That's why I came, Mrs. Kali. To ask you about my mother."

The woman let me go, and we both sat down again. She was sad now.

"Unlucky, my little one. An unlucky baby."

"Did you know my father?"

"Renos? Of course! I was part of their wedding."

"You?"

"Yes, I swear to God. The three of us went to the church, and I exchanged their crowns. Smaragda was already pregnant with you."

"Mrs. Kali, I don't understand. My mother loved someone else. How did she end up with Renos? What happened? You're the only person who can help me."

"I'll tell you what I know, my child, but don't imagine that it's very much. I was a servant in the house. They didn't involve me in everything. I arranged your mother's marriage because your grandmother asked me to."

"My grandmother? Now I'm really confused!"

"Wait. Let's start from the beginning."

CHAPTER 15

Athens, 1971

It took Smaragda a long time to find the courage to cross the threshold of the house where he was waiting for her. She walked twice around the block, scanning for someone who might recognize her. Pointless. The people in the street passed her by without giving her a second glance, lost in their own problems.

She took a deep breath and plunged into the apartment building on Lachanas Street, very close to her own house. On the second floor, Simos was waiting with his heart beating in the same rhythm. She went upstairs and arrived out of breath, nearly bursting with anticipation and shame. There was no other way, though. For months now, the parks, the squares, and the dark corners of Athens had become familiar to them. But the summer had passed, and the first rains had forced them to find a roof for themselves and their love, one close to her house, so they could meet there whenever she managed to get away.

Melpo's illness meant that Smaragda's supervision was much more relaxed. Her mother was inconsolable over her niece's cancer; she often ran to her brother's house to look after him and cook for him since his wife was with their daughter. Also, Smaragda's friend Persa, at whose house the couple had met, was always ready to cover for her. So, Simos borrowed a friend's apartment. The young man pretended to be in school, but in fact he partied happily. Now and then he took a course, so his parents calmly continued to support him. As soon as he learned about Simos's love and the favor he was asking, he agreed with a knowing smile.

"Petros, don't smirk at me like that," Simos said sharply. "And get your mind out of the gutter. The girl is young and I love her."

"Did I say you hated her? Love is what gets this business started!" Petros insisted, winking at him.

"There's no business! We just don't have a place to meet now that it's getting colder."

"OK, friend, you don't have to make excuses to me. Am I her brother or her father? Take the keys now, and do your business!"

Simos huffed angrily, but he had no choice. He snatched the keys and comforted himself with the thought that at least he had no indecent intentions. But when he saw her standing on the threshold, excited and panting with her eyes full of love . . .

Smaragda gave herself trustingly to him. Her lips met his tenderly, as usual, but her body trembled, and he didn't understand how the kiss became deeper, how his hands undid her thin blouse, how he found himself kissing her madly and she kept letting him and at the same time pulling him to her.

There was no embarrassment or regret. Everything seemed natural to Smaragda, and a smile soon lifted the corners of her lips. He continued to hold her in his arms and scattered countless kisses on her face and hair.

"You're mine now," he whispered to her, and she answered with a knowing laugh.

"And you're mine!" Smaragda concluded.

"Ask whatever you want from me, and I'll do it. This moment!" he went on in a voice filled with the intensity of the happiness he felt.

"I want you to love me," she said to him seriously. "Just that."

"Only that? It's the easiest thing," he whispered, disappointed.

"You're wrong. That's the hardest thing, because I want it to last forever," came her answer, and he held her in his arms again.

"Forever, my darling. For a lifetime and beyond that!" he assured her. "Nobody will separate us."

She watched the girl go into the apartment building. She waited patiently on the opposite sidewalk. More than an hour passed. And instead of coming out by herself, she came out with him. They shamelessly kissed on the street, and then they parted. She felt something bitter filling her whole mouth and realized it was her saliva. It was impossible to swallow it, so she spat on the dirty ground. She trembled with rage and with something else she didn't want to analyze. *So the little slut has found a boyfriend . . . and he's so handsome . . .*

Her teeth chattering, but not with cold, Hecuba was in no hurry to follow her sister. Anyway, she knew where she was going. Home, of course, to play the good girl, the obedient, oh-so-sweet one. Her stomach was churning crazily from the excitement; she felt sick, but at the same time a fierce joy flooded her like a wave, and her tight mouth widened in a smile. Suddenly she felt much better. Finally she had found a way to exact her revenge. *That brat should never have been born. Now the time has come for her to regret it and all the rest—even that slap I got on account of her, before that silly party. He must have been there, and that's why she wanted to go by herself.*

She walked back to the house much calmer than she'd left it. Now she had to make sure the doves had a true love nest and that it wasn't some chance event. In the days that followed, Smaragda rushed unawares to the little apartment to meet her lover and her happiness while Hecuba waited on the sidewalk, scheming. Now she could do the damage she had been waiting so long to do. She had no doubts.

That last time, as soon as Smaragda had disappeared behind the glass doors of the building's entrance, Hecuba ran home, and her joy overflowed when she saw that, by some devilish coincidence, her father had returned from work early. Luck was on her side. She slammed the door behind her to attract her parents' attention.

"Where are you coming back from like that?" her mother wanted to know.

"What do you care?" Hecuba asked boldly. "Why don't you ask where your other daughter is?"

"Fotini? At the conservatory? Has something happened?" Chrysafenia was anxious now.

"You have another daughter, I believe! Where did she tell you she was going? To the cinema? Maybe to Persa's house?"

"Hecuba, have you got something to say?" Pericles intervened now, frowning.

"Yes, certainly I have something to say, but I don't know if you'll be able to bear hearing it!" she lashed out nastily. "Because your young, spoiled daughter is in an apartment with her boyfriend. What they're doing there, I think you can imagine!"

White in the face, Chrysafenia jumped up. Pericles did so at the same moment.

"You're telling lies!" her mother scolded her.

"Me? What reason do I have? But if you don't believe me, come and see them with your own eyes walking downstairs in each other's arms and kissing, after—Lord knows what they were doing. Come see for yourself, if you dare!"

They followed her.

Smaragda hadn't even managed to step onto the sidewalk when she heard her father's voice: "Smaragda!"

She staggered, and if Simos hadn't been holding her around the waist, she would have collapsed on the ground. She raised her eyes, and all the blood drained from her face as she saw her father, mother, and sister. She looked at Hecuba reproachfully. *Why, Judas? For how many pieces of silver did you sell me?* But she knew there was no reward for the betrayal. Only the satisfaction it brought Hecuba's nasty spirit. She turned to face her father.

"Yes, Father," she answered him calmly.

"What are you doing here and with your arms around a man?"

He approached her, and the sound of the slap echoed and fled down the street as she would have liked to. Beside her, Simos, who had been caught off guard, recovered, and his body stiffened. He pulled her behind him to protect her from her father's fury.

"Mr. Sekeris, please."

"Step aside, you!" Pericles roared.

Chrysafenia stepped between them. "Pericles! Please! We're in the middle of the street! We're becoming a spectacle."

"Mr. Sekeris," Simos spoke up. "I understand your anger, but I'm an honorable man, and I love your daughter. Smaragda will be my wife."

They were all speechless after this last declaration. Pericles looked more softly at the young man in front of him.

"If you had the intention of asking for my daughter, why didn't you come to speak to me like an honorable man instead of taking her to some little apartment like a prostitute? Why didn't you respect her?"

"You're completely right," Simos said, "but please don't let my irresponsible behavior be an impediment to our marriage."

"Wait a minute, young man—you're getting ahead of yourself. I don't even know who you are, what your name is, what work you do, and here, in the middle of the street, you want me to give my approval to a proposal of marriage?"

"And again, my behavior was unforgivable," Simos apologized. "But the circumstances got in the way of the usual procedure," he said, and a timid smile came to his lips. "My name is Simos Kouyoumdzis, and I'm from an old Constantinople family. My father, Vassilis Kouyoumdzis, brought us all here after the troubles of September 1955. We have a store on Ermou Street, and we're opening another on Patission."

As Simos spoke, he saw Pericles and Chrysafenia looking at each other as if they had been struck by lightning, especially the mother. Her look was filled with something the young man couldn't explain.

"Are you Vassilis's son?" he heard the woman ask.

"Yes, madam," he answered in surprise. "Do you know my father?"

"And your grandfather, Simeon. And your grandmother . . . ," added Chrysafenia, and suddenly her expression became bitter.

"Unbelievable!" Simos exclaimed. "So you know the family I come from." He turned to Pericles now with more self-assurance. "Mr. Sekeris, will you permit me to speak to my parents and come to officially ask for your daughter?"

Simos felt Smaragda trembling behind him and was trying to take her hand to give her courage, when he heard Pericles say, "You have my permission to speak to your parents. Whether they'll come to ask for my daughter is another story!"

"I don't understand you," Simos said, frowning.

"When you speak to your parents, you'll understand," said Chrysafenia. She turned to her husband and said, "Pericles, let's go home, please."

He nodded, angry and stiff. "Smaragda! Come with us, now!"

Without another word, he began walking with his wife beside him. Hecuba followed with her gaze lowered, and Smaragda trailed even farther back. She glanced timidly once more at Simos, who remained rooted in place on the sidewalk.

Nobody exchanged a word the whole time they walked home, deep in thought. Despite herself, Smaragda was weaving dreams. In the end, Hecuba had given her an unexpected gift, her evil plans backfiring, and she must not have been very happy about it. Smaragda wanted to laugh, but she resisted. Even from a distance she could feel her sister's anger, the storm of her unsatisfied soul.

But even Smaragda couldn't imagine the scope of the tempest that now raged in Hecuba's mind. Even in her worst nightmares, she hadn't expected this. *Instead of the little slut getting a real beating, she'll be engaged to a man only I am worthy of!* She seethed at the thought that she had brought about a happy ending instead of the destruction of her opponent.

Pericles walked steadily, without bothering to check whether the three women of his family were following him. He had never forgotten his wife's story, the way she had revealed it to him that first night when a cold had kept Nestor in bed and given him the opportunity to make his move. Nor had her words been forgotten: *"I don't think Vassilis will ever leave my heart."* So what if the girl had gone on then to say she had followed her mother's advice and not cried about a lost paradise. What she said made his ears buzz. *"I don't think Vassilis will ever leave my heart . . ."* The words rang like a bell, again and again. Chrysafenia had never given him the right to doubt her, but deep down, he knew that she had never loved him as much as the man who might soon be his daughter's father-in-law.

Chrysafenia tried to match her steps to her husband's furious pace. She cursed the hour when she had told him not just the facts but also the names. She was so anxious about his reaction that she couldn't be happy about what was now going to happen: after two generations of heartbreak, the third would unite the two families. She wanted to take her husband by the hand, stop him, and say a few words that might calm his unnecessary storm. To explain to him that, after so many years, everything had been forgotten, that she felt nothing but tenderness for her youth, and no love for Vassilis. Perhaps she had never loved her husband as he may have wanted, but she no longer loved her adolescent dream.

They all sighed as they entered the house. Hecuba hurried to shut herself in her room, aching from disappointment. Smaragda again tried to tell her parents something, but her father didn't allow her. He sent her to her room, having first told her that from now on, even when she went to school, she would be accompanied by Kali, who would act as her bodyguard. The couple remained alone, and Chrysafenia was determined to make peace with her distant past.

"I want to know what you're thinking," she told her husband.

Pericles didn't hurry to answer her. First he poured himself a drink and lit a cigarette. He looked at her through the cloud of smoke that came between them, then sat in his favorite armchair.

"If you were in my place, what would you think?"

"At this moment, the only thing I want is for Smaragda to marry, given the situation," she answered in a steady voice. "It's probable that the young man didn't stop at hugs and kisses. She must marry!"

"And you'll get to see your great love again," he said ironically.

Chrysafenia went and sat opposite him. She crossed her arms and met his gaze calmly. "Pericles, you know how old I am?"

"What's that got to do with it? You're forty-one."

"Correct. And when I met and fell in love with Vassilis, I was just seventeen. Since then, twenty whole years have passed, as well as a marriage and four children. Do you understand how silly what you're saying sounds? What do you imagine, then? That, as the bride's mother, my only concern would be falling into the arms of her father-in-law?"

The scene she described was vivid, and indeed, it seemed silly to him too. He took a big gulp of his drink before he looked at her again. "I didn't say that," he said, somewhat mollified.

"Thank God!" Chrysafenia exclaimed. "You've come back to your senses."

"Admit, though, that you were upset when you heard who the young man was."

"Did I deny it? However you look at it, that the women of my family have insisted on falling in love with Kouyoumdzis men is a little strange. It's some kind of destiny. What can I say?" Chrysafenia concluded, frowning now.

"So you know my next question: What's going to happen now? Because destiny, as you called it, hasn't allowed these two families to unite. When that—what's his name? Ah, yes, Simos—when he speaks to his parents, and tells them who he's in love with, do you really think they'll accept?"

"Unlikely, given that his grandmother Roza is still alive, from what I gather."

"And how do you know that?" asked Pericles, suspiciously.

Chrysafenia huffed impatiently. "Oh, Pericles! I've known for years that Vassilis was in Greece. Since he built the jewelry store on Ermou Street. I've never even gone past the store. I didn't want to run into him. It wouldn't have been right. But your sister-in-law Lizeta is a customer, and without knowing anything, she told me about them because she really likes them—both Vassilis and his wife, Lefkothea."

"His wife?"

"Yes, Pericles. He didn't make Simos by himself! The man is married with three sons. Lizeta has met his mother, Roza, too. And it's Roza who turned the world upside down so I wouldn't marry Vassilis. But there's something else you don't know."

His eyes filled with horror.

"You're on the wrong track again," she chided. "What you don't know because I didn't want to tell you is that my mother loved Vassilis's father and they wanted to marry, but his parents rejected her. Three generations, Pericles!"

"It's not possible! Do you mean to tell me that my mother-in-law—"

"Yes. Do you understand now? Three generations, Pericles! Three!"

Silence fell between the couple for a while. Pericles needed another drink, and after the first sip, he murmured, "Unbelievable!"

"Perhaps now you can understand why I was so shocked before and why I'm anxious now. This union isn't lucky for us. What are they going to say when they hear who their son wants to marry?"

After the encounter outside the apartment building, Simos didn't go straight home. He needed to walk and to put his thoughts in order. He loved Smaragda without a doubt, and what he'd told her father was true. He wanted to marry her, despite his young age. However, the papers for his military service had arrived. He would have to serve in the army, and that duty would keep him far away for two whole years. With the help of his father and his contacts, he'd managed to delay it for a while, but he couldn't put it off indefinitely.

It was dark when he returned home, and the family had just sat down for their usual evening meal. They may have left Constantinople years ago, but they observed its ethics and customs faithfully. It was as if his parents, when they left, had packed the city in their hearts and taken it with them. As soon as they'd arrived in Athens, they opened the box that held their lost homeland and built it again unchanged. He took his seat, apologizing for his lateness, and tried to show he was eating while his thoughts turned to all the obstacles he had to overcome. He heard his family exchanging the news of the day, but their voices reached him as if from a distance. He was in a hurry to shut himself in his room, to think in peace, to make his decision, but more importantly, to figure out how to speak to his father.

A shy knock on the door came a few minutes after he had finally gone to his room. When he opened the door, his grandmother appeared, and as always, without asking him, she came confidently into his room. Taking him by the hand, she sat down beside him on his bed.

"What's the matter with my treasure tonight?" she asked, and her hand stroked his hair affectionately. "Why so unhappy?"

He looked at her tenderly and smiled. His grandmother never hid the fact that her firstborn grandchild was her weakness. Not that she deprived his brothers of her affection, but everyone understood that the relationship between Roza and Simos was different.

"Won't you tell me?" she insisted. "You tell me everything. And for you to keep your mouth shut—it must be a big love affair. Am I right?"

"Are you ever wrong?" Simos teased.

"Are you making fun of your grandmother? Shame on you," she said, pretending to be angry. "Enough now, tell me what happened! You've been in the clouds for so long, but it seems as if something went wrong tonight."

Simos looked at his grandmother and sighed. "Yes, Grandmother. I'm in love with a girl."

"Then what were you doing giving me a terrible fright?" she scolded him. "Why are you like this? Is there anything more beautiful than love?"

"You don't understand, Grandmother. She's not just any girl; she's the one I want to marry!"

"Wait a minute, my boy," she said, raising her voice. "You're still very young."

"And she's even younger. But today her father caught us."

"Where did he catch you?" She brought her hand to her mouth to stifle a cry. "Did you interfere with the girl? How young?"

"Seventeen."

"A minor!"

"But I wasn't deceiving her, Grandmother. I want to marry her. And I told her father."

"Wait, young pasha. Let's get a few things straight, because you've told me everything upside down. You love a girl, and in fact, you want her to be your wife."

Simos smiled at his grandmother's roundabout way of saying things.

"Now," she said to him sharply, "pull yourself together and tell me what happened. So, the father caught you in the act. How and where?"

He explained what had happened, and with every word, his grandmother became more agitated until she finally jumped up.

"Ah, you little scoundrel!" she burst out at last and began pacing the room. "Did we teach you to behave like that? Taking a girl to an apartment and getting up to no good. Aren't there any brothels in this town for you to go to? Do you know what a crime you've committed? What harm did the girl do to you for you to shame her?"

"Please, not so loud," Simos complained. "You want me to trust you, and now you're going to announce it to the whole house."

His grandmother sat down again beside him. "OK. I won't shout. And since you're going to marry her—"

"You see?"

"Then why are you so upset? You love her and you'll marry her—the end!"

"Because I have to do my military service for two years. How can I tell Father I'm getting married?"

"That, my boy, you should have thought about a little earlier," she said, surprising him. "But the way things happened, there's no other course but marriage. If you'd respected the girl, we could have given our approval, and you could have been engaged and married as soon as you finished with the army."

"But am I supposed to marry her before I go and leave her with her parents?"

"Who told you such a thing? You'll marry her and bring her to your parents until you come back. That's the way things are done. Now tell me, boy, is she beautiful?"

His expression sweetened at the memory of his beloved, his lips were about to smile again, and his grandmother started laughing.

"Aha! Mush! You flirt! Eh, a strapping young man like you—would you choose an ugly one?"

"Why are you making fun of me?" Simos asked angrily.

"I'm joking, silly boy who plays the tough guy. So, tell me, what's her name?"

"Smaragda. And Grandma, you must know them. Her mother is from Constantinople."

From his first words, Roza's face began to freeze, and by his last it had turned to stone.

"What's her mother's name?"

"Chrysafenia Sekeris."

Roza felt her whole body go numb.

"Her grandfather is also from Constantinople," Simos went on blithely. "His name is Fotis Ververis, and he's a doctor," Simos concluded enthusiastically.

He stopped speaking, and the heavy silence that fell surprised him. He looked at his grandmother, who was staring into space.

"Grandma? What's the matter?" he asked, putting his arms around her shoulders and shaking her lightly.

"Kismet" was all she said.

"But do you know the family or not?"

"Very well, yes."

"Aren't they good people?" When the woman didn't answer, he became irritated. He stood up. "Now who's frightening whom? Why won't you talk to me?"

"Sit down, my dear, and listen to a story you need to hear," she answered with a heavy sigh.

Simos obeyed, and in a short time he had learned a truth that seemed like a fairy tale. Finally, he too was motionless, almost turned to stone as his grandmother had been a little while before.

"Do you understand now?" she said to him gently.

"So that's why her father said I could speak to my parents, but whether they would come and ask for her was another matter."

"That's why," Roza admitted.

"And what happens now, Grandma?" Simos asked, trying to recover. "From what I understand, nothing really tragic has gone on between the two families. Why should the past stand in the way of our love? It's strange, sure, but the fact that it's the third time history has repeated says something. The time has come to put an end to meaningless differences. Isn't it?"

Silence.

Anxious, he asked for reassurance: "Do you think Father will have objections? Or you?"

She didn't answer him.

Smaragda got up late that day and, feeling irritable, took it out on her husband, who seemed slow to drink his coffee and leave. Fotis Ververis, at seventy-three, still practiced his profession tirelessly. For years he had worked at a private clinic, and in the afternoons he could always be found there.

"All right, my dear, finish, and off you go to work!" she said, tapping her foot impatiently.

"Hold on, for God's sake!" he objected. "Are you taking that coffee from under my nose? What sort of rush is this so early in the morning?"

"It's nearly noon, husband. How on earth did I sleep so late? I have so many things to do. The holidays are coming, the house needs a thorough cleaning, the curtains need washing—how will I manage?"

"Sweetheart, don't you have Marikaki to help you?"

"Now you'll really annoy me, Fotis. She should be working while the housewife sleeps? Off with you now, my dear, and go with the Virgin's prayer so I can do my work. You'll see what I have for you to eat at lunchtime."

She nearly pushed him out of the house, making the sign of the cross behind his back. She rolled up her sleeves, but didn't manage to start work before the doorbell rang again.

"Ah, Fotis!" she muttered. "What have you forgotten this time?"

But the words became lodged in her throat. Before her stood not her husband, but Roza.

"Hello, Smaragda," she said calmly, dispelling any suspicion that she was a ghost.

"What are you doing here?" Smaragda asked.

"Do I have to tell you on the doorstep? Won't you let me into your house?"

"I still haven't forgotten the last time I let you in! Have you come to insult me again after all these years?"

The visitor took a step forward to make it clear that she would come in anyway. Smaragda was forced to stand aside. Roza went into the living room and sat down in an armchair.

"I see you've made yourself comfortable," Smaragda said sarcastically.

"Sit down too, Smaragda. You and I have something to talk about."

"I don't know if we have anything to say to each other after so many years. Have you come to tell me how much poison you'll throw at us again? Wasn't it enough that you forced my whole family to leave our country?"

"Whatever you say, you are right," Roza admitted calmly, and Smaragda sat up, disturbed by the reaction.

"Is that all? Roza, are you all right? I want to curse you, and you give me the right?"

"A lot of things have happened since we quarreled," Roza went on sadly. "I lost my husband, as you know."

"Yes, I heard about that, and I was very sorry. And it doesn't matter what you say to me, you should know I wept when I heard he had died."

"I believe it. And I understand."

Smaragda shook her head in confusion. "I feel like I've gone mad. I tell you I wept for Simeon, and you sit calmly and look at me as if you were my friend!"

"Smaragda, I didn't come here to talk about the past. That's lost, as is our city and many of our people."

"So what do we have to talk about?" the woman wondered, but another thought came into her mind, and she burst out: "Don't tell me there's something going on between my daughter and your son! I'll fall like a log at your feet!"

"Mercy, woman!" Roza scolded her. "Are you unhinged?"

"No, but I'm close!"

"It's not your daughter and my son who are involved. It's my grandson and your Smaragda!"

The two women regarded each other. Roza calm, and opposite her a volcano ready to explode. Yet just as the fire began, it ended, leaving Smaragda breathless. The only thing she could do was cross herself.

"Lord Almighty," she added, her voice almost inaudible.

"That's what I said when I heard it from my grandson."

"And you marched right to my house to upset me!" Smaragda said, her voice rising again.

"Is that what you think? I came to tell you that I have no objection to this wedding taking place. And I'll speak to my son to prepare him. It's not a small thing. Years and ages may have passed since then, but it'll be a little hard for him to have a woman he once wanted to marry as an in-law."

"Roza, are you in your right mind?" Smaragda asked.

The other woman smiled bitterly. "Now I am; then I wasn't. I spent my life beside a man I loved with a heart full of poison because he never loved me as much as he loved you. And when our children fell in love, it wasn't the mother who spoke but the wronged woman—my mistake. I had so much evil in me that I set about persecuting you. I wanted to drive you far away. In those days, if I could have driven you from the face of the earth, even that wouldn't have been enough."

"And how did the miracle happen?"

"Before Simeon died, he told me I was wrong. He loved me, but it took him a long time to understand that, and afterward he was ashamed to tell me. We wasted a whole lifetime, Smaragda. And I was to blame then, but I won't make the same mistake now. That's why I came. For us to become friends and close the old accounts. I'm telling you I'll do anything to make this marriage happen. It's our families' destiny."

"Are you telling me the truth?"

"On Simeon's soul!"

They looked at each other again, and simultaneously, they leaned toward each other and found themselves holding hands. Fotis found them like this when he came in. He had forgotten some X-rays and come back to collect them, but he froze when he saw the scene in front of him.

"Have I lived to see this?"

Like naughty schoolgirls, they jumped up and looked at him. Smaragda was the first to speak.

"Come, Fotis, she's here for a good reason today, our . . . in-law." She saw him looking at her as if she was crazy.

"Don't speak, pasha, and we'll tell you everything," she said, leading him toward the visitor.

Chrysafenia woke up with a bad headache, and the atmosphere in the house made it worse. Her oldest daughter wouldn't come out of her room, and the youngest left for school with her eyes scarlet from crying, accompanied, on Pericles's orders, by Kali. Stelios and Fotini were surprised, but they didn't say anything. For the first time after so many years, Chrysafenia thought about going to see Vassilis, not about their own love, but about their children's. Fear held her back. If her husband were to find out she had made such a move, he would certainly react badly, and it would hurt her daughter's chances. In addition, Vassilis must have heard what had happened from his son and made his own decision. Roza was her biggest fear, then and now. She had an ominous feeling, and her headache threatened to dissolve her skull. Her mother's visit took her by surprise—and even more surprising was what she had to say. Every word was a bolt out of the blue, and Chrysafenia's brain was not ready to take it all in.

"And now, my grown-up girl," Smaragda finally said, "roll up your sleeves—we have a wedding!"

"Mother, are you sure? Roza said things like that to you?"

"Well, I haven't gone soft in the head yet! I know what I heard. She'll speak to Vassilis, and that's that! At long last, a Kouyoumdzis will marry a Kantardzis."

"I'll believe it when I see it, Mama. And Vassilis? Will he accept it?"

"Listen to me, Vassilis won't say no. He won't do to his child what was done to him."

"Yes, but there's still the matter of Pericles. You see, I couldn't hold my tongue back when I met him, and he knows—"

"Goodness, my sweet, you too! Should such things be said to our husbands?" Smaragda complained. "What did I tell you all these years? Your husband should know you from the neck down!"

Behind the closed door, Hecuba grew pale as she listened to the two women. Her head swam with scenarios of destruction. She turned around and raced to Smaragda's bedroom. She almost howled with joy when she found the keys that she knew would unlock her sister's secret apartment. She put them in her pocket and snuck out of the house, heading for the locksmith on the next corner. He made the duplicates, and she returned without anyone knowing she'd gone. She'd prepared a plan, but she needed help. Luck was on her side, though. When Smaragda came home, she was full of anxiety. When her parents lay down to rest after the midday meal, Hecuba eavesdropped on her sister's telephone conversation.

"Hi Simos . . . Yes . . . Did you speak to your father? Ah. And what did your grandmother say? Yes, so that means everything is going well. When will you talk to your father, and when will he come? My father won't let me set foot outside the house without a . . . bodyguard. No! Luckily, it's not my sister. I can't even bear to look at her anymore. But Simos, I must see you and talk to you . . . I don't know how, but I'll manage. I'll fall at Kali's feet if I have to. She's a good woman. She'll understand. Not today. Not tomorrow either. The day after . . . I heard my parents are going to visit someone, and I'll find an opportunity. I'll leave with Kali so the traitor won't realize. OK . . . yes, I have the keys.

I'll go in and wait for you, but don't be late because I won't have much time. The day after tomorrow, then. At six. And I love you too . . . if you only knew how much!"

Smaragda hung up the phone, taking every precaution, and Hecuba hid in the shadows again, but now she was smiling. She knew exactly what to do. They would all pay.

Vassilis looked at his mother in shock.

"What did you say, Mama?" His glance moved from her to his son, who was following the conversation as if it didn't concern him.

"You heard me," Roza said sharply. "Simos loves Smaragda, Chrysafenia's daughter. And he wants to marry her. Imagine, one woman finds him, and it has to be her. But will he stay a bachelor? There's no harm, so let it be her."

"Are you trying to make me crazy? How did such a thing happen?"

"Does it take much? They're young, they met, they fell in love."

"Don't you have anything to say?" He turned to his son now.

"Well, seeing as you two are doing the talking, what can I say?" Simos joked, but his smile faded when he saw his father's expression. He became suddenly serious. "Yes, Father, it's like Grandma says. I love Smaragda, and I want to marry her. Also, it's become necessary that I marry her, if you understand." He saw his father raise his eyebrows.

"You've violated her, you mean. And her parents?"

"They know. The next move must be ours."

Simos feared some kind of explosion, but Vassilis, completely calm, lit a cigarette. "Simos, my son, will you leave us alone?"

"But what do you say? Can I marry Smaragda?"

"Simos, do what your father tells you, dear," his grandmother concurred, and the young man hung his head and left.

Mother and son stood opposite each other as if in hand-to-hand combat. Except that their fight had begun many years earlier. Now the time had come for them to end it.

"Aren't you going to say anything, Mama?" said Vassilis.

"What more do you expect me to say?" the woman replied calmly.

"Something like what you told me back then. Where is the mother who raged against me marrying Chrysafenia? What changed now so you have no objections to her daughter?"

"I went to Smaragda, my son. Not the young one, her grandmother. We spoke, and I told her I was sorry for what I did. I think the time has come for me to say the same to you. Whatever happens, this story has to come to an end. You can't quarrel with fate, my son. Tell me now, do you have any objection to the girl?"

"But how can I see Chrysafenia after so many years?"

"You were very young then. It's not the same now. Look at me, Vassilis, my boy. You two didn't get together, but your children are another story. It's destiny."

The family had gathered at the house in Kypseli that evening when Fate revealed what she had written. Chrysafenia and Pericles had returned earlier and discovered that Hecuba was missing, as well as Smaragda and Kali. Another premonition swept over Chrysafenia, who, on the spur of the moment, invited her parents to come for supper. Even on the telephone, her mother could tell that something was wrong. She and her husband arrived a short time later.

"Where are the children?" she asked her daughter, who shook her head and glanced meaningfully at her husband.

Pericles was smoking in front of the fire with a dark look on his face. Again, Stelios and Fotini had caught a whiff of dynamite and disappeared into their rooms, staying there even when their grandmother and grandfather arrived.

"Something's going to happen. I have an awful feeling," Chrysafenia whispered to her mother.

"Enough of that, you," her mother scolded her in the same low voice. "They'll be here any minute, and you'll clear this right up."

"But where are they now, can you tell me? They can't stand each other, yet now they've both gone for a walk with Kali?"

They fell silent as Pericles threw them an angry glance, but in a few moments the front door opened noisily, and Smaragda charged into the room with Kali panting behind her. The girl's eyes were filled with tears, her expression angry.

"So, everyone's here?" she shrieked, on the verge of hysteria. "That's better, I guess, so I don't have to repeat myself. It's over! I don't want to see Simos ever again. The engagement is off!"

Pericles jumped up and approached his daughter. "What did you say?" he hissed between his teeth.

"It's over. What else can I tell you? I don't love him anymore!"

"It's a little late for that," he growled. "When you went off with him to that apartment like a prostitute, you said something else and did something else. Now you'll marry him, and you'll be glad about it."

"I don't want him!" the girl howled, and fresh tears ran down her scarlet cheeks.

Chrysafenia rushed to her daughter. "What happened, girl? It can't be, out of the blue—"

"I don't want him!" Smaragda howled again and buried herself in her mother's arms.

"Kali, where were you? What happened?" asked Chrysafenia.

"I don't know, madam, I swear!" answered the woman, white with agitation.

"Stop the hugging, woman, or you'll all be in trouble here," Pericles shouted. He approached his daughter and shook her until she looked at him. "Where were you tonight? With him? What did he say to you? Tell me!"

A loud slap underlined his words and brought Fotis to his feet. He pulled Pericles off the battlefield to rebuke him.

"Son-in-law, what's all this? I never expected you to raise a hand to your daughter."

"Please, Father, this is my house, and this concerns my honor. And I won't allow my daughter to tarnish it. I have a name and a position in society!"

The older couple exchanged a glance. In one way, their son-in-law was right, and maybe their presence had made things worse.

"Fotis, perhaps we'd better be going," Smaragda said decisively. "The child and her parents can talk."

Despite the pleading look their daughter gave them, they left with their hearts full of agony and their heads besieged by unanswered questions. But behind them, the tension mounted.

"I demand an explanation!" Pericles shouted.

"I have nothing more to tell you," Smaragda insisted. "I don't want Simos, and I won't marry him."

"But why?" her mother intervened. "You loved him and he loved you. What happened to change that so suddenly? Smaragda, dear, you must tell us. We're your parents. You owe us an explanation."

"Leave me in peace!" howled the girl. "I won't give you an explanation."

Chrysafenia's breath caught when she heard her daughter's words. A new slap threw Smaragda to the ground, but instead of withdrawing, she became wilder.

"Whatever you do to me, I won't change my mind. I won't marry him! I don't want him!" she cried out, trembling.

"So, you should have acted like a decent girl. I won't stand being made a fool of!"

"We don't live in the Middle Ages, Father—you can't hit me because I'm not a virgin. It's my life, and I can do what I want."

"Out of my house!" Pericles shouted and managed to hit her again.

"Pericles!" Chrysafenia shouted. "What are you saying to your child?" She tried to calm him. "Please, let's all calm down and talk again tomorrow," she pleaded, coming between them.

Pericles pushed her roughly, furious now, his eyes bloodshot with anger.

"Get out of my way, woman, and I'll kill my daughter tonight!"

He lurched at Smaragda again, who waited, ready for new blows. Her eyes burned, and her lips were split from his punches. She felt her father's hands pushing her toward the front door.

"Out!" he shouted again. "Go away from my house! On the street—that's where you belong! I don't want to ever see you or hear you again! For me, you died tonight!"

"I'd have left in any case. I can't stand you anymore!" she shouted at him, then turned, opened the door, and ran out.

Behind her, Chrysafenia collapsed. She found herself kneeling on the floor and weeping.

"What have you done?" she wailed. "Where will she go? What will she do all alone, the poor thing?"

"It doesn't concern me," Pericles shouted at her, still furious. "Good riddance to her, the slut. And I forbid you to let her back in when she returns. Didn't you hear what she said to me? How she spoke to her father? Like some—I will find out what happened tonight." He remembered Kali, who was still standing petrified at the entrance to the room.

"Come here, you, and tell me this minute where you went!" he shouted and grabbed her by the arm. "Tell me, because otherwise, you'll find yourself on the street too!"

"I don't know, sir!" she began in tears. "She asked me to go with her just down the street. She fell at my feet, and I felt sorry for her. We went to a house. I waited at the entrance because she wouldn't let me come in, and she said she wouldn't be long. She wasn't gone even fifteen minutes, and when she came out she was unrecognizable.

She was crying and hitting herself. Behind her was a young man, very upset too, and he began pleading with her to listen to him. He told her something I couldn't make sense of. He swore he didn't understand what had happened. He told her he loved her. He loved only her—that's what he said. Smaragda hit him and told him she never wanted to see him again, and that he was welcome to the slut he had chosen. After that, we left. She turned around and told him that if he loved her even a little, he should carry that secret to his grave."

"What secret?"

"I don't know. She didn't tell me. I asked her many times, but I couldn't get a word out of her."

"Useless! Get out of my house!" Pericles roared, and pushed her away. He turned with the same fury to his wife. "I'll kill him. He found another girl!"

"But you turned our child out of the house. And she wasn't at fault. Did you hear?"

"You heard the way she spoke to me!"

"What will we do, Pericles?" came her question, full of despair.

"I don't change my mind. A girl who is so cheap as to hide away in an apartment with the first boy who comes along can't be my daughter. And to speak to me that way!"

"Pericles, you may have gone mad, but I'm not following you into this craziness. My child, whatever she does, is my child forever!"

"You have other children."

"How dare you. You threw a seventeen-year-old out because she'd been made a fool of by a bum. Instead of confronting him, demanding he do his duty, you blame her."

"Listen to yourself! Our daughter herself said she wouldn't marry him. How should I make a demand, and from whom?"

"This is no time to talk. Our daughter is walking around all alone in the streets. I'm going to find her, Pericles. You do whatever you want!"

"I forbid you!"

"Did you hear what I said? Do what you want."

Chrysafenia took her coat and disappeared into the darkness to search for her daughter.

The night seemed endless for all of them.

Smaragda felt as if she had been running for an eternity. She didn't even hear the car coming, its brakes screeching madly, nor did she see the driver, who swerved and collided with a tree to avoid hitting the girl who was walking in the middle of the road. The sound of crumpling metal brought her to her senses, and she looked around as if waking from a trance. The car door opened, and the driver climbed out of the vehicle.

"Have you gone crazy, girl?" he shouted as he approached. "You may want to kill yourself, but don't drag me down with you!" Under the pale streetlight, he recognized her. "Smaragda!" he cried.

She squinted at him, racking her brain. She knew him from somewhere, but in her present state, her memory betrayed her.

"I'm Renos, Persa's cousin! What happened to you?"

"I'm sorry," she said so softly that the man could hardly hear her. "Did you get hurt?"

"No. Fortunately, I wasn't speeding; otherwise one of us would have been killed! What happened that you're walking around in the dark as if you were lost?"

Suddenly, her head was on a Ferris wheel at Luna Park, and everything around her was spinning. She fainted at his feet.

"Holy Virgin, what's going on tonight?" he murmured and lifted her in his arms.

He looked around to find a place to put her down, but there was nowhere. He took her to the car and put her in the driver's seat. He tried to bring her around, patting her lightly on the face. The girl opened her eyes, trying to remember the last few minutes.

"Are you all right?" he asked anxiously. "I'll take you to the hospital. You need to see a doctor."

"No," said the girl. "There's nothing wrong with me."

"Then I'll take you home."

"I can't go there. My father kicked me out."

Renos was silent for a moment while he took this in. Fate had thrown into his hands the formerly uppity Miss Sekeris. He'd met her many times at his cousin Persa's house. The relationship was a distant one, but he'd managed to penetrate Persa's fashionable circle. Smaragda had made a big impression on him, but she paid him no attention. Every time he'd tried to approach her, she had pointedly ignored him. When he learned more about her background, he thought that, if she had responded to his flirtation, perhaps he could have married her. With a dowry like hers, his problems would certainly be solved. But Smaragda always treated him like an annoying admirer. And now she had fallen right into his arms. Unexpected luck.

He leaned over her and saw she was crying silently. He stroked her hair tenderly.

"Come," he said, as if he were talking to a child. "Don't be like that—there's a solution for everything."

"You don't know what you're talking about," she whispered through her sobs.

"Does a fight with your father mean the end of the world?" he asked, but the sobs that came as an answer were louder than before. "OK, OK, don't cry anymore. I'm here. I'll take you with me, and tomorrow we'll go together to your parents."

"No! I'm not going back there!" she declared passionately. She looked at him pleadingly. "If you could put me up just for tonight. Until I can figure out what to do next . . ."

Fortunately, the damage to the car was minor enough that it didn't prevent him from driving off, carrying his precious cargo.

As soon as Smaragda had left, Simos went back up to the apartment in a fury. He found Hecuba coolly getting dressed. She looked at him indifferently.

"What did you do?" he shouted at her. "Why?"

"I'm not obliged to answer you," she answered, putting on her jacket.

He grabbed her by the arm and shook her with all his strength. "We're going to your house! Together. And you'll explain your little game to your sister!"

Unperturbed, she broke away from his hands and smoothed her hair.

"Not a chance," she sneered. "And if you dare say something, I'll say you dragged me to your apartment and raped me. Imagine what will happen!"

"Why are you doing this?"

"Because you're not worthy of her."

"What are you saying? I love her."

"And she hates you now because she thinks you were deceiving her. I won, and I advise you to disappear because, if she's spoken to our father, you'll be in big trouble! Pericles Sekeris is not the most coolheaded man in the world. He'll destroy you!"

"And aren't you afraid you'll pay for it too?"

"I'm not afraid of anything. Whatever happens, you can't marry Smaragda now, and that's worth any punishment!"

"You're sick!" The man shuddered.

She didn't grant him an answer. An ironic smile was the last thing he remembered of her before she left with her head high. He remained alone, and his fury abated, dissolving into hopelessness. He felt the walls caving in, the room getting smaller, leaving him no air to breathe. He realized that what Hecuba had said was right. Nothing would be the same now. Smaragda believed that he had duped her and her sister as well. Her parents would think he was warped indeed to have been involved with the two sisters. Whatever he said, nobody would believe him.

Chrysafenia returned home exhausted and with empty hands. She had searched the street, and even dared to go to her daughter's friend Persa's house, but Smaragda had disappeared. The last house where she looked was her mother's, but her daughter hadn't sought shelter even with her grandparents. When she left them, they were very upset.

"I didn't find her," she announced when she returned home. "It's as if the earth opened up and swallowed her."

"You shouldn't have gone looking!"

"Pericles, I don't have the courage to quarrel with you any more tonight. I will find my child, and I'll bring her home. And if you don't like it, you'll have to leave yourself!"

"Do you hear what you're saying?" her husband said angrily. "Why are you driving me out?"

"You drove our daughter away—I'm just paying you back. And if you want to act tough, do it where it's due, don't take it out on the innocent!" She looked around before asking him, "Tell me, did the oldest one come home?"

"Just after you left. She said she was at the cinema and had a terrible headache. She's already in bed. As for what you said, I know my duty, and tomorrow, as soon as God makes the sun come up, I'll do it. I don't need your advice!"

His wife gave him a look full of bitterness and tiredly climbed the stairs. She went to Hecuba's room and found her sleeping deeply. She shut herself in her room, and burning tears fell from her eyes. Without knowing why, she looked for the small metal box that was hidden away in her wardrobe. For the first time in years, she held the tiny gold envelope that Vassilis had once given her in her hands. The pink glow of the lamp on her bedside table fell on the gold letter, making it shine.

"Yet again," she said and put the necklace on. She felt it burning her skin.

Inside the small locket, beside the gold tablet with the words *I love you*, it carried the tears of the third generation too.

When Simos got home, he was white as a sheet. While he was walking back, a sudden squall had come up, but he didn't notice the rain. His head was on fire, ready to burst. He had to speak to his family and then persuade Smaragda that he wasn't responsible for what had happened. His mother was the first to run to him, and behind her, his grandmother.

"Simos!" Lefkothea exclaimed anxiously. "What a state you're in—you'll catch pneumonia!"

"My dear!" his grandmother said, and her eyes filled with tears. "What happened, my boy?"

Without waiting for an answer, they took him by the hand to his room and began to undress him. They rubbed him with a dry towel and cologne and dressed him in warm clothes. Lefkothea ran to make him a hot drink, and Roza watched in surprise as he slumped in her arms and cried. She stroked his head and spoke softly to comfort him. At that moment, his father came into the room.

"What's going on here?" asked Vassilis sternly. "Simos, what's happened?"

"I don't know anymore myself," said Simos, and shamefacedly got up from his grandmother's embrace, wiping his eyes. "It seems like a nightmare."

"Explain, so we can understand."

"I spoke to Smaragda on the phone the day before yesterday. She wanted to meet before we came to ask her parents for her hand."

"Why?"

"I don't know; she wouldn't tell me on the phone. We agreed to meet at the apartment." He paused for a moment as his mother came in with a steaming cup in her hands. "I opened the door to wait for her. Instead of Smaragda, I found her sister stark naked in the bed!"

"What did she say she was doing?" Vassilis asked. "What do you think, son? Do you understand?"

"Before I could ask for an explanation, Smaragda came into the apartment. Just then, Hecuba grabbed me so suddenly that I lost my balance and fell almost on top of her. You can understand what Smaragda saw, and how easy it was for her to misunderstand."

"Christ and the Virgin!" Roza exclaimed. "Didn't you explain to her?"

"I tried. I ran after her and pleaded with her to believe me, but . . ."

"OK, but what business did this sister of hers have in the apartment and moreover in your bed?" Lefkothea asked with the tea growing cold in her hands.

"Hecuba is horribly jealous of Smaragda. She admitted that her aim was to separate me from her sister. But I don't have any evidence, and Smaragda won't believe me. She saw us. How can she deny what her eyes saw? She told me that if I loved her even a little, I wouldn't say a word about all this to anyone. She's probably trying to protect me from her father. Imagine him finding out the story from Hecuba's side! He'd destroy us, and he wouldn't be wrong!"

"But we can't leave things like this!" Roza burst out. "You are innocent, and you must tell the truth. What happens to Hecuba doesn't concern us."

"But Hecuba threatened to say I raped her if I told. Do you understand? Will we go to court now? No matter what happens, there'll be a scandal. They'll drag us all into it!"

Roza approached her son. "The time has come to pay for old sins, my son. My sins. What I did to Chrysafenia in Constantinople has come back to haunt us. I don't mind paying the price for my misdeeds, but you're all paying too!"

She bowed her head and fled the room with a heavy step, her heart beating erratically.

Pericles rang the doorbell of Vassilis Kouyoumdzis's house the next morning, and when the maid led him into the sitting room, he found the entire family there except for the guilty party. Angry, he met the eyes of the man who wasn't only nearly his in-law but also a rival in love. With some difficulty, he stifled his urge to grab Vassilis by the neck and demand an explanation on his daughter's behalf. Their lips were sealed, though, because Simos, who was burning up with fever on the floor above, had asked them not to speak. He would do as Smaragda had asked. He'd take his secret to the grave. Meanwhile, Pericles was getting more and more irritated, and finally he left before he lost his self-control completely. More than anything, he was desperate to avoid a scandal; if he decided to pursue this through legal channels, he couldn't avoid defamation. A silent agreement was made at that moment. Neither Vassilis nor Pericles wanted to continue something that would cost them both their good names.

Back at home, Chrysafenia opened the door and found Renos, who'd taken the initiative to come without telling Smaragda. He explained in a few words how he'd encountered her daughter, and Chrysafenia, relieved, followed him to his place.

At first, Smaragda was angry with Renos for going behind her back, but then she softened and fell weeping piteously in her mother's arms. Chrysafenia joined her tears to those of her daughter. She let her cry as long as she needed to and then asked Renos to leave them alone to talk.

"And now I want the whole truth, Smaragda!" she said to her intently. "Pull yourself together, and tell me what happened yesterday!"

"I can't tell you, Mama. It's better if you leave me. Go now, and I'll make my own way from here on," she whispered, ready to cry again.

"My girl, I can't leave you. I can't! I have to find out. What happened with Simos in the apartment? Kali—from what I understand, he was with another girl?"

Smaragda bowed her head, ready to cry again. "Leave me, Mother," she insisted.

"No, I won't. You'll tell me! Was he with someone else?"

"He was with Hecuba!" she shouted. "Are you happy? I went into the apartment and found Hecuba naked in the bed with him on top of her! What else do you want me to tell you?"

Chrysafenia brought her hand to her heart as if she'd been stabbed. "Smaragda, what are you saying?"

"The bastard was carrying on with both of us! Hecuba told me he loved her and was going to marry her!"

"But that's not reasonable, my dear. He didn't seem like that sort of person when I met him. The love in his eyes couldn't have been false. Anyway, wouldn't your sister have said something at that moment?"

"Maybe that's why she betrayed us to Father. She wanted him for herself."

"Yes, but your father would never have given his approval. She would have undermined her own plans."

"Do you expect logic from her, Mama? Hecuba has always been jealous of me, and I never knew the reason why."

"This doesn't add up, Smaragda. If you were supposed to meet him, why would your sister be there at the same time?"

"Maybe she did it to hurt me. Maybe they didn't calculate the time well. I don't know and it doesn't matter. The image of them in the bed will never leave my mind. Hecuba can have him, and good luck to her! I'm finished with him, but—"

The girl bit her lips so savagely that her mother thought they'd start bleeding.

"Smaragda, what else is happening, my child? Tell me so I can help."

"I can't, Mama. I can't bear to tell you."

The lowered eyes, the way she held her body, the trembling . . . Chrysafenia looked at her daughter, and with an unsteady voice she spoke to her again.

"My girl, look at me, please. Are you pregnant?"

Smaragda's positive reply took her breath away. For a second, she thought she would faint. A buzzing filled her ears, numbing her brain. She took deep breaths to recover.

Outside the door, with his ear glued to the wood, Renos didn't miss a word. Everything would be easy for him from now on.

Simos welcomed his father into his room the next day with eyes almost black from anguish. The fever had left him, but he felt exhausted.

"What happened, Father?" he asked as soon as Vassilis sat down opposite him. "Did Sekeris come?"

"Yes, yesterday evening. I didn't say anything, as you asked me, and he seems to have no idea what happened, just that you were with someone else and his daughter doesn't ever want to see you again."

"As I expected," Simos murmured sadly.

"Naturally, after what happened between you and his daughter, he should have demanded satisfaction and restitution, but the girl doesn't want you anymore. From what I understood, he doesn't intend to pursue a legal case because, like me, he doesn't want a scandal. But what will you do? Will you give her up so easily? You love her, don't you?"

"Sometimes, Father, love isn't enough. Fate has to be on your side."

"You're telling me this?" Vassilis sighed bitterly.

"Yes, of course. I forgot. Grandmother told me you once loved Mrs. Sekeris—her mother—and before that, Grandpa loved her grandmother."

"Yes. But it seems that, in the end, our two families should never have met."

"Did you really love her?"

"Very much. But I was young, like you are now. All the obstacles seemed impossible to overcome. I gave up. And there was only a gold letter to remind her of that love."

In answer to his son's silent question, he explained the history of the jewel his father had designed for the elder Smaragda, and which he himself had made for Chrysafenia. Simos looked at him as if he were lost.

"And where is the letter now?" he wanted to know.

"Chrysafenia must have kept it. Perhaps she should have given it to her daughter. It brought no luck to either of them."

"And Mama?" the question came now. "Don't you love my mother?"

"Very much, but differently. I was able to lose myself in her arms. The pain faded. And I have never regretted marrying her. I'll say the same to you too. You're young, Simos, with your whole life in front of you. One day, a girl will appear for you, and you'll forget this love that wasn't your luck to live and grow with."

"Never!" Simos answered passionately. "Do you hear me? I'll never forget her. And the way we separated will be a thorn in my side forever. I looked so disgusting in her eyes."

"I understand you, my boy. But the best thing you can do now is to leave and do your military service. You'll be away for two years, and that will help you forget and go on with your life. Listen to me—I know something about this."

Hecuba, certain her secret was secure, didn't expect to see her mother charge into her room. Chrysafenia grabbed her, and before the girl could object, she'd already managed to give her a couple of hard slaps to the face. With one hand, she held her fast, and with the other, she hit her wherever she could. Hecuba shrieked, but there was nobody to hear or save her. Kali didn't dare intervene.

"Slut!" Chrysafenia roared. "How could you do that to your sister? What did she do to you, you wicked girl, to make you destroy her?"

Hecuba managed to escape from her mother's hands and looked at her without a trace of shame or remorse. "You always loved her more. But I've fixed you both up nicely!" she howled, beside herself.

"Your father will find out everything!" her mother shouted.

"I'll tell him that Simos raped me, and then we'll see what happens!"

Chrysafenia threw herself at her daughter again. The fresh blows came just as hard, and Hecuba felt tufts of her hair being pulled out. The two women fell to the floor, rolling around. Kali realized that she couldn't delay any longer, and she rushed into the room to separate them. Panting and scratched, like wild cats that haven't sated their fury, they looked nothing like mother and daughter. Kali took Chrysafenia by the arm to lead her out, but she shook the woman off and turned to her daughter.

"For me, starting today you don't exist anymore!" she said, trying to control her breath. "And you'll leave this house. Papadakis asked for your hand. You'll marry him, whether you want to or not, and you'll follow him to Crete. God help the man! And may God forgive me for tricking him. He thinks he's getting a girl, and we're giving him a witch. If you dare object to this marriage, I'll tell your father myself what you've done and let what happens happen. What else do I have to fear?"

She smoothed her hair and left the room with her head high. That evening, she told her husband that Papadakis had proposed and Hecuba had accepted, which improved his mood. He called her in to congratulate her without noticing the poisonous looks mother and daughter exchanged. Chrysafenia showed her disdain for them both with a single glance. One had destroyed her own sister, and the other had written off his own kin without a second thought. She felt something deep inside her catch fire. She wanted to open the door and flee, to take her daughter in her arms and disappear with her forever, but the thought that there were still two younger children who were not to blame held her motionless and trapped. The "must" in her head was well established and defeated the wants of her spirit.

A game of roulette: that was what all their lives were like during that time. The ball ran over the numbers, and Fate, croupier at her casino, watched the players blankly as they agonized about the peculiarities of the little white ball that would determine their future lives.

Chrysafenia didn't dare tell her husband about their daughter's pregnancy. Hecuba was preparing for her wedding. One day, Nestor burst into the house to say that the news from Switzerland was bad. Melpo's condition appeared to be terribly dangerous, and he had to leave. He was going to take his parents with him because Yvonne was ready to collapse from tiredness and needed all the help they could give her. Again, Pericles arranged all the travel papers.

And so, Chrysafenia's hopes that Smaragda could stay with her grandparents evaporated. She remained alone, knowing the truth and trying to find a solution at the same time as she tried to give courage to her brother and her parents, who cried inconsolably over young Melpo. Even when her mother asked her about Smaragda, Chrysafenia managed to appease her with lies.

Chrysafenia said nothing to Smaragda when she went to see her at Renos's; he had become the girl's guardian angel, treating her with exceptional courtesy and kindness. The girl had been through enough; it wasn't necessary to burden her with anxiety about the health of her beloved cousin. She tried to discuss the possibility of terminating the pregnancy, but Smaragda refused, and Chrysafenia didn't know if she felt relief or despair. She decided to tell her daughter everything about their past connection with the Kouyoumdzis family. Perhaps if Smaragda understood that this union had been doomed for three generations, it would soothe her spirit a little. Chrysafenia went back many decades, speaking about the love between Simeon and Grandmother Smaragda, about the gold jewel he had designed but never made. Then came her turn. Her young love for Vassilis, the vows they made, and the stolen kisses in the foyer, with the little candle as their only witness, the locket he had finally made for her and given her as a symbol of their love. When she had finished, Smaragda looked at her mother as if she were seeing her for the first time. Chrysafenia took the locket from her neck and showed it to her.

"I had it locked in a box for years," she revealed, "but when I heard about you and Simos, I felt I had to wear it. Perhaps I should have given it to you. We share the same fate, my child."

Smaragda buried herself in her mother's arms.

"No, Mother. Keep it. At least I have his child to remind me how naive I was."

"But we must make a decision, sweetheart, mustn't we? You can't stay forever in Mr. Karapanos's house. I thought of taking you to Grandmother's, but she left to see Melpo."

"How is she?" Smaragda asked.

"How can she be, daughter? She's fighting for her life, the poor thing, but her mother will soon collapse with exhaustion, so your grandparents have gone to help her a little. Who would have thought we'd have such troubles? I didn't tell them you'd left home."

"Good! Grandma and Grandpa wouldn't have been able to face it right now."

"So what will happen next, can you tell me?"

The answer Smaragda didn't have was given by Renos the same evening. He waited for hours until Pericles left the house and then entered. He knew everything he needed to know . . .

Chrysafenia welcomed him anxiously, afraid that something had happened, but he wore his best smile to put her at ease.

"Smaragda is fine, Mrs. Sekeris, but I wanted to see you so that we could talk."

"Before you say anything else, I want to tell you how eternally grateful I am for the help you've given my child."

"Don't even mention it. It was my pleasure to be able to help. Besides, I'm not completely unselfish," he told her, his expression full of kindness.

"What do you mean?" asked Chrysafenia, frowning now. "What do you want in exchange?"

"Smaragda," he replied, becoming suddenly serious as he began to explain. "Listen, Mrs. Sekeris, I love Smaragda. I've been in love with her for a long time, but knowing her feelings for the other fellow, I didn't dare make a move. What's more, to be honest, who was I to be worthy of her noticing me? I was poor, out of work, with émigré parents who sent me back to their homeland to see if I could make a life for myself. I won't hide the fact that I'm getting ready to go back to them because there isn't much future for me here."

Chrysafenia stood stock-still listening to him, and bolstered by her silence, he went on.

"I know what's going on, and I'm prepared to marry Smaragda and take responsibility for her child," he said, delivering the coup de grâce.

Now the woman took a deep breath.

"Did she tell you?" she asked hesitantly.

"Yes—well, not exactly, but from overhearing snatches of your conversation with her, I realized it, and when I pressed her a little, she confessed."

"And you want to marry her despite what you know?"

"I already told you that I loved her long before this happened. What does it matter to me if she's pregnant? She's still Smaragda—the same girl I'm in love with. Naturally, I wish things had been different, but that's the way it is. I'll acknowledge the child, and I swear to you that I'll look after it as if it were my own. Of course, there's still my wretched financial state . . ."

"Don't worry about that. I have enough money of my own to support you. Perhaps, after the wedding, her father will soften a little since his honor has been preserved."

"Please, Mrs. Sekeris!" he interrupted her, pretending to be touched. "None of that interests me. And if I had a steady job, we wouldn't even be discussing this now. But I'm out of work, and how could I manage things with a wife and baby . . . That's why I came to speak to you."

"And Smaragda? Will she accept?"

"I think she has no other option. I mean, since she has decided to keep the baby, she needs a father for her child and a husband. And seeing as I have your permission, I'll talk to her today!"

"And I'll do the same with my husband, Mr. Karapanos—Renos, my son," she corrected herself. "I hope everything happens as you wish!" she said, very moved, and put her arms around him.

Nothing went as they wished, however. When Pericles asked around about his prospective son-in-law, what he learned made him furious.

"How stupid can you females be!" Pericles shouted at his wife. "You think you can bring me around with this new bridegroom? And that hussy of a daughter of yours—how many men was she carrying on with so that she had a substitute ready? And what an arrogant fool he is! A bum who saw in you suckers a way out of his financial problems. Wherever he's worked, they've fired him!"

"That can't be true!" she objected.

"My information, Mrs. Sekeris, is quite precise! Do you know what they told me? The young man is riffraff! Violent, drunken, and lazy! And if he thinks I'll accept him to cover my shame, he's been fooled. He might marry her, but he'll never be my son-in-law. Don't speak to me again about this, Chrysi. And make sure you get your oldest daughter ready for her wedding. Papadakis is in a hurry."

Chrysafenia didn't know what to believe. She was alone, unable to talk to anyone and get a second opinion. Her parents and her brother were very far away, trying to save a young girl from death, and she was struggling, with no help, not daring to reveal the whole truth to her husband.

The next day, Smaragda agreed to marry Renos, and everything took its course. Chrysafenia gave her son-in-law a generous sum of money to take care of the wedding, and told Kali to give away her daughter. Later, every month, she carefully put aside what she could so that the couple could live.

She dressed her daughter as a bride and tried to hold back her tears for the dreams she'd had of Smaragda's wedding day back when she was first born, none of which had come true. When she saw her in the plain white dress with flowers in her hair and tears in her eyes, she embraced her, and with all the strength of her soul, she begged God to let her daughter be happy. She prayed that Renos would be a worthy husband to the beautiful spirit her daughter carried within her. They all left together for the small church they'd chosen for the wedding.

While they were exchanging wedding wreaths, Pericles received Simos at his house. The young man charged in, and his former prospective father-in-law noticed that his eyes were dull with drink.

"Mr. Sekeris, I want to see Smaragda!" he shouted. "I must speak to her and explain!"

"Why don't you explain to me first," Pericles said, holding back his anger, "because when I went to your father's house, he didn't give me a clear answer. Were you or weren't you with another woman in that apartment? Did she or didn't she catch you in the act?"

"I don't love anyone else, Mr. Sekeris! I only love Smaragda, and I want to marry her! Nothing else matters. Please, let me speak to her!"

"Young man, you're too late! As we speak, Smaragda is getting married," Pericles answered with an unpleasant smile.

"Impossible! It's ridiculous, a lie like that!"

"You can go to the little church of Ayios Yorgos and see for yourself. What did you think? That she was waiting for you? The replacement was ready. Leave my house now because my patience has its limits!" Pericles said, raising his voice, but it wasn't necessary.

Opposite him, Simos looked as if he'd been shot. He left, staggering, and when he was alone, Pericles felt slightly satisfied. The larger satisfaction, the more unholy one, which he didn't dare confess to himself, had to do with his wife. Vassilis and Chrysafenia wouldn't have the satisfaction of seeing their children unite.

Hecuba's wedding took place, but it gave Chrysafenia no joy beyond the relief of getting the girl out of the house. She sent a letter to her parents in Switzerland, telling them instead about the good child, Smaragda, who'd found her Prince Charming. When Chrysafenia read the letter again before putting it in the envelope, it seemed ridiculous to her, but she could hardly go into the whole story when they were at the bedside of their sick grandchild. After a while, Melpo showed signs of recovery, and Chrysafenia's brother was able to return and attend to his work. His manner was strange; he didn't seem to believe her, whatever she said.

"And who is this young man who married my niece in such a hurry?" Nestor said skeptically.

"What can I tell you now? A young man who was in their circle. From what he told me, he loved her," Chrysafenia explained, trying to look cheerful. "Do you remember Persa? He's her cousin."

"And what work does he do?"

"He's looking for work, the poor fellow," she said, trying to excuse him. "His parents are emigrants—they live in Germany. Besides, I haven't told you the best part! Your niece is going to make me a grandmother soon. She's pregnant!"

Nestor sat up straighter, and set about cross-examining her. He was particularly concerned with his brother-in-law's behavior. If Smaragda had married a good man, why did Pericles remain so unfeeling? Chrysafenia tried to blame it on his rigid character, but Nestor left unconvinced.

Chrysafenia wasn't sure of anything anymore. Instead of calming her, the months that passed, bringing the birth of the baby closer, made her more anxious. Pericles's words about their son-in-law came back into her mind again and again. Renos had made no effort to find work, but he had begun to drop hints about the money she gave them, saying it seemed meager. He persuaded her to talk to her husband and tell him to give them what they were entitled to. Chrysafenia searched her daughter's expression to see how she was, but Smaragda lowered her eyes.

Chrysafenia managed to see her grandchild and learn that the child shared her name shortly before she and her son were killed in a car crash. She had given him the wheel that cursed day. A sudden turn, a pedestrian who stepped out abruptly, and everything was over. Chrysafenia Sekeris and Stelios died almost instantaneously, and her last thought was for the daughter she was leaving almost alone. Renos was left with a wife and child to take care of without the help of his mother-in-law, and without fear of anything or anyone. The mask fell . . .

In an attempt to find a solution to his financial problems, he dared, two months after the deaths that had struck his father-in-law's house, to call on Pericles Sekeris and ask him for his daughter and granddaughter's legal rights. He expected to find a man destroyed by grief, and therefore vulnerable, but instead he found a wild beast. As soon as Pericles heard his request, he charged forward and would have struck him had Fotini and Kali not intervened. With a great effort they managed to rein in his fury.

"Get out of my house!" he roared loudly at the stunned Renos. "If you thought I'd pity you, you made a mistake. I don't have a daughter called Smaragda. She died! Do you understand? Go drown yourself and the slut you took up with! Leave! Get lost!"

Renos turned around and raced out of the house, while behind him Pericles was still shouting. He'd played and lost! He'd imagined the wealth of Sekeris in his hands, and now he was stuck with the man's penniless daughter and her baby.

CHAPTER 16

Kypseli, 2016

After Kali's revelations, Melpo guided me into the house, and Karim ran to help us when he saw what a state we were in. I didn't even remember leaving the retirement home. The woman had finished her story and found two women standing like statues in front of her, breathless, white with shock. I faintly remembered her bringing us a little water and a dessert we didn't touch. Then my mind dimmed as all the things I'd found out refused to fit in my brain.

We sat in the office. This little place had become a refuge—a crucible for confession and memories. But now we didn't even have the courage to speak. Karim didn't know what to do to bring us around and resorted to the obvious: sweets and coffee. Mechanically, we both took our first sip at the same time and lit cigarettes. I didn't even realize I was crying until sobs shook my whole body. Melpo, sitting beside me, held my hand tightly.

"Cry, sweetheart," she advised me. "You have every reason."

"I don't want to cry!" I shouted, but in vain; it was impossible to stop. "I want to go and beat Hecuba to death. I want to trample her. She destroyed so many lives. Like a domino that didn't leave a single piece standing. Simos and my mother would have lived happily together, and I—"

This time, together with the sobs, came a howl. It came from deep inside me and let my wounds bleed. But there was something else, a very small relief. At least that rapist monster wasn't my father. What happened was still sick, naturally, but the same blood didn't flow in our veins.

"I'm the daughter of Simos Kouyoumdzis," I said out of nowhere. "After all these generations, a Kantardzis woman is also a Kouyoumdzis."

"What are you going to do now, Fenia?" my forever practical aunt asked me.

"I don't know. Do you have any suggestions? Where is Simos today?"

"That shouldn't be difficult to find out."

"Yes, it's what comes after that's difficult."

Unconsciously, I touched the necklace at my throat. I turned to my aunt inquiringly.

"Melpo, tell me the truth: How did this necklace come into your hands?"

"When his sister, your grandmother Chrysafenia, was killed, my father came here and collected some of her personal belongings to keep as mementos. The gold letter was among them. I suspect that was the day the final rift was created between the two families. He gave it to me before he died. OK? You solved another of your mysteries. Today we learned so much that I don't know if it was good for us. I'm still shaking. And I wonder at you! You got your composure back so quickly that I'm worried."

"What do you suggest, that I cry for days about something that can't be changed?"

"That would be more natural."

"My sweet, dear Melpo," I began affectionately, "I'm not a young girl. I've seen and lived through a lot. At this moment, as much as I'd like to go and beat up my aunt, inside me there is a sense of relief. What I suffered wasn't done to me by my father, but a stranger. I feel—I feel"—I searched for the word—"I feel lighter, Melpo! Mrs. Kali took my worst burden away from me. And I also feel numb. My whole life has been turned upside down. I'm the daughter of a person and not a beast. I was always afraid of his blood in my veins, and now I'm simply somebody else. Today's revelations were like a transfusion."

"And now that you know, shall we find your real father? You can restore your mother's memory. She didn't betray him, she didn't have a substitute ready—she thought she had to protect his child with this marriage. My poor Smaragda." A tear rolled from Melpo's eye.

What happened next, my good aunt didn't expect. I got up so suddenly that Tiger was startled, and with a long yowl he leaped and hid behind the armchair.

"Let's go!" I called out.

"Where, my child?"

"To Ermou Street. Isn't that where the Kouyoumdzis family jewelry store is?"

"Fenia, have you gone mad? It's nighttime. It'll be closed."

"That's exactly why I want to go. Are you coming, or should I go by myself?" I was already at the door.

Of course I wouldn't have gone if there had been the slightest chance of finding someone at the store. I didn't even know if the business still existed. Karim, who had come to call us for dinner, was afraid.

"Madam!" he shouted. "Where are you going? What happened?"

"Food later, Karim," I said hurriedly, dragging Melpo by the hand.

I was in a great hurry. Fortunately we found a taxi immediately, and the roads weren't busy. It was a very hot summer, and the Athenians had been driven away. I asked the taxi driver to let us off at Syntagma Square, and arm in arm, Melpo and I marched down the central street of Athens. The shops were closed, but their windows were lit up, and everywhere there were signs advertising tempting sales. At each intersection, the bars were full of people. The scorching breath of day had given way to the cool of night. Candles on the tables cast a happy glow on smiling faces, and some couples exchanged kisses in the half-light. I quickened my step as my eyes scanned the street, and suddenly I stopped. In front of us, all lit up and very elegant, was the window of a jewelry store. Over the storefront was a sign. On it, ornately written, was the name KOUYOUMDZIS, and below it in smaller letters, SINCE 1955. With cowardly footsteps, as if I was doing something wrong, I approached and peered through the metal grating that protected the plate-glass windows. In the display cases were a few pieces of jewelry, certainly nothing of great value, since the valuable ones would be stored safely inside the store. I tried to imagine my father working here. Perhaps he was with his children.

I felt Melpo's tender hand on my shoulder.

"All right now?" she asked. "Have you calmed down? Let's go, and I'll buy you a drink so we can relax."

The way I felt, it would have been impossible to go home anyway. We telephoned her husband, who arrived at a café a little later to keep us company. Melpo caught him up on what we had learned, and my uncle had to take a large gulp of the whiskey he had been sipping.

"Now I've heard everything!" he exclaimed.

"Do you understand what evil my witch of a cousin did?" Melpo burst out.

"Excuse me, but your uncle wasn't far behind! Stubborn and nasty. Pericles was always like that!" Paschalis responded. "He threw his child out and disowned her because she went against him. What if he'd found out about the pregnancy?"

"He would have killed her."

"What a shame!" he murmured sadly and ordered another drink. "If everyone had just spoken honestly—forgive me for saying so, but your aunt Chrysafenia was also at fault, Melpo."

"There were a lot of mistakes," his wife agreed. "Some were out of evil, and some were out of an attempt to do good. My poor aunt thought she was doing the best she could for her child."

"If she'd done the simplest thing, maybe all the rest would have worked out," I joined in. "If she'd gone to find Vassilis herself—"

"We're making a fundamental mistake," Paschalis interrupted. "We're judging what happened from today's point of view. Chrysafenia was raised to believe that a woman doesn't have a say. And her husband certainly agreed—wasn't Pericles a supporter of the junta? Let's not forget their slogan was 'Fatherland, religion, family.' Whoever deviated from the virtuous path was thrown into the gorge on Mount Taygetus, like the Spartans did with unwanted children. These days, a child born out of wedlock doesn't provoke disgust in anyone, or even surprise. Then, it was different. And by today's standards, Simos, the poor fellow, was just a boy. Their reactions may seem excessive now, but at the time the actions took place, they were completely normal. The question is, what now? What will you do, Fenia?"

"What do you suggest?" I asked him.

"The only logical thing. Go and find your father and tell him who you are. He has the right to know he has a child by Smaragda."

"What'll come of that?"

"You'll find out."

"Why should he believe me and not think I'm lying to try and take over his fortune?"

"Come on!" my uncle responded. "If he doubts what you say, there's such a thing as DNA! A test can show what's been hidden for forty years. But I believe you must go and see him."

We all returned to the house an hour later, and I was surprised to see Karim sitting on the entrance stairs, his anxiety written so clearly on his face that I felt ashamed. We had relaxed over drinks at Syntagma Square while he was suffering. To make it up to him, we all sat at the table and ate together. I wasn't hungry, but I took care to empty my plate. Afterward, though, I shooed everyone out. I wanted to be alone. I needed the thoughts that silence brings.

It was long after midnight, but despite the two drinks I'd had earlier with Paschalis and Melpo, there was no question of sleep. I didn't even bother to go to my room. As soon as I was alone, I made a strong cup of coffee and went back to what was by now the familiar and loved space of the office to spend the hours until daybreak. I hoped the complete quiet would help me make my decisions. I opened the two windows wide and sat on the sill of one of them with my coffee and cigarettes. I looked at the apartment buildings that rose up around me. Some had light in the windows, some didn't, and quite a few had completely closed shutters, indicating that their owners had probably headed off for some seashore to spend their holidays. My eyes fell on the deserted street.

Suddenly, my heart skipped a few beats. I opened and closed my eyes several times, certain that my mind was playing tricks on me. Across the street, in a parked car, a driver was smoking in the semidarkness, faintly lit by the streetlamp. It couldn't be him . . . There was no reason for his presence outside my house, when he should have been thousands of miles away.

CHAPTER 17

Munich, 2013

With shaking hands and a voice she tried to keep steady, Fenia was reading the fairy tale to little Ino to put her to sleep, as she did every evening. The five-year-old girl, unaware of the drama about to strike their house, listened until her lids finally grew heavy and closed. The woman beside her left the book and turned out the light, having made sure the girl was well covered up. She didn't hurry to leave the room. The child's rhythmic breathing calmed her and helped her absorb what she had found out a little earlier but had not been able to take in.

Yannos had called her into his office, and as soon as the door shut behind them, he almost collapsed in her arms. When he was finally able to explain, she felt the floor giving way under her feet.

"It can't be!" she'd whispered. "There must have been some mistake in the tests."

"If only," he said, the tears running down his face. "There's no doubt. Savina is doomed. The cancer has spread."

"But how? Out of the blue? There was nothing wrong with her!"

"Unfortunately, my wife ignored some signs. If she had told me . . ."

He didn't continue, overcome by guilt. Despite being a doctor, he hadn't noticed, hadn't done anything in time. She touched him shyly on the shoulder, and this simple gesture brought them close. Arms around each other, they wept, full of pain and hopelessness.

"Does she know?" Fenia asked.

"Very little. I didn't let my colleague tell her the whole truth."

"But won't she find out? The treatments have side effects."

"We'll start with radiation to shrink the tumors. Fenia, I won't lie to you: all the doctors who've seen her say it's useless. That we shouldn't even put her through the treatments."

"But you can't just let her die!" Fenia objected.

"Of course not!" he burst out angrily, then softened. "But we must be prepared. I'll do anything to prolong her life as much as I can."

They came out of his office knowing that, from that moment on, nothing would be the same.

Savina Pantazis didn't ask any questions, which Fenia knew was a sign that she understood but was going along with the game of secrecy her loved ones were playing. When Yannos told her in the most natural way he could manage that they'd have to start chemotherapy, Savina smiled calmly.

"Whatever you think is best. Of course, we'll have to adopt a new hairstyle!"

The two people opposite her were expressionless while she smiled still more broadly.

"Come on now, you two are looking at me like I'm a ghost! It's hair: it'll grow back."

But Fenia was there ten days after the first chemotherapy session when Savina went to comb her hair and a tuft of it came out in her hand. Her face froze, and her eyes stared at Fenia's in the mirror.

"It's started . . . ," she said tightly.

"Yes," Fenia agreed and then smiled at her. "Like you said: it's hair, and it'll grow back," she went on with a coolness she didn't feel. "Do you want me to comb it for you?"

"Why? If you're the one with the comb, will it be too shy to fall out? Leave it. I'll get used to it."

Over the next few days, Savina had pulled almost all of her hair out, although it took no effort. Fenia was always there to take it from Savina's hands, and she shuddered when she felt it between her fingers. A few days later, as soon as Yannos had left to take Ino to school and then to go on to the hospital where he worked, his wife shut herself in her room, and Fenia heard the sound of the electric razor. She bit her lip and stayed where she was until the door opened and Savina appeared with a scarf around her head.

"It's finished," she said simply. "Let's get on with it."

"What do you mean?" Fenia asked.

"I don't even know. The only thing I want is for this nightmare to end."

She marched past Fenia into the living room and settled down there with a book. But soon, Fenia could hear her sobs, loud and clear. She didn't know what to do—whether to go to her or not. Her feet moved of their own accord, and she found herself kneeling in front of the grieving woman. Savina clung to her, hugging her in despair and continuing to cry until she finally calmed down and remained motionless in the comforting arms.

"Thank you" was all she said.

"Savina, I don't just work here; I love you very much, and you know it," Fenia told her gently. "So I have to tell you that you're facing this situation all wrong. Stop being a heroine and trying to give us courage, instead of letting us do that for you. It's time to weep about what's happening to you, because if you don't, you'll find it ahead of you later."

"How much later, Fenia?" she asked, and the complaint in her voice was like a slap. "I don't say anything, I play along, but I know and I understand. There won't be any later for me."

"What are you saying?" Fenia tried to object, but Savina stopped her, putting a finger affectionately to her lips.

"Don't underestimate my intelligence. I agreed to the chemo for Yannos's sake. So he won't feel guilty that he didn't try to save me or at least buy a little time. I found the results of my tests that he hid, and I read them. I know everything. Maybe in a little while I won't be able to have this discussion with you, because from what I read, the metastasis has reached my brain. And now that we both know, I want you to listen carefully to me. I'm not afraid to die, but I won't pretend I'm not sad to be dying so young. I'm especially sad for the child."

"Savina," Fenia said, weeping and kneeling at her feet.

"Fenia, listen to me! I'm sorry I'm leaving, but I'm at peace because you are here in their lives. I want you to swear to me that you'll never leave them. That you'll bring up my daughter as if she were your own. Swear!"

"You know I will," Fenia said, as steadily as her sobs would allow.

"Thank you. And not a word to Yannos about this."

Savina leaned back and closed her eyes, tired from the effort. Fenia got up, then bent and kissed her tenderly on the forehead. What she really wanted to do was to bow to the greatness of a human soul.

Time was Savina's greatest enemy. Her brain betrayed her first. Her speech became slower; she searched for words that were hidden inside her. Her exhaustion was more and more intense. The chemotherapy cycle ended, but the test results were not good. Savina now spent her time in bed; she seldom got up, and when she did, she needed help. It was impossible for her to stand by herself or to walk to the armchair two steps away. Fenia didn't know who to help first in the house, and they each had different needs. Ino couldn't understand what was happening. Sometimes her mother didn't recognize her, and the child cried pitifully. Yannos tried to be brave for his wife's sake, but he wept like a child in Fenia's arms when they were alone. Savina demanded more and more of Fenia's energy and soon needed care twenty-four hours a day. When Fenia herself was on the verge of collapse, Yannos realized how bad things had gotten and brought in another woman to help.

The dawn of New Year's Day 2014 found Fenia awake beside Savina, together with Yannos. Her condition had deteriorated a great deal, and the oxygen mask she wore seemed to bother her. Her chest rose and fell with effort, and each breath was agony for her, each exhalation a terrifying whistle. Yannos got up from the chair where his legs had fallen asleep.

"I'm going to drink a little water," he whispered as if he were in danger of disturbing the patient. "Do you want anything?"

"Bring me some water too," Fenia answered. "And make sure you eat something," she added. "You haven't eaten since yesterday."

He nodded before he left the room, but Fenia knew he wouldn't put a bite of food in his mouth. She turned again to the tired face and froze as she realized that Savina was watching her. A hand, thin as a branch, pushed aside the oxygen mask. A moment of clarity.

"Where's Yannos?" she asked.

"He went to get some water. I'll run and fetch him," Fenia answered, jumping up.

"No." The woman stopped her. "Better that he doesn't see me go. Just you. Remember what you promised. You'll never leave them!"

Fenia bent over her, and the two women exchanged a look full of love and understanding. Then Savina's eyes closed, two more rough breaths, and with the third her soul slipped to where it would no longer suffer.

Absolute silence spread over the room that had, until a short time before, been filled with pain and anguish. Fenia took Savina's waxen fingers in her hands. Yannos found her in the same position a few minutes later. The glass of water fell and smashed to pieces on the floor. He ran to his wife, who had already begun her journey. Fenia moved aside and let him fall on his dead wife to weep.

The period that followed was difficult for all of them. Fenia gave all her attention to the child, who kept asking for her mother. As was to be expected, she clung to Fenia with an insistence that was sometimes perturbing. At first, she didn't even want to go to school for fear that Fenia might leave too. With patience and persistence, Fenia did what her conscience dictated, and slowly the child calmed down. But when she came home, she wouldn't let Fenia out of her sight. Fenia decided to fill the afternoons with various activities, some of which took the child out of the house. She didn't know if she was doing the right thing, and Yannos was in no condition to discuss it. He had chosen to fill the void left by the loss of his wife with endless hours of work. The house suffocated him. He looked around and saw Savina. He never set foot in their room but slept in the living room. Again, Fenia took the initiative. She put all his clothes in her room and slept in the couple's bedroom, having rearranged it. The rare times that Yannos was at home, he shut himself in his office, but he needed her presence. She took a book and sat in an armchair without speaking unless he asked her to. Then Fenia told him about what was going on at home, and about his daughter. It comforted her that he listened attentively and sometimes suggested some solutions himself.

After some months, a pleasant, calm routine was established; they all needed it. The good weather drove the snow, cold, and gloom far away. Ino felt more secure again and spent her afternoons happily with Fenia. The structured activities continued, and now the child was crazy about her art lessons, her ballet, and her sports team. Yannos seemed calmer, he worked less, and he began to accompany them on some spring walks in the city. Whoever had seen them from far away would have thought they were watching a happy family.

The familiarity that had grown between Fenia and Yannos didn't surprise either of them. It came naturally, without them seeking it. When Ino slept, they passed time with a game of chess or watched a film together, eating lots of popcorn that Fenia made. They loved comedies and exciting adventure films and shared a passion for miniseries. Their relationship had changed into one of companionship without them being aware of it.

A high fever brought the change. Ino came home that afternoon from her art class and complained that her throat was sore. Later that evening, the thermometer climbed to 103, and Yannos called the pediatrician. The pills he'd given Ino to lower the fever hadn't done much, and he suspected she would need antibiotics. The child was burning up all night, and neither of them left her side. Sitting in armchairs on either side of the bed, they held her hands and almost counted her breaths. Tiredness overcame them at one point. The girl was sleeping peacefully, and without realizing it, their heads dropped onto the mattress and they fell asleep. They jumped up nervously at the same moment because they had forgotten themselves, and their hands met on her forehead. It was almost cool. The tips of their fingers, though, seemed to have caught fire from that touch. They looked at each other and both knew there was no need for shame; despite that, they lowered their eyes like guilty people.

Ino recovered very fast thanks to the antibiotics, and had no idea that the situation in the house had changed. Fenia pretended nothing was wrong, but when she was alone, she rebuked herself.

It's Yannos, you useless creature! she kept thinking. *Yannos, who picked you up from the streets and offered you a home. Yannos and Savina! Do you remember Savina?*

She blushed every time she had to speak to him and avoided spending time with him in the evening, pretending she still had housework to do. She had the honesty to admit to herself that her feelings for the gentle, sensitive man had changed. Almost from the first moment, they'd had a special relationship, but the existence of Savina, and Fenia's love for her, had obscured any other feelings for him. But that touch in the night on the forehead of the child she adored was the fuse for a great explosion.

For his part, Yannos wondered what had happened to make him suddenly see Fenia in a different way. He had never thought of her as a housekeeper, nor as a nanny for his child. In his mind, she was always a good friend, and now even that wasn't enough, and his guilt consumed him. He hardly dared to look at his wife's photograph because of the shame he felt.

By a common but unspoken decision, they both kept their distance, without suspecting that this was the best way to strengthen their feelings. The calm evenings with chess and movies stopped, and Yannos began to work long hours again, and returned exhausted but still unable to sleep. Mere yards separated him from the object of his obsession, sleeping unawares in the next room. He couldn't know that she was also awake, counting her heartbeats in disbelief. She'd been sure romantic attraction was not for her. The way she'd experienced sex in her life, first by force and later for money, had made it a terrifying thing, evil. She felt repulsed by herself, by her own body that woke and desired, this time with the participation of her heart.

One evening, when it was raining very hard, Yannos was late coming home. She put the child to sleep and shut her own door, feeling like a wild animal in a cage. She lay down and tried to lose herself in a book. She wanted a drink more than anything, but she knew it wouldn't stop at one—she'd spend the night with her arms around a bottle because she couldn't have what her arms really longed for. She had no idea how long she'd been asleep when the noise of something breaking made her jump out of bed. She ran to the child's room, but the little girl was sleeping deeply. The sound of Yannos's voice came to her; he was cursing, and something else broke with a crash. She raced downstairs and saw him in the living room searching in the little bar for a bottle of whiskey. The first one, which had woken her, was in pieces at his feet. She approached nervously; he never drank.

"Yannos," she said, and her voice came out in a whisper. "What are you doing up at this hour?"

He turned and looked at her with bleary eyes. His breath smelled of alcohol.

"I wanted . . . ," he began to say to her but didn't finish his sentence. Standing in front of him was the reason for every gulp he had consumed. With her hair untidy from sleep, and her body half-naked under a thin nightgown. The alcohol flowed inside him, all inhibitions had relaxed; he couldn't even think. Besides, there were those eyes of hers . . . like melted gold. They haunted his nights, and now they were looking at him again, shining in the half-light. He didn't know if it was the shadows that deceived him, but what he saw there gave him courage.

He reached out his arms and pulled her to him, as she welcomed something she had never known in her life. Her fingers buried themselves in his hair, then squeezed his shoulders, and she didn't object when she felt her nightgown being ripped away. With trembling hands she undid his shirt, tearing the buttons off in her own impatience. She felt his arms lifting her, and she wrapped her legs around his waist as he supported her against the wall. Without his lips leaving hers, he removed all the other impediments so he could lose himself in her body, finally finding hell and paradise together. Fenia felt that her body was about to be crushed between the wall and his strength. His arms gripped her tightly, and she felt herself being raised in the air. She clung to him until she felt her back sink into the soft couch. She arched back to take him deeper, like a flower trying to swallow a bee. She had never experienced anything like it. She realized that she had not lost her innocence until that night; only with Yannos had she known the true, magical dimension of love.

CHAPTER 18

Kypseli, 2016

I stared at the parked car as panic came over me. The phantom of my imagination, because there was no way it could be true, had now gotten out of the car and was looking back at me. Trembling, I closed the window. I stood in the dark, measuring the time with breaths, until I heard the doorbell. I couldn't move. Another ring at the door, more demanding now. He knew I was inside, awake. Tiger, curious about the night visitor, appeared at the top of the stairs, meowing loudly. Like an automaton I pressed the buzzer that opened the door and stood beside my cat, sure that my dream would finally dissolve and the visitor would turn out to be somebody else. He took the stairs two at a time, dispelled the illusion. No more darkness, no shadows.

"Yannos . . ." I dared to look him in the eyes.

It was as if not a day had passed: the same dark features, the same graying hair, the same bearing.

"I was worried I'd have to break down the door!" he grumbled.

I didn't know what to say to him; my brain felt empty.

"May I come in?" he asked, and not a trace of light appeared on his darkened face.

Without speaking, I stood aside, and he entered the hall. I showed him the way to the office, and in a moment, we were standing again, facing each other, without speaking. Tiger sat still, watching us. After a while, he lost his patience and rubbed against my legs meowing, wanting assurance that I was all right.

I realized how ridiculous the scene was and gave a dry cough to clear my throat.

"I'm sorry," I said awkwardly. "I didn't expect to see you here. How did you know where I lived? And why aren't you in Germany? Where is Ino?"

"An interesting change," he observed quietly. "From complete silence, we've progressed to an outburst of questions. Let's leave Ino out of it for now. As for me, I'm here because I tore up the world trying to find you. If it hadn't been for a stroke of luck, I'd still be searching in Germany. When you disappeared, I didn't imagine you would be heading to Greece."

"I didn't disappear," I responded angrily. "I wrote to you—"

"Right! That long letter in which you explained the 'reasons,' after six wonderful months of discovering how much we meant to each other, you had to leave forever."

"What else do you want me to say?" I wondered.

"Something that makes sense, maybe? Maybe you should have told me you don't love me, that our time living together meant nothing to you."

"I couldn't have written lies," I admitted and lowered my eyes. "I thought—"

"You thought I needed to know your father raped you and that after he died you worked as a prostitute? You thought I'd think you weren't worthy of me, and when I started talking to you about my dreams, you got afraid and left?"

"More or less," I whispered.

"Didn't you realize you were destroying me? Didn't it pass through your mind that there was another point of view, that after so many years of living with you, I'd fallen in love with the real Fenia? You left me a letter filled with the story of a wounded child who developed into a woman deprived of love, but that wasn't you. I am crazy about a woman who gave love, affection, tenderness, and passion with no bounds. I love a woman who stood beside me through all the difficult times and became my friend, my lover, and a mother to my child, together. That's the woman I fell in love with, and I can't imagine life without her. Does this woman exist, Fenia, or did I imagine her?"

Again, I had no breath to answer with. The truth was, after that magnificent night in the living room, there was no room for evasions. We were madly in love, and we acted on it intensely. We even learned not to feel guilty. We'd cry for Savina in each other's arms, and the next moment, make love like two crazy people. Ino found nothing strange in our behavior; she only laughed happily, and sometimes a shy "Mama" escaped her when she asked me for something.

And later, Yannos began to speak of the future and his dreams for us. In my head, I pictured terrible scenes from the past pursuing me. Suddenly, that young girl Renos managed to twist and nearly destroy threatened to suffocate me. All at once, the prostitute who sold herself to any man for the right price grabbed me by the neck. Then it was the Fenia with a bottle of alcohol who slept on the streets until she was like a rag, another piece of garbage. What right did this woman have to dream about a beautiful, calm life beside a respectable man and a child who thought of her as a mother? Fear turned into terror and then panic. I wrote to Yannos, telling him my life story, and said I was leaving, believing that he wouldn't ever want to see me again.

But he was in front of me now, furious. He grabbed me by the arm and shook me, snapping me out of my memories.

"I'm waiting for an answer, Fenia! Does the woman I love exist? Nothing else interests me. I never asked about your past!"

"It was different when I was just a housekeeper and nanny."

"You're wrong," he insisted. "I took you into my house, and I trusted you. And you earned that trust every day. You became part of our family, and when my wife got sick, you couldn't have looked after her with more love or devotion even if you had been her sister. If I could trust and care for the woman I found covered in blood on my doorstep, why should the past matter now when I love her so much? You had no right to do that to me," he finished, shouting. "I didn't deserve it. And now I want an answer. Tell me! Are you the woman I love?"

He shook me again, and the tears rolled down my face until he pulled me to him. There was no room for tears anymore, and it was I who pressed my lips to his. My taste, my breath, my sense of smell and feeling all returned. I clung to him to recover the strength I had felt leaving me more each day.

The next morning, we nearly gave Karim a stroke. He came into the office and found us asleep in each other's arms, half-naked on the little couch.

"I'm sorry, madam," my Syrian friend yelped. He ran out, closing the door behind him.

Yannos looked at me in surprise. "What was that?"

"*That* was Karim," I answered and began getting dressed.

"And what's he doing here?"

"He lives here, with me. Yannos, there are a lot of questions, and last night neither of us had the patience for them."

"Yes, you're right. We need time," he said and looked hard into my eyes. "Do we have it?"

"We'll see. It doesn't only depend on me."

"Wrong!" he responded forcefully. "It does. My intentions were and are quite clear. From the day you left, I've searched, and now I've finally found you."

"Yannos, I want to make a few things clear before we say anything else."

"Please. I've been waiting."

"So first and foremost, I want you to know I love you, and it's the first time in my life that has happened to me. You know now what I've lived through, and you can understand what I mean. I'm at an age when I didn't think I'd ever feel what I've felt with you."

"You say that like it's a problem—"

"Let me speak. I didn't leave because I didn't love you, but because I was scared of what I was carrying inside. I came to Greece without expecting anything, just wanting to forget and to stop hurting; then everything got turned upside down. A lot of things have happened that you don't know about—and I'll tell you about them, but I don't plan to return to Germany. Everything there hurts me. Even the language grates on my nerves. Besides, I have a lot of things to put in order before I could devote myself to you. There are some accounts still open with my past, and if I don't close them—"

"You keep talking, and you don't let me tell you—" he complained.

"And nor will I let you—not yet—not before you learn, before you understand—"

"Stop!" he ordered. "Why is it so important to you for me to understand? Nothing about your past concerns me, only your present and your future, and I want to be a part of those."

"Yes, it is important. Because everything that's happened since I came to Greece has given me back my self-respect and revived my spirit. I'm not what I thought I was."

"Then I'll listen to you. And then we'll talk about us."

"Thank you. Do you have time? Where's Ino?"

"She's with me in Greece, as is a woman who's looking after her. She knows we're coming to find you, and she can't wait to see you."

"I can't see her, Yannos. Not yet."

"I know—your old accounts."

"Yes."

"Before we immerse ourselves in your ledgers, whatever they are, do I deserve a coffee?" he asked, a little smile on his lips.

I led him by the hand to the kitchen. I had to explain things to poor Karim too.

My friend was making me breakfast, and from his nervous movements, I could tell how upset he was. As soon as he saw us, he began speaking, but he was so mixed up that half of it was in his own language, and we didn't understand a word. I went up to him, took the spoon he was holding, and smiled.

"Calm down, Karim," I said. "You did nothing wrong."

"Madam, I am ashamed. Didn't know. And now madam angry. I am so sorry, so sorry," he said in English.

I put an arm around his shoulders, and he fell silent in surprise.

"Madam?" he asked. "Not angry? Not send away?"

"No, Karim," I said to him, smiling. "Come and meet Mr. Yannos."

The two men faced each other to be introduced.

"Yannos, Karim is a refugee from Syria and the first friend I made when I came to Greece. He lost his parents and nearly all his family in the bombings, and he's come, like thousands of others, to save himself. Despite the fact that he could be my son, he looks after me as if I were his child. Karim, this is Yannos Pantazis. He's the man I love."

Yannos's face lit up with a broad smile, and he grasped Karim's hand warmly. Karim's face also lit up. As soon as we sat down at the table, he began to prepare and offer us endless delicacies for breakfast.

Yannos leaned over to me. "Does he feed you like this every day?"

"Almost. He thinks I must eat well and get strong, and it's the way he shows his love. Today he's happy, so—"

"Yes, but I can't eat any more," he complained softly so as not to offend the young man, who was searching the refrigerator for something else to put on the table.

I smiled. If Ino had been sitting in the empty chair next to me, my happiness would have been complete, but I had to take care of a lot of things before I could have the life I had always dreamed of. I stroked Yannos's cheek to make sure he was really there and then turned to Karim.

"Enough, my dear. There's always lunchtime. This isn't our last meal."

Karim smiled sheepishly. "Then, madam, I go do work," he announced and disappeared with a small bow.

A few minutes later, I heard him in the little office opening the window, a sign that the cleaning would begin there.

"And now, the two of us," Yannos said, and his expression told me what he wanted: the truth.

It took me nearly two hours to tell him briefly all that had happened since my return to Greece—the inheritance, my meeting with Melpo, and everything I'd learned about a family I'd never known. The coffee Karim had made was gone, but I made a pot without interrupting my narrative. Yannos didn't miss a word, his face revealing surprise or distress at every turn. The further I progressed, the more his eyebrows drew together until the revelation of my true father made his mouth open in surprise.

"Now you know everything," I said, and like an epilogue, I showed him the gold letter around my neck.

"So that's it," he said, and touched it in awe.

"Yes, a letter made of gold. It carries a lot of tears."

"Unbelievable. It's completely surreal what fate sometimes contrives for people!" he said and took my hand.

"I was just a tiny grain of wheat under the grindstone of destiny, Yannos. Even my aunt Hecuba was only the instrument of a fate that for some peculiar reason didn't want any descendant of the Kantardzis family to join the Kouyoumdzis family."

"Except that you yourself are the result of that union, Fenia."

"Exactly. Maybe that's why fate made me pay for it."

"And now? Whose turn is it?"

"You're the man I love. And now I don't feel unworthy of you. I'm descended from a respectable family. I have roots too, Yannos."

"So what you're telling me is that, in some way, you've been redeemed in your own eyes."

"Yes. And not in some way. In every way. I'm not alone now—I have a family, and some part of it loves me. I want them in my life. I lived all those years thinking that I was cursed, without roots and with a monster for a father. Now I have aunts and, more importantly, cousins. My father loved my mother, and I want to meet him. I don't know if he'll accept that I'm his daughter, but I have a duty to tell him and vindicate my mother's memory."

"And then?"

"Then you and I must find some common path to walk because, as I told you, I don't want to set foot in Germany. Maybe it sounds bad, but not even for you would I return there. I have the feeling that that country is responsible for all the terrible things in my life."

"At the moment, most Greeks think the same," he observed, smiling, and he stood up.

I looked at him curiously as I too stood up. He took me in his arms and kissed me tenderly.

"So, my golden girl," he began, "like you, I have a lot of things to think about and do. And we have a week to get it all done!"

"What do you mean?" I asked and felt suddenly lost.

"I'm going back to my daughter, who's waiting for me. I'll show her around Athens, and I'm sure she'll adore it. I want her to know the city where her parents grew up. I give you seven whole days to solve all your problems. To think about what you want to do in the future—apart from marrying me, of course; that's a foregone conclusion."

"What? What did you say?" I whispered. Fortunately, he was holding me, or I would have collapsed.

"Fenia, I didn't turn the world upside down looking for you so that we could spend a night together. I want your days, your nights, and your years—you, yourself, for life. Finish what you have to do and come and find me. I'll be waiting for you with Ino. We're staying at the Astir Palace at Vouliagmeni."

He left so suddenly that I staggered. I leaned against the table and heard him saying a cheerful good-bye to Karim.

Melpo and Paschalis had exactly the same expression when I told them what had happened, looking as if they'd met someone from another planet. Even when I concluded with a grin, they stayed still.

"What's the matter with you?" I asked impatiently. "Don't you have anything to say?"

Melpo finally recovered and jumped up to hug me.

"You crazy girl!" she said, pretending to scold me. "And you didn't tell me anything all this time? You let me believe that your whole life had passed in agony, and you didn't mention the most important thing: love?"

"So now," Paschalis asked, "what will you do?"

We all sat down.

"I have a lot to think about," I admitted. "I'm not alone anymore. Apart from you, there's also Karim. I'm responsible for him, and he can't hide in this house for the rest of his life."

"I think I can help with that," Paschalis said, and we both turned to look at him in surprise.

"What do you mean?" his wife asked.

"I didn't want to say anything until I figured out whether there was a way. Some old acquaintances owe me favors. Karim has the right to apply for asylum in our country, and that way, his residency will become legal."

"Paschalis," I gasped. "How can I thank you?"

"Don't thank me yet. Today or tomorrow I'm expecting a telephone call. Then I'll go to the fellow on the committee that reviews such applications, of which, you understand, there are thousands. The truth is I've never asked for this sort of favor in my life, and I feel a bit awkward, but good luck to the boy! He looked after you, and I know you care for him."

I sat on the edge of Paschalis's armchair and hugged him affectionately. In the end, my first impression—that he was just like Saint Nicholas—had been right.

"And now we come to the other subject," he continued, and I leaned back to look at his eyes, jolly behind the little glasses.

"Yes, and that is something I must handle by myself," I said simply, and he hugged me again approvingly.

I didn't sleep a wink the night before the most important visit I would make in my life. Yet by morning I was rested and strong. I bathed and did my hair the way the hairdresser, whom I now visited regularly, had taught me. I chose the prettiest dress of the ones I'd bought but not worn yet. It was light green with fine stripes. It made me feel pretty when I put it on. I made myself up carefully and slipped on my only piece of jewelry, the gold letter. I ignored Karim's pleas that I eat something and left the house as if I'd been hypnotized. I had called a taxi so as not to search in vain in the Athens summer heat, and in a few minutes, I was at Syntagma. A light breeze was blowing. I looked at my watch. It said eight thirty, still very early. I found myself opposite the Public, and the smell of their coffee encouraged me to sit down. A final moment of peace, a recuperation of my energy, and a strong coffee. That was what I needed before I walked down Ermou Street to meet the cause of my coming into the world. I found a table and ordered, then lit a cigarette as I waited. Others followed until only the foam of my iced espresso remained in the glass. I looked at my watch: half past nine.

An inexplicable coolheadedness held my feet and my heart steady as I stood, a minute later, outside the Kouyoumdzis jewelry store. This time, the shutters were up and the windows shone. I stood for a moment and persuaded myself I was admiring them, while in reality I was peering secretly into the interior of the shop. It was long and narrow, and on the walls were display cases, also full of jewelry. At the back I could see a desk and a man sitting behind it. I pushed the door open and entered the cool shop. Simos Kouyoumdzis was drinking his coffee, and he got up to welcome me. I had a few seconds to observe him before he approached. Tall, erect, with pure white hair and a face that scarcely showed his age. I observed that the corners of his well-shaped lips turned slightly down, a sign that my father had forgotten to smile for years. I took him in briefly, above all his lips, and that dimple in his chin; I'd always wondered where I'd inherited that from. He satisfied my curiosity.

"Good morning," he was saying now, smiling politely. "What can I help you with?"

I noticed his professional manner and the fact that he hadn't really looked at me yet. I chose not to answer him so that he'd have to. And indeed, Simos Kouyoumdzis slowly raised his eyes, and we were so close that I could see the lightning flash in them. I looked like my mother, and I could tell that my face had violently stirred his memory. Now he was silent too as his eyes searched my features. His face darkened; his mind tried to reject what he saw.

"Mr. Kouyoumdzis," I said to break the heavy silence.

His vision cleared.

"Yes. Do you know me?" he asked unsteadily.

"My name is Fenia Karapanos," I continued, and unconsciously fingered the gold letter at my throat.

The movement attracted his attention again, except that now his eyes were open wide. He may never have seen the necklace that his father had made, but he knew about it, and now here it was in front of him.

His reaction surprised me. He reached out and took the letter between his fingers. I stood still, holding my breath. I let him examine it. He found the mechanism, and the little gold tablet with *I love you* written on it fell into his hand. He looked at it as if he were lost and took a step back. It took a few seconds before he focused on my face again.

"Who are you? That locket—" His voice gave way, catching in his throat.

I calmly took the gold tablet and put it back in its place before I looked back at him confidently.

"I know," I said. "This gold letter was designed by Simeon Kouyoumdzis for Smaragda Kantardzis, but it was made by Vassilis for Chrysafenia Ververis, my grandmother. I'm named for her."

I paused for a second, giving him time to take this in. Simos was deathly pale. He turned around and sat at his desk again. I took a chair opposite him.

"Whose daughter are you?"

"Smaragda's."

I watched him close his eyes and take a deep breath before he was ready to face me again.

"Smaragda got married and left for Germany with her husband."

"Yes." I nodded and got ready to launch the final volley. "Except that, when she married Renos Karapanos, she was already pregnant by you."

Now I was silent. In front of my eyes, I saw on his face all the reactions of a man who has been stabbed in the chest. Surprise, pain, doubt, and then the stillness of death. Except that Simos Kouyoumdzis was still alive.

"You're lying!" he shouted loud enough to break the windows of his store. "You're a miserable liar. Smaragda would have told me if she was pregnant with my child! She wouldn't have married someone else."

"She came to tell you and found you in bed with Hecuba," I said, holding on to my self-control. "Do you remember? She asked you to meet her at the apartment. Except that my dear aunt trapped you. And then Sekeris threw my mother out of the house, and that animal Karapanos swooped in. The day you went to find her, my grandfather said she was marrying someone right at that moment. But what you never knew was that she only married him to give a name to your child."

I watched him lower his face and hide it in his hands, unable to believe that his life could be upended so.

"Impossible," he murmured.

"I have no reason to lie to you," I said quietly. "I know how you feel."

"No!" he shouted. "You don't! I never loved anyone but Smaragda. My whole life I never found anyone to take her place. I grew old alone with my memories. And you expect me to believe that we lost a lifetime of happiness because of bad timing and the whim of a few small-minded people? Do you expect me to accept that, all these years, I had a child and didn't know it?"

"There are many things you don't know. But perhaps it's not the time." I got up and placed a piece of paper in front of him. "Here is my address, although you already know it well. It was my mother's family home. I live there now. I'm ready to submit to any genetic tests you want to establish that I'm telling the truth, which I only found out recently from Melpo."

"Melpo?" he said, and his expression brightened. "Smaragda's cousin! She loved her very much and thought she had lost her."

"Yes. Except that she recovered, and when she learned about me, she came to see me and tell me the whole history of my family. Though I wouldn't have found out the last part if I hadn't tracked down Kali."

"The housekeeper," my father remembered.

"Exactly. She knew my mother was already pregnant when she married. That and more. Listen, I haven't come to ask you for anything. I thought it was my duty to tell you that you have a daughter and that my mother wasn't anything like her father said. If you have other questions, or if you're interested in getting to know your daughter, come and find me."

I left without a look back. My resilience had almost run out. I ran up Ermou Street and hailed a taxi in the square. In a few minutes, I was home, and there I could cry at my leisure. What could I expect, after all, from a man who had arranged his life around his loneliness? Did I think he'd take me in his arms? Cry with me? Become the father I'd always wished for?

Melpo and Paschalis were waiting at the house, together with Karim. They were all worried. Sitting in the living room, they watched me fly past like a bullet and run upstairs. Melpo was the only one who dared to follow, and she found me crying miserably, facedown on the bed. For a little while, I had the illusion that my mother had come back to life, as she took me in her arms and let me cry, stroking my hair softly.

"Hush, my girl," she kept saying. "Don't cry; everything will be all right." Between my sobs, I told her what had happened.

"Give him a little time, Fenia," she said. "I don't blame him."

"I don't either," I admitted, biting my lips to subdue the resentment that threatened to overcome me. "But it hurt to look at him, Melpo. If Hecuba hadn't done what she did, if my grandfather hadn't driven my mother out—"

"Sweetheart, don't make me talk in clichés. *If* is a word that exists only to drive us crazy. It's meaningless."

"I know," I said with a sigh. "Time only moves in one direction." I looked at her, and a shy smile appeared on my lips. "He's handsome, Melpo—my father. Very handsome."

"I remember him. They were a beautiful couple, he and your mother. No wonder they produced such a beautiful child! Enough crying now, my dear. You're not a young girl anymore, and there's a man who loves you. A new life is waiting. You did what you had to do; now give the man some time to decide what he wants to do. Right or wrong, whether we like it or not. Let's go downstairs. Paschalis has some good news for you."

"What's happened?"

"Tomorrow he'll take Karim, and they'll go arrange his situation. In a little while, your dear friend will have legal papers and be free to stay in Greece."

I threw my arms around her. How much I loved this woman!

Yannos's one-week deadline was approaching. We hadn't even spoken on the telephone. I knew him well. He would count the hours and the minutes, but he would remain faithful to his word. At the same time, plans were revolving in my mind. They had all come at once, while at the edge of my heart, the thought of my father kept watch.

My legs gave way when I saw him two days after our first meeting, standing on my doorstep. Karim was away with Paschalis doing his legal paperwork, and I was alone in the house. Simos came up the stairs and stood at the top.

"Welcome," I said and stood aside to let him into the living room.

He looked around him, and a bitter smile twisted his mouth. "The last time I was here, I thought my heart had stopped," he said quietly. "When I heard that your mother had married."

"Like her heart stopped when she saw you embracing her sister," I answered him with a calm I didn't feel.

He looked at me hopelessly. "That wasn't my fault!"

"It wasn't hers either, yet she's the one who paid most dearly for Hecuba's wickedness and your cowardice—"

"My cowardice?"

"If, when you found out about the wedding, you'd run to find her, everything would have been different. Instead, mouths remained closed, words went unspoken, and time took a sad toll on a destroyed life. My mother's life." I couldn't stop the hardness of my tone.

"Wasn't my life wasted?" my father complained.

"First listen, and then you can judge," I told him.

Yet again I had to repeat the story, but I framed it around her life and mine from the time Renos came into it. I didn't mince words. I told him everything just as it happened, sometimes graphically. I knew how hard I was being on him, and I didn't understand why. On the one hand, my behavior was childish; on the other, I took a small satisfaction from punishing him for not fighting for us.

When I finished, he was sweating. I was suddenly worried and ran to fetch him a glass of cold water. He drank it greedily and wiped his damp forehead with his handkerchief. Then he jumped up and began pacing the wooden floor. It creaked in complaint at his suffering. After a while, I got up and stood in front of him, blocking his path. He was like a vehicle that someone had suddenly pulled the hand brake on. He grabbed me in his arms, and I stood like a statue, not knowing how to respond. He leaned back to stroke my hair and put his hand on my dimple, identical to his.

"Everyone in the Kouyoumdzis family has it," he said, and his eyes shone with tears.

"So you believe me?" I asked in a broken voice.

"I believe you. And for the rest of my life, I'll try to win your forgiveness."

"If you want us to do a paternity test—" I rambled, feeling pathetic.

"There's no need," he said. "But we have to get to know each other. There's so much I need to know about you. And I want to know about her too."

"I told you what we lived through."

"Not that. Together we'll remember the real Smaragda, her smile, her eyes that were the same as yours, her beautiful spirit. And I'll ask forgiveness from God and from you. I was young and cowardly—you're right. Like my father and grandfather. We put it behind us instead of fighting for our love, for the happiness of the women we worshipped. We have a lot of things to talk about and just as many to experience together."

I knew from Melpo that, when she came from Crete, Hecuba stayed with her sister Fotini. She didn't know nor could she have imagined what awaited her when she opened the front door. When her eyes moved from me to the man at my side, she looked ready to faint. She tried to slam the door in our faces, but my father raised his hand and stopped her. He shoved the door open wide, and Hecuba took a step backward.

"What do you want here?" she shrieked.

She stumbled into the next room and collapsed into an armchair. We followed, and I noticed another chair with a woman sitting in it. As I guessed, this was my aunt Fotini. She looked at us at first with an empty gaze, but then something lit up inside her; she rose and approached me.

"Smaragda," she said, and fell into my arms. "My little sister," she went on, weeping.

I sensed my father's fury beside me. He hadn't taken his eyes off Hecuba, and now he approached her. I broke away from Fotini's arms, worried about what he might do. He loomed over my aunt.

"What do you want?" she asked without looking up at him.

"I only came to tell you that, whatever harm you did to me and Smaragda, it was nothing compared to the crime you perpetrated on our child!"

It was as if an electric current passed through her.

"What child? What are you saying?" she asked now and stood up with the last remnants of her courage.

"Smaragda was pregnant, Hecuba! That's why she came to me that afternoon when you played out your wretched game!" my father yelled. "You condemned your sister to an executioner who, once he'd managed to annihilate her, then spent years abusing her daughter."

Hecuba's eyes flicked back and forth over me.

"It's me, Aunt," I said to her drily. "Smaragda and Simos's daughter."

"Impossible," she managed to whisper.

"I don't know what you had against my mother. Nothing I've learned about our family explains the hatred, the jealousy, and finally the evil. Grandfather gave you the weapons, as did the times you lived in. But there's no excuse for the harm you did."

I took a step closer and she edged back in fear.

"Don't be afraid of me," I said calmly. "I won't hurt you, despite the fact that, from the time I found out the truth, I've fantasized about beating you to a pulp."

"We came to tell you," my father took over again, "that despite you and all the others, a descendant of the Kantardzis family will, from now on, take the family name she deserves. So, let me introduce you to Chrysafenia Kouyoumdzis. Now, as long as you live, I want you to know that the only thing waiting for you is the hell you deserve."

He took my hand and we left. The only thing he neglected to do was to spit behind him, but it was as if he had. For one crazy moment,

I imagined I could see Fate herself howling with fury that all her evil games had finally been in vain.

My information was correct. Mr. Pantazis and his daughter were in the sea. The time had come for me to meet them, and I'd taken a taxi to Vouliagmeni.

I went to the spot a polite hotel clerk showed me and took off my sandals to sink into the golden sand. My eyes searched for my familiar, beloved faces among the many other swimmers, and when I spotted them, I smiled, watching them play in the blue water. Ino's hair was pulled back in a little braid, and her skin had taken on a golden color. My eyes filled, and a lump rose in my throat. I had missed my little one so much . . .

I took another step. I knew very well what I wanted and what I would do in the future. I would turn the house I'd inherited into a fancy restaurant, and Karim would make the Athenian public familiar with his country's cuisine. My father had already set in motion the necessary process for me to take the name that belonged to me. In the next few days, I would meet the remaining members of my family: Melpo's children, on my mother's side, and my uncles Damianos and Loukas with their families on my father's side. Grandmother Lefkothea was still alive, but not Vassilis. But I was sure that, wherever he was, he could make out the gold letter that shone at my throat and would always stay there.

Without hesitating, I walked toward the beautiful life that was waiting for me, not caring that my dress was getting wet. When they caught sight of me, their faces shone even brighter than the sun. Ino shrieked happily, and her lips clearly formed the word *Mama* before she wrapped her arms around my neck, ready to drown me in her joy. Yannos's arms closed around us both. Never in my life had I felt such fullness, such security, such peace. All the terrible things, all the difficulties were behind us, and there were endless solutions for the problems of the future. I didn't know yet that, like me, Yannos had been making decisions about the future. Aside from planning our wedding, he'd begun to organize their permanent resettlement in Greece.

I looked at him without hiding anything that I was feeling.

"I love you," his lips said above mine.

"I love you both," I whispered, and a loud, clear laugh, transparent as the water that surrounded us, flew out of me.

I tilted my head, and the rays of the sun struck the letter on my neck. Gold mixed with gold, and the brilliance finally blinded evil Fate, whom I saw burning. She wouldn't bother us anymore.

AUTHOR'S NOTE

A few words about me . . .

And this time I mean it . . . just a few words about me. They're chatterboxes, the heroes of this book. They have a lot to say, so I don't want to add much. Besides, this particular book could be characterized as being anything from strange to tormented.

It began one morning at dawn. I had made up my mind to take a long break from my computer, and it was now . . . a long, slow pause . . . five a.m. . . . I opened my eyes and saw my husband looking at me, and quite naturally, I was really anxious. I'll repeat the conversation to you exactly as it took place so that you don't have any doubts.

"Yorgos, why aren't you asleep?"

"I've been thinking about it all night: I have an idea for a book!"

"You're going to write a book?"

"No! You'll write it. It came to me as I was watching those commercials aimed at people who buy jewelry. So, imagine a woman going into a shop like that and she's wearing a piece of jewelry that the shop owner recognizes. Someone in his family made it—probably—I'm not sure. But it has a history, that piece of jewelry," he concluded. "What do you think?"

While he was talking, both sleep and my decision to take a leisurely break had gone out the window.

"You like it!" he realized proudly. "And now it's your turn to stay awake. Good night."

He turned over and went to sleep while I . . .

That's how *The Gold Letter* was born in my mind. I have to confess that such a piece of jewelry exists. It was a gift from him, a custom order, which, because of a theft, is sadly no longer in my hands. The novel, however, is in yours.

The second adjective I used to describe this book was "tormented." A violent interruption occurred when the person who gave me the idea for it became ill. You know about that already; I told you about it along with all the other things that concern me. As we said: you and I have a different relationship that you respect and so do I. From here on, I can tell you something else: I've never been so frightened in my whole life. In addition to losing him, I was in danger of losing the reason for my own existence . . .

The main thing is, we're fine—on our feet again. And besides God, I warmly thank two people who, as I wrote once on Facebook, held his heart in their hands and saved him. Victor Papayiotakopoulos and Nikos Baikousis, I thank you. What you don't know is that, by saving him, you saved me, and gave me back my smile and my strength.

When we returned home, during the difficult period of Yorgos's recuperation, I escaped into my words, into the games I played with them. My heroines were waiting for me. Smaragda, Chrysafenia, and all the other members of the family gave me peace of mind and restored my balance. The pages I filled were a refuge, their adventures and love story a relief. Also, yet again in my life, the truth of the saying "never say never" was borne out. I thought that I had freed myself of Constantinople with Theano, one of my earlier heroines, but as it turned out, the city wasn't finished with me. My story wandered again in its own haunts. Except that now I had learned more, and had a lot more to say.

And something else strange about this book: I don't know if I loved it. Perhaps I didn't have enough time. It came out of me violently, as if it was hiding, and as soon as it found a way out, it slid indignantly onto the white pages and mocked me, the ungrateful wretch! I know what I felt, though, when I had finished and was revisiting it for a second reading to make any corrections or additions before I wrote the words *The End.* I felt myself bound to it with unbreakable bonds. Something familiar but also previously unknown to me. Usually, when I finish a book, I bury it deep in my mind, together with the others, and I almost forget it. But this was and is different. As if it had moved in with me.

What's more, it is the only book that my husband didn't read as I was writing it, but only after I had finished. And that too was a first.

Writing these words, I realize that now I'm saying good-bye to it. Good-bye, Smaragda; good-bye, Chrysafenia; good-bye, Fenia. I'd especially like to give you a kiss. We became good friends. Apart from your own life, you know about the tears, the agonies, and the sleepless nights I suffered for Yorgos. So, here's to you, and to him too . . .

Lena Manta

ABOUT THE AUTHOR

Photo © 2016

Lena Manta was born in Istanbul, Turkey, to Greek parents. She moved to Greece at a very young age and now lives with her husband and two children on the outskirts of Athens. Although she studied to be a nursery school teacher, Manta instead directed her own puppet theater before writing articles for local newspapers and working as a director for a local radio station. Manta was proclaimed Author of the Year in both 2009 and 2011 by *Greek Life & Style* magazine. She has written thirteen books, including *The Gold Letter*, her second book to be translated into English, and the bestselling *The House by the River*, which has sold almost 250,000 copies. Hers is a voice to be reckoned with, and each new book is a tour de force in the Greek publishing world.

ABOUT THE TRANSLATOR

Gail Holst-Warhaft is a poet, translator, musician, literary scholar, and the poet laureate of Tompkins County for 2011 and 2012. Her books include the poetry collections *Lucky Country* and *Penelope's Confession* as well as the nonfiction works *The Cue for Passion: Grief and Its Political Uses*, *Dangerous Voices: Women's Laments and Greek Literature*, *Theodorakis: Myth and Politics in Modern Greek Music*, *Road to Rembetika*, and *The Fall of Athens*, a memoir in prose and poems. She has translated *The Collected Poems of Nikos Kavadias* and *I Had Three Lives: Selected Poems of Mikis Theodorakis*. Her poems and translations from Greek, French, and Anglo-Saxon have been published in many journals and anthologies, including *Literary Imagination*, *Per Contra*, *Translation*, *Southerly*, *Antipodes*, and *Stand*. Holst-Warhaft lives in Ithaca, New York.